Speed Tile

Speed Tile

John Leben

Writer's Showcase presented by *Writer's Digest*
San Jose New York Lincoln Shanghai

Speed Tile

Published by Writer's Showcase presented by *Writer's Digest* an imprint of iUniverse.com, Inc.

For information address:
iUniverse.com, Inc.
620 North 48th Street
Suite 201
Lincoln, NE 68504-3467
www.iuniverse.com

ISBN: 0-595-09640-9

Printed in the United States of America

Thanks to my family for putting up with my speed tiles and slabs, suiters and propeller heads…and for allowing me to use their crazed antics as inspiration for this novel. And a big thanks to Mark for holding my hand while writing this book.

Contents

Foreword

John Leben shares some interesting facts about his semi-autobiographical novel, *Speed Tile*

FACT: I built my first facsimile of a speed tile almost 20 years ago in my basement studio in LaGrange, Illinois. I cut it out of aluminum bar stock and brass studs. It was a quarter inch thick and an inch square with four brass nubs, one in each corner. I made the speed tile right after a romantic week-end in Saugatuck with my wife, Marcia. I hiked the dunes that week-end. The dunes over Singapore.

FACT: My video production business went to hell soon after I built the speed tile. I spent a lot of time in those days drawing speed tiles and making them out of aluminum and brass. They became an obsession which left little room for clients. I had fantastic dreams of speed tiles and the strange world they came from. After a few tough years, Marcia and I closed down the Chicago office of Leben Productions, sold our house in LaGrange and moved to Saugatuck.

FACT: After successfully ignoring the speed tile for several years after moving to Saugatuck, the damned thing crawled back out of my subconscious and became a symbol for the technological trauma my production business was experiencing. Again, I made speed tiles. I made them by the bucket, hundreds of them. I painted them, sculpted them, drew them and made shrines to them. Then I exhibited my precious speed tiles at Good Goods Gallery in Saugatuck.

FACT: I wrote *Speed Tile* in an attempt to make sense of my obsession with speed tiles and the power they hold over me. The novel takes place in Saugatuck, Michigan and concludes on deserted South Manitou Island after a spirited sea voyage on DANCER, my sailboat. If you live in Saugatuck, you may very well recognize many of the colorful characters who populate this novel of artistic inspiration and technological trauma. You'll certainly recognize many of the locations.

FACT: There are others in Saugatuck and surrounding communities who have been affected by the allure of speed tiles.

FACT: My daughter Hilllary really does spell her name with three l's.

Prologue

Westerly winds blowing off Lake Michigan constantly form, erode and rebuild massive dunes made of sand over the ghost town, a town once known as Singapore. A small artifact, a square, metallic, quarter-inch thick wafer with bolt-like nubs on its weathered surface slowly emerges from under the blowing sand. Over and over, the wind covers it gently (again) with a new blanket of sand, then carefully brushes it away to allow the artifact to sparkle in the sun, to gather strength, uncovered at last.

The artifact attracts a hiker (an artist) awed by the mystery of the place. It reflects a flash of sunlight into the artist's eye drawing him to the sand dune where the artifact hides. It waits as the artist scans the dunes, searching for the source of the flash. The silver-colored wafer signals again, drawing the hiker near. The wind picks up, teasing the hiker with needles of blowing sand, spraying more sand over the artifact. The wafer vibrates briefly, coming alive. It pulls more sand over itself as if shy, trying to hide from his curious eyes (not yet).

Intrigued, the artist approaches, brushes sand off a badly eroded grid-like structure imbedded in the dune, and finds the artifact planted precisely in the middle of one square cell, partially covered, gleaming in the sun. Smiling, the artist reaches for the metal square, then hesitates, simultaneously repelled and attracted by the object. Then he picks it up, turns it over in his hand and abruptly pockets the odd object for a more careful examination later.

Back in his rented room, the artist secretly hides the artifact in his briefcase, away from the thoughtful eyes of his wife and partner. He never touches it again, but its now tenuous grip on the artist's mind would grow more firm with time...symbiosis begun.

The artifact, awakened, grows stronger in the artist's briefcase. Blueprints, proposals, storyboards, video scripts (papers hinting at the artist's vocation) make their periodic visits to the home of the wafer-like icon, giving the artifact purpose.

Then, trauma...Strange, unwelcome hands...A snapping of the symbiotic link (temporary)...sailing through air...immersion in the murky waters of industrial waste...retrieval. Exile to a dark corner of an attic room...the briefcase retired, forgotten, discarded.

But the artifact continues its work in the dark, closed confines of the leather briefcase (nest?), spurred by the lines and notations of blueprints, proposals. Small, jagged sparks, dim at first, random, zap sporadically out of the bottom of the still and silent artifact. Feathery filaments of white strand delicately billow out of the lines of the old, filthy blueprints. Sparks and strands noiselessly, endlessly dance, bounce randomly off the confined sides of the case, slowly forming a grainy, muddy substance (shell?) around the square metal artifact. It secretly, quietly mutates.

Months...years. Then, a dim, barely audible static sound emanates from the brass-like nubs of the tile—pulsing, zapping, (communicating?). Pointy, wire-like, prickly thorns grow in spurts out of the bottom of the muddy shell enclosing the artifact within. A fog-like shroud of dirty yellow gas spits out of the nubs, envelops the shell, and adds slowly, relentlessly to the hardening surface.

More years. More growth. Unnatural. Impossible. Slowly, in the dark corner of the attic, the briefcase begins to bulge, straining at the latches that bind it. The grainy shell inside hardens, shapes itself into a rectangular form. It continues to grow. The tile within, now secure (safe?), emits a continuous irritating buzz made up of single blips of static. Too fast. Too far.

Finally, the case bursts open in an explosion of leather fragments and brass latches. The slab within, enveloped in a semi-transparent cloud of foul yellow gas, slowly floats out of the case. As the shroud of gas dissipates, the slab snaps and pops (bigger) with a screeching, unworldly groan. It's an almost perfect rectangle now, with a concrete-like surface and red, angry, wire-like tendrils dangling from the bottom. It floats to the ceiling and remains there, straining at the beams of the roof, trying to get out, still growing.

Chapter 1

The Chicago River

The water. It was a dull, grayish green color. Not that garish, bright green of St. Patrick's day when the City of Chicago pours hundreds of gallons of green food coloring into the Chicago River, but a sick, diseased color, like old pea soup. Puke green.

I paused on the bridge looking down at the ugly torrent of thick water flowing below me, white foamy stuff collecting in the eddies, dark, oily patches clinging to the banks. A rat carcass, a shoe…A polluted river, the price of progress in this city.

My name is John Hunter. I'm an artist and a video producer. Actually, I pretended to be an artist back then. I wanted to be an artist. But I was in business to make videos. That's how I made a living. That's how I earned money. I had just gotten off the train from the western suburbs. I lived in LaGrange with my wife, Marcia and two pre-teen daughters, Hannah the ballerina and Hilllary, the lunatic. (No, that's not a typo. She spells her name with three l's. She says the extra "l" is for extra lunacy.)

That was the day I lost it, that gray day in Chicago. That was the day I flushed my sanity into the sewer-ravaged waste of the Chicago River.

The sky was gray-green like the river. It looked like rain. It was March. I was on my way to a meeting about a video I was producing for a downtown development company. They were building yet another

massive skyscraper in Chicago. I was making a video that would extol
the virtues of this new slab, this glass and steel monster, this economic
boon that would bring even more faceless suiters across this bridge and
into this crowded city. I thought of the script and storyboard in my
briefcase with bitterness. Bile rose in my throat. I popped a Rolaids in
my mouth.

I thought of the dunes. That's where I'd rather be, even in March, the
rolling dunes of Michigan. No buildings there. No skyscrapers. No
McDonalds, No sidewalks or bridges or scurrying suiters. Only sand.
Mountains of sand. The only sign of man's intrusion to these dunes is
the occasional stone foundation, badly eroded, partially buried, a testa-
ment to man's folly in building a town there. Singapore. A ghost town
in the dunes. That's where I found it almost nine months ago.

I didn't believe in this project. I didn't believe in much of anything just
then, just the speed tile. I was obsessed with it. I dreamed about it every
night. I thought about it every day. I drew it. I painted it. I even started
making speed tiles. In fact, I made hundreds of them, meticulously cutting quarter-inch by one-inch aluminum bar stock into one-inch squares,
filing the edges to look worn and weathered, drilling holes in the corners,
inserting brass nubs in the holes.

I should have been working on the script for this skyscraper video, or
prospecting for more work, more video projects. My business had been
failing in recent months, ever since that weekend in Saugatuck, but I
couldn't help it.

I filled up an old wooden cigar box with speed tiles, then a big galvanized bucket. Obsessively, I cut, filed, drilled—making replicas of
the speed tile I found in the dunes. As I worked, as I made each tile,
I imagined more about this odd artifact. I started creating a history
of the speed tile in my imagination, making up a long list of exotic
powers and uses, powers that became ever more real to me as I filled
the galvanized bucket.

I moved away from the railing and pulled up my collar to keep the cold, damp wind from blowing down my neck. I joined the flow of foot traffic heading east, toward the massive buildings of the loop, toward downtown Chicago, toward my meeting with Kaminski.

In this city, north-south streets are kind of hectic and helter-skelter. Pedestrian traffic goes this way and that, each person with an important destination. Each person lost in his or her own purpose, bumping and pushing and dodging around others like bumper cars at an amusement park. But east-west streets are different, especially west of Wacker Drive in the mornings and evenings at rush hours. In the morning, everybody goes east, heading for work. Hundreds of people, thousands, all walking at a purposeful clip, all heading in the same direction, at the same pace, heading for the concrete slabs, going to their gray cubicles to start another day of work—a team, an army of uniformed business people, an east-bound stream of faceless humanity. I joined the gray suits, the black overcoats, the ties, the hats, the umbrellas—linear, predictable, manageable, I joined the team.

I hated myself for being so selfish, so unproductive. I couldn't justify my preoccupation with speed tiles. I had a family to feed, a mortgage to pay. I should be doing things to earn money, to pay for Hannah's ballet lessons and Hilllary's piano. I pretended that it was my art that inspired me. My art. Wasn't that important to pursue? Wasn't that my destiny? Wasn't that reason enough to make my family suffer?

Marcia and the girls were patient with me. They liked what I was doing. Marcia had been after me for years to spend less time in the stressful vocation of video producer and more in the relaxing occupation of artist. In her eyes, that's what I was doing. Hannah said I was a dork, but she made me teach her how to make a speed tile for herself. Hilllary didn't see anything strange in my behavior at all. I guess someone who spends days painting massive caterpillars with fangs on her bedroom walls wouldn't think that an obsession with speed tiles was strange.

So I made speed tiles. And I lost interest in making video programs for my clients. I went through the motions for a long time: going to meetings, writing scripts, drawing storyboards. But the inanity of the work got to me. Clients irritated me. Their requests seemed irrelevant, petty. Maybe it would have happened without the speed tile, but the tile gave me an excuse. The tile became my art. And I became…Well, I guess I became its slave.

I stopped in front of Kaminski's building and looked up at the massive skyscraper. Kaminski was the developer, the man who would be building another one of these things. This meeting would be to resolve the point of view of the video. Helmut Schmidt, the architect, had his own grand ideas. Ideas that Kaminski looked at with disdain. The client, a Dr. Wong representing some Asian research company would also be at the meeting. It was Dr. Wong's building we would be discussing.

I entered the building through the revolving doors and stopped at the security desk to gain clearance. For some reason I needed a badge to prove I belonged there.

Badge? Badge? I don't need no stinking badge…I thought of Humphrey Bogart and his confrontation with the Mexican Federales in Treasure of the Sierra Madre. The guard looked at me suspiciously and called Kaminski's office to check on my appointment. I was fifteen minutes late.

After wandering past several elevator banks and finding the one that stopped at the 17th floor, I squeezed into the crowded box, watched the doors close and stared at the counting numbers above the doors. Everyone stared up at them, averting their eyes from each other, trying to act natural in a small box full of strangers. Ten, eleven, twelve, fourteen, fifteen, sixteen…

We continued to stare, waiting to hit the jackpot, waiting to win the prize, watching for our number, our floor. I stared too. I waited. Ding! Seventeenth floor. I won. The prize? A two hour audience with a Polish general, a German clown and an Asian prince.

I pushed my way out of the elevator and wandered the empty hallways looking for Kaminski's office. I heard him before I got to his office. Joe Kaminski was a big, overweight Polish guy from the south side of Chicago. He was a self-made man and he didn't mince his words. He was ranting about progress and what an economic boom this new building would generate in Chicago. That's what he wanted to stress in the video. I entered his outer office and was shown into the conference room by Kaminski's secretary. Kaminski and Schmidt were so engrossed in their argument they didn't even acknowledge my presence. I was invisible.

Schmidt didn't agree with Kaminski. He was babbling about the beauty of his design. He was a slim, dapper man with wire-rimmed glasses and an aristocratic air. He was especially excited about how he incorporated microwave dishes, radio/TV antennae and cell towers into his design.

"She will bloom on the Chicago skyline like a flower. The six wings of the building will shoot up like petals. The radio and TV antennae will radiate like pistils and stamen from each tower."

Oh brother, I thought. I hope he doesn't want to say that in the video. I took a seat at the big table and nodded to a stout Asian man across the table from me. He must be Wong, the client, I thought. He was completely bald. Shaved head. He wore wire-rimmed glasses, giving him a bookish air. He was thick-set, but I sensed a muscular body beneath his gray suit. His face was expressionless. I thought of Odd-Job in the James Bond movies. I glanced around the room looking for his lethal derby. I looked back at Wong and our eyes met. He nodded.

I pulled out a notebook and prepared to take notes while Kaminski and Schmidt continued their banter. Half listening, I started doodling, drawing speed tiles on my note paper…four sides, rounded corners, bolt-like nubs, then another one right next to it…

"The towers! The towers! Pistils! Stamen!" he shouted, startling me. "We have to relate them in the video," he continued, confirming my dread. "We can use computer animation and special effects to compare the antennae to a flower."

Another hundred-thousand dollar program on a twenty-thousand dollar budget, I thought. I started another row of speed tiles under the first row, somehow hiding my frustrations in the meticulous rendering on my paper.

"Yeah, yeah, fine! Pistils, Stamen," mimicked Kaminski. "I don't give a shit about flowers. I just care about profits. This building is gonna bring a lot of money downtown. It'll be an economic boon to Chicago. That's what we gotta drive home. Money! Growth! Progress!" Joe looked to his client for confirmation but Wong just sat there impassively, saying nothing.

I looked at Wong, trying to figure him out, my right hand absently rendering my speed tiles, the arrangement becoming ever more complex on my paper.

"Isn't the occupancy rate for downtown buildings at an all time low right now?" I asked. But nobody seemed to hear me. I shrugged and turned back to my "notes." I drew wires emanating out from the bottom row of tiles; connections to…what? The design I drew was elegant and symmetrical. I liked it better than Helmut's building.

"It's a revolutionary design! That's the thing to stress!" shouted Helmut, trying to get Wong on his side. "The first building ever designed with the antennae fully integrated into the design…"

"Ahh, bullshit!" from Joe. "Who cares? Who even looks up at a building? Who even notices antennas?"

Wong looked at each man as they spoke, but he remained noncommittal.

They went on like this for another twenty minutes while I pretended to take notes, working on my wires, my speed tiles. Three drafts of the script and as far as I could tell we hadn't even settled on a concept yet.

Half listening to Helmut rant about his flowers, I sighed and looked up from my doodling. My heart skipped a beat. Wong was leaning forward, staring down at my speed tile drawing, his forehead creased in thought, his attention focused. As he looked up and stared into my eyes, I saw his lips form the words and thought I heard him whisper silently, "speed tiles."

Clumsily, I dragged Helmut's ridiculous blueprints over my drawing, hiding it from Wong's intrusive eyes. I looked at Helmut, then at Kaminski. They hadn't noticed the exchange. I looked back at Wong. He was rising from his chair.

"Excuse me, gentleman," he said politely. He glanced at me, paused, then abruptly turned and left the room.

Helmut and Kaminski continued their argument in spite of Wong's absence. They went on rehashing the same themes over and over. Depressed and a little agitated by Wong's unwanted attention, I quietly opened my briefcase. I shoved the cluttered contents to the side to make room for my "notes" and carelessly revealed the speed tile sitting on the floor of the briefcase, its metallic golden nubs glowing, emanating reflected light from the ceiling florescents. I recoiled from the shiny square, surprised to see it in these unlikely surroundings. I thought about the damned thing every day, dreamt about it every night. How could I have forgotten that it was still there, still in the briefcase where I hid it from Marcia in Saugatuck last summer?

Hid it from Marcia? I thought in a flash of recognition. Did I really hide it from Marcia?

I didn't really think consciously about hiding the thing until now, but then it hit me. I didn't want her to see it. I wanted to keep it to myself. But why? I never keep things from her. I can't. She reads my mind. I realized that I never even showed her the speed tile. I never intended to show it to her because it was mine. I stashed it in my briefcase after my hike in the dunes. I hid it from her.

I quickly looked up at Helmut and Joe to see if they noticed my speed tile. An irrational feeling of greed passed fleetingly through my mind. They hadn't seen it. I looked back down and stared at it, remembering the day I found it in the dunes of Michigan. I smiled. It calmed me at first, but then a chill went up my spine as I thought of Wong, then of Helmut's pistils and stamen, of the proposals and the scripts. I covered the speed tile with my drawing, hiding it from…(who?) I closed the lid, clicked the latches. Sweating now and confused, I quietly stood up, sighed, and left the room. They didn't even notice.

As I closed the door to the conference room I heard Helmut shouting: "The wires! The fiber optic lines! They are like the roots of a flower digging deep into the Earth."

"Fuck the Earth," mimicked Kaminski.

I used to be able to laugh off meetings like that, but this time I couldn't. It was tough coming up with the script in the first place and there wasn't any end in sight. Without an agreement on direction, the video would turn out to be a compromise at best, and it wouldn't reach either Kaminski's or Schmidt's audience. In fact, I wasn't even sure who the audience was. The mysterious Mr. Wong certainly didn't offer any clues. The video would just be another piece of fluff that would be easily forgettable by anyone who watched it. And it would be expensive. What a business. What a waste. I'd rather make speed tiles.

I couldn't wait to get out of there. I felt nauseous, trapped, and a little frightened by Wong. I hated this project, this building, this city.

Angry, I waited ten minutes for an elevator I could fit into. When I finally got to the mezzanine, a suspicious guard stopped me to inspect my briefcase. He was the same guard who let me in, a big black guy with a badge and a gun.

I felt an irrational surge of panic (the tile!). Trying to think logically, I knew I didn't have anything to hide. I was here on legitimate business. (What if he found my speed tile? What if he took it?) As I opened the briefcase, he looked at me instead of the briefcase, using a technique customs agents use to ferret out smugglers. He was looking for fear in my eyes, and he found it. He started unpacking everything, searching for the source of my uneasiness. He even called Kaminski's office to confirm my meeting with him and the flower-crazed architect. As he waited for Kaminski's office to call back he saw the speed tile, my precious speed tile.

"What's that?" he asked, pointing at the square metal artifact on the bottom of my briefcase.

"Uhh…It's a…uhh…speed tile…" I stammered, beginning to shake.

"Say what?"

"A, uhhh, speed tile…I found it…It's mine…" I tried to explain. This was ridiculous. It was only a piece of metal I found. It wasn't important. Why was I getting so upset?

"Yours, huh? Where did you find it? And what the heck is a speed tile anyway?" he asked.

"I, ahh…I don't really know…It's a…uhhh…I don't know what it is," I explained. I was losing it. My eyes darting this way and that, looking for a way out. I was sweating bullets now. I was in a panic. For some reason, I couldn't have him looking at my speed tile. I couldn't let him touch it.

"Don't know? You take this from one of the offices upstairs, buddy?" He was getting a little gruff. He sensed my panic, my weakness.

"No. It's mine. I found it in the sand…I need it," I blubbered.

"Ain't no sand 'round here. Whachou mean sand? Here, lemme see that." And he reached for the speed tile.

I gasped.

Just then the phone rang and the guard turned to answer it, leaving the speed tile untouched. It was Kaminski's office calling to confirm my meeting. But there was some confusion because the secretary thought I was still in the meeting. I listened as he talked on the phone, staring at the speed tile, trying to think of some way out. The nubs seemed to glow, like they did in the meeting upstairs. They seemed to be alive, squirming like little golden worms. I shook my head and rubbed my eyes. Probably reflections…I thought, from the lights.

I continued to stare at the squirming nubs, half listening to the guard on the phone. The reflections began to pulse softly. "So who is this guy if John Hunter's in a meeting upstairs. He's got this speed tile thing. I think he took it. You know anything about a speed tile?"

Mesmerized, I watched the pulsing grow more distinct, the guard's conversation muted, distant. "Uh huh, yea…OK…Doctor Wong? Twenty-third floor? Yeah, maybe he'll know something."

He turned to me. "You in big trouble, boy." I looked up at him, frightened, the spell broken. "I think you stole this little thing and I'm gonna call upstairs to the twenty-third floor and see if anything's missing."

He reached for the speed tile. It was definitely alive, pulsing from within. "Don't touch that!" I warned, but he ignored me. I held my breath, sweating, feeling weak. He picked up the glowing speed tile. He ran his fingers over the nubs, turned it over, felt the smooth polished back surface, fingered the rough, weathered edges of the sides.

I felt a jealous rage come over me as if he were violating one of my daughters in front of me. I didn't want him touching it, caressing it. It was mine! I gripped my umbrella tightly, fighting the urge to punish the guard. I felt the fragile wires inside the umbrella buckle and break as I clutched it tighter. I watched the guard's face change from angry to curious as he looked at the tile and continued to finger it. He was obviously enjoying the speed tile in his hand, and I hated him for it.

I was breathing heavily, tears coming to my eyes. He dialed Wong's office and asked for him. "Uh huh. Uh huh," he said, looking back up at me, a little confused by the instructions he was getting. He continued to handle the speed tile and I watched his hard face continue to soften.

"Okay, Doc," said the guard. He put the phone down and reluctantly turned back to the brief case. He hesitated, not wanting to give up the speed tile. I saw it in his eyes. I saw him struggle to let go of that precious and wonderful object. Finally, with a sigh, he placed the speed tile back in the brief case. He put all my papers back on top of it: my proposals, storyboards, Helmut's pistil and stamen building blueprints. Then he took the speed tile sketch I had made in the meeting and looked up at me. He frowned. He carefully folded it twice and put it in his shirt pocket, then he closed the lid and latched it. "Okay, you can go now," he growled, looking me in the eye. Then he turned away.

Relieved, but frightened and confused, I picked up the briefcase and headed shakily toward the door. What's going on? I thought. Is that damned thing really that important to me? I almost beat him with my umbrella. Oh brother, what's happening to me? And why did he take my drawing?

I left the building and tried to blend into the flow of traffic heading toward the train. I was in a daze of confusion, simultaneously relieved to have my speed tile back and repulsed by its sick, pulsating glow. I stumbled, shaking, into a bar. I had to sit down. I had to calm myself. I sat at the window drinking a martini, clutching my briefcase, recovering my composure, watching the people go by.

One drink, then another, the alcohol dulling my senses, magnifying my confusion. I lost track of the time as I sat and drank, sedating the chaos in my mind. Pistels and stamen...Fuck the earth...Speed tiles...Hiding the thing from Marcia...The buckets of speed tiles I was making, collecting...The alien visions I was painting...Why? What did it mean?

I must have been there for hours because when I looked out at the street the foot traffic had switched direction. It was now headed west, back to the trains, and it was raining.

No longer shaking but in a foul, muddled state of mind, I left the bar and went out on the street. The drizzling rain ran down the back of my neck. I pulled up my collar and tried to open my umbrella but the broken and splintered wires ripped through the fabric and offered a misshapen tangle of metal and nylon for protection. I remembered the guard fingering my speed tile and my irrational urge to beat him with my umbrella. I mindlessly raised the mess over my head and joined the team heading for the trains.

I walked south bouncing like a pinball off random foot traffic, trying to go far enough to reach the relative calm of a westerly flow. I staggered down the street with random thoughts, dark thoughts, darting in and out of my mind. I didn't like this. I wanted my old life back, a life without speed tiles, a life where I could laugh off Helmut's rantings about pistil and stamen towers.

Or was it something else? Maybe a new life. Didn't I want a life without idiotic clients, without faceless crowds and black umbrellas and bulging briefcases? A life without skyscrapers, where sand dunes were the tallest things around.

Finally, reaching the cross street, I turned west, joining the throngs, marching to the trains. We were almost in step, walking at a steady pace. The rain was quickening, but we were civilized, orderly. Weren't we accomplishing something? Weren't we going home?

I looked around me. No one looked back. Then I thought: Another building? Another ten thousand people here, doing this? I remembered Wong's penetrating stare…eerie, scary. I couldn't imagine producing a video about Helmut's ridiculous pistil and stamen building. "Fuck the Earth?" Isn't that what Kaminski said? What am I doing here? What am I doing with my life?

I slowed down, rain pouring down my collar, fearing the tile's power. I was on the bridge going over the Chicago River. I didn't notice people bumping me from behind, going around me, stepping on my feet, pushing me. I was out of step, no longer one of the lemmings, no longer part of the team.

I looked up, and standing by the rail, out of the flow of traffic, I saw a man with an old-fashioned sandwich board over his shoulders. I blinked. Was he real, or is this my mind playing tricks? In my agitated state, half drunk, I didn't trust my perceptions. Rain was falling steadily now, streaming down the man's face, cascading over the sandwich board. I strained to look at the board. I moved closer…bump, push, shove…It was the man's resume, blown up big and hung around his neck. He was a consultant. A gravity consultant. What the hell is a gravity consultant?

I looked up at his face. His eyes stared back at me, dark, empty. His hair was long and scraggly, dripping rainwater over his face and shoulders. He had a thick mustache and long, bushy, old-fashioned sideburns. I looked down at his clothing. He was in some kind of costume, dressed like a seaman. Britches of old, coarse fabric, black boots, a long black coat with a wool scarf around his neck. He was soaked from the rain. Incongruously, his resume listed several sailing ships he had captained, ships with old-fashioned names—the S.S. Farnsworth , the Audrey Rose, the F. B. Stockbridge—names that evoked images of wooden hulls and square sails. What's the connection, I thought. What does gravity have to do with sailing ships?

I felt dizzy, confused. I looked around me. No one paid any attention to the gravity consultant, the sea captain. After all, who would hire a consultant in a crazy costume with a sandwich board standing in the pouring rain on a bridge over the Chicago River? And sea captains? They don't work downtown. They don't wear sandwich boards.

Through the pouring rain, he looked me in the eye and smiled, darkly. Then he turned and silently walked away, disappearing into the crowd…

Frightened and losing control, I pushed my way to the rail where the captain had been standing. There, floating impossibly in the air, spattered by rain, right where the gravity consultant had stood, was a speed tile. Rain drops pounded it. The small tile looked just like mine, but it was hot, the nubs pulsing yellow, the raindrops evaporating as they hit, hissing and steaming. It hung suspended in front of me. Absurd. Impossible.

My mouth dropped. Gravity. The visions I was having, my thoughts and daydreams as I built my own speed tiles in my basement—they predicted this anti-gravity thing. But I thought it was a joke, a figment of my over-active imagination. Am I dreaming? What's going on?

I rubbed my eyes, blinked, and shook my head. Suddenly, one of the passing suiters bumped the levitating speed tile and knocked it through the railing. I pushed my way to the rail and watched it plunge into the

Chicago River. The gravity man's speed tile was gone. So was my sanity. Did I really see that speed tile? Maybe I imagined the whole thing; the sea captain, the speed tile, the guard. I felt nauseous and confused.

I looked down on the thick, muddy water of the Chicago River, churning, bubbling like lava below. Pouring rain pocked the raging waters, splattering the waves. The futility of it, I thought, of rain cleansing these rancid waters.

Rain poured over my head and down my collar. Could the rain wash out my own rancid thoughts, my nightmare visions? I caught a chill, lifted my collar and raised my wounded umbrella over my head.

What happened next was startling in its suddenness and its clarity. I held my briefcase in my hand, heavy with the project's proposals and the building's blueprints and the unfinished video within, heavy with the awesome power of the speed tile. Rain spitting, splattering through my broken umbrella, I paused on the bridge and looked down, again, at the murky water below.

"I just want to be an artist," I whispered.

Tree branches, garbage and raw sewage flowed by, taking my dream of being an artist downstream, out of reach. I felt choked, constrained by the miles of film, tons of videotape that I shot, ashamed of the bucket of speed tiles I made. After a brief hesitation, I whispered "no"—then heaved the bulging briefcase filled with proposals, blueprints, scripts and storyboards (and the speed tile)—heaved it into the Chicago River…

I smiled, weakly. My knees shaking.

But my relief and satisfaction were short-lived. I realized that my precious speed tile was gone. I felt like Tolkien's Golem when he lost the ring: insane with dread.

"No!"…I wailed, frightening the suiters around me. I turned and struggled against the grain of the faceless masses heading toward the train. I pushed my way back through gray suits, around black umbrellas and newspapers under arms, over briefcases in hand and past sexless women suiters in running shoes, fighting my way to the far end of the bridge. In a panic, I clambered over a chain link fence, scaled a concrete barrier and shimmied down a post to the water's edge. Spotting the briefcase, still floating, I dived into the gray-green water after it...

By the end of that dismal March, I was diagnosed and treated for a nervous breakdown. It was soon after leaving the hospital that I left the dripping shame of the Chicago River behind and moved my family to Saugatuck.

Our new house was in a rural setting on the edge of a forest, along a pleasant, meandering creek. Moving trucks. Bank closings. Pack, unpack, store this, sell that.

The briefcase, now warped and stained from Chicago's polluted waters, found its way into a corner of the attic where it sat undisturbed for ten years while I made a new life with my family in Saugatuck.

The speed tile? A dim memory, a bad dream. I tried to forget about it, to forget that it was sealed away in that old briefcase, stashed in a corner of the attic. I continued my life in Saugatuck, resurrecting my vocation as a video producer, forgetting my obsession with speed tiles, forgetting my ambitions, putting aside my dream of being an artist—working, preparing, waiting.

Waiting for the speed tile to tell me what to do.

Chapter 2

The Night Visitor

My name's Hilllary...with three "l"s. I'm 13 years old and I live in Saugatuck, Michigan with my Mom and my Dad and my cats, Spinnaker and Spooky, my dog, Sandbar, and my parakeet Salt. I used to have another parakeet named Pepper, too, but Spinnaker ate him. Spinnaker's really my stupid sister's cat. He's big and yellow. He's a beast. And, oh yeah, my demented sister Hannah. She lives here too. She's a whore. She just got her driver's license.

I'm real skinny, like my Mom. She's always been skinny. Dad says she eats like a horse, but never gains any weight. Mom's real pretty too. She looks a lot younger than she really is. She's got long blonde hair, but it's not real blonde. She gets it out of a bottle. I've got brown hair. It's long too. Dad says Mom's hair would probably be the same color as mine if she didn't hit the bottle every couple of weeks. Mom says she's worth it.

Mom says that Dad asked her if she ever broke her nose on their first date. Dad's a real romantic. Mom was pissed but she married him anyway. Dad says he likes her nose, but it's got a little bump on it that Dad mistook for an old fracture. It's really a feature. Mom's part Czechoslovakian and part Polish. Dad's part Slovenian and part Lithuanian. Dad says that makes me a mutt.

Dad's kind of tall. Six feet. He's got brown hair too, but he insists its blonde. He must be color blind. I don't know how he got through art school. He's got a mustache and kind of long hair, but not long enough for a pony tail. His mustache is blonde. Maybe that's why he thinks he has blonde hair...or is it gray? Dad's around 50 years old. Pretty old, but he looks a lot younger than that, kind of like Mom.

Dad and Hannah aren't as skinny as Mom and me. They're not fat. They're just not skinny. Hannah wishes she was skinny like me because she's a ballerina. Tough shit, Hannah. She's got long brown hair like mine. She puts it up in a bun when she goes to ballet class. Hannah's really strong. She beats me up all the time. She's also real pretty. Boys are always calling her up or coming over and acting stupid. Hannah laughs a lot. Dad does too.

We live outside of town along Goshorn Creek. Sandbar loves the creek. He's a big yellow Lab. So does Dad. He says it sure beats the Chicago River. Ursulla DeWitt, our neighbor, owns all the property across the creek...about 50 acres. Ursulla usually lives in town in an apartment behind her bookstore, The Singapore Bank Bookstore. She calls her house here on Goshorn Creek her country house...even though it's only three miles from town. Ursulla doesn't want anyone to build on the property across the creek, so its kind of nice. It's just so...dark...and empty...especially at night.

I'll bet you wonder how we wound up in Saugatuck. We didn't always live here. We've only been here for about ten years now. We used to come here on vacations. We had a really great time when we rented a house on the beach with our friends, the Weavers. Dad also started keeping Dancer in Saugatuck. Dancer's our sailboat. We used to spend week-ends and vacations on Dancer at Tower Marina. Anyway, we sold our house in LaGrange. That's near Chicago. Then we bought this house.

Mom said we moved here to get away from the urban scrawl of Chicago...whatever that means. And to bring us kids up in a small town instead of Yuppieville where we used to live.

I think it had something to do with Dad's swan dive into the Chicago River…yuck! I was pretty little then, but Hannah says Dad lost a few marbles that day. Dad jokes about it now. He says it was a very refreshing and invigorating swim. But I don't remember Dad looking very invigorated when Mom brought him home from the hospital that night. We moved right after that.

I like it here, but Hannah's a big city girl at heart. I think she's a big slut at heart…just kidding. I really like Hannah, sometimes, but I think she'd go back to Chicago in a minute if she could. She's sixteen now. A couple more years and she might just do that…join a dance company somewhere. Hannah dances with the Grand Rapids Ballet. She's really a good dancer. But she's not your typical anorexic, little twig like some of the snooty girls in her ballet company. Mom says she will probably get into modern dance or jazz or something as she gets older.

Anyway, even though Hannah says she hates it here, Mom thinks Hannah likes it better than she says. She says sixteen year-olds either "hate" or "love." There's no in-between.

"Why do we have to live in hick town, Saugatuck?" asked Hannah. "There's nothing to do here, Mom!"

"Nothing to do?" said Mom. "It's a real hardship living in this awful place. It's tough being a bike ride from the beach…having beautiful dunes and forests to hike in…being able to walk the streets at night without being mugged. It's agony to have to go sailing on your Dad's sailboat on Lake Michigan. Yeah! Kids the world over should pity your deprived existence."

"Bikes are for dorks. Hiking sucks. Walking? I'm sure! And sailing is so boring…I hate it here!" said Hannah. "There's nothing to do."

Mom definitely does love it here. She loves the water and the harbor and the boats. She loves the dunes and even the tourists. She says tourists pay most of the bills in a vacation town like Saugatuck. I guess it is pretty here, but when you live in a place, even a beautiful place like

Saugatuck, you start to not notice the beauty. You become, like Dad says, short-sighted or near-sighted or something.

When we first moved here, Dad worked out of a couple of rooms in the house. He's a producer. Video. He produces TV programs. Documentaries. And stupid programs about training. And programs about how great his client's companies are. He calls them corporate propaganda. But he always wanted to be an artist.

"Arts, farts, applecarts," he said to Mom right after we moved here. "Who's gonna pay for Hannah's ballet lessons and Hilllary's art supplies? How are we gonna pay the mortgage on this house? What about payments on the boat, and the mooring fees at the yacht club? Artists don't belong to yacht clubs you know?"

"Artists sell paintings. They make a living too," answered Mom.

"I'd have to sell a lot of paintings to support our lifestyle," said Dad.

We all wanted Dad to be an artist, but he told us that for him to be a full time artist would be a very selfish thing to do. I think he was kind of afraid to be an artist, especially after what happened in Chicago before we moved. So he made videos and turned our house into a TV studio…cameras, computers, editing systems…all crammed into two of the five bedrooms in our house.

I guess Dad's business was good because after a couple years he bought a small gray house in town to move his business into. That place really sucked at first. It smelled like cigarette smoke. There were cracks in the walls and the carpet was ripped up and the stove was covered with taco grease. Yuck. But Mom and Dad fixed it up.

Dad found some weird devil-worship stuff in the basement. He threw it all in the dumpster. He hauled it all out through the outside basement door, a kind of flat, trap door leading out to the back yard. It was a kind of secret door, hidden in the bushes. It looked like the storm cellar door on the Kansas farm in The Wizard of Oz. Dad would also use that door to get in the house when he forgot his key, sneaking into the house through the dark, spooky basement.

He also found a bat. Mom was upstairs at the time trying to clean the stove. I had just stopped off there after school with my friend, Suzie, to squeeze some money out of Mom for the soda fountain. Dad was in the basement ripping out an old wall. We heard a blood-curdling scream from the basement, then we heard heavy footsteps running up the stairs.

Suzie's mouth dropped. Mom and I looked at each other, scared. "Dad found a dead body," I thought. "Or a hideous monster. And it's after him!"

"A bat! A bat!" Dad stammered as he burst into the kitchen and slammed the basement door behind him. "It's this big." He held out his hands to show Mom a wingspan three feet wide. "And it started chasing me!"

"What?" Mom looked toward the basement, waiting to hear the giant bat beat its massive wings on the door, expecting to see it burst into the kitchen.

"It's this big..." Dad blubbered, showing an even wider wingspan.

Suzie backed quietly out of the kitchen, eyes wide with terror. Then she turned and ran, slamming the front door behind her...the chicken.

"Bats don't get that big," said Mom, calmly. "It must have been a wild turkey if it was that big." She turned back to the stove.

I tried to picture a wild turkey flying around the basement before I realized that Mom was teasing him. But Dad was still shook up.

"No, really!" Dad insisted. "It fell out of the wall! I picked up a board to hit it, but it started flying around...chasing me. I hate bats!"

Mom had a big laugh at Dad's expense. Dad hired an exterminator. He called him the exorcist. We never saw any more real bats in the house, but we bought Dad a furry stuffed animal bat that hangs from a suction cup sticker. We put it on the front door. When you push its belly, its red eyes light up and it squeals with an eerie "EEEEE, eeee, EEEEE, eeee". Now we call Dad's office the Bat House. Dad uses the stuffed bat for a doorbell. I never liked going in the basement over there. The basement is like hell at the Bat House.

We had a pretty normal life in Saugatuck, even though we hardly ever had dinner together. Dad usually worked late. Hannah had ballet class or rehearsals in Grand Rapids most nights. I was always rehearsing too…usually for some play at Holland Civic Theater. If we did have dinner it was at 10 or 11 o'clock at night. We were a pretty busy family.

Mom worked with Dad at Hunter Productions, but she also drove me and Hannah around a lot, at least until Hannah got her license. School was fun. It still is. Especially with my best friend, Suzie. We started a singing group last month. So far our best songs are "Going to the Chapel" and "My Boyfriend's Back."

One day my Dad dug out an old picture he drew and hung it on the wall in the kitchen. I remembered the picture from when we lived in LaGrange. It was called The Visitor and it shows a blurry skinny guy with a bright light behind him. It's a little picture. Colored pencil. It's a picture of an alien…a UFO guy. Dad drew it around the time he was making all those weird speed tiles before we moved here.

"Oh oh!" said Mom. "Where'd you find that."

"I dug out quite a few of these old pictures." answered Dad. "Remember them? Remember all the speed tiles?"

"How could I forget," said Mom.

"I don't know. I just want to put a couple of these up," said Dad. "I really like some of the colored pencil work I did on these."

"Uh huh," said Mom suspiciously.

I looked at the picture. It was a typical, corny alien, like the kind you see on TV or on the covers of cheap science fiction books. The head was too big for a normal person, and the body was too skinny and delicate…no clothes, no real detail, the eyes, hidden. The weirdest thing was the two rows of speed tiles lined up above the alien's head. It was as if the speed tiles were causing the light, or giving the alien some kind of powers or something. Speed tiles. I had forgotten about the speed tiles.

Slam! I jumped. But it was only Hannah getting home from ballet class. "Sandbar! Sandbar! Pupalupagus!" screamed Hannah. "I missed you so much!" She started rolling around on the floor with Sandbar. She acted like she hadn't seen our dog for months, but she'd only left for class three hours ago.

"Hannah, calm down," pleaded Mom, but Hannah was still full of energy from ballet class.

"Gimme that!" shouted Hannah, as she chased after Sandbar's toy hamburger. Sandbar loved his hamburger. He loved being chased even more.

Hannah tackled Sandbar and ripped the hamburger out of his mouth. The yellow lab sat bolt upright and cocked his ears, waiting to see what Hannah would do next. Then, at point blank range, three feet away from Sandbar's face, she fired the hamburger at his nose. Snap! Catch! He caught it! He usually did.

"Hannah, give the dog a break!" said Dad.

"He loves it." said Hannah, and he did. All animals have this thing about Hannah. They all love her, and she loves them. She even kisses them. It's sick.

Hannah went into the kitchen to get some lemonade, but she stopped at Dad's alien picture. "Hey! It's a portrait of Hill! Looks just like you, dork, skinny legs and all!"

"Shut-up Hannah," I was a little sensitive about my skinny legs. "That's one of Dad's alien drawings."

"I thought there was something inhuman about you, Hilllary." Then she turned to Dad. "I remember this picture, Dad. Where was it anyway?"

"I had it stashed away with all my other paintings in the storage space," answered Dad. Then sheepishly, "I just wanted to see it, that's all…"

Then Dad turned and went into his bedroom. He seemed a little defensive or something. Mom just shook her head.

I woke up late that night. My bedroom is across the hall from Hannah's. And both our bedrooms are in another wing of the house, like a thousand miles away from Mom and Dad's. I had a nightmare. I don't even remember what it was about anymore. Mom and Dad tell me

I have a very active imagination. Anyway, I was scared, so I woke up Hannah. You think she'd help? Right.

"Get out of here you little twerp. Hilllary, you butthole. Don't ever wake me up again. I'm sleeping!"

Whatever my dream was, I was really scared, and I needed some kind of reassurance. I was only 12 then. I was also pretty scared about waking Mom and Dad up. They were trying to keep me out of their room at night. They said I was old enough to deal with my own dreams.

Anyway, heart pounding, I quietly sneaked across the house and carefully opened their door. I tip-toed into their room, mind racing, scared, vulnerable.

Then: a quick movement. (Someone? Something? Or just a shadow…a cloud passing over the moon?)…

Thump, thump thump…(Footsteps? A dog scratching?)

A quiet click. (Door latch?)

A wheeze. (Sandbar snoring? Yes, Sandbar snoring…)

Relief.

Oh, Sandbar…I was comforted by the snoring of our dog. Sandbar sleeps in Mom and Dad's room. If they let him out of their room at night he'd chase the cats and bark at them. He also bites people…but that's another story.

I went over to Dad's side of the bed. I knew Mom wouldn't understand, but maybe Dad would. I stood there quietly for a few seconds trying to decide what to do. Should I wake Dad up and tell him about my dream? Luckily, he rolled over toward me. It looked as if I wouldn't have to wake him up after all. I thought, great, he'll take me in his arms and I'll feel safe again.

So, there I was, standing quietly at the side of his bed watching him turn over. He turned and saw me standing there. Then: his eyes popped wide open and he started screaming!

"Aghhh!" His eyes were bugging out…"No!"

What he saw in his groggy, sleepy condition was that stupid alien figure from his drawing. I was skinny then, my big head silhouetted against the patio doors, moonlight behind. He saw me looming over him, threatening him.

I started screaming, Mom woke up, Sandbar leaped into action, barking, jumping, snarling.

"Aghhh!" Dad was yelling and pushing me away…"Not again!"

I couldn't believe it. What was he doing? What did he think I was doing there? What's going on? God, he scared me. I thought he was really pissed so I started crying.

Sandbar was barking Woo! Woo! Woo! I was crying! Mom was screaming! I guess she thought we were being murdered or something.

Finally, Mom turned on the light and Dad saw it was me and we all stopped screaming and barking. Dad started hugging me. I was crying, Sandbar was still jumping around, excited, wagging his tail now.

Dad said he thought I was an alien or something. I thought he was nuts. He looked at me and gave me another hug and looked outside.

When things calmed down, he got real quiet and went over to the sliding glass door overlooking the deck. He looked back at me and smiled, then looked out at the dark woods in back of our house, Ursulla DeWitt's Woods. Mom kissed me and sent me back to bed, but I didn't sleep much. I had this feeling like it was all starting up again, like before. I guess you'd call it a premonition. I was afraid. Afraid for Dad.

Chapter 3

Trouble at the Bat House

I laid awake for most of the night after Hilllary's alien fiasco. Sandbar went back to his little dog nest under Marcia's sewing table. Marcia fell asleep again, but not before razzing me about my antics. "You gotta stop reading those Whitley Streiber books, John," she teased. "Aliens…UFOs…Next thing you know, Sandbar will start looking like the wolfman."

I don't know why I thought Hill was an alien. I must have been dreaming. I had never been abducted by aliens, I knew that. As far as I was concerned, alien abductions were a fiction, and the alien I drew with my colored pencils was just a symbol, a popularized fabrication of what aliens were supposed to look like.

But the alien image I drew lingered in my mind. The speed tiles over his head, the dirty yellow light behind his emaciated figure. And the other speed tile drawings: the wires, the little bolt-like nubs, the sailing ship with the speed tile hull. There was an undeniable truth to those drawings. Was it the speed tile that drew me, that tugged at my mind? I had not thought about the speed tile for years, not until I pulled out those old drawings. I guess I repressed those bad memories: the murky waters, the weird look on the guard's face, my homicidal fury as he caressed my speed tile.

I remembered the speed tiles I made in my basement studio in LaGrange so many years ago. Where were those speed tiles? I knew I had saved them, put them somewhere. And the strange history I made up as I cut and drilled and shaped that aluminum into exact replicas of the speed tile I found in the dunes. Hmm, the dunes…Singapore. Did I make that up too?

Sleep gently tugged at me as I closed my eyes, thinking, tomorrow I'll have to find those speed tiles…Alien speed tiles…Anti-gravity devices…

Old ambitions wash over my semi-conscious mind as I finally drift into sleep: Old dreams of being an artist…of painting, drawing. (A drawing) A sea captain, a dark, empty stare. He's wearing a sandwich board, his resume…Rain cascading off the board…(A painting) A big black man in a uniform. A guard…A confused look…He moves. (Now, a video) Dim memories of the guard carefully folding a drawing in the lobby, (Cut to) a close-up of the drawing. Speed tiles, meticulously rendered, rows of speed tiles, with wires, brass nubs, worn, weathered edges…(Insight) It's my drawing. (Wide shot.) The guard, slipping the drawing into his shirt pocket…Sleep.

Fitful sleep with the siren call of creativity tugging at my brain. Art. Speed tiles. Repressed needs. A deserted sand dune, a decaying grid-like structure buried in the sand. Speed tiles lined up, one in each square, growing, birthing, generating, getting bigger, bigger…The tile, once small, grows impossibly large. Bloated, slimy, dripping mucous. Disgusting, growing…Oh my God, too big, floating up, over my head…No!, it can't be…Now, a slab. A dripping muddy slab. River waste running down its sides. Wires, popping bigger, bigger, then: bang! It explodes.

My eyes pop open. It's the bedroom door slamming, waking me up. Hilllary, now playing the part, stomps ominously into my room. She's wearing a full length pink leotard, a big pink towel wrapped around her head. She's got big paper eyes, drawn in crayon, cut out and taped on her forehead. She walks with her arms sticking out, motionless in front of her like the monster in an old Frankenstein movie. She has the big barbecue tweezers in one hand and a suction basting bulb thing in the other hand. She reaches the bed, hovers over me and says: "I am an alien creature from the planet Pluton. I am now going to abduct you and perform agonizing experiments on your brain."

I sit up in bed, smiling. Hannah bursts in, camera in hand, Sandbar underfoot, mouth open, tongue hanging, tail wagging, thrilled to be part of the joke. As Hilllary grabs my head with the tweezers and begins "injecting" air from the basting bulb into my forehead, Hannah, laughing, snaps our picture (flash) and Sandbar starts barking.

"Hey Dad!" shouts Hannah. "I heard you had a close encounter of the third kind last night."

"Well," I said, "believe it or not, Hill looked more convincing as an alien last night than she does now." Then I grabbed Hilllary and started tickling her.

"Wo, Wo, Wo, Wo, Wo!" Sandbar hates it when any of us in the family hug each other. I think its because he's so nearsighted. He can't tell us apart when we're close together.

"No! Dad," cried Hill, "I'll get you for that…, Come on Hannah!" Then Hannah jumps on the bed and starts tickling my feet and legs, the place they learned long ago was my most vulnerable spot.

"Wo, Wo, Wo, Wo, Wo!" barks Sandbar.

"Get him. Hold him down," commands Hannah.

Thrashing, tickling, rolling, barking, laughing, three bodies roll off the bed in a heap, Sandbar joining the fray, pink towel unraveling, bringing Hilllary's head down to normal size. Crayon eyes, forgotten, crumpled in the maelstrom. Sandbar, jumping, snarling, barking…getting in the act, part of the fun.

"OK you guys. Cut it out!" The Mom. "Time to get ready for school. Enough of this alien abduction stuff. Hannah, stop!"

Hannah grabs my leg one last time and gives it a fierce tickle; more like a scratch now. She gets up to run, but I time my swing perfectly and lay a loud slap on her retreating butt.

Hilllary, not yet aware of the retreat, is still tangled in the sheets at the foot of the bed. I grab her and hug her close. "My little alien," I say, and give her a big kiss.

Mom. Patient Mom: standing with her arms crossed, smiling. She shakes her head and follows Hannah out of the room. "Come on Hill. Time to get ready for school."

Hilllary looks after Mom, back at me, frowns, looks into my eyes with all the innocent wisdom of a twelve-year-old and says: "You OK, Dad?"

"I'm fine Hill. Sorry about last night."

Still worried, she studies my face, searches the growing darkness in my eyes.

"Really. It was just a dream," I say. Then smiling, "now go on. Get ready for school."

Hilllary smiles back, delivers a quick kiss on my cheek and runs out after Mom, then pauses at the door, "Wait 'til you see what I do to you tonight," she threatens. "It involves a savage beating and a thorough soaking with a water hose." She smiles an evil, mocking smile as she leaves the room with Sandbar at her heels.

I gather up the sheets, the pillows, throw them back on the bed, lay down and smile, looking up at the ceiling, thinking: What a night! And Hilllary! What a kid!

(Then: A flash of memory. A grid. The sand. Singapore.)

I showered slowly, thinking about the night, planning my day. No pressing appointments, some office work, scripting, a few phone calls to clients, not a heavy day, but another day of battle with the business of media.

Jed Lincoln, our only employee, was hard at work in the editing room when I got to the Bat House. He was editing a one hour documentary about Tulip Time, a two week orgy of Dutch tradition…and a celebration of the humble Tulip. It would be about the sixty-year history of the festival told through interviews with local historians and festival volunteers.

Tulip Time in Holland, Michigan is the second largest flower festival in the country, right behind the Rose Bowl in Pasadena. Millions of tulips, dozens of parades, thousands of silver-haired tourists. Mostly members of the geriatric set…four hundred thousand every year. It's a spring ritual. They come to see the flowers and the Klompen Dancers and the scrubbing of the streets (They really do scrub the streets to make them clean for festival parades.) Four hundred thousand people, a big potential audience for a documentary on the festival; a video they could buy from us and watch at home. But we were running out of time. It was already early-April and Tulip Time would begin in early May. Only three or four weeks to finish the edit and get copies out on the streets and in the stores.

I sat down on the couch in the editing room to watch some of the edit and see how it was progressing. I was surrounded by videotape decks, computers, time base correctors and editing devices. There were cables and wires and monitors everywhere, a constant electronic hum in the air: an intimidating place. It was at the center of most activities at Hunter Productions. I had an odd relationship with this room as I did with the technology of media in general: a love-hate relationship that lately was tilting toward the hate side.

The room was an old dirt-floor garage just a year ago. Somewhere during the ancient history of the house, it was a stable, converted to a garage, then to a storage area. Now it's a high-tech edit suite, built mostly by a colorful local with the unfortunate name: Dick Beaver. Dick divides his time between music (the blues), and carpentry. His blues group, "Dick Beaver and the Bunns," had gained some notoriety in local clubs and he had several blues CDs on the market, but most of his income came from the work he did as a builder and a carpenter. Oh yes, and he also moved houses, an odd specialty that was much in demand in these parts.

"How's it going, Jed?" I asked.

Jed was a tall lanky guy with blonde, thinning hair. His sharp, brown eyes missed little, revealed less. He was a private person, passionate about his work, capable of working unsupervised: a prerequisite for working in the loosely structured environment of Hunter Productions. He was impatient, his mind several steps ahead of the poky video machines methodically performing their edits. As he rapidly hit the keys on the editing computer and changed tapes in the video machines, his left leg nervously, quietly, pounded out a rapid beat: thump, thump, thump, thump thump…

"I don't know," replied Jed, pointing at the screen. "This dippy street scrubbing segment. Do we really need it? There's only one picture to support this guy's long boring story. It puts me to sleep. And the Hi-8 deck is acting up again. It just won't lock on the edit points I give it."

Jed joined Hunter Productions permanently about a year ago. He started working with me one summer between his junior and senior year at the University of Michigan. He was majoring in filmmaking and he found Hunter Productions phone number in a local phone book. He called on a lark to see if he could find a summer job doing something that was closer to his major; something that wasn't in a factory. There was something about his quiet, no nonsense manner, his intensity, so I hired him for that summer and, again, the following summer. After he graduated, I hired him full time.

"Street-scrubbing's a pretty odd practice, you've gotta admit that. Edit it back a bit if it's boring. And use some of the footage we got from the TV station to visualize it." I said.

Cleanliness-obsessed Dutch immigrants brought the practice of street scrubbing to this country from the Netherlands where families would regularly scrub the streets with soap and water outside of their homes. In its Americanized, Tulip Time incarnation, hordes of street-scrubbers, hundreds of them, armed to the teeth in Dutch costumes and brooms, would open the Tulip Time Festival every Spring in a parade. Even Michigan's Governor would traditionally participate with his family.

"Yeah, OK," he relented, "but what about this Hi-8 deck?"

"You sure you got the Hi-8 deck synched properly?" I offered. "You know Peg was in here yesterday doing some editing."

"Peg? I see…" He got up from his chair and moved around to the back of the video machines so he could study the dozens of cables coming out of the back. "Peg has some kind of weird karma with this system. All she has to do is walk in the room and it crashes."

Jed fumbled with the wires. "We synched to that little black burst box, or to Video F/X now? Somebody keeps changing it."

"Well, Dick was in over the week-end, and you know how he edits," I confessed. Instead of paying Dick Beaver for building the edit room, I bartered editing time on the system. Dick's a dabbler and an all around jack-of-all-trades. He knows how to do just about anything and he's interested in just about everything, but his methods are sometimes a bit unconventional. He never really understood the way the editing system works, but he always, somehow, gets his little projects edited by randomly hitting keys and clicking on pull down menus until something happens. When his methods backfire, he calmly says "Oh puke," then continues clicking the mouse and punching the keys. Sometimes he starts recabling, convinced that the fault is in the wires, not his methodology. We try to keep an eye on him when he's here.

"Yeah, he's been back here all right. He left a trail." Jed pulled out a brightly colored cabling chart and started tracing wires to their source, checking the label on each cable to make sure it was going to the right place. He drew the chart months ago, frustrated by the ever-changing configurations of our equipment, and by the insufficient documentation supplied by our equipment manufacturers.

We were a small production company and all our equipment had to serve multiple purposes. We often ripped video decks out of the edit suite, cables hanging, for other jobs, like duplication of multiple copies for our clients, or time code window dubs on VHS for referencing video we already shot, or for digitizing video footage into our non-linear editing computer in the other room. Most of the time, these rapes of the edit system were performed in haste, with impossible deadlines and careless follow-up. Stringent management of our resources could probably have avoided a lot of technical problems at Hunter Productions, but we were a bunch of loose, laid back creative types. We lived for the moment, solved only the immediate problem…damn the torpedoes, full speed ahead.

Manufacturers of our high tech systems weren't much help. They can rarely predict how their systems will be used and configured, especially by a bunch of flaky creative types like us. Our systems were a constant frustration because they were a hodge podge of equipment and software from half a dozen different vendors, cobbled together in odd combinations. Video manufacturers kept coming out with newer and better video formats. Computer manufacturers kept making bigger and faster computers. When something new came out that we could afford, we crammed it into the system and made it work.

We were on the phone a lot.

"I'm sorry Mister Hunter, but you're trying to control our Sony BetaSP machine with editing software I've never even heard of."

"You can't make that computer control a Hi-8 deck, they use different protocols."

"No, it's not our hard drive that's giving you problems, it must be the computer. Did you call Apple?"

To make matters worse, the core of our editing system was Video FX, a combination of hardware and software that allowed us to edit video through our Macintosh computer. Digital FX, the company that manufactured Video FX just went bankrupt and we could no longer call them for technical support.

Our ancient three-year-old editing computer was growing whiskers but was forced to control Betacam, 3/4-inch and Hi-8 format videotape editing machines. It was crammed with special circuit boards for video editing, digital audio recording and a high resolution monitor. It clicked and whined and hummed in a schizophrenic symphony as we made it edit video, audio, animation, illustration, print layouts, web pages and word processing. SCSI cables to CD-ROM, external hard drives and a scanner; control cables to a video editor and three video editing decks; communication cables to a printer, the video editor, the internet and our trusty Wacom Graphics Tablet…and that was just the downstairs computer. A bigger computer rigged for digital editing resided in the upstairs edit suite, overlooking the main room through a curved glass window Dick found abandoned in a Herman Miller warehouse.

We were not engineers. That was obvious. Our motivations were creative, not technical, so our most challenging problems were artistic ones. We would often force our equipment to do things it wasn't designed for. We were often frustrated by its limitations.

Jed fumbled with his cables and his chart, changing this cable and that connection. Multi-colored lines hopelessly criss-crossed each other on his chart running from the computer to the edit controller, back to the time base correctors and on to the edit machines. The chart was drawn by Jed, so it was completely indecipherable by anyone else.

"So, now that Digital FX is out of business, when are you gonna get a new edit system. This one sucks and it will only get worse." Jed was turning into a technology junky and we wouldn't be getting any more software "fixes" to feed his habit.

"We have absolutely no money right now," I said, "and don't let Marcia hear you talk about 'buying' anything. She's a little sensitive about money." Marcia, my wife, was our bookkeeper and our fiscal conscience. We were stretched to the limit at the bank, still making payments on equipment that was now hopelessly obsolete. The life span of video and computer equipment was getting shorter every year, and somehow, the competition always seemed to have a newer computer or a better camera than us. But our equipment was not what attracted our clients, we pretended, it was our creativity.

The announcement of Digital FX going bankrupt put a definite damper on our future plans. While a software update to bring our technology up to date was relatively inexpensive, buying a brand new edit system was hopelessly out of our budget range. But without constant updates, we would be left in the dust of our competitors, dinosaurs in an age of faster, escalating technological change.

"You know, Pritchett called this morning," said Jed as he continued to fix Dick's cabling nightmare, "about that video newsletter you're bidding on."

"Oh yeah? What did he say?" I was especially interested in the Pritchett project because it would mean four videos a year, and an ongoing contract.

"He said to call him," answered Jed. "He mumbled something about Avid editing…"

"Oh great!" I moaned. Avid was a sophisticated editing system that was capable of outputting finished video directly out of the computer, bypassing the need for videotape decks. Avid stored video images digitally and allowed the editor to work in a non-linear fashion. Non-linear, digital editing was doing for video what word processing did for typing. Scenes could be rearranged, added or deleted easily without affecting the flow of the program. Before non-linear editing, a video program had to assembled in a linear fashion, carefully, scene by scene from beginning to end. Any deletions in the finished program would leave a gaping hole and would require a complete re-edit from that point on.

We had a digital, non-linear edit system called the Hitchcock in our upstairs edit suite, but it was manufactured by Digital FX, the same company that made our Video FX analog editing system. Unfortunately, they went bankrupt before Hitchcock took the leap to an online system. The video quality coming out of the Hitchcock was grainy and low in resolution, not good enough to qualify as finished video. We only used the Hitchcock for preliminary edits in which the computer would keep track of every edit decision. To finish a program edited on Hitchcock, we would have to repeat the edit on our analog system using good old-fashioned video edit decks that would be controlled by the computer; a tedious repetitive process.

"They want to finish their news video on an Avid?" I asked.

"It makes sense," replied Jed. "With all their late-breaking news and last minute stories coming in, finishing the video digitally is the only way to go. You'll just have to get an Avid."

"Right," I said. "The bank's already breathing down my neck. We haven't even paid for Hitchcock yet. I'll give Frank at Pritchett a call."

"Better call him right away," said Jed as he put away his chart. "Frank sounded anxious."

I went up the four stairs to the main part of the house and dialed Pritchett's number from my phone on the bookcase in the conference room. I didn't really have an office at the Bat House. All the rooms were used for various "video" needs or for storage of videotapes and masters. The conference room was once a dining room and I liked making phone calls standing up so I could pace and wave my arms around as I talked. Marcia walked in as I was dialing.

I waved. "Hi!, can I talk to Frank Johnson?" to the phone. "Hi Marsh. Where you been?" to Marcia.

"I was over at Sally's shop," she answered as she went to her desk in the room that was once the living room.

"Hello, Frank? It's John at Hunter Productions. How ya doin?"

I didn't like his tone as he answered, "Oh, I'm doing OK. This video newsletter project is driving me nuts, though."

"Oh yeah?" I said. "Jed said you called this morning. You getting ready to start on the first issue?"

"Yes, we are, John." He said, then cleared his throat nervously. "But unfortunately for you, we're gonna award the contract to Digicam Video in Holland."

I sat down. I didn't know what to say. "But we've been doing your video for years. Why go there?"

"Avid," he said, "that's why. I'm sorry John. We need a Digital system and your Hitchcock won't do it. Avid is what we need."

"Wait a second!" I stood up again. Marcia looked at me, sighed, shook her head, went back to her pile of bills. "People do edits, not machines. The Avid's a tool. Who's gonna run it? Who's gonna make the edit decisions? Frank! You're making a mistake, here. What about those awards we won last year for those videos we did for you?"

"That was last year," said Frank. "Avid's the 'in' thing now. Digital editing. It's the wave of the future."

"Frank, you're setting yourself up. It's a trap," I pleaded. "When you start thinking that technology, that Avid, is gonna solve all your problems, you're gonna start producing crap for video. You gotta hire people, not machines!"

"Sorry, too late," he said. "We hired Avid." Then he hung up.

"Yeah. Keep in touch," I mumbled, then slammed the phone down.

"Shit! We just lost another one," I said as I walked over to Marcia's desk. "We just can't compete with all this out-dated equipment."

She held up a handful of envelopes: invoices, past due bills, reminder notices, "It's getting harder to keep up with all these out-dated bills too."

"Maybe Tulip Time will pull us out of this," I groaned as I sat down next to her, referring to the video we were producing.

"Yeah! And maybe Santa Claus will come at Easter this year," she said. "I've got some more good news for you," she said, trying not to look me in the eye.

"Great," I said. "Now what?"

"I was just over at Sally's shop," she started, "and Sally's looking for a part time sales person. Someone who can work about three days a week."

Sally Clark was one of our first friends when we moved to Saugatuck. Her daughter, Suzie, was one of Hilllary's best friends. Sally's husband, Ted, owned Clark Systems, a growing company in

Holland that manufactured high tech work stations for manufacturing facilities. Sally started a retail business in an old Victorian mansion she and Ted bought in downtown Saugatuck. She called it "Sally's Nook" and it was one of the more creative shops in Saugatuck, selling upscale clothing, jewelry, crafts and ethnic artifacts. She was in the process of gently evicting the long time tenants on the second and third floors of the building so she could expand her shop and grow her business.

"So what?" I replied. "You've got a job. You work here."

"I've never even gotten a paycheck from this place," she said sarcastically. "I just work here for fun. I told Sally I would take the job."

"What?" I cried. "Who's gonna do all this stuff?" I pointed at the bills and the ledger book.

"I'll still work here two days a week," she answered. "And week-ends if I have to. We can really use the money, John. These bills aren't gonna pay themselves."

"But what about shoots and meetings?" I asked desperately. Marcia often worked as the production coordinator for our shoots, scheduling actors and freelance crew members and interfacing with the client.

"I guess you'll have to use Peg," she replied.

"But I have to pay her!" I said.

"Exactly!" she said, and looked me in the eye.

"John, we have to do something," she said softly. "The ship's sinking fast." Then she held up a handful of bills again.

"Hey Marcia, I'm glad you're here," interrupted Jed. He had been in the edit room until now. "Can you order a couple more cases of 20-minute 3/4SP mini's. We ran out of tape stock for the Tulip Video."

Marcia looked at Jed, then back at me, frowning.

"Good timing, Jed," I said. Then I left the room.

Chapter 4

A Bucket of speed tiles

Dad's been a real grouch lately, ever since Mom started working at Sally's Nook. He's kinda mad at Mom. He accuses her of being a traitor, he says she's deserting a sinking ship. Mom says, "Women and children first."

Dad's at the Bat House a lot lately, but I think it's because of the stupid Tulip Time video, not because of Mom. He and Jed are editing their brains out, trying to get it done in time for the Festival. It's funny when I call Dad at work. I can always tell when he's editing.

"Dad? It's Hill. (silence) Dad, you there?" Dad really gets into it when he edits. It's hard to get his attention. Jed's the same way too.

"Uhhh…what?" says Dad. I could tell that his mind is still on one of the scenes he's trying to edit. He still doesn't even hear me. I try shouting to get his attention.

"Dad?…Dad!"

"Huh? Who is this?" I think I finally got through, but I know if he hung up the phone now, he would immediately forget I called him. It's spooky. It's like he gets into some kind of trance or something.

"Dad, it's Hill. Are you editing?"

"Uhhh, yeah. Okay Hill. Yeah, I'm editing. Can you hang on a second. Let me just get this scene marked."

I wait, listening as he keeps working. I hear him typing away on the keyboard. I hear "siht, ot deal doul pilut eoh noitarbelech limis a tat tought eo doul OH!" the silly backwards talking at high speed as the machines back up, looking for the scene Dad marked, the clickety-clack of the tape decks cueing up to his edit point.

"Dad?"

"Just a second, Hill."

Then a final clickety-clack as the machines start to record. I hear the narrator: "Who would have thought that a simple celebration of the Tulip would lea...!" Then Dad again: "Shit!" I hear him hitting more keys, making some kind of correction. Watching Dad edit is like watching paint dry. I usually can't tell what the heck he's doing. Listening to him edit on the phone is even weirder.

"Dad! Stop! Listen to me!"

"What Hill? I'm editing. What is it?"

"Okay Dad, now concentrate on what I'm saying. Turn away from the computer and listen to me." I speak very slowly and distinctly. "Mom wants to know when you're coming home for dinner. Dad? Dad?" I could tell that his mind was still on the edit. He was thinking about what he had to do to fix the scene. But I was making progress. I was starting to get through to him.

"Dinner?"

"Yes, Dad, dinner. What time will you be home?"

"Dinner, dinner, dinner..." he mumbles, one part of his brain trying to put meaning to the word, "hmmm,...Oh Dinner! Yeah, dinner. Uhhh, what time is it now?"

I did it. I got through to him. "It's 7 o'clock already, Dad."

"7 o'clock? Really?" (silence)

"Dad?"

"Yeah, Hill. Uh, let me just finish this one edit and I'll be home...15 minutes, max."

I usually triple Dad's time estimates. "He'll be home about quarter to eight, Mom."

It's not that Dad's an idiot, although Mom calls him that sometimes. It's just that he gets to concentrating so hard on what he's doing with those edit machines that he blocks out everything else. Its like talking to a brick wall trying to get his attention. At our house, we call that condition "Edit Brain."

Anyway, Dad was in the Edit Brain mode a lot lately. So was Jed.

But Dad also got into his speed tiles again. That was even more weird. He found an old cigar box full of speed tiles in the garage, and a big bucket of them too. I don't remember much about when he made the speed tiles. But I remembered enough to know what they were. I knew they were speed tiles. He made them a long time ago, when we lived in LaGrange. Hannah remembered more than me.

"He was such a spaz, Hill. He spent, like, hours in the basement, making those stupid things. Filing and drilling. He showed me how to make them too. I made one, but, God! It was so boring. I can't believe he made so many of them."

We watched him when he first brought the tiles in from the garage. Mom was in the kitchen making dinner. I was sitting on the couch, drawing. Hannah was pretending she was studying. She was really writing one of her stupid letters to Jason, her latest so-called boyfriend. We pretended to keep drawing and writing. Dad didn't notice that we were secretly watching him.

"God, Hill, this is spooky," whispered Hannah. "This reminds me of LaGrange."

Dad was picking out the speed tiles one by one. He studied each one. Then he started lining them up in rows on the dining room table. I looked at him and I realized he was in "Edit Brain" mode. He was really into those stupid speed tiles.

I leaned over and cupped my hand over Hannah's ear. "What are speed tiles anyway?" I asked.

"They're alien pods from another planet," she said quietly, her eyes darting back and forth, looking into my eyes, one by one, measuring the effect of her words.

I half believed her. "What do you think he's doing with them?"

"He's setting up a force field," she whispered, her eyes sparkling more brightly and her tone becoming conspiratorial. "It's like a beacon that only UFOs can see."

"A beacon? UFOs?" I swallowed, my voice shaking.

"Yeah," whispered Hannah, coming closer. "And when he gets the tiles just right, a space ship is gonna land on the roof and kidnap you and stick needle-like probes into your eyeballs and your stomach. They're gonna artificially impregnate you and clone an inferior race of dorks just like you."

Finally, realizing I was being teased, again, by my big sister, I stuck my tongue out at Hannah and looked back at Dad.

He kept picking out the speed tiles one by one, lining them up in neat rows on the table.

"Dad?" I said quietly.

He didn't hear me. He studied another tile, then, rejecting it for some reason, put it aside. He reached into the bucket for another one.

"Dad!" I said louder, and this time got through.

"Huh?" said Dad, a little startled.

"What are those things anyway, Dad, and what are you doing with them?"

"Oh, these things," he said, holding up one of the speed tiles, then looking at Hannah, "They're alien pods from another planet."

He turned back to me and smiled as my eyes grew wider. Then he looked back at Hannah and winked. I guess he did overhear us after all.

"I told you Hill!" said Hannah. "The aliens are gonna get you, 'cause you're such a hopeless dork!"

Dad sat down across from us. "No, Hill, these are speed tiles. I made them in LaGrange a long time ago. I don't know what they're for, or what I'm gonna do with them."

"You should have one of them implanted in Hilllary's head," teased Hannah. "It'll be bigger than her brain, anyway."

I ignored my stupid sister and looked at Dad, curious about what he was saying.

"I'm thinking about making a sculpture or a construction of some kind using these things," said Dad. "I don't know why I call them speed tiles. Just something I made up, I think."

He looked up and stared at the fireplace, thinking, remembering.

Then, shaking his head, he continued. "I made up this thing about speed tiles having unusual powers, anti-gravity properties. Like they came from another time, another place…just a story, I guess."

Mom came in with two glasses of wine. She handed one to Dad and sat down next to him. "Do they have any kind of income-generating powers?" she asked.

Dad turned to her and frowned. "Maybe," he replied. "Maybe there's a market for speed tiles. People buy pet rocks and Chia Pets don't they? Why not speed tiles?"

The phone rang. I leaped to my feet and beat Hannah to answer it. "Hello?"

No answer. I listened. It was the breather. We were getting more and more of these crank phone calls lately. The breather scared us at first. The calls started a couple months ago, but now they were kind of a joke. We didn't feel threatened, we kind of felt sorry for whoever it was.

"It's for you, Hannah." I held out the phone to my big sister.

Hannah smiled. She was expecting a call from Jason, her Neanderthal boyfriend. "Hello, this is Hannah," she said, expectantly.

"Hello! Hello!" she repeated. I watched her as she listened. I was sure she heard the crank breather now, her eyes registering recognition. She looked at me. She knew she had been had.

She slammed the phone down. "I'll get you for that, you whore." Then she came after me.

"Who was it, Hannah?" asked Mom.

"The fricking breather, Hilllary's long lost lover," she shouted as she chased me out of the room, Sandbar scrambling to his feet, joining in the fun.

At dinner that night Dad talked about the Ronald McDonald House video he was helping to produce as a public service project. The video was about a house in Grand Rapids that was built by the Ronald McDonald Foundation. It was there for families to live while their children were being treated in local hospitals. Usually the kids were really sick, some of them dying, and the people who ran the house thought of it as a kind of support group for families going through traumatic times. Anyway, he asked Suzie and me to sing the theme song for the video. It was a kind of corny song, nothing like "My Boyfriend's Back," but we were going to record it the next day in Dick Beaver's studio.

I sang in Dick's studio once before around the time he was building Dad's edit suite and it was really fun. He asked me to sing the little kid part in a Christmas song he wrote. I got to wear earphones and sing into a big microphone. It really sounded great. It was a sad song about a man who got a divorce and had to leave his home. His little daughter stayed with his ex-wife. Anyway, the man became a department store Santa, and who should sit on his lap one day, but his daughter, who didn't recognize him. The chorus of the song, sung by me, was that all I wanted for Christmas was for Mommy and Daddy to get back together…sappy, but, hey, it was fun.

Anyway, I was looking forward to the recording session. So was Suzie. Dad was going to pick us up right after school and take us to Dick's studio.

After dinner, Dad went back to sorting his speed tiles and Hannah and I did the dishes. Mom went into the library to watch TV. Hannah and I joined her after the dishes. Dad looked like he was in a trance again as I walked past him on my way to the library.

Mom went to bed early, and Hannah went to her room to call Jason on the phone. She was mad because he didn't call her. I watched the rest of the Dick Van Dyke Show on Nick at Nite, an episode about a whole closet full of walnuts or something. I thought of Dad and his speed tiles. After the show ended, I shut off the TV and started into the dining room to see how Dad and his speed tiles were doing.

After the laugh track on Dick Van Dyke, the silence seemed amplified. I heard crickets and a soft wind blowing through the leaves. Living right on the edge of the woods, we had a lot of trees around our house. So many trees that we seldom got any real sunlight through our windows except through the big skylights Dick Beaver helped Dad put into the dining room over the table. On a clear night you could see the moon and stars through these skylights.

Frogs croaking in the creek, a hiss and meow from a distant cat fight, a barking dog down the block, continuing rustle of wind in the trees. With the TV off it was very dark in the house. I walked quietly into the dining room and froze. My heart pounding, fear gripping my throat, I fought back a scream.

There was Dad, standing over the dining room table, staring blankly at the speed tiles arranged there. It should have been dark, but somehow there was a sick yellow glow reflecting off the speed tiles, shining up on my Dad's face, lighting his features from below like a cheap Halloween mask. The light reminded me of Dad's drawing with the putrid yellow light silhouetting the alien's skinny form.

I looked down at the table and gasped, thinking of the walnuts pouring out of the closet in Rob Petrie's dream. The entire surface of the table was covered with speed tiles, each tile meticulously placed in even rows, one after another, tiles perfectly arranged perpendicular to the edges of the table. It also reminded me of the scene in the Stephen King movie, The Shining, where Jack Nicholson typed page after page of a single phrase "All work and no play makes Jack a dull boy." I thought of insanity and obsession.

The yellow glow seemed to be coming from the little brass bolts in the corners of the speed tiles, softly, persistently, beaming reflected light up to Dad's face. Thousands of silent rays of filthy yellow light zapping him, pelting him with alien thoughts, dangerous dreams.

"Dad?" I said shakily, breaking the spell.

"Huh?" He slowly turned and looked at me blankly, not seeing, still thinking. Still an edit brain.

Then, slowly, a cloud passed over the moon, erasing the sick light reflecting off the speed tiles from the skylights above.

Shaking his head to clear it, Dad leaned clumsily on the table, knocking off some of the speed tiles arranged there. He brought his hand up shakily to his forehead, rubbed it and looked at me. "Hill, you still up? I thought you went to bed."

"I was just going to bed," I said. "But I wanted to see how you were doing first. You scared me."

"Scared you?" he asked. "Why? How?"

"Dad, you were in some kind of trance or something, like a zombie, and those speed tiles, and the light. You looked possessed."

Dad laughed nervously and walked me back through the library to my bedroom. He gave me a quick hug and said good night. I watched Dad leave my room and close the door.

I watched him go back to his precious speed tiles.

Chapter 5

Audio Dick

The next morning, all the speed tiles were cleared off the dining room table. Dad was in the kitchen drinking coffee with Mom. Mom needed the car so she offered to drive us to school. Hannah and I both hate the school bus. I yelled "Shotgun!" and my sister hit the ceiling. She's not what you'd call pleasant in the morning.

"No Hilllary! You got shotgun yesterday!"

Shotgun is the front seat next to the driver. Hannah hates to ride in the back seat. I don't mind the back seat myself, I just like to get to Hannah every chance I get.

"I don't care, I called it," I said.

"OK you little whore, wait 'til I get you in the car to drive you somewhere. I'll take you out to Fennville in a snowstorm and kick you out of the car and leave you there and you'll die."

"I'll sit in the back," said Mom. "You can drive, Hannah."

"Yes!…How about if I just drive you to work, Mom? I'll keep the car and Dad can drive you home later?" Hannah was always pushing her luck with Mom.

"Because I need the car today. I've got to go into Holland to do some shopping later."

Dad looked up, "Where you going?"

"I've got to pick up some foam core at the office supply store…for the Tulip Time video displays."

Dad looked at the clock. "Why don't you stop off at Dick's studio later. Hill and Suzie are gonna record the Ronald McDonald song."

"Come on you guys, let's go!" Hannah always liked to be early. She hated to wait for anyone else.

"Hannah, chill! I haven't even brushed my teeth yet. It's early," I said.

"It isn't early, you retard, it's quarter to eight. I have to meet Mickey." Mickey is a girl. Hannah's best friend at school. Mickey hates me because I'm smarter than her. Of course just about everybody's smarter than Mickey. I call her Mickey Mouse, but she's more like a rat.

"Mom, can we stop and pick up Mickey on the way?"

Mom looked at the clock. "No, it's too late. She's probably already on the bus."

"She's probably in back of the Coral Gables rooting around in the garbage with all the other rats."

"Hiller…you don't want to live, do you? Go brush your teeth…" Hannah grabbed an old scrub brush from under the sink, the one Mom uses for cleaning the toilet bowls, and threw it at me. "You'll need this."

Mom looked at Dad. "Such loving children. I'll try to meet you at Dick's this afternoon, but don't count on it. I'd like to watch the session, but I've got a busy day."

We got into the car and went to school. Dad went to work. We drove down 64th street, past Clearbrook Golf Course and out to Blue Star Highway. We drove past the "Men with Beards" auto repair place. It's really called Riley's, but all the men who work there have great big beards…and big dogs too, greasy, oil-stained dogs. Dad says the dogs help with the oil changes. Then we went past Blue Star Storage, where my Dad rents some warehouse space, and turned right on Old Allegan Road toward the high school.

We got stuck behind one of the school buses and who do we see smashing her face against the back window, but Mickey, acting like a jerk, sticking her tongue out, laughing, making obscene gestures with one of her fingers. Hannah, laughing, beeped the horn and screamed, "Oh my God...what's she doing? What a dork!"

Mom leaned over the seat to take a look. "Good grief. What's she doing? Hannah, pay attention to your driving."

Mom leaned back just in time to miss the next event. I looked up and saw what I thought was a pair of really fat cheeks against the inside of the bus window. Then Hannah started shrieking and beeping the horn. Mom had a cow. "Hannah! That's enough!" Then I saw Jason, Hannah's Neanderthal boyfriend, turn around. It was his fat cheeks in the window; his butt cheeks. He was laughing and waving, at least until he saw my Mom lean over again.

Hannah's got really good taste in friends.

Finally, we got to school and pulled up behind Suzie's Mom's car. Her name is Sally. She's the one who owns Sally's Nook where Mom works. Luckily she didn't witness the butt cheeks in the window. Suzie's mom is a little conservative. She's the president of the school board. Hannah jumped out of the car and ran to catch Jason getting out of the school bus. Jason was buckling his belt as he jumped down the bus stairs.

"Hannah! The keys..." yelled Mom.

"Oh yeah. Here..." and she threw the keys to Mom and ran off.

Of course Mom didn't catch the keys, she dropped them. Mom's not a very good catch. Suzie's mom was watching out her car window, frowning. She's kind of afraid of Hannah. She won't let Suzie sleep over when Hannah's home. She thinks Hannah's gonna corrupt her little daughter. But I think it might be just the opposite.

"Hi Hill! What's up?" yelled Suzie as she danced up, pushing past Drew and Todd, a couple of passing 9th graders. Then she stepped on the back of Todd's shoe and grabbed Drew's hat and threw it up in the air. "Drew's hat is up." Suzie's my best friend, but she's such a flirt; even a worse flirt than my sister Hannah.

I caught Drew's hat and ran toward the school with it. Suzie joined me.

Suzie's Mom called after us: "Suzie, behave yourself," and got out of her car to talk to Mom. I knew they'd probably talk about Suzie and I singing at Dick's studio. As I went into the school I saw Mom and Sally smiling and shaking their heads. I could just imagine them saying something like "What are we gonna do with these crazy children."

After school, Dad picked up me and Suzie and we drove to Dick Beaver's studio. Dick's studio is on the same property as his house, on an old farm about halfway between Saugatuck and South Haven, about 15 miles. On the way there, Dad told us about how Dick got his audio studio.

"Dick's a great musician," said Dad, "mostly sings the blues and plays the piano. He's very talented, but he makes his living as a carpenter and a builder. He's a pretty independent guy, likes to do it his own way. A lot of builders around here don't like to work with him. He's stubborn and obstinate, but if he likes you, he'll bend over backwards for you."

"He likes you, huh, Dad?" I asked.

"We wouldn't be going there if he didn't, Hill." answered Dad. "Anyway, Dick puts all his extra money into his music, into his studio. He's really proud of that studio. He built it and bought most of the equipment in it about five years ago. That was the year he learned how to move houses."

"Move houses?" said Suzie. "No way!"

"Way, Suzie," said Dad. "He's an expert now. Nobody knows exactly how he does it. But he hasn't always been an expert. He learned how to move houses with a big 2-story house from the lake shore. And he moved it, somehow, single-handedly."

"He moved a 2-story house all by himself?" I asked in amazement.

"Yep, by himself," said Dad, then he continued. "You know what the shoreline's like around here?"

"Yeah," said Suzie, "50 foot cliffs leading down to the beach."

"That's right, Suzie," said Dad. "The erosion from Lake Michigan is always threatening the houses that people build too close to the edge of the cliff. Well, one year an elderly lady who Dick worked for quite a bit decided to build a new house back from the cliff. Her old house was right on the edge, and the spring storms that year were doing more damage to the cliff. It wouldn't be long before the old house simply toppled into the Lake."

"My uncle Jack's house, in South Haven, fell in the lake one year," bragged Suzie.

"It happens all the time." said Dad. "Anyway, once the old lady moved into her new house, she figured she'd just let Lake Michigan demolish the old one, but Dick asked her if he could have it. She liked Dick and was happy to give it to him, but only if he moved it off of her property."

"So, how did he do it?" I asked. "And where did he take it?"

"That's the mystery," said Dad. "One day it was teetering on the edge of the cliff, the next day it was gone, disappeared, poof."

"What do you mean, poof?" asked Suzie. "Did it fall off the edge? Or did Dick move it?"

"Actually, it turned out that Dick moved it," answered Dad, "because a few days later, it turned up in Douglas. He got it there all by himself. Nobody remembers him asking for help. Nobody remembers seeing the house moving down the street or along the road. Nobody remembers the day he plopped it down in Douglas. One morning it was just there."

"Right, Dad," I said. "What's the punch line?"

"No punch line," said Dad. "It's a true story. Apparently, Dick bought a piece of property on the Kalamazoo River in Douglas and moved the old house there…about ten miles. It's that big house right next to the bridge going over the river. It disappeared from the lake shore, and three days later, reappeared in Douglas."

"Come on, John," said Suzie. "He must have had it moving on some back roads over those three days."

"Probably, Suzie," said Dad, "but you would think someone would have seen him, or taken a picture or something. Of course, moving houses is no big deal around here. It happens all the time. You know, our neighbor, Ursulla's bookstore in Saugatuck is in a building that used to be in Singapore; you know, the ghost town that was once at the mouth of the Kalamazoo River."

"My grandmother's house too," said Suzie. "It was moved from Singapore before my grandmother was even born. My Dad says they used to move houses in the winter when the water froze on the Kalamazoo River."

"Really, Suzie?" I asked. Then I turned to Dad. "Why does Ursulla call it the Singapore Bank Bookstore?"

"I guess it used to be a bank in Singapore at one time, Hill," answered Dad. "Anyway, Dick fixed up the old lady's house a little after he moved it to Douglas, then he sold it. Got a good price for it. River front property. Then he put all his profits into his audio studio.

"He's been moving houses ever since, too. His audio studio is in a building that came from some farm down the road. His wife's studio was moved from somewhere else. He gets these buildings for free and just picks them up and moves them. Dick is like a legendary house-mover around here."

Dad found Dick's driveway by looking for a fallen down rusty sign on the side of the road. It said "Audio Dick." That's the name of his studio. Dick props up the sign every once in a while, especially when he knows someone is coming. It would be easy to miss his driveway without it.

"There it is," said Dad, and he turned onto a really nasty road with lots of holes and ruts. "This road gets worse every time I come here. I'm gonna need a 4-wheel drive vehicle to get in pretty soon."

We drove around some trees and past an old rusted out boat hull leaning on a pile of concrete blocks. We passed a big truck that looked like a UPS delivery truck. It was sitting at a weird angle, one of its tires deep in the mud. It was painted about ten shades of dirty purple with peace signs and crazy designs all over it. "That's a leftover from Dick's hippie days," said Dad, "I think his chickens live in it now."

A dog with a bent ear and only three legs ran along with our car, barking at the tires. We drove past Nancy's studio, a little frame house painted white with a little front porch. Nancy's an artist. It was on the right side of the road. Across from Nancy's studio was Audio Dick, Dick's studio. It was a wood frame house, a lot like Nancy's, but bigger. It was painted puke green with purple trim. Another leftover from Dick's hippie days, I guess. There was a neon sign at the peak of the roof. All it said was "DICK" in big capital letters. It was flashing on and off: DICK, DICK, DICK.

Suzie hadn't said much since we turned into Dick's driveway, but her eyes were pretty big. "I told you this was a weird place," I said to Suzie.

"Gross," muttered Suzie as her upper lip curled into a grimace. She was looking at Dick's 3-legged dog taking a dump on the side of the road. With only one back leg, it was quite an acrobatic feat. Chickens were clucking around, pecking at the ground, but keeping a safe distance from the dog. A goat was on a rise near Dick's big stucco house, grazing, trying to keep up with the overgrown grass.

Dad turned into a more or less level part of the road that looked like a parking area. Dick's old rusty Mercedes was parked there, so I guess it was the parking lot.

We heard a door slam and looked up to see Dick sauntering down the hill toward us. He had his three-year old daughter, Jenny, up on his shoulder. She was laughing and having a great time. Dick really loved his Jenny. The 3-legged dog finished his business and ran up to greet him, tail wagging.

Dick looked even bigger than he was because we were looking up at him as he came down the hill. He looked like he could move houses. And I guess tiny Jenny helped the illusion. She was quite a contrast to Dick's 6-foot, 4-inch frame. But in spite of Dick's size, he was not scary. He was a gentle giant. You could tell by the way he handled Jenny. He always had a big smile and a twinkle in his eye.

"Hi Dick, hi Jenny," said Dad. "When are you gonna fix that road?"

"Road?" answered Dick. "Why? What's wrong with it?"

"The ruts, the holes," said Dad. "You can hardly get through."

"Don't drive in the ruts," was his answer. "I always keep to the side, straddling one of the ruts. You think it's bad now, you should see it when it rains." He plucked Jenny off his shoulder and held her out in front of him, "Right Jenny?"

"Right," she repeated, then started giggling as Dick tickled her under her arms.

"What happened to your dog?" Dad asked. "I remember counting four legs on him last time I was here."

"I don't know," answered Dick. "Came home one night with only three legs. Guess he had a run in with our neighbor's tractor."

The dog was jumping up, wanting Dick to pet him. "Didn't need that extra leg anyway. Gets around OK without it."

Suzie still had her lip curled up in a grimace as she looked around Dick's place. Suzie's not very tolerant. Dick noticed her distasteful look. "Hey Suzie, wanna see the pigs? I just hosed 'em down. You can ride one of 'em."

"N-No thanks," she said. "I don't ride pigs."

"Ever try it?" teased Dick.

"No, I haven't," replied Suzie, hands on hips.

"How 'bout the ostrich?" he continued. "Wanna ride the ostrich?"

"You've got an ostrich?" asked Dad in disbelief.

"Nah! Don't have any pigs either." replied Dick. "But I can strap a saddle on one of them chickens. How 'bout it Suzie? Wanna ride a chicken?"

"I don't think so." replied Suzie, finally catching on that she was being teased. "I came here to sing."

"And sing you shall!" said Dick. "And sing you shall."

We followed Dick into his audio studio. We stepped into the entryway and made our way around stacks of amplifiers, speakers and microphones. There were big black cases piled high on either wall, equipment that Dick and his band, the Bunns, use for gigs. We followed him into the control room, equally cluttered with cables, microphones, keyboards and computers. The room was dominated by a huge audio board with about 30 rows of switches, dials and levers. Next to it was a Macintosh computer and an 8-track recording machine. In front of the audio board was a big window looking out over an open studio cluttered with speakers, instruments, a big drum set isolated by the same curved glass partitions Dick used in my Dad's editing suite. Between the glass window and the audio board was a mass of cables and wires, casually hanging to the floor, snaking their way into various speakers, amplifiers and microphones. It was a mess.

"When are you gonna clean this place up?" asked my Dad.

"I just did," answered Dick.

He put Jenny down on the couch facing Dick's audio board and gave her a picture book to look at. I sat down next to her. "Suzie. Sit down." I said, gesturing to the couch on the other side of Jenny. Jenny held up the book to Suzie, winning her over. Jenny's very sweet. Suzie smiled and sat down.

Dick started hitting keys on his computer and tapping on a microphone to see if it was on. He switched switches, pushed buttons, ran around the back of his audio board and pulled cables. It seemed like he was just randomly trying things until he could get something to work. He plugged one cable in and got a loud high-pitched screech. "Nope, not that one," said Dick.

He pulled a couple more cables out and plugged one in on the other side of the board causing big sparks to shoot out. Dick jumped backwards to escape and at the same time, the lights went out on his side of the room. "Oh puke," said Dick dejectedly. "Blew a fuse."

He rummaged around in the dark, found a flashlight and switched it on. Nothing. He tossed it on a pile of cables in the corner. "Hey Hill," he said to me, "point that lampshade this way." I tilted the lampshade next to me so that more light spilled on Dick's side of the room. He opened a fuse box on the wall and unscrewed a fuse, tossed it on the pile next to the flashlight and screwed another one in its place. The lights went on.

"So, you got all this cabling pretty well documented, Dick?" teased Dad.

"Yep," answered Dick. "About as well documented as your edit suite."

I laughed and looked around the messy room. Dad said Dick's the most fatalistic person he's ever met, whatever that means. Nothing ever bothers Dick. If something goes wrong, he just finds some way to work around it. Dad says Dick's attitude has something to do with the booze and drugs he consumed in great quantities as a hippie.

My eyes scanned the walls where Dick had hung some awards he had won, past his three framed album covers, over the cables and microphones and switches. Finally, my eyes landed on a little metal object on the corner of the audio board. I probably wouldn't have noticed it at all if my Dad hadn't spent half the night arranging them on our dining room table, but there it was, a speed tile. It was more primitive and irregular than my Dad's speed tiles. The nubs weren't really bolts, like Dad's, just gold-colored nubs, but it was, for sure, a speed tile.

I looked over at Dad and saw that he noticed it too. He was staring right at it. He was pale. He had a blank look on his face. His eyes were kind of glassed over, like a zombie, like the night before. I looked at Dick, fussing with his wires and cables. Dick looked at Dad, saw his dead stare, than turned to see what he was looking at. I thought I saw surprise in his eyes, and hate, jealousy, irritation, something like that, something completely foreign to Dick's easy-going personality. Dick moved quickly toward the speed tile and casually snatched it up and put it in his pocket. He didn't say anything about it, but it was weird. Dad looked at Dick. Dick looked back at Dad. Then some kind of recognition registered in both of their eyes.

Jenny squealed with laughter, pointing at a picture in the book. Everyone looked at Jenny and smiled. The whole thing took less than 30 seconds and I'm sure Jenny and Suzie didn't even notice anything happened. But I did. What was it about those speed tiles? And where did Dick get the one he put in his pocket? Why didn't Dad ask him about it?

When Dick finally got everything working, he hooked Suzie and I up with headphones and put us in front of a microphone in the studio.

Everybody seemed to get into the song and Dad seemed to forget about the speed tile. Suzie and I sang the Ronald McDonald song. Dick recorded it and mixed it with the instrumental tracks that Dad brought with him. Dick even let Suzie and I sing "Going to the Chapel." It was really fun.

It was getting late. The sun was starting to set and Suzie had to be home for dinner. We got into Dad's car and Dad started back down the driveway, taking Dick's advice about straddling one of the ruts. I looked out the back window of the car as we drove away. I saw Dick pull something out of his pocket. We were pretty far away, but I think it was the speed tile. He looked at it, frowned, looked at our car, then put it back in his pocket. In the failing light I watched him walk back up the hill to his house, holding Jenny's hand, head down, walking slowly. He looked sad.

Chapter 6

The Balloon House

I watched Hilllary and Suzie in the recording session, but I couldn't get my mind off Dick's speed tile. I knew that's what it was. I couldn't believe he had one too. But why shouldn't he? Why shouldn't lots of people around here have speed tiles? I found it in the dunes. So could anyone else. And the look he gave me. Whoa. He really didn't want me looking at his speed tile...his precious speed tile. What is it with those things?

I forced myself to concentrate on the recording session. I'd have to ask Dick about the speed tile sometime, but, for some reason, I dreaded bringing it up. I was curious, but afraid, and angry. Why angry? Why should I be angry about Dick having a speed tile? Why should I be the only one? Why should I care if everyone in town has a speed tile?

As I drove the girls back to Saugatuck, I thought about my speed tile, the real one, the one I found in the dunes. I think it was still in that old briefcase...the one I threw into the river so many years ago. Where was that old briefcase anyway? I know I kept it. I think I put it up in the attic...somewhere safe, warm, dark. Yes, in the attic. I remember. It's safe there. It'll be OK there.

"Dad!" interrupted Hilllary. "Is that the house Dick moved?"

We were just approaching the bridge going over the Kalamazoo River and there it was on the right side of the road, down a little hill leading to the river's edge. "Yeah. That's it."

"No way, Dad," said Hill. "No way he could have moved that house himself."

Then, Bang! It hit me in a flash of insight. I hit the brakes. The tires squealed. The car in back of me weaved just in time to miss rear-ending me. Horn blowing, he passed on my left. Suzie and Hilllary, both in the back seat, were thrown forward against their seat belts. "Dad! What the heck?" said Hill.

Sweating, I looked at Dick's house. I had passed it a thousand times over the years, but now I knew how it got there. I knew. I saw it. I felt it. A distinct image dissolved into my mind, blocking out everything else.

"Dad!" yelled Hill, her voice distant and muted.

"What's he doing?" asked Suzie. "Why did we stop here?"

I stared at the house. A picture. Early morning, before sun-up. Thick fog rolling in over the Kalamazoo River. Dim light. The house. The two story house. Hanging there. Impossibly floating…suspended in air. Moving, drifting, bobbing slightly in the morning breeze like a big balloon, surrounded by fog, yellow fog, dirty yellow fog quietly blending into the mist from the river. Heart pounding, eyes wide, wider.

"Dad! Dad!" A faint echo…muted…from across the river, far away.

(Cut to) The lumbering form of Dick Beaver moving methodically around the house, the balloon house, placing concrete blocks. Some here, some there. (Closer) The corner of the house, moving, drifting, swaying quietly in the dim fog, concrete blocks inches below. A whisper of breeze in the muted thickness of yellow fog. Concrete blocks in place. (Cut to) Dick's hand reaching under the house, tugging, gently tugging, extracting a small square wafer: a speed tile. A soft groan of wood beams and sagging timbers. Next corner, then next. Four speed tiles, one in each corner of the rectangular house. (Wide shot) Soft settling of wood. A final creak and snap as the balloon loses its buoyancy and settles, finally, on the blocks, a house once more. (Cut to) Dick's face. Eyes wide, possessed, demonic, bathed in yellow light. He looks up, toward the road, the bridge, our car. He looks down, opens his hand, four speed tiles. He quickly closes his fist over the tiles and looks up again. Panic. (Zoom) Eyes wider, surprise, possessive urgency, (Closer) into soulless, selfish orbs of hate, (Faster now) simmering, smoldering sparks of venom (His speed tiles. His!).

"Dad! Hey Dad!" A pull on my shoulder, shaking me. "Dad! What's wrong, Dad?" A frightened voice. Hilllary. The car.

Snap! Back in the car. "Yeah, Hill," I said, snapping out of it, sweating, shaking. "Dick's house. There it is."

"We saw it," said Hill. "What the heck Dad?"

"Weird…" said Suzie. "Your Dad's weird. I think I wanna go home now."

I turned around and looked into the back seat. Two frightened girls looked back at me. "Dick's house," I said lamely. "The one he moved. I just wanted to take a look at it."

Hilllary and Suzie looked at each other, then back at me. I shrugged. "I just wanted to look at it," I mumbled again then drove over the bridge, Dick's impossible house filling the rear view mirror.

The next morning I pulled myself away from my bucket of speed tiles and went to the Bat House early. I had to get ready for a shoot at Clark Systems, Ted Clark's company in Holland. Ted was Suzie's father and a good friend. He was also the husband of Sally, Marcia's employer at Sally's Nook. Clark Systems designed and manufactured high-tech work stations for manufacturing operations. Ted wanted to shoot some of the features of his workstations on video and edit them into a short sales piece his marketing people could use to help sell the product. The shoot wouldn't be very demanding, but I was distracted by thoughts of speed tiles, by my vision of Dick Beaver's floating house.

Jed showed up soon after I arrived. He would be the cameraman on this shoot. He had finished editing the Tulip Time video only two days before and he was still a little groggy from the marathon edit. "It's gonna be so great to be shooting today and not editing," he said as he came down the stairs. "I'm so sick of that Tulip Time video."

"Yeah," I replied, "but you'll be sick of this project too before long." Jed put so much of himself into our projects that they completely consumed him and wore him out by the time they were finished.

"The dupes of Tulip Time come yet?" asked Jed. He started pulling the equipment we would need for the Clark shoot out of the cabinets.

"Not yet," I answered. I started thumbing through the Clark script. "They're supposed to arrive this afternoon. A thousand copies. Marcia's ready to jump on them as soon as they arrive to get them into the stores. Of course, I have no idea how we're gonna pay for those thousand copies. We better sell a bunch of them."

Jed opened one of the large Porta-brace cases, loading cables and microphones into its deep pockets. "How 'bout that government job you bid on?" he asked. "The one on the environment. You should make a lot of bucks on that."

"If we get it. There's a lot of competition out there. A lot of production companies willing to work for nothing."

"You bid it pretty low, didn't you?" he asked.

"Yeah," I answered, "and this one is not being awarded strictly on cost so I think we've got a good chance. They're looking for a company with a lot of documentary experience, and that's something we've got tons of."

"When you gonna hear?" he asked.

"Soon. I sent in the bid two weeks ago. Over one hundred pages of stuff, ten sample videos. It took me two weeks to pull it all together. I'm really hoping we get it. We can use the work."

"Didn't you say it's a year's worth of work?" he asked.

"Yep," I answered. "It'll keep this place popping."

"What about that 'Chair' video?" he continued. "You hear about that one."

I put the script down and looked up at Jed. "Yeah," I sighed, "it went to Digicam Video in Holland. Another Avid thing. They wanted digital editing. Everybody wants digital editing."

Jed closed the microphone case and looked up. "You're gonna have to bite the bullet eventually," he said. "You know, the whole world's going digital. If you get the government job, maybe you can use some of the profits for a new editing system.."

"Dream on," I said. "Maybe we can use some of the profits to pay some bills. You know, we probably wouldn't even be able to use a digital system on a documentary project anyway. How can you digitize 30 or 40 hours worth of footage into a computer. We'd need an incredible amount of storage space."

"You'd have to work on it in sections," he answered.

"Maybe. But that kind of defeats the purpose of nonlinear editing. It might be more efficient for that kind of project to just edit analog, the old-fashioned way. Look at the Tulip Time video. There's no way you could have edited that one on an Avid."

Jed pulled out the Sony DXC-537 and started unscrewing the back. The 537 is a 3-chip modular camera that can be re configured to shoot DV (digital video), Hi-8, BetacamSP or 3/4SP formats. He pulled the Hi-8 dockable recorder out of the padded box and took it out of the plastic wrapping. He carefully screwed it onto the camera. "You know…I think there's something wrong with the zoom control on this camera. The last time I used it, it only worked once in a while. It would, like, click, click, click and not zoom sometimes."

"That's just the loose parts of your brain rattling around in your head," I teased. "There's nothing wrong with the zoom."

"No, really, here, watch." Jed slipped a battery into the camera and turned it on. Sure enough, there was a clicking noise, and the zoom didn't work.

"Umm, that's happened to me before," I said. "Just check the screws holding the zoom control onto the lens. I'll bet they're loose. The zoom gears aren't engaging."

"Hmmm…they are loose. I hope that's all it was." Jeff changed the screwdriver blade and inserted a smaller Phillips head blade into the handle. He tightened the screws.

I looked up at the clock. "Where's Peg?"

As if in answer, the phone rang. Jed picked it up. "We were just talking about you. You working today, or what?"

Jed listened, laughed. He put the phone down. "OK if Peg meets us there? Clark's real close to her house." Jed put his hand over the mouthpiece and whispered, "she just doesn't want to help carry the equipment."

"We can handle it," I said. "Tell her to meet us there at 9:30."

Jed picked the phone up again. "Nice going Peg. I'll do all the work, as usual." He listened and laughed again. "See you in a bit." He hung up the phone.

Peg is a local producer who works with Hunter Productions on a per job basis. Sometimes she's the producer. Sometimes, like on this job, she's the production coordinator. Sometimes she works as a narrator or an actress. She grew up in Montana and worked for many years with a traveling theater group as an actress. She's married to George Morgan, a professor of Theater at Hope College and she's got a precocious 2-year old daughter, Sherry, who inherited her mother's intense brown eyes…X-ray eyes that miss very little.

I stuffed the shooting script into my briefcase. "Let's bring both lighting kits. I'm not sure how much of this table of his we have to light."

I helped Jed load the station wagon…an old Taurus that has seen better days. We loaded up the camera case, monitor, tripod and a couple of other dark blue Porta-brace cases with gadgets and batteries and cables and videotape. We put in a big, beat-up black case with three 500-watt Lowell lighting fixtures and a couple of little Fresnels. Then Jed struggled to find room for a newer black and orange case with three 1000-watt Desisti fixtures. "Why don't you get a new van or something. Every time we go on a shoot you want to bring more stuff. A nice new van with Hunter Productions on the side. How about it?"

"Why not just put a neon sign on top of the van too? And a big arrow: Attention criminals. $50,000 worth of electronic equipment. Help yourself!"

"Our competition in Holland has a van," whined Jed.

"Yeah, but the only place they shoot is in Holland," I answered. "There aren't any criminals there. The Dutch have genetically eliminated all criminals from their gene pool."

The phone rang again and I ran inside to answer it. "Hello, Hunter Productions, can I help you?" I said, a little breathless from my sprint to the phone.

"Mister Leben?" said the phone.

"You got him," I replied.

"Mister Leben, this is George Wilson. I'm a lawyer. I represent the Holland Tulip Time Festival."

"Pleased to meet you, George," I replied, excited to hear from a Festival official. We had hoped to get our Tulip Time video into their hands for wider distribution and I thought George may be calling about that.

"Did you produce a video called Tulip Time: A Colorful History?" he asked.

"We sure did!" I said. "We just finished it a few days ago."

"It's come to our attention that you are planning to sell that video at the festival this year," he said, a little too formally.

"Yep," I said guardedly. "That's why we produced it. We plan to get a thousand copies into the stores by the end of the day tomorrow."

"Mister Leben, Tulip Time is a registered trademark of the festival," he said, "and I'm afraid you do not have the right to use that name on your video, or to sell any products related to the festival without a contract from the Tulip Time Festival."

I slowly removed the phone from my ear and looked at it. I couldn't believe what I was hearing. "What? OK, who is this? Is this some kind of joke?"

"It's not a joke, Mister Leben," said the lawyer. "We have to protect the Tulip Time name from abuse."

"Abuse?" I said in disbelief. "The video we produced is a celebration of the festival. It's not an expose."

"Nevertheless, Mister Leben," he continued. "We can't allow you to sell the video without a contract."

I took a deep breath. "Look George, we've been working on this video for months. We've interviewed dozens of festival officials. Everybody connected with the festival knew we were producing a video. Why would this contract thing come up now? Why did you wait so long?"

"Our office was not contacted, Mister Leben," he sniffed. "We handle all rights to the Tulip Time name. We take a commission off the top of all sale of products related to Tulip Time"

"A c-commission, what kind of a commission?" I stammered.

"Oh, twenty to twenty-five percent of gross is customary, Mister Leben."

"Twenty…" I paused, fuming inside, wishing I could reach my arm inside the phone line and wring this worm's neck. But I also knew we had a thousand copies of the video arriving in just a few hours. I would have to be careful how I handled this. "George, let me explain something to you. I'll try to keep this very simple for you. This video is a good video. This video will help promote the Tulip Time Festival. This video makes the Tulip Time Festival look good. It will bring more people here. It will help make the festival even bigger and more popular. This video will bring more people, more business, more dollars into Holland, and you're telling me we can't sell the video at the festival without giving you twenty percent?"

"Mister Leben," he answered, "perhaps the video is a good video, but the committee will have to review it and you'll have to sign a contract with us to be able to distribute it."

I put my hand on my mouth, afraid of what would come out next. I tried again, patiently, "Uh, huh. Contract. Yeah. A contract. Fine, I'll tell you what, George. I'll tell you what you should do." Just then, Marcia walked in the room carrying an armload of Tulip Time Video displays that she would be filling up later in the day with Tulip Time Videos. She smiled and waved at me, then, noticing my red face and the smoke pouring out of my ears, she put the displays down and stopped smiling. "I'll tell you what you should do George…Mister Lawyer, Mister Tulip Time lawyer. You send me a contract right now. You fax it to me, because I've got a thousand videos going into stores this afternoon."

"Oh, I'm afraid that's impossible, Mister Leben," he answered. "The committee reviews products and endorsements in February. We'd be happy to review your video for next year's festival."

"Next year's festival!" I shouted. "I've got thousands of dollars tied up in this video. I can't wait until next year!"

"I'm afraid that's all I can do, Mister Leben," said the slimy lawyer. "You can't distribute this video without going through the proper channels. If it has the words 'Tulip Time' in the packaging or in the body of the video, you'll be breaking the law by trying to distribute it. If you try to sell the video we'll have a judge issue a restraining order and have all the copies confiscated and destroyed."

I lost all restraint. "Listen you slimy son-of-a-bitch. I'm selling that video. I don't give a shit what kind of order you issue." But Mr. George Wilson didn't hear most of my threat. He hung up on me. I sagged into the nearest chair and looked up at Marcia.

"What was that all about?" she asked.

"That was a Tulip Time lawyer," I answered. "He said we can't sell the video without a contract. We have to give them twenty percent of sales and he says we can't even have a contract until next year."

"Can't sell the video?" she said calmly. "He said we can't sell the video at the festival?"

"That's what he said." I rubbed my eyes, then my temples. I felt a massive headache coming on.

Just then, Roger, the UPS man stumbled into the front office carrying two large boxes of videos…Tulip Time videos. "Hi John, Marcia, where do you want these boxes. I've got 18 more of them in the truck."

Jed came in the back door. "We going on this shoot or what? Aren't we supposed to be there by now?"

I looked at Marcia. She looked at me. She shook her head. "This is silly. There's no reason why they shouldn't want the video to be out there. It's to their benefit to have the video on sale."

"Tell Mister Fucking George, Goddamned Wilson, asshole Tulip-Time Lawyer that."

"What's going on?" asked Jed.

"I'll just stack up these boxes on the porch," said the UPS man, diplomatically, then he quietly left the room.

"The Tulip Time videos came?" said Jed, "Great!"

I stood up, "Yeah, great! But now they won't let us sell them."

"We'll just see about that," said Marcia. "Why don't you and Jed go on your shoot and let me make a few phone calls. It's just some kind of bureaucratic mix-up. I'm sure they'll listen to reason."

On the way to Clark Systems, I told Jed the whole crazy story. He agreed that this Judd lawyer guy was probably some minor bureaucrat and Marcia would probably be able to sort things out with the Tulip Time people that we knew, the people who have been helping us with the video these past months. I calmed myself and tried to focus on the coming shoot. It wouldn't be fair to give Clark Systems only part of my attention that day. Jed convinced me that Marcia would solve the Tulip Time problem by the time we finished shooting.

By the time we got to Clark Systems, Peg was waiting in the reception area. "What took you guys so long?" she asked.

"Don't ask," answered Jed.

"Sorry, Peg," I said. "Been waiting long?"

"Since 9:30, like you said," she answered.

"No way," said Jed. "You mean you were not late for the first time in your life?"

"That's right, Jed," she bragged, "and you weren't here to see it. I was on time." She glanced over to the glass partition separating the reception area from the conference room. Ted Clark was having a rather animated meeting with Bill Kramer, his marketing manager. "It doesn't look like they're quite ready for us anyway."

Peg looked at me with her X-ray eyes. She knew I was upset about something. "OK, what's wrong John?"

"Ah, some problems with a Tulip Time idiot..." I answered. "Probably nothing. I'll tell you about it later."

Jed laughed, "Yeah, some lawyer from Tulip Time called this morning, just as we were leaving." He turned to me, 'What did you call, him? A slimy son-of-a-bitch...was that it?"

Peg looked at me, "Uh oh. Sounds like trouble."

Slam! Just then, Bill Kramer stomped out of the conference room and walked up to me. "You're not gonna believe this, John, but Ted had another busy week-end."

I looked over Bill's shoulder toward the conference room. Ted was gathering up some working drawings on the table. He was smiling. I asked, "you mean Ted redesigned the prototype again?"

Ted was a creative type, a designer who was happiest in his workshop. Bill was more pragmatic. He was happiest when he had a product to sell. Ted and Bill didn't always see eye to eye on things. Ted's designs were brilliant. Ergonomically correct workbenches, hydraulic tables, integrated wiring and endlessly adjustable surfaces...a revolution in workbenches for high-tech manufacturing, but he kept fussing and revising his designs.

Ted came out of the conference room and put his hand on Bill's shoulder. "I just changed a couple of little things. We can still shoot today. It was too hard to reach the hydraulic foot pedal for the main countertop."

Bill shrugged Ted's hand off. "What about the table top. Will you please tell me why it has to revolve 360 degrees. Who's gonna work upside down?"

Ted thought for a minute. In fact, he looked a little confused. He frowned, "Well, ahh…zero gravity, that's it."

Zero gravity. That got my attention. I looked at Ted and thought about my vision of Dick's house floating like a balloon.

Ted continued, "what if one of our work stations had to work in zero gravity?" He smiled and slapped Bill on the shoulder.

"Zero gravity…" Bill muttered and walked away. "I've had it. How can I sell a product that keeps on changing."

Peg looked at me and smiled. We both knew our job would be easier that day. Only one client to deal with.

Ted led us into the factory where the prototype was still being reworked. "Is there any way we can simulate zero gravity on videotape?"

I looked at Ted and thought of speed tiles. "We can always mount the camera upside down. But jees, Ted, you planning to send your workbenches into outer space, or what?"

"Just curious…".

Peg would really be directing the shoot and keeping track of all the shots. Officially, I am the director, but with new clients, someone has to run interference and keep the client from helping out too much. Peg and Jed would do all the work. I would keep Ted and Bill occupied, that is, if Bill even showed up for the shoot. I learned long ago that for every client you invite to a shoot, you have to double the time it will take for the shoot. The same goes for the edit. One client in the edit suite and the program might take ten hours to edit. With two clients it will take 20 hours. With three clients, it will take 40 hours…

The script was a simple description of Ted's workbench with all its features and attachments. Our job would be to simply gather video footage that illustrated all the features described in the script. The trick would be to methodically zero in on each feature, arrange the lighting so that we could record a good video picture, then shoot the feature in action, if possible. Most videos fail, or have an amateurish look, because the crew doesn't take enough time to set up and light every shot. We had already recorded the narration track and timed each segment. After shooting, we would go back to our studio and edit all the scenes and narration together into a continuous program, adding music, sound effects titles, and any other special effects that were needed.

As Jed and Peg worked with the lights and camera, I chatted with Ted. "You know that old two-story house in Douglas, Ted, the one Dick Beaver moved?"

"Yeah, Old Cynthia Ryan's house, about five years ago," he answered, "from the lake shore."

"Who did he get to help him move that house?" I asked. "He couldn't have done it himself."

"Why not?" he answered. "Anything's possible with the right physics. It's just a matter of leverage."

"But a two-story house?" I countered. "That's a big house."

"Dick's a big guy." replied Ted. "What made you think of that house, anyway?"

"I don't know." I looked up at Ted. "Just your zero gravity comment, I guess."

Ted shot a piercing glance back at me, a little too fast, too severe. "Zero gravity?" he asked.

"Yeah, zero gravity," I continued. "With zero gravity, it would be easy for Dick to move that house."

"I don't think Dick has access to that kind of technology," mocked Ted, looking away nervously. "But I read about some interesting research going on at this new lab in downtown Chicago...in Scientific American or someplace...I think they're affiliated with Argonne National Laboratories. Can't remember exactly. It was on the Web."

Ted was a real Web junkie. He was also insatiably curious about things, how they worked, how they ticked. His wife, Sally, told me Ted spends a couple of hours every evening surfing the Web. "I have a friend at Argonne…a physicist." I replied. "Will Reed. He lived across the street from us in LaGrange."

"Ask him if he knows Jan Wong…I think that was his name," said Ted. "Doctor Jan Wong."

Wong. The name hit me…a Chinese name. I shot a glance at Ted, then looked away, remembering. (A dream?)…Wong…Hmm. A familiar name. Downtown Chicago. Something about this…

He continued: "He's finding a lot more geographical variation in the gravitational pull of the earth than anyone anticipated. Apparently there's an area right here in Michigan, around South Manitou Island, that has an especially light gravitational pull. Nobody knows why."

"What about this 360 degree rotation feature," interrupted Jed as he carried the camera back further for a wide shot. "Do we really need to shoot that?"

"You bet," replied Ted. "Who knows. They might need one of these things on South Manitou Island." Ted got up and moved toward the work table to show Jed how the rotation control worked.

I stayed where I was, thinking about that meeting. So many years ago. Is it the same Wong that wanted to build a building in Chicago? The Hong Kong Corporation. Helmut, the crazy architect and Joe Kaminski, the Polish developer. And later, the guy with the sandwich board resume. Did I really see those things? The sea captain? The floating speed tile? I shook off the thought and joined Ted and Jed at the table.

The day's run of bad luck continued. The tape ejection mechanism in the camcorder jammed. We had the Hi-8 portable recording deck attached to the camera and the ejection mechanism was one of the few delicate features of this normally fool-proof camcorder combination. It had jammed a couple of times before and I knew it would require professional servicing. This was especially bad news because we already owed a considerable amount of money to the video engineering company that serviced our equipment. Hunter Productions' mounting debt would make it difficult to get the recording deck working again anytime soon.

Jed took the aging Taurus back to the Bat House to pick up the Sony BVU150 portable 3/4SP deck. We would use that deck for the remainder of the shoot by changing the back of the camera and running a control cable to it. We didn't like changing formats in the middle of a shoot, but we didn't have any choice if we wanted to finish Ted's program.

Peg and I joined Ted for a cup of coffee. "Have you ever sailed to South Manitou, John?" asked Ted.

"It's one of my favorite places," I answered. "I love South Manitou."

"What's a South Manitou?" asked Peg.

"It's an island in Lake Michigan, about 15 or 20 miles from the mainland." I answered. "It's part of Sleeping Bear Dunes National Park."

"There used to be a thriving community on South Manitou," continued Ted, "but now it's part of the park and I think it only has a couple of residents now. It's pretty deserted."

"Sailing to South Manitou is quite an experience." I told Peg. "It takes about six hours from Frankfort. Approaching the island from the water reminds me of the island in the old movie, King Kong…It's really very beautiful and mysterious. Marcia and I will probably sail there again this summer."

"Is there a resort or a hotel on the island?" asked Peg.

"No accommodations," answered Ted. "The park is letting nature reclaim the old farms and the village that used to be there. There's wilderness camping, though, and boaters and sailors like John like to anchor off the island."

"There's a great, natural harbor," I interrupted, "protected from all directions but the east. It's like another world. But you have to be self-sufficient to spend any time there. No stores, no restaurants, only a ranger station and an old lighthouse that isn't even used any more."

"And some kind of anomaly in the gravitational pull," said Ted.

"Say what?" said Peg.

"That's what brought the island up in the first place," I told Peg. "Ted was telling me about an article he read about gravity research, and apparently, South Manitou is a place that was identified as having an unusually weak gravitational pull."

"Yeah," teased Peg. "Gravity research…Comes up all the time in my conversation." She smiled and continued, "that would make South Manitou a great place for a Weight-Watcher's convention."

Ted laughed, "The article said there will be a scientific expedition to the island this summer led by Jan Wong, the physicist I was telling you about. Maybe he'll be there when you go this summer."

"I'll have to ask Will Reed about Jan Wong and his gravity research," I said. "This is getting very interesting." I paused and looked at Ted. I didn't mention that I had once known a Wong, long ago in Chicago. I didn't know if it was the same man. Wong was a common name.

Ted was deep in thought. He looked a little distracted. "Why are you reading articles like that anyway, Ted? You know, about gravity research. What's that got to do with work tables?"

Ted frowned, thought for a few seconds, looked at me, "I don't know, John. I really don't know. I just ran across it on the Web. I subscribe to a search service that automatically identifies articles and web sites that might be of interest to me. One of the key words in my search criteria is 'Saugatuck', so it points me to any mention of Saugatuck, where we both live. It's really a pretty nifty service." Ted leaned closer and looked me in the eye. "Saugatuck was mentioned in that same Gravity article, John. Apparently, Saugatuck is similar to South Manitou, in an area of weaker than normal gravitational pull."

Ted continued to stare into my eyes. My heart began beating faster. Peg looked at Ted, wondering what was going on. She looked at me. "So, a Weight Watcher's convention in Saugatuck, then…" she joked, breaking the spell, "Easier to get to. Better restaurants."

We all laughed. I looked at Ted. "Is Wong coming to Saugatuck this summer too?"

"Not according to the article," answered Ted. "Saugatuck's only a little weaker than normal. I guess South Manitou is the most pronounced area of weak gravity in the Western Hemisphere. He wants to find out why." Ted rose to his feet. "I'm gonna make a couple of phone calls while we wait for Jed to get back. Rattle my cage when he gets back."

Ted left and Peg looked at me. "Duh, duh, duh, duh. Duh, duh, duh, duh," she said, imitating the theme song from The Twilight Zone TV Series. "Spooky. And what was that look he gave you when he told you about Saugatuck. What do you guys know that I don't know?"

"Oh, it's nothing, Peg," I answered. "We were just talking about Dick Beaver and his house-moving exploits. We were joking that Dick would have an easier time moving houses in zero gravity."

Peg looked at me suspiciously. Her X-ray eyes penetrated mine, trying to determine if there was more to this gravity thing. "Uh, huh, OK," she said, and waited, still looking in my eyes.

It was late when we finished shooting, so Jed and I quickly unloaded the equipment at the Bat House and I went home. I wanted to see how Marcia had done with the Tulip Time people. It would be a devastating development if we couldn't sell the tape. I was worried.

Sandbar greeted me, as usual, as I drove into our driveway, tail wagging and tongue hanging happily out of his mouth. He was a friendly, happy dog to his family, but a legendary monster in these parts to strangers and delivery men. A husky, 90-pound yellow lab, he didn't hesitate to charge and bite anyone who would dare trespass on his turf. Potential boyfriends calling on Hannah and Hilllary thought twice about entering our yard.

We had an electronic fence installed around the perimeter of our one-acre lot. Sandbar wore a collar that would zap him with an electrical shock if he tried to leave our yard. He learned to stay close.

Sandbar followed me into the house and waited, sitting patiently, staring up at the bowl of doggie biscuits near the back door. If I forgot to give him one of them, he would bark to remind me. I gave him a biscuit and went into the kitchen.

Marcia sat at the kitchen counter, glass of wine in hand. I knew by her look that she didn't have good news for me. "We can't sell the Tulip Time video," she said. "They want to review the finished program next February so that we can sell it at next year's festival."

"Shit," I said and poured myself a large glass of Merlot. "This is very bad news. We were counting on the money from tape sales this spring."

"I know," she said. "What are we gonna do?"

"Isn't there any way around it?" I asked.

"I talked to everyone I could find," she said. "They all agree that it would be silly not to introduce the tape at this year's festival, but I guess that lawyer guy's committee...what's his name, George Wilson. His committee is pretty powerful and he won't back down."

"Especially after I called him a slimy son-of-a-bitch," I said.

"Everybody I talked to kind of thought of him in those terms," she said. "And more bad news. You better sit down, John."

I sat next to her at the kitchen counter. She got to her feet and picked up a big package in a Federal Express box that was sitting on the kitchen table. She brought it to me. "Recognize this?" she said.

I looked at it and realized it was the same package I sent to the Environmental Protection Agency two weeks before, the project Jed asked me about earlier that day. It was my bid for the government job...for a year's worth of work producing programs about the environment. It was a little battered around the edges, but it looked as if it wasn't even opened. Marcia pointed at a note taped to the box next to the address label. It read: "DELIVERY REFUSED. This bid package received at 10:14 am, April 27, past the deadline of 10:00 am. Federal provision number CG12-607-9 prohibits this bid from being considered for a government contract."

"When it rains it pours," said Marcia as she poured herself another glass of wine.

Chapter 7

Struck by Lightning

Suzie and I ducked into the old hallway, slamming the door in their faces. Jerky Jason and stupid, French Fry Freddie were chasing us and we just made it ahead of them through the door leading up to Ursulla's bookstore. Suzie started the fight, as usual. She squirted one of those little ketchup things you get from Burger King onto Freddie's face and called him a potato head. He had really short hair and his head was kind of lumpy, and brownish gray, just like a potato. She said he needed some extra seasoning. Freddie the French Fry, she called him.

We giggled as we held the door closed, waiting for them to push on the door, to come in after us.

"I'm not goin' in there," I heard Jason say. "Ursulla the Witch lives in there. With all her rats and bats and stuff. We can get them back tomorrow."

"Yeah, old Ursulla will probably put a curse on 'em anyway," said Freddie to Jason. "Suzie! Just wait 'til tomorrow," he shouted from the other side of the door. "I'm gonna make you drink a whole bottle 'a ketchup…if Ursulla doesn't get you first."

Suzie giggled again, but her smile slowly faded as she looked around. "Hill…th-th-this place is spooky," she whispered quietly.

We both looked up the steep stairs to a dim, bare light bulb at the top. "You smell that?" I whispered back. There was a dusty, rotten smell in the narrow hallway, like some kind of animal, a mouse or a bat or something, had died, long ago, and was sealed up behind the walls. The dusty part probably came from the red carpet snaking up the middle of the stairway, worn, threadbare patches in the middle of each step. Dust particles drifted in the yellow light. Music, if you could call it that, came from the rooms upstairs. It was a chant. I thought of brown robed monks in a dank stone monastery.

"Smells like Jason," said Suzie, laughing nervously. "Sounds like him too."

We both started giggling, holding our hands over our mouths to muffle the sound. We started slowly climbing the stairs.

I had known Ursulla DeWitt for a long time, ever since we moved to Saugatuck. She had a house right next door to us, her country home, she called it, but she stayed in an apartment in back of her bookstore most of the time. I had never been to her bookstore before. It was on the second floor of the old Singapore Bank Building that was moved from Singapore over 100 years ago. Some of the kids say Ursulla was in the house when they moved it here. She was pretty old, but not that old.

"You sure about this?" asked Suzie.

"Yeah, come on," I said. "Don't believe everything you hear, Suzie. Ursulla's really nice."

"Nice, huh?" she whispered. "As nice as the Wicked Witch of the West?"

"Shhh," I said. "Come on."

We climbed all the way to the top of the stairs, then stopped to look around. There were tall shelves on three walls of the room we were in, filled with books. The chanting continued from somewhere far away. We could see into two other adjoining rooms that also had overflowing bookshelves going up to the ceiling. Huge, gaunt plants, starving for light, reached for the windows with their spindly branches, grasping for what little sun came through the tall, dirt-encrusted windows. There were big overstuffed chairs and couches, coffee tables and end tables and a big dining room table…all of them stacked high with books. The room was crowded and really old-fashioned looking. It smelled kind of musty and dry, the dead animal smell left behind on the stairway. We heard a rustling sound and turned to see Ursulla coming out from behind a heavy drapery separating her apartment from the book store. As she opened the drape, the chanting got louder.

She was a tall, thin woman with a prominent nose, a pointy chin and bright, intelligent eyes. She looked to be in her 70s. She really did look like the Wicked Witch of the West, except for her color. She wasn't green. She left the drape open carelessly. The soft, warm light from the room she left followed her in with the chant. It glowed through the strands of gray hair escaping from the bun arranged haphazardly on top of her head. "Hillary…" she purred, "what a nice surprise, yes, yes."

"Hi, Ursulla," I answered. "This is my friend, Suzie."

Ursulla turned to Suzie and nodded. "How nice, yes, how nice."

"I've never been here before, Ursulla," I blurted. "You sure got a lotta books."

"Oh, yes, yes," she replied. "We have a lot of books, yes, yes. How's your mother and father, dear?"

"Oh, they're okay," I lied. Dad, especially, was having a hard time. I guess business wasn't so good lately and he was kind of quiet and depressed.

"And that big old yellow dog of yours, he bite anyone lately?" she asked, smiling.

Ursulla had witnessed Sandbar's biggest triumph about a year ago. She was outside doing some gardening on the wooded strip between our two houses. A door-to-door salesman was selling bibles or something religious. I was watching out the window. Ursulla turned him down, I saw her frowning and shaking her head. She didn't like salesmen bothering her. Then I saw her pointing at our house. I think she purposely sent him over to our house because she knew Sandbar was out. She smiled as he started for our driveway.

The salesman happily strolled up our walk toward the house, swinging his case of bibles and whistling. But his smile faded quickly as he spotted our dog. Sandbar started slowly, head down, shoulders hunched over, eyeing the intruder, a low growl coming from deep within. As the man stopped cold and started slowly backing up, Sandbar charged. He attacked, growling and snapping as he came. The man backed away faster, swinging his case, but too late. Sandbar bit him right on the crotch, ripping his pants as well as doing some more serious damage within.

Dad was home at the time, and he ran out to get Sandbar, but it was too late. Dad drove the man into town to Dr. Payne's office for a couple of painful stitches to his private parts. Ever since then, the story's become pretty exaggerated, and mixed up with another Sandbar story. About a week later, our house was burglarized while our mighty watchdog slept right through it. But the burglary story and the salesman story somehow got combined. Now, legend has it that Sandbar caught a burglar in our house and ripped his balls off...a mistaken notion that Dad rarely tries to correct.

"Oh Sandbar's fine," I said. "He nips somebody once in a while, but nothing serious. Nothing like the bible salesman."

"Yes, yes, that's good, dear, yes," said Ursulla, then she turned to Suzie. "And who are your parents, dear?"

"Ted and Sally Clark," she answered, "You know, Sally's Nook."

"Oh, yes, dear, yes, Sally...And Ted Clark, yes, yes," she went on. "And that must make you Mabel Clark's granddaughter."

"Yep," answered Suzie. "Mabel's my Grandma."

Mabel Clark lives in the only other house in town that was moved down the river from Singapore in the winter over 100 years ago. Some of the kids tease Suzie that Mabel was in her house when it was moved too. Ursulla and Mabel are about the same age.

"Well, how nice, yes, yes," continued Ursulla, her head nodding absently but her eyes bright and alert. "And what brings you girls here today? Yes, yes, uh huh? yes..."

"A class assignment," I answered. "We have to do a report for history on Singapore."

"Oh, yes, yes…" she said, "the ghost town on the lake. That's where this building came from, you know."

"We know," Suzie and I said at the same time. We looked at each other and giggled.

"Yes, yes, Singapore," muttered Ursulla as she shuffled through a stack of books. "It's here somewhere. A book… by Kit Lane, yes, yes, Kit Lane…Singapore…"

Suzie and I looked at each other and fought back another giggle.

"Here it is!" said Ursulla in triumph. She held up a large format paperback book with a white cover. "Kit does a nice job of writing the official history of that little town…that doomed little town, yes, she did, yes…"

We watched Ursulla as she came toward us with the book. I saw her eyes darken and her brow furrow in thought. She gestured for us to come near. She looked away, thinking, then back to us. The chanting music seemed to get louder. She whispered, "But Kit doesn't write about the insanity, or the sand…yes…the drifting sand, yes, yes…"

Suzie and I exchanged glances, eyes wide, a little frightened. The chant droning on in the background.

"No…no, Kit really had no way of knowing," said Ursulla, thinking back, remembering. "This house knows. This house knows the real history of Singapore, yes, yes it does."

She looked at Suzie. "And your grandmother's house, Suzie. Yes, yes, I'm sure Mabel knows, yes. Her house knows…"

"W-W-What does the house know, Ursulla?" I asked. "What insanity? What sand?"

She looked at me, thinking. She sat down in one of the old overstuffed chairs, holding Kit Lane's book in her hands. She sighed and gently pulled a lace handkerchief out of her sleeve and absently patted her eyes, looking away, considering, thinking. "It was a long time ago, yes, yes it was. The people left Singapore because they were afraid…afraid of the sand. The drifting sand. And those odd little square coins. It made them crazy, you know, yes, yes they did…" The chant, the droning chant.

"Coins?" asked Suzie.

"In those days, banks issued their own currency, you know," continued Ursulla. "Yes, yes, and those square metal coins were considered very valuable. This bank," she said, looking around the room, "the Singapore Bank, had hundreds of those odd little square coins on deposit, but they made men greedy, like gold, yes, yes, like gold. They wanted more and more."

I thought of Dad's speed tiles, his square metal speed tiles. "Ursulla, what did these square coins look like?"

"Oh, they're very beautiful, yes they are…lovely," she said, wistfully, staring off into space, thinking, remembering. "They're such a comfort, you know." She looked at me with sad eyes. "They keep me company, yes, yes…They're like my children."

I glanced sideways at Suzie, then back to Ursulla. "Your children?" I asked, a little confused now.

She looked at me suspiciously. Then she looked at Suzie. Her eyes narrowed. Her brow furrowed. Finally, reconsidering, she shook her head and started rising from the chair. "Here, I'll show you. I found some of them here in the attic."

Standing, she shuffled off to her apartment. She closed the drape after her. The droning chant got quieter, muffled by the heavy fabric.

"This is too strange," said Suzie, her eyes wide.

"Spooky, huh?" I replied.

"I've heard of gold fever when, like, prospectors get real greedy and stuff," said Suzie. "But here? In Singapore?"

The chant got louder, the droning chant. We looked up as Ursulla shuffled back into the room holding an ancient red change purse in one hand and the Singapore book in the other. She set the book down on a nearby table and sat down again in her chair. We watched her as she struggled with the purse, her old wrinkled fingers squeezing the latch. It opened at last and she turned the purse to shake out the coins within. The chant music was coming to a conclusion, and, as if on cue, it stopped just as a single speed tile dropped into her hand with a metallic "click." The silence was thick, overwhelming. I looked at the thing in her hand and gasped, "It's a speed tile."

Ursulla reacted with a jerk. She leaned away, quickly closing her wrinkled fingers over the speed tile, over the brass-like nubs protruding from the four corners, wheezing, the breath knocked out of her. She hissed, "What did you say?"

Afraid, I looked into her eyes, now like slits, dark, impenetrable slits. "A speed tile. It's a speed tile."

Recovering, Ursulla leaned closer to me. "How did you come by that name, dear, yes, yes, how did you know this is a…speed tile?" Then she opened her fingers again to reveal the square object.

It was older and more worn than the speed tiles my Dad made, more like Dick Beaver's speed tile. It looked like it had a finer mesh of scratches inscribed over its silver metallic surface, scratches that seemed to have a pattern, a purpose. And the nubs in the corners, they were not brass bolts like in my Dad's speed tiles, they were more irregular, like careless drips of gold, one in each corner. The nubs also had a fine mesh of scratches, or lines, running over them. Ursulla's speed tile looked important, precious.

"My Dad's got one of those," interrupted Suzie.

Ursulla gasped again, her eyes widening in surprise, looking now at Suzie. Her comment surprised me too.

"I-I think he got it out of G-Grandma's house…" stammered Suzie, "…out of her attic. I didn't know what it was called, though."

"And I saw another one too," I offered, "a couple of weeks ago out at Dick Beaver's studio."

"Dick Beaver?" asked Ursulla with a croak, closing her eyes and clutching her hand to her chest.

"Yeah, the musician. You know, Dick Beaver. He lives out toward South Haven. He's a house mover too."

Ursulla's eyes snapped open. "A house mover? Dick Beaver?"

I was beginning to worry about Ursulla. It seemed like everything we told her caused a shock. She was really acting weird. Now I knew why the other kids thought she was a witch. She took a deep breath, looked directly in my eyes, held out the speed tile and said, "Speed tile, yes, yes, now why did you call it that, dear? Why?"

"My Dad's been making them, Ursulla. He's been making them for years, first in LaGrange before we moved here, now in the garage, in his workshop. He says they're speed tiles. But they don't look quite like this one, Ursulla. He makes them out of aluminum and brass bolts." I reached my hand out, drawn to the object. I wanted to touch the tile in the palm of Ursulla's hand.

She snapped her hand closed, opened her old red coin purse and dropped the ancient object in with a quiet clunk. I wondered how many speed tiles she had in that old purse. I wished she would give me one. I looked at Suzie. She looked back, eyes swimming, struggling to understand.

"Hmmm," moaned Ursulla. She looked up to the ceiling. "It's starting again, just as I feared…yes, yes…" she sighed loudly. We heard the distant rumble of thunder outside. I saw a tear drop silently out of the corner of her eye. She took out her lace handkerchief again, dabbed her eye. "Yes. It's starting again."

We left Ursulla sitting in her big over-stuffed chair, clutching her red coin purse, her speed tile purse. She was deep in thought, troubled, her body gently rocking back and forth, her head nodding absently. She scared Suzie. She scared me, too. Ursulla was almost in some kind of trance or something.

I looked over at the big, dirty windows, at the skeletal plants in profile. It was getting darker. The rumbling of thunder was louder, the wind picking up. Light spatters of rain hit the glass. We didn't know what to do about Ursulla, so we just left.

Out in the street the rain came down harder. It was one of those early summer thunderstorms that appear out of nowhere, a squall off Lake Michigan. We ran down the street for Sally's Nook where both of our mothers would be. We ducked into the shop and stood there, just inside the door, catching our breaths, looking at each other, eyes wide, trying to understand what had just happened at the bookstore.

"That was so fricking weird, Hill."

"I know."

"It's starting again, it's starting again," mimicked Suzie. "What is fricking starting again? What is a fricking speed tile, Hill? What is going on around here?"

"I don't know, Suz. You think Ursulla will be okay?"

"That witch? God, Hill, I'm just glad we got out of there. I'm glad we're okay."

"She's not a witch, Suzie. I think she was just as scared as we were."

"She is a witch, Hill."

"She is not!"

"She is!"

We were both staring each other down, both angry and confused when a terrific thunderclap and a bright flash of lightning made us practically jump out of our skin. Reflexively, we jumped into each other's arms for protection. We both screamed at once, then looked at each other, our noses almost touching, then we started giggling hysterically. The thunder brought us together again. The lightning settled the argument.

"God! That was close, Hill."

"I know."

Just then, the phone in Sally's Nook rang and Mom answered it. We went into the shop. Sally was behind one of the counters. She waved to us.

"Hello. Sally's Nook." said Mom politely. "Oh, hi, Hannah."

She listened and her smile faded slowly. "What? Our house? Are you sure?"

Her mouth dropped open as she listened. Something was wrong. "Okay, okay, Sally's here. I can come right home. Hill's here too. Where's Dad?"

"In the attic?" We all watched her, wondering what had happened. She listened more, nodded, "Okay, good. We'll be right home."

"Come on, Hill. Let's get home." Mom looked at Sally. "Do you believe it, our house just got hit by lightning."

"Oh, my God," said Sally. "Is John okay, everybody okay?"

"No fatalities, but I better get home."

We ran to Mom's car in the rain. It was really coming down hard now. We were soaked. Mom drove as fast as she could in the driving rain, but we could hardly see the road. I didn't know what to expect when we got there.

Finally, we pulled into the driveway. It was so dark by now and the rain was coming down so hard that I couldn't even tell if we had a house any more. Another thunderclap and a flash of lightning startled me again, but it lit up the house from behind. I was relieved to see the dark profile of our house. It was still there.

We ran into the house, dripping wet, and saw that Dad had pulled the attic stairs down out of the ceiling in the utility room. I looked up into the darkness of the attic and gasped as another flash of lightning lit up the outline of a man, my Dad, standing at the top of the stairs, staring out at the sky through a big, jagged, splintered hole in the roof, rain pouring down on him through the hole.

"John, John," called Mom. "Are you okay?"

Hannah ran to us in the utility room, crying, frightened. "Okay? Are you kidding? He's nuts, Mom. Get him down from there, Mom. What if another lightning hits. Get him down!"

We all looked up at him. He turned and looked down on us. "My speed tile. It's gone," he said quietly. He looked back out at the sky: lightning, thunder, rain; wind gusts whipping the branches of the trees.

"John! Come down!"

"Dad! Please."

He turned to us again and finally started down the attic stairs, dripping wet. "I better call Dick. We have to get that hole covered."

The rest of the night was surreal, spooky. The power was out so Mom gathered up all the candles she could find and an old hurricane lamp. Against the dancing shadows of candle light, Dad called Dick Beaver to help him cover the hole in the roof. Water was already dripping out of the ceiling in the library, just below the section of roof that was hit. We worked fast to pull the books off the shelves and stack them in the living room where it was dry. Mom tried putting buckets and bowls around the room to catch the water, but it was coming from so many places that she finally gave up.

Dick came over right away with a big blue tarp and some boards. He looked up the attic stairs at the hole in the roof, then he looked at the dripping ceiling in the library. "Well," he joked, "good place for a skylight."

"Let's get up there and cover it," said Dad.

"Shouldn't you wait until it stops?" asked Mom. "It's dangerous up there."

"Safest place in the world," laughed Dick. "Lightning never strikes in the same place twice."

They climbed up on the roof in the pouring rain. We heard them arranging the tarp over the hole and hammering boards in place to keep it there. Finally, the rain eased up, a soft rumble of thunder in the distance as the storm moved east.

Dad and Dick came down off the roof and sat, dripping, at the kitchen counter. "Want a beer?" asked Dad.

"Sure."

Mom brought in a couple of towels as Dad handed Dick a beer.

"Got my shower out of the way tonight," joked Dick as he toweled off his hair. "Should have brought some shampoo up on the roof with me, though."

"You often take showers on the roof, Dick?" teased Dad.

"Only when it rains," laughed Dick.

"Ever see lightning damage like that, Dick?" asked Dad.

"I've repaired a couple of hits," he replied, getting a little more serious. "But nothing like this. Nothing this big. And the damage. The roof boards. It looks more like something hit the roof from the inside. The splinters and jagged boards are all facing out. Lightning. It's weird. You can't predict what it's gonna do."

Dad looked at Dick. "Like something hit the roof from the inside…" he mumbled. "Something from the inside. Something trying to get out."

Chapter 8

Jeremiah Bullfrog

Two more squalls blew through Saugatuck that night, testing the tarp Dick and I had nailed over the hole in the roof. I woke early the next morning after a troubling night of odd dreams. Floating slabs, speed tiles, lightning bolts, Dick Beaver's balloon-like house...ghostly images of sand-covered grid-like structures, wood frame houses buried in the dunes and a frightening Asian man with insanity in his eyes, an old woman...someone I recognized, an oracle...a seer. And I dreamed a new dream: a sunken ship, a freighter...seagulls circling, cawing...a constant, incessant bird-like flutter, sprinkling feathers and guano on the exposed bridge, painting it white...the deserted and broken pilot house poking up out of the water at an alarming angle...a sentinel, a marker.

I dressed quietly, relieved that the power was back on. I started a pot of coffee, fed our dog, our cats, and climbed the stairs to the attic in the gray light of dawn. The tarp Dick and I had covered the hole with cast a bluish tint over the rubble in the attic. In the dim light, with the soothing, contradictory sounds of birds waking and chirping outside, I inspected the damage. Soggy cardboard boxes were strewn haphazardly with flaps sagging and contents spilling out. Charred and splintered wood lay in large and small chunks all around. The hole in the roof was impossibly large...about six feet across.

I looked for my briefcase, the one with the speed tile. I knew I wouldn't find it. I knew it was gone. But I did find it. I found it in bits and pieces of ripped and torn fragments in an explosion of leather all over the attic floor. I also found scraps from the plans of Helmut Schmidt's Chicago skyscraper…blueprints for a slab. Soggy papers and proposals from an old life lay torn and shredded, mixing with the leather fragments. A brass latch and a sturdy handle ripped from their home, from their places on the briefcase, were thrown across the attic into a corner, their purpose forgotten.

I picked up the homeless handle, remembering that night in Chicago so long ago, when I gripped that handle tightly, swung the briefcase over my head and hurled it into the Chicago River. Then I remembered last night. The thunder. The lightning. The impossibly loud crash and the sickening, splintering sound as the roof gave way. Hannah's frightened face as I looked up toward the attic, panic in her eyes.

I thought of the impossible visions my mind had been suppressing for so long and I knew they were true. The slab, the hanging, dripping, oozing wires, the growing slab-like thing that grew around the speed tile…a perverse rendering of Helmut's design. I pictured it bursting out of the briefcase, spraying leather fragments everywhere, pushing at the roof beams, struggling to get free, struggling to escape the leather prison I had trapped it in.

I remembered last night, pulling down the attic stairs, heart beating wildly, frightened, afraid I might lose my precious speed tile. I remembered ignoring Hannah's hysterical pleas as I dashed up the stairs, storm raging, lightning flashing, determined to recapture my prize. I remembered standing in the gaping hole, rain pouring down my face, longing for the slab, the disgusting floating slab like thing. I remembered watching it through the splinters and the charred wood, illuminated only briefly by flashes of lightning, an ominous, ponderous, floating chunk of gray concrete-like material with wires and tendrils swaying in the wind, impossibly floating west and north, against the wind, heading for the lake, heading for Lake Michigan. I knew I would follow it. I had to.

I heard activity downstairs so I went back down to the kitchen as my family got ready for the day. I poured myself a cup of coffee and sat at the island counter, waiting for them to appear. I set the handle down on the counter next to me.

"Everybody sleep okay?" I asked as my family scurried in and out of the kitchen. Hannah and Hilllary were getting ready for school, Marcia was getting ready for work. They dashed into the kitchen one at a time, grabbing a quick bagel or a bowl of cereal, a glass of juice, a cup of coffee. The sun was out now, drying the outside, but the inside of our house, the library, was damp, the walls soggy, the ceiling sagging.

"Sure, Dad, fine," answered Hannah, smearing large gobs of cream cheese on her bagel, "like sleeping in a fricking puddle. Ughhh, what's that?" curling up her lip and pointing her knife at the soggy, mutilated briefcase handle.

"That's what's left of my briefcase…from the attic."

"Looks like a turd," she commented delicately and went back to her cream cheese.

Hilllary came in, looked at the briefcase handle and mimicked in a baby voice, "That looks like a pooper!"

We laughed, remembering our first Fourth of July in Saugatuck. Hilllary was a baby, just learning to talk, suffering the trials of toilet-training. She had only two "l"s in her name then. We were watching the fireworks from the bridge going over the Kalamazoo River, the same bridge that overlooks the house Dick moved. As the fireworks exploded, the wind picked up long dark clouds of smoke, extending them into sausage-like configurations.

Hilllary was more taken with the sausage clouds than the bright fireworks. "That looks like a pooper," she announced in all seriousness, pointing at the cloud.

We all roared with laughter and Hilllary was delighted. She told her first joke. She drove it into the ground that night, though. Every rocket, every star burst, was followed by "That looks like a pooper!" We laughed every time, more uncontrollably with every burst. I think Hilllary's sense of comic timing was born that night.

"How did you sleep, Hill?" I asked.

"I slept great," said Hilllary. "I dreamt about waterfalls." Hilllary noticed Hannah's over-indulgence with the cream cheese so she grabbed the knife out of Hannah's hand. "God, Hannah, leave some for the rest of us."

"You whore." Hannah snatched what was left of the cream cheese and held it protectively so Hilllary couldn't use it. "Gimme that knife back, you little bitch."

Hilllary quickly picked up Hannah's bagel, still on the counter. "Fine, I'll just eat this one."

"Think again, you little twerp," and Hannah attacked.

I sat, smiling, with my cup of coffee, as Hannah chased Hilllary around the center island in the kitchen, followed closely by Sandbar, joining in the fray, as usual, barking, tail wagging, paws sliding, slipping on the hardwood floor.

Hilllary, realizing she couldn't escape, came to me for protection. "Dad, help me…"

Hannah lunged at the bagel. I tried to protect my coffee. Sandbar jumped on Hannah's back. Coffee splashed across the counter as Hannah knocked the bagel out of Hilllary's hand. Out of control, the airborne bagel shot like a rocket straight up in the air and with a sickening "thwoop", stuck on the ceiling with cream cheese oozing out the sides.

At that instant, Marcia walked into the kitchen and saw all of us, including Sandbar, looking up at the ceiling. She looked up to see the bagel, drooping slightly, the cheese, loosening. Then, with a wet, suction-like "schlup", the bagel fell.

Sandbar, utilizing the countless hours of training catching doggy toys and tennis balls, snapped at the falling bagel and caught it before it hit the ground. Not believing his good fortune, he took a quick, guilty look at Marcia, and two bites later swallowed the bagel.

We all burst into laughter, Hannah, as always, the loudest. Sandbar, tail wagging, hoped we would continue this game, but Marcia brought us back to reality. "Hannah, get up there and clean that off the ceiling…What were you thinking?"

"Me? Hilllary started it. She took my bagel."

"And you over-reacted," said Mom, "as usual."

"Hilllary, I'll get you for this. I'm gonna cut your hair off when you're sleeping tonight."

Hannah got a sponge from the sink and a step stool and started wiping the goop off the ceiling while Hilllary smirked, toasting another bagel in the toaster-oven.

"How can you let them get so crazy?" asked Marcia as she poured herself a cup of coffee.

"I don't know. They amuse me. We need a good laugh around here."

"You'll get a good laugh tomorrow morning," said Hannah, climbing down off the stool, "when you see Hilllary's bald head." Hannah threw the sponge across the room, hitting Hilllary in the forehead, leaving a residue of cream cheese in her hair.

"Hannah!" yelled Hilllary and Marcia simultaneously.

After depositing our loving daughters at school, Marcia and I drove to the Bat House. We didn't expect much at Hunter Productions, just a stack of bills and 20 boxes of Tulip Time tapes. We had to make some decisions about how to deal with our precarious financial condition.

The smell hit us immediately as we walked in the front door. It was a pungent, electrical smell, like ozone, that tickled the nostrils and made you want to sneeze. "Oh oh," I said. "Now what?"

Marcia opened some windows to air the place out while I went down into the basement to check out the circuit breaker box. Several breakers were thrown, but when I tried to flip them back they popped again. Something was wrong.

Even with the windows open, the smell continued, as if something was burning in the walls or in the attic. I called the fire department and they told me to cut the main breaker for the house. Then I called the power company.

Jed showed up just as the power company truck pulled into the driveway. "What's up?" he asked.

"Some kind of electrical problem in the office," I answered. "Did you leave anything on last night when you left?"

"Oh-oh," he said, thinking. "The whole dubbing station was left on. I was dubbing ten tapes for Ted Clark. And I also left the big computer on...and the BetaSP deck. It was rendering some animation when I left."

"Great!"

The man from the power company determined that the same storm that put a hole in our roof caused a major power surge in the Bat House. "Hope you got insurance," he said. "Anything you left on in here is probably fried."

"We've got surge protectors on all the equipment," said Jed, hopefully.

"This was a lightning strike," said the power guy, holding up a charred surge protector that he found in back of the dubbing bay. "A very high voltage lightning strike. We've been up all night restoring power around here. There's been a lot of damage."

As the man from the power company fixed the lines coming into the Bat House, Jed and I surveyed the equipment. Several surge protectors were destroyed by the lightning strike. We just hoped they did their job and cut the power before burning out.

A few minutes later the power guy came in to let us know the lines had been repaired. We could turn on the power again. I flipped the main breaker and we spent the rest of the morning testing equipment. The ten VHS tape decks we used for duplication were zapped. The distribution amplifier that sent the same video signal to all the tape decks was fried.

The time base corrector used for stabilizing the video signal...baked. The 3/4SP video deck we were using to feed the VHS decks...dead.

We checked the Macintosh computer Jed was using for rendering animation...also dead. The BetaSP video deck we used to record animation frame by frame...gone. The high resolution computer monitor, the RGB video monitor, the 8 gigabyte hard drive, the scanner...all zapped by the power surge.

Marcia checked the security system...dead. Her desk calculator... dead. The central air conditioning unit...dead. Everything in the house that was turned on at the time of the lightning strike was no longer working.

"We better call Herc," I said to Marcia, referring to our insurance man. "We've gotta call him about the house anyway. The insurance should cover repairs on all this stuff. But what do we do in the meantime? How do we service our clients without any equipment?"

Marcia went to her desk and fished out a file folder from the file drawer. "Better sit down, John. I've got more bad news for you."

She showed me an insurance bill that was ninety days past due. The notice informed us that our business insurance had been terminated. We weren't covered. "This is one of those bills we just couldn't pay, John," she said, and sat down across from me.

I looked around calmly. I thought of Dick Beaver and his fatalistic ways. Oh, puke, that's what Dick would say, I thought. Actually, I was almost relieved that circumstances had finally brought us to a decision we should have made months, maybe years ago. Selfishly, incongruously, I thought of my art...the speed tiles and floating slabs, nightmare images building up inside of me, bursting to get out like the slab in my attic. I smiled. "I guess we're out of business," I said to Marcia. Then, looking at Jed, "You better start looking for another job, Jed."

Steve Kirby, our accountant, had seen us through hard times before. Steve was an old friend, a college chum of mine, who we had depended on for years to keep the IRS off our backs and to keep us out of jail. He advised us to declare bankruptcy and seek protection from our creditors. I refused, feeling personally responsible for the money we owed people, even though Hunter Productions was a corporation.

We called all our creditors, one by one, and explained our situation, buying time until we could cash in some of our assets. They were all appreciative of our frankness and honesty. Marcia and I negotiated payment terms and discounts to get us over the hump. All our creditors decided to wait for payment rather than force us into bankruptcy and receive only a fraction of what we owed them.

We cashed in some stocks and bonds and put the Bat House up for sale. Jed talked Peg Morgan into forming a partnership to take over what few clients we still had. They borrowed money and bought most of the video equipment at a healthy discount, including the stuff that was zapped. Marcia went full time at Sally's Nook as store manager. I focused on marketing the large library of video programs that we had produced over the years. And I finally got back into my art, seeking solace in my paintings and drawings, producing them at a prodigious rate, feverishly trying to flush the trauma of failure from my soul.

We cut back on everything. Hannah and Hilllary took it hard, but it made them more independent and self-sufficient. They both found summer jobs in Saugatuck; Hannah scooping ice cream and Hilllary bussing tables at a local restaurant. Slowly, we reduced our debt to a manageable level.

The one luxury we were not able to part with was our sailboat, Dancer. Sailing had become an important part of our lives, a release, an escape. We cherished our day sails out into Lake Michigan, our cruising vacations, our romantic dinners at anchor. Somehow we worked the boat payments and the dockage fees into our budget.

Eventually the trauma of losing our video production business turned to relief. Marcia enjoyed working at Sally's Nook far more than juggling bills at Hunter Productions. I relished the solitude of my new lifestyle as an artist and the healing salve of creating art out of my experiences.

By mid-summer, the Bat House was sold to an art dealer with the unlikely alias of Jeremiah Bullfrog. He bought the building with cash, no mortgage, so we never learned his real name. He planned to open an art gallery in the old Bat House called "The Ecclesiastical Absurdities Foundation." * Like Marcia and me, so many years ago, he said he was escaping from the urban sprawl of Chicago. Jeremiah's purchase allowed us to pay off moldy old bank loans on equipment we no longer owned.

Jeremiah Bullfrog was an odd and mysterious, but charming man. He was a real showman. We met him for the first time at the closing when we transferred ownership of the Bat House to him. My first thought when I saw him was Salvador Dali, the Spanish surrealist. He had a long, stringy mustache, a Fu Manchu beard, and a regal air about him. He had penetrating eyes that looked right through you, but revealed little. My second thought was that I knew this man from some-where. He looked familiar to me. Maybe I had met him many years ago when I lived and worked in Chicago.

He also had Dali's sense of silliness and absurdity. He didn't think like a normal person. "This house," he said to us, stroking his beard. "Is it possessed?" He looked at us suspiciously, with his eyebrows raised. His face was very expressive.

"Possessed?" I asked.

He smiled, losing his suspicious air. "Oh yes. I certainly hope so. Possessed by the spirit of creativity and art…yes, I know it is. I felt it the first time I entered the house, yes, possessed."

"Well, I don't know…"

Then he became suspicious again. A real schizo, I thought. "Ahh, but all those bits and bytes…all those, ahem, computers." He spit out the word with disgust, then continued. "We'll have to flush them out, of course…clean house, as it were, yes, clean out the bits and bytes."

"Bits and bytes?"

"Oh, yes. They won't do in my gallery. They're imbedded in the walls, in the floor. All that cyber stuff's gotta go." Then he straightened up, looked right at us, eyes bulging, and shouted, "I won't have it!"

This unexpected outburst made us jump. Marcia and I looked at each other nervously. I asked, "Ahh, you mean computers?"

He grimaced, putting his hands over his ears, "No! Don't say that word in my presence...I'll be infected."

"Don't worry, Mister, er...Bullfrog..."

"Jeremiah," he interrupted, smiling, changing again, in an instant. "Please, call me Jeremiah."

"Okay, ahh, Jeremiah, but we have removed the computers and all the other equipment..."

He grimaced at the 'computer' word. "Ah, but the bits and bytes, the residue...it remains..." he said, shaking his head. Then he brightened, "But, not to worry." He leaned closer to Marcia and I, looked around him to see if anyone else was listening, cupped his hand over his mouth as if to tell us a secret. Then he whispered, "Magnets."

"Magnets?"

"Shhh!" He looked around again to see if anyone had heard, then he drew us closer and continued in a conspiratorial whisper. "Yes, magnets. I have thousands of them."

He straightened up and absent-mindedly brushed off his jacket and straightened his tie. Marcia and I looked at each other. Marcia rolled her eyes.

"Well, okay, Mr. Bull...Ahh...Jeremiah," I said. "I'm glad you have a solution."

"Solution? Of course!" He looked at us again and winked. "The house is perfect, It will make a wonderful gallery..." Then he laughed. "Just kidding about the magnets."

Marcia and I looked at each other again. I turned to Jeremiah. "I can't wait to see it...I think."

He smiled.

But the odd Mr. Bullfrog was opening a new gallery in Saugatuck, and I would soon be looking for a gallery to show my work, so I was curious about him and his plans. I also had this nagging memory. Someone I met, long ago, someone like Bullfrog. Marcia was cautious. "Be careful of that guy, John. There's something about him. I don't trust him."

But I had to start selling my artwork. I hoped I would have a chance to get to know Mr. Bullfrog a little better in spite of Marcia's misgivings. That opportunity came up sooner than I expected.

It was only a few days after we turned over the keys to the Bat House to Jeremiah. I was at home, painting. I had converted one of the bedrooms into a studio and had a large three-by-four-foot canvas on the easel. I was painting a picture of a man screaming in fear and frustration. His contorted face filled the large canvas. He was wearing a propeller hat, but the propeller had stopped turning. He was in a panic. He didn't know what to do without the security of his propeller hat. In the background was a city in flames. The man's world was crumbling.

The phone rang. I dropped my brush into a coffee can filled with muddy water and picked up the phone. "Hello."

"Mister Hunter, this is Jeremiah Bullfrog."

"Oh, hi," I answered. "How's the bits and bytes problem over there, Jeremiah? Get 'em all exorcised yet?"

"The bits and bytes?" he asked, forgetting our conversation at the closing. "I know nothing about bits and even less about bytes. I'm calling about the bats."

"The bats?" I thought of my episode with the bat when we first moved in.

"The bats, yes, the bats!"

"You have bats?" I asked.

"I've been told that you called this place the Bat House, Mister Hunter. You didn't tell me about the bats."

"That was just a nickname, Jeremiah." I paused. "Why? Have you seen bats, Jeremiah?"

"It dropped out of the rafters in the basement this morning. Why didn't you tell me this house was infested with flying vermin?"

I guess I was a little amused by his plight. I wondered if it was the same bat that had terrorized me. "Well, I told you about the bits. I warned you about the bytes. I guess I forgot to tell you about the bats." I looked at the screaming man on my canvas, thinking how Mr. Bullfrog's Fu Manchu beard might look on him.

"Very funny, Mister Hunter," he said sarcastically. "I'll just roar with laughter every time I get one of my rabies shots."

"Rabies shots?"

"Yes, Mister Hunter. The bat bit me. Then it flew away, out the basement window."

I tried to picture Jeremiah Bullfrog in the basement with bats dropping down out of the rafters. I smiled, but I tried to be more sympathetic. "Oh, I'm so sorry Jeremiah. I didn't realize you had been bitten. I wouldn't have joked…I'm sorry. And, Jeremiah, call me John. Everybody else does." I wondered where he was bitten.

"Okay, ahem, John…" he said my name as if it were a disease. "But back to the bats…"

"Well, yes, bats," I began. "One dropped out of a wall I was tearing out of the basement many years ago…when we first moved in. But we had an exterminator over and he found no sign of infestation. Your bat is probably an isolated case, just like my bat." I looked at my painting, wondering if I should include a bat in the background somewhere.

"Hmmm…" he said.

"Maybe it's the welcome bat?" I joked.

"The welcome bat?" he asked, thinking I was serious.

"Another joke, Jeremiah." I thought of painting a whole flock of bats coming out of one of the buildings in the background.

His sense of absurdity got the better of him when he realized I was joking. "If it were the welcome bat," he mused, "it wouldn't have bitten me so viciously…John…now would it? Hmmm?"

I considered that for a few seconds, "No, Jeremiah, your typical welcome bat, the ones around here, anyway, will only nip you…affectionately…not bite you viciously."

Jeremiah considered that. I didn't expect him to laugh at my joke. Laughter would be too revealing, too out of character for a man who was always acting a part. But he played along, so I knew he was beginning to enjoy the conversation. "Then, John, if we have determined that this particularly vicious bat was not of the…ahem, welcoming sort…then when would you surmise that I might expect a visit from the welcome bat? Hmmm?"

I laughed, enjoying the game. "No, really, Jeremiah. I only saw that one bat, and that was many years ago. And Jeremiah, I'm really sorry about the shots."

"Shots? What shots?" He abruptly changed the subject. "I want to see your artwork…for my gallery. When can I see it?"

I was getting used to Jeremiah's abrupt mood shifts. "My work? Yes. I'd love to show it to you."

"But I must warn you," he said, seriously.

"Yes?"

"No bats. I won't hang any bats in my gallery." Then he hung up.

I hung up the phone, smiling, and looked at my painting again. I decided that a flock of bats wouldn't be a good idea after all.

Gallery name courtesy of Bruce Cutean of ThirdStone Gallery in Saugatuck, MI.

Chapter 9

Bullfrog's Visit

My Dad really calmed down after he sold the building to 'Jeremiah was a Bullfrog'…that's what Hannah and I called that weirdo. Mom said going out of business was good for him. Dad, I mean. I noticed he didn't worry as much as he used to, and he was in a much better mood…most of the time, anyway.

The bad part was that Dad didn't have money any more. He told Hannah and me that we would have to fend for ourselves, make our own money. It kinda ruined my summer. I was gonna spend most of my time at Oval Beach with the other kids, but now I had to work at the Auction House, a restaurant in town. It was gross, cleaning up other people's messes, picking up dishes and silverware and stuff.

Dad spent most of his time drawing and painting, or working in the garage on sculptures. It was like he was erupting with art. He kept bringing big canvases out of his studio to show us, or weird little constructions made out of speed tiles and wires. He was preparing for a show at Bullfrog's gallery, The Ecclesiastical Absurdities Foundation. I have no clue where Bullfrog got that name. I still thought of it as The Bat House.

But even though Bullfrog was a big spaz, it was really fun to go to his gallery. Unlike most of the galleries in Saugatuck, Bullfrog showed some really far out stuff, not just landscapes and flowers. There were big, colorful, sloppy paintings that looked like they were painted by a three-year old. And a whole bunch of little sculptures that looked like miniature church alters made out of cheap plastic knick-knacks and last year's dime store action figures. There was one artist who showed old-looking, 50s-style science fiction pictures of outer space. And another artist who made weird totem-pole things with gargoyles and monsters stacked up on top of each other. Dad said that a lot of the stuff Bullfrog showed was challenging. I just thought it was funny.

It was also pretty funny the day Bullfrog came to our house to decide if he would show Dad's art in his gallery. Dad was kinda nervous because he wanted to impress Bullfrog. I was in the kitchen. Somehow, I had gotten roped into doing the morning dishes. Dad said my training at the Auction House was coming in handy around our house. I saw Bullfrog's funny, squashed-looking car turn into the driveway. Dad said it was an old Citroen…a French car. I also saw Ursulla doing some gardening next door.

Uh oh, I thought. I wondered where Sandbar was? I watched as Bullfrog got out of his car. He straightened his jacket (he always wore a jacket and tie), stroked his skinny beard, looked up at our house, and started walking toward the side door. I glanced over at Ursulla and saw her smile. I looked back at Bullfrog and saw him stop cold, color draining from his face. It was Sandbar. He was outside sitting on the side porch when Bullfrog arrived. Snarling and barking fiercely, he charged Bullfrog, thinking he was an intruder. Bullfrog turned and sprinted back to his car. Somehow, I didn't think of Bullfrog as the running type, but he made it back to his car in a flash. When he got there, he fumbled with the door handle, looking over his shoulder at the approaching dog with horror.

He finally got his car door open and dived, head-first, into the front seat, Sandbar at his heels, snapping at Bullfrog's shoes. Dad came rushing through the kitchen and dashed out the side door, trying to call Sandbar off. I glanced back at Ursulla to see her still smiling, then back at Bullfrog to see his car door slamming closed. Sandbar, our vicious dog, was jumping, barking at the side of the car, trying to get him.

Dad grabbed Sandbar by the scruff of the neck and dragged him back to the house. "Hill," he yelled. "Put Sandbar in my bedroom and close the door. I gotta see if Mr. Bullfrog's okay."

By the time I got back to the kitchen, Dad was outside, talking to Bullfrog through his car window. I went out to see what was happening. I waved at Ursulla. She waved back, shaking her head, still smiling. I hadn't really seen her much since that spring day when Suzie and I went to her bookstore.

"Jeremiah," pleaded Dad through the closed window. "It's okay. You can come out now. We locked Sandbar up in the house." But Bullfrog wouldn't even open his window. He looked around suspiciously for more hidden dangers.

I watched him as he scanned our property through his car windows, fear still etched in his face. I saw him stop when he saw Ursulla, some kind of recognition in his eyes. I quickly glanced back at Ursulla and saw the smile fading from her face as she stared back at Bullfrog. Hmm. Something going on between those two, I thought.

Finally, Dad got Bullfrog's attention. He rolled down his window, looked around again and said, "First you sell me a building infested with man-eating bats, now you invite me to your…your…zoo! And you turn a vicious wolf dog on me."

"I'm really sorry, Jeremiah," said Dad, trying to laugh it off. "I thought he was inside."

"I suppose he has rabies too," said Bullfrog, gesturing toward the house. "I saw him foaming at the mouth."

"He's really a nice dog," I tried, "when you get to know him."

"I'd rather get to know a—ah—a snake, a python…something less vicious," spluttered Bullfrog.

"Please, Jeremiah," said Dad. "Come on into the house. It's safe, now."

Reluctantly, Bullfrog opened his car door and climbed out. With a scowl on his face, he brushed off his jacket, straightened his tie, trying to regain his dignity, his composure. He glanced back at Ursulla, frowned and said, "this artwork you want to show me. Where is it?"

"It's in the house, Jeremiah," said Dad, then with a twinkle in his eye, "Sandbar's keeping an eye on it."

Bullfrog shot a piercing stare at Dad.

"Just kidding, Jeremiah. Sandbar's locked in a room all the way on the other side of the house."

"You're just full of jokes, aren't you," said Bullfrog as we all started walking toward the house. "Sick, sick jokes."

I looked over at Ursulla and saw her waving to me, gesturing for me to come to her. I left Dad and Bullfrog and went to see what she wanted.

"Yes, yes, Hilllary, how are you, dear?"

"I'm fine Ursulla. How are you?"

"Oh, fine, yes, yes, I'm just fine, dear, yes, thank you for asking. But, tell me, dear," she paused, getting more serious. "Who is that man with your father, dear?"

"Oh, that's Jeremiah Bullfrog, Ursulla. He's the man who bought my Dad's building in Saugatuck."

"Jeremiah Bullfrog…Jeremiah," she mumbled, thinking. "Yes, yes, Jeremiah."

"I saw him look over at you. It looked like you knew each other."

"Knew each other?" Ursulla frowned, looking toward our house. She thought for a few seconds, her head nodding absently. She looked back at me. "Oh yes, Hilllary. I know him all right. Yes, yes. I know him, but by a different name, yes."

I waited for her to continue.

"You must come by the bookstore tomorrow, Hilllary. You forgot your book about Singapore, you know."

"That was a long time ago Ursulla. School's out. I finished that report. I finished Singapore."

"Finished Singapore, Hilllary? No, I don't think so. No, it's not finished. It's just beginning. Come by the store tomorrow. There's something I want to show you. Yes, yes, something to show you." She looked me in the eyes. "Will you come see me, Hilllary?"

"S-sure, Ursulla, I guess. Can I bring Suzie?" I was getting very curious about Ursulla's mysterious request. I wondered what she wanted to show me, but I was afraid to go back to her bookstore alone.

"Yes, yes, of course, bring Suzie. Little Suzie Clark. Mabel's granddaughter. Yes, yes. Bring Suzie."

I looked back to our house to see Dad and Bullfrog just entering the side door. It took all that time for Dad to convince Bullfrog that it was safe. I started jogging toward the house, away from Ursulla, when I heard a blood-curdling scream. I stopped dead in my tracks. It was Bullfrog. Sandbar must have gotten him. I started running toward the house again, faster this time.

When I got in the side door, I saw Bullfrog back against the side wall, holding his chest, eyes wide, staring. Across the room, I saw Hannah's big yellow cat, Spinnaker, standing on the utility sink next to the washer and dryer with his back up in an arch. He was hissing. I looked back at Bullfrog. Spinnaker was hissing at Bullfrog.

Hannah came running in from the other room. She's very protective of her cat. She grabbed the cat off the sink and held him close, petting him. He was almost too big to pick up and hold like that. Hannah struggled with him.

"Is there no end to the horror you will put me through?" asked Bullfrog, looking at Dad. "What's next?"

Hannah looked at Bullfrog with fire in her eyes. "You scared my cat. What did you do to him?"

"I scared your cat?" said Bullfrog. "Look here, young lady, that beast tried to attack me."

"He's not a beast!" Hannah turned and stomped out of the room, struggling to keep Spinnaker in her arms.

"It's just a cat, Jeremiah," said Dad. "You don't get along with animals very well, do you?"

"Animals?" he asked. "That was a beast from hell. That was no animal."

"That was my daughter's cat, Spinnaker," explained Dad, patiently. "You must have scared him somehow, surprised him or something. How about a glass of wine?" asked Dad, changing the subject. "It'll calm your nerves."

Bullfrog's eyes lit up. "Wine? Yes. I would like a glass of wine. Thank you."

Bullfrog followed Dad into the kitchen, brushing off his jacket and straightening his tie again. I came in after Bullfrog, sitting on one of the kitchen stools. Dad pulled a big, half-empty bottle of Gallo Sauvignon Blanc out of the refrigerator. Bullfrog scowled, looking down his nose at Dad's jug wine.

Dad noticed Bullfrog's reaction. He shrugged, "I'm an artist, Jeremiah. What did you expect, some kind of fancy French wine?" Dad poured a glass for Bullfrog and one for himself. "Let's go into my studio."

"Before we do, please tell me?" asked Bullfrog, "Do you have any more vicious animals lurking around here? My nerves can't take any more surprises."

"Hmm," thought Dad, that twinkle coming back into his eyes. He looked at me. "Hilllary, where's your pet Iguana?"

Bullfrog gasped. I picked up on Dad's joke right away. "Oh, he's catching flies on the back porch." I turned to Bullfrog. "You wanna see him?"

"No, please...I..."

Bullfrog turned pale. He turned around and started for the door. He wanted to escape, but Dad stopped him. "Jeremiah, stop. She's just kidding. So am I. We don't have a pet Iguana."

He looked at us both. "Another joke?" he asked. "Another one of your sick jokes?"

I looked at Bullfrog and then at my Dad and I thought there would be no way in hell this man would want my Dad's stuff in his gallery. Not after the way we treated him that day. But I was wrong. Bullfrog loved my Dad's work.

At first, he sat on the couch in my Dad's studio, sulking, sipping his wine. Dad brought out the big painting of the screaming man with the propeller hat, "This one's called When the Propeller Stops," explained Dad. "It's about our dependence on technology."

"Hmm," said Bullfrog, brightening up a bit.

Dad brought out another big painting. This one showed two bald-headed men in suits. They were in a wicker basket attached to a hot air balloon. They were fishing off the side of the basket using a briefcase for bait. They were rather agitated because they had attracted a big cement slab, also floating in the air below them. Dad called this one, The Bald-headed Suiters, Fishing for Clients, Attract a Floating Slab. It was one of my favorites.

"Yes, I see," said Bullfrog. "The slab…tell me about the slab."

"Oh, it's kind of crazy, Jeremiah." answered Dad, trying to keep the explanation simple. "There are other slabs in my work. They're like a symbol for runaway development…you know, civilization. The paving of America"

Dad brought out another big painting. It was a briefcase like the one Dad used to have in the attic. It was open and sitting on a bed of speed tiles. The speed tiles were arranged in neat even rows, like the rows of speed tiles Dad arranged on the dining room table that night. A big cement slab with red wires sticking angrily out of the top surface was growing out of the briefcase. "Here's another slab painting, Jeremiah. It's called Birth of a Slab."

"Hhhhh," said Bullfrog, inhaling in surprise, eyes wide. "The slabs grow?"

"Yes," answered Dad. "They grow out of briefcases."

"And there…down there, on the bottom." He was excited now. "What is that? What is the briefcase sitting on?"

"Speed tiles," answered Dad. "They're speed tiles."

"I knew it!" he said happily.

"You knew it?" asked Dad. "You knew what?"

"I knew they were speed tiles," he said, leaning closer to the painting.

"Dad found a real one in the dunes once," I volunteered.

"A real one? In the dunes?" Bullfrog looked at Dad, excited. "Where in the dunes? Where did you find a speed tile?"

Dad shot a glance at me as if I was giving away some kind of secret. I answered for him. "He found it in the sand covering the ghost town at the harbor entrance. He found it in the sands of Singapore."

"You have it now?" asked Bullfrog, turning his attention back to Dad. "Let me see it. Let me see this speed tile."

Dad tried to explain. "It was just a piece of metal. A scrap. It's gone now. I don't have it any more." He looked at me. "It was just a creative exercise, Hill. I made up all that stuff about speed tiles."

"But its not made up," I said. "Lots of people have speed tiles around here."

Bullfrog sat, watching us, listening.

"Remember, we saw one at Dick Beaver's," I said. "When we did the Ronald McDonald song."

Dad continued to look at me, a surprise registering on his face. He didn't know I saw Dick's speed tile.

"And Suzie's father has one too. Suzie told me he found it in her grandma's attic."

"Attic? What attic?" asked Bullfrog.

"Suzie's grandma's attic. Mabel Clark, over on Holland Street." I answered.

Dad sat down in the old, paint splattered-wooden chair he used while he was painting. He stared at me with a confused, distant look on his face. I saw a look of sad resignation draw slowly on his face. I realized he had been denying the reality of speed tiles.

"And Ursulla, too." I continued. "She has a whole purse full of them at her bookstore."

At that, Bullfrog practically squealed with delight. "A whole purse full?" he asked. "How many? Who's Ursulla?"

I looked at Bullfrog, confused by his sudden glee, "You know. Ursulla. Our neighbor. I thought you knew her. I saw you looking at her outside."

Bullfrog leaned toward me, grabbed me by my shoulders and looked straight at me, eyes dancing with madness. "How many, girl? How many speed tiles does Ursulla have?"

I pulled away from him, repulsed by his touch. I frowned. "I don't know. She only showed me one of them."

Bullfrog leaned back on the couch, eyes bright, thinking, scheming. I looked back at Dad.

"Ha," said Dad, finally recovering, now smiling a little. He slapped his hand on his knee. "Whaddaya know. Speed tiles." Dad looked at me. "Why didn't we ever talk about this before, Hill? I thought I was the only one. I thought I was going nuts or something."

"I don't know. It just never came up, I guess."

Dad turned to Bullfrog. "One more picture I want to show you."

It was one of Dad's crazier pictures. It was a street scene. It's raining and there's a scruffy looking guy, like a seaman or something. I knew he was a seaman because Dad called this one The Sea Captain Looks for a Job. Anyway, this old time sea captain is standing in a crowd with suiters going by him with their black umbrellas up. He's dripping wet, but he's standing there, kind of impassive. But the strangest part of the picture was that the sea captain is wearing an old fashioned sandwich board, and his resume is printed on the board. But he's not looking for a job as a sea captain. His resume says "Gravity Consultant."

Dad propped the picture up on his easel and I looked at Bullfrog. His eyes went dark and his expression became grave. "Where did this image come from?" he growled.

His reaction confused me because the picture was kind of funny and playful. The modern-day suiters were almost doing a dance or a ballet in the rain with their umbrellas. They were a funky contrast to the serious, old-fashioned look of the sea captain. No one looked at the captain. You could tell that his efforts to find a job this way would be futile.

I looked at Dad and noticed that he was staring at Bullfrog, leaning toward him. He rose slowly from his chair, glanced at his painting, then back at Bullfrog. He pointed at Bullfrog, his eyes growing wide. "You!"

Bullfrog was flustered by Dad's pointing finger and he reacted defensively. "This picture!" He demanded. "Why did you paint it? What does it mean?"

Dad pointed back at his picture. "It's you! I knew I had seen you somewhere before."

Bullfrog frowned. "Nonsense. What do you mean, it's me? What's me?"

"This picture. It's from an old memory of Chicago." Dad looked at Bullfrog from one angle, then another, cocking his head this way and that. "Yes! You have a beard now, and you shaved off those bushy sideburns. But it's you I saw in the rain. It's you!"

Dad looked at me and clapped his hands together. Bullfrog jumped in surprise at the clap. He pointed at Bullfrog "It's him, Hill. It's him!"

I didn't know what the heck Dad was doing.

Bullfrog stood up. He straightened his tie. "This is ridiculous. I don't know what you're talking about. I must be going now."

Dad continued to smile as Bullfrog headed for the door.

"I like all the paintings except that last one," said Bullfrog. "I don't like it. It doesn't make any sense."

"Uh huh, Bullfrog. Sure. I understand," said Dad, still smiling, humoring him, now. "I've got plenty of work to fill your gallery. We don't have to use that one."

"I won't have that painting in my gallery! I won't have it!"

"Fine, Bullfrog, fine."

Bullfrog left our house then, and Dad told me about the sea captain.

"He's the same guy, Hill. I know it! He won't admit it, but I know it's him."

"Who Dad?" You know who's him?"

"The sea captain, Hill. The guy in the painting. I really saw him. He really was wearing a sandwich board resume."

"Right, Dad. Uh huh, sure."

"No, really, Hill. It was just before I threw my briefcase in the Chicago River."

"Oh, that day," I said, now understanding a little better. "Wasn't that the day you popped your cork, Dad?"

He looked at me and frowned. "You don't believe me do you?"

"Well…"

"Ahhh…" He waved his hand at me and turned away. "It doesn't matter." He turned back to me. "But I just know it's him."

He sat next to me on the couch and gave me a big hug. "He sure acted funny when he saw that painting, didn't he?"

"I don't think he liked it much."

"No, he didn't. Brought back bad memories, or something."

But the sea captain wasn't the only mystery Bullfrog left behind that afternoon. Why was he so interested in speed tiles? And what was it with Ursulla? How did she know him? I found out the next day when I went to see Ursulla at her bookstore.

Suzie really didn't want to come with me. "Go see that old witch again?" she asked. "Think again, Hill."

"Come on, Suze," I pleaded. "I don't want to go myself. Ursulla asked me to come."

"Hilllary, you think I'm crazy? That's like walking into the flames of hell on purpose."

I thought fast. Maybe if I make it sound more like an adventure. "Maybe she'll tell us about the madness in Singapore, Suzie. Remember that? And the drifting sand? Come on. She's spooky, but she's got some good stories."

"I don't know, Hill." I saw that she was starting to weaken.

"You're just a chicken, Suze," I tried. "Pluck pluck, pluck, pluck!" I started prancing around her living room, my hands jammed in my armpits, flapping my wings, nodding my head, doing my best imitation of a chicken.

"I am not!"

"Yes you are! Pluck, pluck!"

"An not!"

"Pluck!"

"Shut-up Hill! Okay! I'll go!"

When we entered the hallway leading up to Ursulla's bookstore, we heard someone talking to Ursulla. We climbed the stairs quietly, listening.

"But I want to pay you for them, woman," came a familiar voice from upstairs. "You haven't changed a bit, have you, Ursulla. You're as stubborn as ever."

I grabbed Suzie's arm, put my index finger up to my lip, "Shh, wait," I whispered. "That's Jeremiah Bullfrog up there, talking to Ursulla."

"Stubborn? Maybe. But, you can't have them. I want to keep them. Yes, I do, yes," said Ursulla's voice. "They're my children, you know."

"But I want them! I'll give you a hundred dollars each for them."

"Oh my, that is a lot of money, but I'm sorry, Jeremiah Butler, or Bullfrog, or whatever you call yourself, now. You see, they're not for sale, at any price, yes, yes, I must keep them, yes."

"Why did she call him Butler?" whispered Suzie.

"Shh! I don't know." I whispered back. "Listen."

"A thousand dollars each for them."

Suzie and I looked at each other, eyes wide. We both silently mouthed 'a thousand dollars,' Bullfrog's last offer. We silently crept up a few more stairs so we could hear better.

"How many do you have, Ursulla? I'll take them all."

"How many? Oh my, I don't know. No. I really don't know, Jeremiah. Not that many. You took most of them with you when you left, Jeremiah. Yes, you did."

"How many do you have?" hissed Bullfrog.

"I don't know. I haven't counted them. No, Jeremiah. I haven't counted them. But you wouldn't understand that, would you? You see, I've never counted them. No, never."

"I need those speed tiles." Bullfrog sounded desperate. "You have no use for them any more. You're old now. Sell them to me! I need them, I tell you."

"Yes, yes, Jeremiah. Yes, I can see that you do," said Ursulla coldly. "But, you see, I need them too. Yes. I still need them. They keep me company. And if you'll take my advice, Jeremiah, you'll forget about my speed tiles. Yes, forget about them. I'll never give them to you. Never. Not after what you did in Singapore."

"Damn it, woman! Name your price. I must have them!"

"Good day, Mister Butler," she said politely but firmly. "Yes, good day. You must go now. Yes. Please go now, yes, yes."

We heard Ursulla shuffling back to her apartment and we saw Bullfrog appear at the top of the stairs. He saw us, frowned and started brushing off his coat and straightening his tie, a nervous habit I had seen him do many times.

We must have looked guilty as we scrambled to our feet trying to get out of his way as he came down the stairs. He paused as he passed us on the stairs, eyeing us suspiciously. He grunted a quick greeting, then he was out the door and on the street. He looked pissed.

"Whew," said Suzie. "He knew we were listening, Hill."

"I know. Did you see the look he gave us?" I started up the stairs. "Come on, Suze."

We went the rest of the way up the stairs, walking loudly now so that Ursulla would hear us. She peeked timidly from behind her curtain to see who it was. She sighed in relief when she saw that it was us and not Bullfrog. "Ahh, Hillary. And Suzie. What a surprise. How nice, yes, yes, how nice."

"Hi, Ursulla," Suzie and I said in unison.

"I see Mister Bullfrog was here," I continued.

"Yeah. What a creep!" said Suzie.

"Yes. He is a very unpleasant man, that Mister Bullfrog. Yes, quite unpleasant." Ursulla brought her shaking hand up to her forehead and leaned heavily on a table next to her.

"Are you okay, Ursulla?" I asked, and went to help steady her.

"Yes." she sighed again, leaning on me. " Thank you, dear. Yes, thank you."

We walked unsteadily to the big chair she sat in the last time we were here. She sat down with a soft moan. "Yes, I was afraid this might happen again. The greed. The madness. I could see it in his eyes. Yes, it is starting again, yes."

"You were calling him Jeremiah Butler, Ursulla. I heard you." I said. "Is that his real name?"

"Yes, yes. Butler. That's his name. His real name. I checked the journal again this morning when I came in to open the store. The journal. I wanted to make sure it was him. Yes, the journal. I want to show it to you." She tried to rise, but decided against it, dropping back into her soft chair. "Hillary, I'm not up to it right now, dear. Can you get the journal for me? Yes, it's right inside the curtain. An old book. On the table. Bring it here to me, dear, please, yes, yes."

I left Suzie and Ursulla to look for the journal. I pushed aside the curtain concealing her private rooms and went in. The room was dimly lit by an old glass-shaded lamp, a Tiffany lamp. It was furnished in old mahogany antique tables and chairs with leather-bound books and gold-framed oil paintings scattered about, a cluttered room. Dark, flowered wallpaper covered the walls and gold-trimmed, red upholstery curtains accented the walls. It was a quiet, cozy refuge. It looked as old as the woman who lived there. I looked around for the journal she mentioned. It was sitting on the table just inside the curtain, an old dusty book with a faded orange ribbon tied around it. The cover looked like it was once black, but was now faded to a dull gray. The corners of the book were reinforced with leather, cracked and brittle with age.

I picked up the book and started back, then stopped. Right next to the book was the red purse that held Ursulla's speed tiles. I glanced toward the curtain, toward the bookstore. I looked back at the purse. "I can't find the book," I shouted, stalling for time.

"It's right inside the curtain, dear," replied Ursulla. "On a little table."

"Okay. I'll find it," I said, then picked up the purse. I was so shocked that I almost dropped it. The purse had no weight. The bulky speed tile coins within should have made the purse heavy, but it was like picking up a balloon. Quickly, I opened the latch on the purse and looked inside. Speed tiles, beautiful, glowing, pulsating speed tiles. Golden nubs, squirming, calling to me. I felt an overwhelming wave of emotion: laughter, tears, joy and sorrow…reaching out from the tiles. They scared me, but they were so beautiful.

I gasped, remembering my Dad arranging speed tiles on our dining room table. Appalled, I clumsily closed the purse again and put it back on the table, just where I had found it. I dashed back into the bookstore with the book. I handed her the book, hoping she wouldn't notice my shaking hand.

Ursulla untied the string and opened it. The pages were yellow and crumbly. There were pictures and hand-written entries on each page. "I found this book under one of the floorboards in the back bedroom many years ago. Yes, many years. When I first brought this building here. Yes, yes, many years ago. It was right after this building was moved here from Singapore. Yes, right after it was moved."

I looked at Ursulla, at her wrinkled face and her trembling hands. I remember from the report I wrote for school that this building was moved here in 1890, over 100 years ago. Ursulla must be confused. She wasn't even born yet when the building was moved.

"It's my father's journal. He hid it there himself, under the floor-boards…a warning, a record of the madness, the drifting sand. Yes, the sand." She looked at Suzie and me, gestured for us to come closer. "And the speed tiles. A record of the speed tiles, yes."

She paged through the book, looking for something. She handled the book carefully, delicately, so as not to damage the crumbling pages any further. I glanced at Suzie, her eyes were wide with anticipation. Ursulla found the page she was looking for. "Here it is. Here is Mr. Jeremiah Bullfrog's page."

Suzie and I leaned over, sitting on either side of Ursulla, perched on the arms of the old chair. We peered down on the page and saw a faded photograph of a man with thinning hair, a long mustache and bushy sideburns. Except for the beard, the man looked just like Jeremiah Bullfrog. He was wearing a long black coat and black boots He had a heavy woolen sweater on. He looked like a seaman. He was dressed like the man in my Dad's painting. He was standing on a wooden porch, Lake Michigan in the background, a big canvas bag in his left hand. He was smiling, proudly holding up the bag, posing for the picture. The bag was bulky. It looked heavy, but the Bullfrog look-alike was holding it up as if it weighed nothing at all.

I looked closer at the captions, the writings, scribbled on the space around the old photograph. They were written in another language. Ursulla said it was Dutch. She translated for us. "This says the man here is Captain Jeremiah Butler,"

I gasped. "Captain?" I asked.

"Yes. yes, Hillary. He was a sea captain back then. Yes. He was also the estranged brother of William Butler, one of Saugatuck's founding fathers. Yes, fine man, his brother. William was a fine man."

The man in the picture looked just like Bullfrog, but that was impossible. It couldn't be Bullfrog. The photograph was over a hundred years old.

"But, Ursulla," I argued. "That picture is really old. It couldn't be Jeremiah Bullfrog."

"It must be someone who just looks like him," added Suzie.

Ursulla sat staring at the page, staring at the picture of Jeremiah Bullfrog. Her hands shaking, she slowly closed the book and carefully tied the faded orange ribbon around it. She looked up at me, distressed, then turned to Suzie. She looked back down at the book on her lap. She sighed and shook her head sadly, "Yes, yes. I know. It is impossible, isn't it? His age..."

She held up her left hand, her wrinkled, shaking hand. She looked at it, turned it around in her gaze, flexing her fingers slightly. A perplexed look came to her face as if she was seeing her hand for the first time. "Yes, Hillary. His age. He would be well over a hundred years old, now, wouldn't he? Well over a hundred." She stifled a short laugh, bringing her hand to her mouth. "Oh dear, how time flies, Hillary. Yes, yes, he would be over a hundred years old. I didn't think of that. Yes, yes. But he hasn't aged at all, has he? Not like me. No, not like me. I've aged, but he hasn't. Now that is a puzzle, isn't it?"

She looked up at me, turned to Suzie, then back to me again. "You see, Jeremiah Butler and I are the same age. Yes, yes we are. We went to school together. Yes...a long time ago. We went to school together in Singapore."

Chapter 10

Dick Loses It

I often took Dancer, our sailboat, out into Lake Michigan while Marcia and the girls were at work. I would bring my sketchbook with me on these excursions, anchoring off the beach, working on pen and ink drawings and watercolors of the surrounding landscape or developing images from my subconscious…nightmare images of slabs and speed tiles and digital spoons, darkly humorous portraits of troubled people in technological trauma. Sometimes, I would simply sail the boat, daydreaming and enjoying the wind and the waves on Lake Michigan. Hannah and Hilllary euphemistically called the sailboat "the office."

Hannah was sitting on the floor in the living room trying to get her socks away from Sandbar. "So, Dad, how's the wind today?" she asked. "Going to the office?"

"As a matter of fact, Hannah, I am going to the office." I held up my sketchbook. "I've got a lot of paperwork to do today."

"I wish I could go. Sandbar! Drop it!" she yelled.

Sandbar let go of her socks and sat, ears up, head cocked, waiting for the game to continue.

"I have to frickin' scoop ice cream today," she complained.

Hannah put one of her socks on, then reached for one of her tennis shoes.

"What do you think you're doing?" I asked her.

"I'm putting my shoes on, Dad, what does it look like."

"Wait," I continued. "You're doing it wrong. How many times do I have to tell you. You have to put both socks on before you put any shoes on. It's sock-sock, shoe-shoe, not sock-shoe, sock-shoe."

Hannah rolled her eyes, familiar with this ongoing argument of ours. "Here, Dad, sock this!" She looked up at me, smiling, mocking. She continued putting her tennis shoe on, leaving one foot sockless and shoeless.

"No Hannah!" I started toward her. "Haven't I taught you anything as a father?" I grabbed the tennis shoe out of her hand.

"Dad! Give me that!"

"Put your other sock on first!"

She gave me a sly smile and put her other sock on. But then she ripped the first one off quickly and threw it up in the air. Sassing me, she grabbed the remaining shoe.

Sandbar caught the airborne sock and started wagging his tail, holding it just out of Hannah's reach, hoping she would chase him for it. Giving Hannah a disapproving look, I dropped to the floor and grabbed her, reaching for the other shoe.

Laughing, Hannah fought to get her shoe on. Sandbar joined in, jumping and barking. I grabbed the sock out of Sandbar's mouth and tried to forcibly put the sock on Hannah's sockless foot.

Marcia walked in from the bedroom to see us rolling around, wrestling on the floor, Sandbar barking, Hannah screeching, shoes flying. "What is going on around here?" asked the Mom.

"It's your daughter," I said, sitting up. "She's putting her shoes on wrong again. She's doing sock-shoe, sock-shoe. Do you believe it?"

"Dad!" said Hannah, giggling. "You are such a spaz!"

"Oh, that again," said Marcia, shaking her head and going back to the bedroom.

"You need a ride to the Ice Cream Shop?" I asked, tossing Hannah the tennis shoe. "I'm going to the boat. It's on my way."

"You mean...the office?"

"Yeah, the office. You want a ride?"

"Sure. I just wish I could go to the office with you."

Hannah finally got both shoes on, her own way, and stood up. "Let's go."

"Okay. Just let me throw a couple of beers in the cooler. Marsh!" I yelled.

She came into the kitchen. "Shhh! Hillary's still sleeping. Suzie's here too. She slept over last night. I'm surprised you guys didn't wake them up already."

"We're taking off," I said.

"Dad's going to the office Mom. He's gonna drop me off."

"Okay. Be careful, John." said Marcia "It's blowing pretty hard today."

Hannah took the car keys out of my hand. "I'll drive."

We started for town. "Dad?" she asked.

"Yeah?"

"How old do you think Ursulla is?"

"Oh, I don't know. In her mid to late seventies, I would guess."

"Hill says she's over a hundred years old."

"No way," I said with a laugh. "Hundred-year-old people are pretty rare."

"No, over a hundred years old. Way over. Hill says she's like a hundred and twenty or a hundred and thirty years old."

"That's nuts, Han. What makes her think that?

"She told me last night that Ursulla used to live in Singapore before it was a ghost town. She said Ursulla went to school there."

"Right." I said and looked out the window. "She's teasing you."

"And get this, Dad," she continued. "She said Jeremiah Bullfrog's the same age as Ursulla."

"Ha! Jeremiah's younger than I am."

"Ursulla told her and Suzie all this yesterday…at her bookstore."

"Uh huh." I said, waiting for the punch line. "What's the joke?"

"No joke, Dad. They were kinda serious."

"Bullfrog's only about forty. What's she talking about?"

We got to the Corner Ice Cream Shop, so Hannah pulled the car over to the side, double parked, and got out of the car.

"Hannah," I said as I got into the driver's seat.

"Yeah?"

"I really didn't want to tell you this, but your sister, Hilllary, is really a sixty-year-old woman, in disguise."

"So that makes me sixty-three, right Dad?"

"Right." We laughed. "See you later, Han."

"Bye." She kissed me on the cheek and dashed into the ice cream shop.

I drove to the Saugatuck Yacht Club on the west shore of Lake Kalamazoo, where Dancer was docked. The Saugatuck Yacht Club is a modest, family club; more of a sailing club than a yacht club; a place where locals could get together for parties and friendly small boat racing. Hannah and Hilllary learned to sail there in little square-ended prams when they were younger. There's also a fleet of Laser sailboats at the yacht club: sleek, athletic little boats, shaped like surfboards and capable of frightening speeds in a good wind. Older kids and adults raced Lasers and the smaller kids raced prams every Wednesday and Saturday during the summer months.

It was Wednesday morning and there was a lot of activity around the club. Sailors young and old were scurrying around, rigging sails and launching their boats. It was race day. I saw Ted Clark lowering his Laser into the water over the rollers built in to the edge of the sea wall. He was an avid Laser sailor. He looked forward to the twice-weekly races. I waved to him as I walked down the dock, dodging sails and weaving around young sailors preparing their prams for the big race.

Ted lowered himself down on his Laser and struggled to get it under control. It was a windy day and a Laser is a handful in a breeze. He zipped past me under sail and shouted over the noise of halyards clanking and sails flapping from the other boats, "Why don't you race with us today? You can use Sally's Laser. She's not sailing today."

"Thanks, Ted, but no thanks," I yelled back. "I'm going out on the big lake. I've got some work to do," and I held up my sketchbook.

"It's blowing like snot out there," he answered as he pushed the rudder away from him and came about. The wind caught his sail and he had to lean over backwards, using his body weight as ballast to keep it upright. When he gained control he sailed toward me as I climbed into the cockpit of Dancer. Just before crashing into Dancer's stern, Ted released his main sheet, luffing the sail and, again, pushed the rudder away from him. His Laser turned and glided softly alongside as Ted grabbed the stern ladder to stop the boat. The sail flapped softly in the wind.

"What? Showing off again, Ted?" I teased. It was a tricky little docking procedure in the stiff wind.

"Nah, but you really should race today. It's gonna be a fast race."

"I want to get some drawing done," I explained. "I've got some ideas I want to sketch out."

"Ha!" he laughed. "You'll be working the sails out there today, not drawing. Hey, speaking of drawing, when are we gonna see some of your artwork? You've been keeping it to yourself."

"I showed some paintings and drawings to Jeremiah Bullfrog the other day. You know, the guy who bought the Bat House. He likes them. He wants me to hang some stuff at the Ecclesiastical Absurdities Foundation."

"The what?"

"The Ecclesiastical Absurdities Foundation. That's what he's calling his new gallery. I guess he doesn't have the sign up yet."

Ted laughed at the crazy name. "Now I'm really curious. What kind of stuff have you been doing that you can exhibit in a gallery with a name like that?"

"Ahh, you'll see soon enough, Ted. It's mostly about technology: drawings, paintings…stuff I've been thinking about for years. I think you'll like it." For some reason I had been keeping my artwork to myself. I only shared it with Marcia and the kids. I thought it was because I was afraid of rejection. Maybe I was afraid my friends wouldn't like it. Maybe I was afraid my friends would think I was nuts.

"I can't wait to see it. When is Bullfrog's Foundation place gonna give you a show?"

"Soon. I'm gonna hang it in a couple of weeks, before we leave on our cruise. I'll let you know."

"Going north?" he asked.

"On our cruise?" I asked. "Yep. Gonna go to South Manitou." For some reason South Manitou made me think of Hannah's questions in the car about Ursulla's age. "By the way, Ted, how old do you think Ursulla DeWitt is?"

"She's about the same age as my mother Mabel, why?" He looked a little surprised by my question.

"Uh huh," I continued. "Hilllary wondered." I paused. "That would make her, what, 75 or so?"

Ted looked down and started arranging his lines, either ignoring my last question or thinking about what to answer.

"Older than that?" I asked.

He looked up. "Yeah. older. You don't want to know. Mabel would kill me," he joked. Then he changed the subject. "I'm gonna get out there and see if I can figure out this wind. I want to win a race or two today." Ted was very competitive. He loved contests. "Have a nice sail out on the big lake," he shouted as the wind caught his sail.

I waved to Ted as he stretched out backwards, balancing his boat, the Laser slicing quietly through the water, reaching top speed in seconds.

I opened the main cabin and deposited the cooler and my sketchbook below. I spent a few minutes securing everything, putting things behind fiddles and wedging the cooler between two cushions. If it was blowing hard out there, the boat would heel and stuff would fly if it wasn't secure.

I took off the mainsail cover and stashed it below. I attached the main halyard to the top corner of the mainsail and raised it up a few feet. I wouldn't raise the main all the way until underway. I looked out over Lake Kalamazoo and saw that Lasers were turning over everywhere. Laser sailors are used to getting wet, so I wasn't alarmed, but it did give me an indication of what the conditions would be like out on Lake Michigan. I reefed the main, reducing the maximum amount of sail that could be raised once I was underway.

I went below, turned on the power, flicked on the depth sounder, the speed log and the auto pilot from the main circuit breaker panel. I turned on the VHF radio and switched to a weather channel. Ted was right, I wouldn't be sketching today.

Fifteen to twenty-five knots of wind out of the west with four to five foot seas. I thought about the dinghy. Conditions were a little severe for towing a dinghy, but the sun was out and the radio predicted that conditions would moderate by mid-afternoon. I decided to bring it in case I wanted to anchor and row to shore.

It takes about twenty minutes to reach the big lake from our dock at the Saugatuck Yacht Club. While some sailors dislike Saugatuck Harbor because of this long river ride, I like it. The river is beautiful. It's flanked by wild forest and dunes for most of the trip and the twenty minutes out and twenty minutes back under diesel power keeps my batteries topped off nicely.

The Kalamazoo River goes mostly parallel to the coastline, north and south, between Lake Kalamazoo and the big lake, snaking east and west here and there. In the forties, the Army Corps of Engineers changed the entrance to the harbor by digging a new channel that would eliminate a large, oxbow-shaped bend in the river. The settlement of Singapore was nestled at the far north bend of the oxbow, a couple of miles from the natural mouth of the river. Now, the river emptied into Lake Michigan right where the settlement once was. Every time I sailed out of the harbor I passed through the ghost of Singapore.

The dunes still hid the remains of the old town under tons of sand. It was in these dunes that I originally found my speed tile so many years ago. Nearing Lake Michigan, I looked out over the sandy beach, toward the dunes. In the distance I could see a man. I could tell he was a large man, even from this distance. He had a shovel. He was digging in the sand. I was curious, but preoccupied. The water gets especially turbulent just at the mouth of the harbor entrance and Dancer was being tossed by the waves, riding up their crests and slamming down in their valleys. It would be a spirited sail, but I had to get Dancer out of these confused seas.

I steered Dancer under diesel power out into the lake and turned north, the wind on my port beam. I switched on the auto pilot and pulled out the jib. Dancer accelerated, dancing across the wave tops, surfing down the troughs. I cut back on the diesel's revs, put the transmission in neutral and pulled the diesel cut-off switch…Quiet.

I always treasured this time. With the diesel off, all I could hear were the wind and waves and the dinghy cutting through the water behind. I trimmed the sails, adjusted the course of the boat and tied off the loose mainsail left over from reefing the main. I went back to the cockpit and leaned back at the wheel. Eat your heart out Ted, this is sailing. No wet Lasers for me. I took another yank on the mainsheet to tighten her up, checked her heading to see if any other boats were around, then checked the dinghy to see if it was doing okay in the waves. It was following nicely, so I went below for a can of beer.

I sat at the wheel, sipping my beer, watching the dunes flow by on my right, the auto pilot, Tito, as Hilllary called it, keeping us on course, heading north. I thought about my artwork. With every speed tile that I made, with every drawing and painting, I imagined more secrets were revealed about the power of the speed tile. Logically, I considered these secrets to be the result of my over active imagination, but I couldn't help remembering Chicago and the apparition on the bridge. Maybe there was some unknown forces at work here. If not, it was fun to think there was anyway. I popped another beer and watched the dunes.

I imagined that speed tiles came from a time before history, and that they were very old and very powerful. The speed tile was a technological commodity then, like today's microchip. It was used in everything from eating utensils to flying machines. People used speed tiles as currency and wore speed tiles as jewelry. They had a strange, giddy effect on their users. They made life seem simpler, eased the wearer's burden. But they were much more than a gadget or a token. They were dangerous. When used excessively, they were like a narcotic. People became dependent on them, and some went mad when deprived of their powers. Speed tiles came from another time and place (Another planet? Another dimension? A long lost civilization?) making them very dangerous and unpredictable. And they often have a dark, menacing effect on their users, an effect unleashed only by the conceit and greed of men.

Their purpose? Why they exist? Who made them? Is there an actual soul or life force embedded in the mysterious interior of a speed tile? Are they the devil's work, emerging now, at the dawn of a new millennium, to destroy us? Or are they like Adam and Eve's apple, a test, created by angels to gauge our character and test our resolve? Do they signal an end? Or a new beginning?

I had been using the speed tile as inspiration for my art, as an escape from an unsatisfying career. But was I using it recklessly, naively allowing it to infiltrate my mind, influence my thoughts? That's what happened in Chicago. I didn't relish another dive into the river.

I thumbed through my sketchbook thinking about the drawings. A stout sailing ship with speed tiles lining the hull. I knew that if I built this craft, water would never touch the boat, that it would move through the water without friction. A bed of speed tiles with a heavy, slab-like object floating above it, defying gravity. Patterns of speed tiles lined up in rows inspired by that doodle in Kaminski's office so many years ago. I fantasized that the patterns would generate an immense amount of energy if fully realized.

I flipped the page to a close-up of a speed tile with miniature circuits and wires and connections hanging off of the bottom of it. I shuddered and felt the horrible danger of dissecting such a strange and wonderful object.

How did I learn these things? By making more and more speed tiles, obsessively, repetitiously. By extracting bits of their history and purpose as I cut and filed and drilled. By adding to their story with each tile I made. Was this history coming from my imagination, or was the speed tile somehow playing back a prerecorded message into my subconscious? I don't know. I thought it was my imagination at first, an artist's ripe imagination, a psychological release, a mind game. But the obsession was getting more real every day.

I frowned and sipped my beer. The motion of the boat was too severe to really get any drawing done, so I sat back and enjoyed the sail. I thought of Ted's elusive answer about Mabel's age, about my conversation with Hannah. But that day, I wouldn't let my imagination run away with me. I relaxed and relished the solitude, the wind, the waves. I watched as the sun slowly made its arc across the sky.

Later, I woke from my reverie, surprised to see the stacks of the power plant at Port Sheldon off Dancer's starboard beam. I was fifteen miles north of Saugatuck, three hours closer to South Manitou Island, the place where I imagined my speed tile had gone. Soon...I'd be going there soon. I came about and headed home.

I thought of South Manitou Island and the voyage Marcia and I had planned for later in the summer. I looked forward to our annual cruise, our family vacation, coming up in another five weeks, after opening my show at Bullfrog's gallery. We planned to sail north, our whole family, harbor hopping along Michigan's western shore, all the way to South Manitou Island, about 130 miles. We had sailed there many times before. I was always struck by the primitive beauty, the isolation, the mystery of the place. I don't know what I expected to find there this time. A slab, my slab, floating in the air, my speed tile within? Absurd. Impossible.

It took a couple of hours before I passed the Holland harbor entrance. Another six miles to Saugatuck. I watched the "Big Red" Lighthouse pass on my port beam. By then, the wind had died down and the seas were becoming calmer. I shook the reef out of the main to increase the sail area, but Dancer's speed stayed at a slow three knots. At this rate, it would be dark before I got home. I turned on the diesel and furled up the jib, increasing Dancer's speed to six knots. I hugged the shore, watching the dunes go by, approaching the spot where Singapore once stood.

I remembered the man digging in the dunes on my way out. I grabbed my binoculars and scanned the beach. There he was, still digging. I had been out sailing for about five or six hours. This man had been digging for a long time. I wondered what he was doing, what he was looking for. Maybe speed tiles, I thought. That's the same area where I found my speed tile. I approached the harbor entrance and continued to watch the man digging. He looked frantic, obsessed. He was digging randomly, tossing shovels full of sand over his shoulder. He wasn't digging in any one place, but moved around digging here, then there. His image got bigger in the binoculars as I got closer.

By now the wind had died completely and the seas were getting calm. The sun was approaching the water in the western sky. I motored closer to the beach to watch the digging man. As his big shoulders filled the binoculars, he turned and looked out at me. I realized with a shock that the man was Dick Beaver. His hair was wet and stringy and covered with a powdering of sand. Sweat dripped from his forehead, attracting more sand, crusty and brown. His shirt was wet with perspiration, his shoulders stooped. He looked exhausted, but his eyes were wide and intense. I couldn't hear him but he seemed to snarl at my approach. I thought of our dog, Sandbar and how he would protect his food if anyone bothered him when he was eating.

I cut the engine and drifted quietly, fifty yards off the beach, watching Dick through the binoculars. He continued to dig but his tired body betrayed him. He lifted less and less sand with each shovel, looking up, looking at me between digs, his eyes insane, obsessed. I waved, but he didn't respond. He just kept digging. At this distance he wouldn't recognize me without binoculars, but I thought Dick would recognize Dancer. He didn't. Something was wrong.

I checked the depth sounder. Twelve feet deep. I went forward and prepared to anchor. It would be unwise to anchor overnight in Lake Michigan, but the water was calm now. It would be safe here for a little while. I pulled the pin releasing the CQR anchor from the bow roller, pulled 25 feet of chain and another 35 feet of line out of the anchor locker. I dropped the anchor into the water and let all sixty feet of rode out a little at a time as the boat drifted backwards. I tied the anchor line off to the deck bollard. When all the line was out, I gave the line a strong tug to dig it into the sand bottom.

I dropped the mainsail and gathered it around the boom, securing it with black nylon straps. I looked out at Dick and saw that he was still digging. He had stopped looking over his shoulder. It looked like he had forgotten I was there.

I went below and grabbed a couple of beers out of the cooler. Dick looked like he could use a beer. I brought them topsides and lowered the stern boarding ladder into the water. I pulled the dinghy alongside and dropped a throw cushion into the little boat, then a couple of life jackets. I thought of lifting the three horsepower Yamaha outboard off the transom to use in the dinghy, but decided to use the oars, instead.

My back was to Dick as I rowed, so I didn't know if he was watching me or not. I reached the beach, jumped out in the shallows and pulled the dinghy up on the shore. I looked up into the dunes and saw that Dick was still digging. I could hear the shovel digging into the sand in the distance. He didn't pay any attention to me.

I took the two beers out of the dinghy and hiked up the dune to where he was digging. I could see now that he was digging around the buried foundation of one of the lost Singapore houses. I could hear his heavy breathing as he dug. "Dick?"

He kept digging, ignoring me. I went to his other side so he would have to see me. "Dick?"

He looked up, a crazed look in his eyes, sweat pouring down his face, mixing with tears of frustration coming from his eyes. My heart skipped a beat. Dick had definitely fallen off the deep end. He grunted and went back to digging. "Gotta find 'em," he mumbled, breathing hard. "They're here, somewhere…They're here. I know it."

Frightened now, I tried to distract him. "Dick. How about a beer, Dick. Take a break. Have a beer." I reached for his arm to stop him from digging.

"No!" He wailed. He shrugged off my hand and went back to digging, faster than before, frantic, obsessed, mumbling between breaths. "The tiles. The speed tiles. I need more. More."

"Dick. It's okay. Just take a break for a minute. Have a beer. You must be tired, Dick." I grabbed his arm again and he was so tired that he dropped the shovel. In frustration he dropped to his knees and started digging crazily with his hands, scooping sand, searching.

He looked up at me, tears streaming down his cheeks. He looked down, took one last handful of sand, then collapsed, his head in his arms, sobbing. "I need them…Oh God, I need them…"

I looked around, wondering what to do with this anguished giant, this nut case. I sat next to him in the sand and put my hand on his shoulder, trying to comfort him with the only words I thought might reach him. "Beer, Dick. I have a beer for you. Snap out of it, Dick."

Dick sobbed for a little while longer, then quieted down. He looked up at me, his crazed look gone now. He sat up in the sand, wiped the tears and sweat from his face. He spoke quietly. "My speed tiles, John. I lost my speed tiles."

I handed Dick the beer. He took it, popped the top and took a sip. We sat in the sand drinking our beer with the ghosts of Singapore, watching the sun dissolve into Lake Michigan.

Chapter 11

Confession

Dick Beaver was a real mess when I brought him home that night. He was sweaty and covered with a thick crust of sand. He looked like I had just dug him up out of the dunes. I thought of the old Mr. Sandman song that Hilllary and Suzie were practicing to add to their repertoire. I hummed the tune in my head, Mr. Sandman, bring me a dream…A nightmare was more like it.

Marcia was in the kitchen, doing the dinner dishes. Hannah was rooting around in the refrigerator, as usual, looking for food, I guess. Hilllary was practicing her piano in the living room.

"Sorry I'm so late," I said. "I hope you weren't worried about me."

They all looked up, surprised to see Dick with me, especially in his disheveled state. "Oh yuck," said Hannah, looking at Dick. "Gross!"

Dick looked up at Hannah, still a bit dazed and confused. He looked down at his clothes and realized how he looked. He smiled weakly, a little twinkle returning to his sagging eyes. "You wanna dance, Hannah?" he croaked. Then he slowly lifted his heavy arms as if to embrace her.

Hannah shied away, closing the refrigerator, not really getting the joke. "No way, Dick. You stink." Hannah will never be famous for her diplomacy.

Of course, Sandbar thought Dick was a real feast for the nose. He liked the way Dick smelled and he couldn't get enough of him, wagging his tail and sniffing away.

"Don't like my, ahh, after shave, Hannah?" asked Dick, wearily. He reached down to pet Sandbar. "Sandbar likes it."

Dick stumbled a little as he reached down. "Whoa…" He caught himself on the kitchen counter, then brought his other hand up to his head, rubbing his temples. He was still dazed, tired. He recovered his balance and patted Sandbar on the head. He whispered, "I look like your name, Sandbar, don't I?"

Marcia wiped her hands on a dish towel and came closer, a look of concern on her face. She put her hand on Dick's shoulder. "You okay, Dick? You look exhausted."

Dick looked up. "I'm fine." He cleared his throat. "Just a little tired." He looked at Hannah and smiled again. "I'm too tired to dance, anyway."

"He's been dancing with a shovel all day," I said.

"Should I call Nancy?" asked Mom, referring to Dick's wife.

Dick looked up quickly. "No! Don't call Nancy."

Marcia shot me a questioning glance. I shrugged. "I'll drive him home later."

I gave Dick a towel, one of my jogging outfits and a can of beer and sent him into the bathroom to take a shower.

"What's the matter with him, Dad?" asked Hannah. "He looks so…confused or something. Is he drunk?"

"No, he's not drunk, Hannah, just upset," I answered. "He lost his speed tiles. I found him on the beach. He's been digging all day, looking for more speed tiles to replace the ones he lost."

"Dick was looking for speed tiles?" asked Marcia, surprised. "Your speed tiles? In the dunes?"

"No, Marsh," I began. "Real speed tiles. He was looking for real speed tiles." I had just begun admitting to myself that there was such a thing as real speed tiles.

"Real speed tiles?" she asked. "What's that? I thought you made speed tiles?"

"God! Speed tiles," moaned Hannah. "What is it with those stupid things? Everybody's so obsessed with them."

"There are speed tiles for real, Mom," said Hilllary. "Suzie and me were at Ursulla's bookstore the other day and Jeremiah Bullfrog was trying to buy Ursulla's speed tiles."

"Bullfrog was?" I asked as I popped a beer for myself. I was a little surprised to hear that Jeremiah was so interested in speed tiles. Then I remembered how interested he was in the speed tile imagery in my paintings.

"He offered her a thousand dollars each for them," said Hilllary.

"Whoa!" said Hannah. "No wonder Dick was digging."

"Yeah," I said, "but Dick wasn't digging so he could sell 'em."

Hannah's eyes lit up. "A thousand dollars each, Dad! You've got a whole bucket of 'em. You could sell 'em to Bullfrog. We'll be rich!"

I smiled, amused by Hannah's capitalistic instincts. "No, Hannah, those aren't real speed tiles, I just made them up."

"Real speed tiles? You're telling me Ursulla has real speed tiles?" asked Mom, sitting on the stool at the kitchen counter. She turned to me. "I thought they were your invention. I thought you made them up."

"So did I," I said, "but apparently there's more to speed tiles than I originally thought."

Marcia looked at me, a look of confusion on her face. "Like what? I don't get it? What the heck is a real speed tile?"

I couldn't ignore the reality of these strange artifacts any longer. Too many unexplained secrets. Too many half-truths. Maybe if we talked about speed tiles openly, discussed these impossible happenings, these selfish longings, maybe Marcia could help me understand.

I sat on the stool next to her and took her hand. I looked into her eyes. "I thought speed tiles were something out of my imagination, Marsh, but now I'm not so sure…I mean, I am sure. I'm sure they're real. And I'm sure they affect people in crazy ways." I gestured toward the bathroom. "Look at Dick."

Marcia still looked confused. "Dick's always been a little odd."

"You should have seen him on the beach," I said. "He was obsessed. And, somehow, I kinda know how he feels…his needs…his longing for speed tiles."

"Speed tiles have supernatural powers, Mom," Hilllary added.

"Yeah, right," said Hannah, punctuating her remark by throwing Sandbar's toy hamburger at Hilllary's head. "You're such a dork!" Hilllary ducked and Sandbar went scrambling past her chasing his toy. He brought the hamburger back to Hannah for another throw.

"I think there's some truth in what she's saying, Hannah. I know there is." I looked back at Marcia, at her questioning expression. I took a deep breath and decided to level with her. "I found a real speed tile once in the same sand Dick was digging in."

"Huh?" said Mom. "When? Where is it?"

"It was a long time ago. Before we moved here. Ten years ago. We were here for a weekend, staying at the Park House. You went shopping in town, I went for a hike. Remember that weekend? I didn't think anything of it at the time, but for some reason, I didn't tell you about it. I hid it in my briefcase."

Hannah and Hilllary were listening intently to my confession. Marcia frowned. "You hid it in your briefcase? You hid it from me?" She took her hands back. "What else have you hidden from me?"

Dick came out of the bathroom, dressed in my jogging outfit with a towel around his neck, giving me a brief reprieve. He looked a lot better now and less confused. Of course, the outfit was too small for him and he looked funny in it. He smiled at Hannah. "Okay, Hannah, I'm ready to dance now."

Hannah threw Sandbar's hamburger at Dick. "Here, dance with this."

Sandbar went scrambling after his toy but Dick caught it. He handed it to Sandbar, paying no attention to Sandbar's disappointment and confusion. "What's the matter, Sandbar? I thought you wanted it."

"God, Dick!" said Hannah. "He wants to chase it. He doesn't want you to just hand it to him...God!"

"Oh, sorry..." Dick reached for the hamburger, but Sandbar pulled back, keeping it just out of reach, teasing Dick. He gave up on Sandbar and looked up at Marcia and me. "So, what else have you hidden from her?" he joked, repeating Marcia's question. He went back to grabbing at Sandbar's hamburger.

"We were just talking about speed tiles, Dick," I started. "I was telling Marcia that they are real."

At the mention of speed tiles, Dick flinched and looked up suddenly from his game with Sandbar. "Oh, they're real, all right."

"I was telling Marcia that I found one in the dunes at about the same place you were digging today."

"I had four of 'em," admitted Dick. "I found 'em a long time ago, when I was a kid. I found 'em in those dunes. I had a feeling you knew something about 'em. I saw it in your eyes. At my studio."

"Suzie's Dad has one too," said Hilllary to Marcia.

Marcia looked at Hilllary, her brow wrinkled, skeptical. She turned to Dick, then to me, "So, let's see the one you found," she said sharply, hiding the hurt in her voice. "Let's see this mysterious speed tile that you've been keeping from me for all these years."

I saw disappointment and pain in her eyes. I had betrayed her by keeping this secret for so many years. I thought of the cigarettes I hid from her so many years ago when I was trying to quit. I hid the tobacco smell with breath mints. She eventually found out. She looked at me the same way then. Betrayal.

I looked at my wife, my life long partner, embarrassed by my secrets, embarrassed by the absurdity of what I was about to tell her. "It's gone now. It got away. The night of the lightning bolt. It left."

"Left?" asked Mom. "What do you mean, left?"

Dick made a quick lunge for Sandbar's hamburger and snatched it out of his mouth. "Yeah, what do you mean, left?" mimicking Marcia again.

I looked at my wife. "It was in the briefcase I threw into the Chicago River. The speed tile. That was the real reason I dove into the river. To get the speed tile back. Anyway, I stashed the briefcase in the attic when we moved here. It grew in there. It grew for ten years in that briefcase."

"Yeah," confirmed Dick. "You can't lock 'em up. That's dangerous." He threw the hamburger into the living room over Hannah's head, sending Sandbar scrambling after it.

I looked at Dick, surprised by this new bit of knowledge, "You can't lock 'em up? You know that?"

"Sure. I tried to bury one once. It kept digging its way out."

Marcia looked at Dick and back at me. Her look of displeasure at my secretive ways now mixed with disbelief. "You guys are totally out of your minds."

I looked at Hannah. She was sitting on the floor now with her mouth open and her eyes wide, staring at Dick. She was getting an earful tonight. So was Hilllary. A confession of secrets from her Dad, now this, revelations of supernatural occurrences…impossible happenings.

Sandbar started barking. Dick's last throw landed under the couch and Sandbar couldn't reach it. Hannah snapped out of it. "Sandbar!" she wailed, impatiently. She crawled over to the couch and reached under, feeling for the slimy toy. She found it, sat up and tossed it at his face from point-blank range. Sandbar snapped it out of the air and pranced off proudly toward Dick, tail wagging.

I took another deep breath, knowing Marcia could never believe this, but hoping she would, "It burst out of the briefcase…I don't know when, maybe the same night as the storm. Anyway, it got out the hole in the roof. It was like a big, slimy slab thing. But I know the speed tile was inside of it…I know it."

"Oh my God," she said, getting up off her stool and backing away. "This is too weird for me. You guys are nuts. Listen to what you're saying."

"I thought I was seeing things, too," I admitted. "I thought my mind was playing tricks on me, causing visions, hallucinations, but I distinctly remember seeing the slab floating just outside the hole in our roof, floating north, over the trees."

"Could I have another beer?" interrupted Dick, then he tried to confirm my story. "Yeah, the roof looked like it exploded from the inside, remember?"

I went to the refrigerator for Dick's beer and was dismayed to see Marcia backing away from me, suspicion in her eyes. I think she felt trapped in a house full of lunatics. I tossed a can of beer to Dick and took one for myself. "Beer, Marsh?"

Marcia looked at me as if I were from the moon. "I think I need something a little stronger." Still watching me suspiciously out of the corner of her eye, she crossed the room to the liquor cabinet and took out a bottle of Scotch.

"Dick!" said Hannah.

"Huh?"

"So, what happened to your speed tiles?" she asked. "You said you had four of 'em? What happened to 'em?

Dick looked down at his beer can. He ran his hand over his face, rubbing his eyes. He looked up at Hannah. "Don't know. Kept 'em in my studio. I went in there last night and I knew. Before I even went in, I knew they were gone." He looked up at the ceiling, his voice trailing off. "Gone…"

"You think somebody stole 'em?" asked Hannah.

"Maybe. I tossed and turned all night, thinking about 'em. About where they went. Not many people knew I had 'em." Then he looked at me, suspicion growing in his eyes.

"Don't look at me, Dick," I said. "You know me better than that."

"Dad!" said Hannah, her eyes wide with excitement. "This is so cool," she said. "These speed tiles. What do you think they are? Are they alive? Are they from another planet or what?"

"They're from Singapore," said Hilllary, answering for me. She had been quietly absorbing our confessions and revelations. Now she was ready to contribute her own. She had a very serious, determined look on her face.

"What do you know, dork?" said Hannah, treating Hilllary, as usual, with disdain.

"I know lots of stuff, Hannah!" yelled Hilllary. She turned to me. "Ursulla's got this book about them. She said her father made the book a long time ago. It's all yellow and faded. Its like a journal. It's all about speed tiles. She showed it to Suzie and me."

Marcia dropped a couple of ice cubes in a glass and poured herself a Scotch. "You people are all out of your minds. This kind of stuff only happens on TV programs like the X-Files."

"It is happening, Mom," said Hilllary, still serious, wanting Mom to believe. "Ursulla's got a whole purse full of speed tiles and I think they somehow keep her from getting old. She calls them her children."

"Ursulla is pretty old, Hill," said Mom.

"I know," said Hilllary. "She's at least 120 years old."

Marcia almost spit up her last mouthful of scotch.

"And Ursulla's the same age as Jeremiah Bullfrog," added Hilllary.

Marcia looked at Hilllary with her eyes wide with disbelief. I had been observing these strange speed tile happenings a little at a time and digesting them over a period of years. We were laying all this on Marcia in one night. I couldn't blame her for being skeptical. But this last bit of information, that Ursulla and Jeremiah are over 120 years old, sounded far-fetched, even for me to believe. "That's a bit hard for me to swallow, too, Hill."

"And Dad!" continued Hilllary. "I saw a picture in Ursulla's journal. Ursulla said it was Jeremiah. The guy in the picture was dressed just like the guy in your painting. And the caption said his name was Captain Jeremiah Butler. He was a sea captain."

I looked at Hilllary. Another revelation. "Oh my God!"

"Okay, that's it," said Marcia, "I've heard enough of this nonsense." She took her Scotch and went into the library. We heard the TV go on. Sandbar followed her in with his hamburger.

"Dad!" said Hannah. "What's a real speed tile look like? Does it look like the ones you make?"

I looked at her, thought for a few seconds and shook my head. "You know, Hannah, I guess I can't really answer that. I had the damned thing for ten years, but most of the time it was in my briefcase. I was kind of afraid to look at it. I think the only time I really looked at it was the day I found it in the dunes."

"I looked at mine, plenty," said Dick. "They're kind of hard to describe."

"Yeah," added Hilllary. "They're kind of blurry, sometimes."

"Blurry?" asked Hannah.

"Yeah," added Dick, "That's a good way to put it. Blurry."

"And there's a kind of yellowish light that seems to come out of the gold nubs," continued Hill. "They're not brass bolts like Dad's speed tiles."

"It's almost like the nubs are alive," added Dick.

"Yeah, they are," said Hill. "I opened Ursulla's purse to look at her speed tiles and I almost screamed. The nubs looked like little worms. They almost looked like they were moving, squirming. This sick, yellow light was coming out of 'em."

"And they're light as a feather," added Dick. "They look heavy, made out of some kind of metal, but their weight, it's more like they're made out of Styrofoam."

Hannah was looking back and forth from Hill to Dick as they described the speed tiles, her eyes getting wider with each detail.

I saw a little twinkle appear in Hilllary's eyes. She knew she had Hannah's undivided attention. "And if you press on one of the nubs," she said very seriously, looking right into Hannah's wide eyes, "the speed tile will play a Beatles song."

"Really?" she asked.

"Yeah, a different song for each nub."

"Wow, cool."

I smiled. Dick looked at Hilllary with a perplexed look on his face, then recognition.

He caught on. "I don't know, mine play Frank Sinatra."

Hannah looked at Dick, then back to Hilllary, realization dawning on her face. "You little bitch!"

Dick and Hilllary started laughing. I joined in. "Hannah, you are so gullible," I said.

"I'll get you for that, Hill! You're dead meat. Just wait." Then Hannah started laughing too.

I got a couple more beers out of the refrigerator and handed one to Dick. Hannah sat back down on the floor and looked up at Dad. "So, how much of this speed tile thing has been a joke?"

I took a sip of beer and looked down at Hannah. "I wish it were a joke, Han. It's not. Just the last part about the Beatles songs."

"Yeah," added Dick. "Everybody knows they only play Sinatra."

We all started laughing again, a little too hard.

Dick started yawning after he finished his beer. He looked really beat. I asked Hannah if she would help drive Dick home. Dick and I had consumed a lot of beer and I didn't want to drive. Hilllary asked if she could come too. She didn't want to miss anything.

I went into the library to tell Marcia we were leaving. I sat down on the couch next to her and put my arm around her. She was still pouting about my secrets.

"Marsh," I tried to explain. "It was kind of a mind game at first. I didn't think I was keeping anything from you until lately. Now all this speed tile stuff is coming true. It's happening."

"I'm more worried about these delusions you're having than your secrets." She looked into my eyes. "You sound like you're going off the deep end, John. Like in Chicago. I don't want to lose you."

"You won't lose me," I said. "Just bear with me. Gotta take Dick home." I kissed her and got up off the couch.

"Be careful," she said with a mischievous smile. "Don't get abducted by any UFOs. And watch out for Bigfoot...and oops, there's a full moon tonight. The wolfman's out."

"Okay, okay," I said, glad to see her joking. "I get the point. We'll be right back."

Hannah drove south on Blue Star Highway. Dick was so tired he was nodding off in the front seat. When we got to the bridge going over the Kalamazoo River, I looked out the window at the house Dick had moved. "Dick?" I asked.

"Huh?" Dick woke with a start.

"Dick, I've been having these visions," I said. "These pictures appearing in my mind. Coming home from your studio a couple months ago I kind of imagined you moving that house using speed tiles. You had one in each corner. The house was floating like a balloon."

"Visions?" Dick mumbled.

"Yeah, like a balloon," I repeated. "That house. The one you moved."

"Balloon?"

"Yeah, Dick," I continued. "I've been imagining that these things have some kind of anti-gravity powers. You know, speed tiles."

"Uh huh," confirmed Dick sleepily. "Anti-gravity...like a balloon."

We waited for him to continue. He yawned again, turned around and looked out the back window at the house he had moved. He looked at Hilllary and me in the back seat. "I thought that was why I needed 'em...the speed tiles. It sure makes moving a house easy." His eyes narrowed and he got very serious. "But I need 'em. If I never moved another house again, I'd still need 'em. I gotta have more speed tiles...gotta have 'em." He ran his hand over his face, rubbing his blurry eyes, regaining control.

Hannah was listening intently, watching out of the corner of her eye. She looked a little frightened of Dick's intensity. Dick turned to her, his eyes softening. "I guess I just can't live my life without Sinatra."

Chapter 12

Wong

"Come on, Hill, ask him," pleaded Suzie.

"No Suzie! I can't. I have to work." I tried to make it clear to her. "Jack's got nobody else he can call today. I'm on the schedule."

Jack Lancaster was the owner of the Auction House Restaurant where I worked bussing tables. Suzie was trying to get me to take the day off and go to the beach.

"But Hill, it's such a great day, and all the kids are going to the beach. Jason's putting up a volleyball net."

"I'm gonna be there, but not 'til after work. I brought my swim suit."

"God, Hill! The sun'll be going down by the time you get out of here."

"No, it won't, Suze. I really want to go, but I told Jack I would work. God! I hate this job! I'll meet you there after I get out of here. About two-thirty."

A horn beeped out on the street. Suzie looked out the window at her Dad, waiting in the car. "Last chance, Hill. My Dad's waiting."

"Go on."

"How you gonna get there?"

"I brought my bike."

"Okay, Hill," she said sadly. "I'll see you at two-thirty." She dashed out the door.

It was only ten-thirty. Another four hours to go before I could leave. I looked around at all the people still eating breakfast. There were only a few tables empty now, messy with leftover food and dirty dishes. There were people waiting in the hallway for a table. It was a busy morning at the Auction House. It was a popular restaurant, especially in the summer.

Jack came out of the kitchen. He was a tall skinny guy, kind of nervous and high strung. He worked hard and fast and he expected everybody else to work fast too. "Hill, we still got breakfast people coming in. You gotta get those tables cleared."

I sighed. Why wasn't my Dad rich? Why did I have to work on such a beautiful summer day? I grabbed one of the big gray tubs and started stacking dirty dishes from a table for two.

"Get the big table in the corner first, Hill. There's a group of six in the hall waiting for that table."

"Okay, Jack." I smiled, trying to appear cheerful. I went to the big table and started clearing it off. Jack grabbed another gray tub and started helping me. He worked fast, as usual, clattering dishes and cups and silverware into his tub. I tried to keep up with him, even though I was especially grossed out by this table. It had the usual half-eaten food on the plates. It had those luscious lipstick marks on the coffee cups. And it had, my favorite: cigarette butts in one of the water glasses. I must have had a sneer on my face as I picked a soggy napkin out of the ash tray because Jack let me off the hook. "Tell you what, Hill, I'll finish this table. You go up front and seat that big party. Drop off your tub in the kitchen first. By the time you get them here, I'll have the table ready."

I dropped my tub off in the kitchen with Pete, the dishwasher. Pete was Jack's son. He was a couple of years older than me, but I liked to tease him. "Here, Pete, there's a couple of cigarette butts in here to feed your habit." Pete liked to smoke, the jerk. I picked the glass out of the bin and handed it to him.

"Thanks a bunch, Hill."

"And there's a cup in there with mouth marks. I know how you like to French-kiss the lipstick stains."

Pete grimaced then snapped his towel at me, stinging my retreating butt. "Get out of here, you little wench."

Frowning and rubbing my wounded pride, I went out to the lobby to seat the group. I grabbed a handful of menus and smiled at a group of six snobby-looking ladies. "Your table's ready. Right this way, please." They were probably rich ladies from Grand Rapids; a shopping expedition, here to spend their rich husbands' money in Saugatuck. All of them had dark, freshly painted lipstick on. Great. More lipstick stains for Pete to lick off.

As I led the group to the table, I glanced out the window and groaned. I saw Jeremiah Bullfrog getting out of his squashed Citroen. A bald-headed man with glasses was getting out of the passenger side. I saw Bullfrog gesturing and pointing, smiling broadly; typical Bullfrog behavior, bragging to his guest about our little town. He was swinging a rolled up paper, like a blueprint or something, using it to point at stuff.

I showed the rich ladies to their table just as Jack was finishing with the napkins. He looked up when he saw Bullfrog come in and whispered, "Why don't you seat those two, then come back here with some water glasses." He took the menus from me.

I sighed, dreading Bullfrog's greeting. "Hello, Mister Bullfrog."

He looked at me with his eyebrows all arched up, eyes wide. It took him a while to remember who I was. "Ahh yes! The little eavesdropper. Hillary, isn't it? Hillary Hunter."

"Yep. Can I show you to a table, Mister Bullfrog?"

He ignored me, turning to his guest. "Oh, what luck! Doctor Wong, this is Hillary Hunter. She is the daughter of John Hunter, the artist I was telling you about. Now isn't that a coincidence?"

I tried again. "Would you like a table, Mister Bullfrog?"

"Hillary, I'd like you to meet Doctor Wong. Doctor Wong is here from Chicago, Hillary." Bullfrog turned to Dr. Wong. "Hillary's one of our promising young talents here in West Michigan. A wonderful future she has. Oh, very talented."

He was so full of it. "Nice to meet you, Doctor Wong." I turned back to Bullfrog. "Can I show you to a table now?"

"A table?" Bullfrog looked at me with surprise, as if he didn't know the meaning of the word.

"Yes, a table," I explained. "Would you like to sit down?"

"Of course we want to sit down, my dear," his expression now exasperated, his brow wrinkled. "You wouldn't expect us to eat standing up now, would you?"

I looked at his friend, Wong. He seemed to roll his eyes, impatient with Bullfrog's act. "Okay. Right this way."

I took them to a table for two near the window, a small table already set with silverware and napkins.

"Oh my, no, Hillary. No, no, no. This will never do." Bullfrog didn't like the table. "We will need a much bigger table." He looked around the room. He was beginning to attract attention from the other diners. "How about that one over there," he said, pointing to a table set for four near the kitchen. He smiled his phony smile and arched his eyebrows, waiting.

"Fine. You can have that table." I led them to the bigger table.

Bullfrog and Wong followed me, Bullfrog nodding and greeting everyone he passed, acting as if he knew the whole town. I knew he didn't. And I could tell Wong wasn't impressed. He didn't care who Bullfrog knew.

Bullfrog stopped at Todd Camper's table. Todd was the editor of our local newspaper, the Commercial Record. It came out once a week, sixteen pages of local news and ads. I called it the Comical Record. Todd was a kind of rumpled, burned-out newsman from Chicago. He had been on the job here for about a year. Some people said he was hiding out from some political scandal in the big city. Lately his big story was the rash of burglaries at people's houses around town, or I should say, break-ins, because at each break-in, nothing was reported stolen. He was sitting alone, reading a type-written story, his camera sitting on the table next to him. "Todd! How nice to see you!" said Bullfrog, ignoring Wong and me.

Todd looked up, "Oh, hello Mister Bullfrog…"

"Jeremiah, please. Call me Jeremiah."

"Yes, ah, Jeremiah."

"You must stop by my gallery," said Bullfrog, smiling. "You'll want to write a story about it, I'm sure. It's very unusual. Very New York."

"New York?" asked Todd.

"Oh yes…"

Wong cleared his throat and looked at his watch.

Bullfrog looked at Wong, then back at Todd. "Oh, excuse me, Todd. I must go. But promise me you'll stop by."

"I promise," said Todd, not sounding completely sincere. Todd went back to his papers.

I brought Bullfrog and Wong to their table "Oh yes! This is perfect. Good job Hillary. Good job." He turned serious, furrowing his brow and bringing his hand up to his temple in an exaggerated gesture, "Hillary, you must bring me a glass of water right away…I have a splitting headache and I must take a powder immediately!"

"Okay, Mister Bullfrog, right away." Good grief. What an actor. A powder? What's that? I went to the sink for Bullfrog's water.

I filled up two water glasses with ice, then water, and rushed them back to Bullfrog's table. Bullfrog had a small paper package like a sugar packet, but bigger. He ripped the corner off one end as I approached. "Oh, finally! My water!" It only took me 15 seconds to bring it to him, but he acted as if it took an hour. I set the water on the table. Bullfrog was not happy with his water. He frowned and pointed at his glass. "Ice?" he asked. "Ice? I didn't ask for ice. I can't have ice." He looked up at me and said, "Hillary, I can't have water with ice. I must have a glass of water…plain water."

I retreated, muttering obscenities. Why did he enjoy making people feel small? I hated that. I returned with a glass of water without ice.

He poured the contents of the package into the water glass as Wong sat there, impatiently drumming his fingers on the table, watching him. He stirred the white powder into the water, oblivious to his guest or the other diners that were now watching him. He held the glass up to the light and studied it to see if all the powder had dissolved. He wasn't happy with what he saw, so he stirred it more and held it up again. Happy at last, he drank down the cloudy mixture and with a loud "Ahhhh!" set his glass down with a bang. I saw one of the snobby ladies jump, then glance over her shoulder at Bullfrog.

I went back to the sink to get water for the snobby ladies, glad that I wasn't a waitress at Bullfrog's table. I glanced over at Wong as I carried a tray of glasses to the big table. Wong was Chinese or Japanese looking…Oriental. With a name like Wong, I guessed he was Chinese. He was close-shaven and he wore wire-rimmed glasses. He had no hair. He was completely bald. He must be one of those guys who shaves his head every morning, I thought. He was wearing a tie and sport coat. He looked smart, well-groomed, conservative. He was quite a contrast to Bullfrog. Wong also looked like he didn't really want to be here with Bullfrog. Lisa, a new waitress who was kind of nervous and timid (and not very smart), went over to take their orders.

I cleared off one table, then another, glancing occasionally at Bullfrog and his guest. I saw Lisa shrugging, pointing at the menu, shaking her head. Twice she ran back to the kitchen to ask about some special request. I met her in the kitchen with one of my gray tubs of dirty dishes. She was almost in tears. "What am I gonna do with your friend in there, Hillary? I don't know what to do. He keeps asking for stuff we don't have. I just don't know what to do."

"Sorry, Lisa…He's not really my friend, you know. Not really."

She dashed back to the dining room.

I followed her with another gray tub.

Jim Fletcher and Linus Beagle came in for a table…two out of the four policemen that keep our town safe from criminals. They were both in their mid-twenties…both a little full of themselves and overly proud of their uniforms. They swaggered through the room as Jack showed them to a table. I saw Jim check himself out in one of Jack's mirrors as he passed, straightening the holstered gun on his hip.

I looked back at Bullfrog's table. Lisa finally got their order. With a big sigh of relief, she went back to the kitchen. Bullfrog looked up, searching the room. He saw me, but I quickly put my head down, trying to look busy clearing a table. It was no use. I couldn't hide from him. "Hillary!" he bellowed too loud. Everyone in the room looked up at him. I wished I could crawl into the gray tub and hide. "Hillary, come here please, Hillary!"

I couldn't hide. I went to see what Bullfrog's latest request would be. Another glass of water?

"Hillary, please clear off these other place settings. I need room to spread out this chart."

I should have cleared the other place settings when I sat him down, but I forgot, with all the water requests and stuff. I quickly gathered up the place mats, silverware and napkins and tried to get away.

"And Hillary. Bring me a glass of water, please."

Rolling my eyes, I went to the sink and filled up a glass with water. No ice. I brought it to Bullfrog. He looked at it as if it were poison, then looked back up at me, "It's a very hot day out there today, Hillary. It would be so much more refreshing to have a glass of ice water."

My mouth must have dropped open. "But, but…"

He interrupted. "Please get me a glass of ice water, Hillary."

I took the glass of plain water away thinking, what a jerk. I should pour it on his head. I hated the way he bossed people around. By the time I got back with his ice water he was already unrolling his chart on the section of the table I had just cleared. I recognized it right away. It was a nautical chart. My Dad had lots of them. He placed a napkin holder on one side to weigh it down. He looked around for something else to weigh down the other side. "Hillary. Bring me another one of these…these things," he demanded, pointing at the napkin holder.

I dashed off to the kitchen to get him another napkin holder. Lisa was just coming out carrying a tea pot with steaming water and a wicker basket of tea bags. I had never seen a tea pot at the Auction House. We usually used those little metal one-cup water containers with the lid for tea. I wondered where she had found this tea pot. It must have been one of Bullfrog's demands. Lisa rolled her eyes as we passed.

I grabbed a napkin holder and rushed back to Bullfrog's table. Bullfrog was shaking his head and pointing at the tea bags, "I was hoping you could brew us a proper pot of tea, Lisa. I just don't like these new fangled tea bag things. Can't you take the tea out of the bags and brew the tea normally?"

Wong interrupted. It was the first time I had heard him speak. "Bullfrog! Stop bullying the woman." He looked up at Lisa. "We'll use the tea bags."

I was surprised that Bullfrog didn't object. He stopped bullying Lisa and let her set the teapot and the cups on the table without saying another word. Then he saw me. "Ah, Hillary. Yes. You've brought a weight for the other side. Put it on the chart over there, Hillary."

He unrolled the chart, making room for the weight. I recognized the location of the chart right away. I set the napkin holder down in northern Lake Michigan right off the western shore of South Manitou Island. I paused, looking at the chart. I couldn't believe it. We would be sailing for South Manitou Island in another couple of weeks. Why were Bullfrog and his friend Dr. Wong looking at a chart of South Manitou Island?

"Okay, Hillary. You may go now," said Bullfrog, dismissing me regally.

I watched them as much as I could while I cleared tables. I was really curious about South Manitou Island. They kept referring to the chart. They seemed to be arguing about something. Wong quietly shaking his head, Bullfrog waving his arms, gesturing like a corny actor in a silent movie. "In the sand…In the dunes…" I heard Bullfrog shout, pointing at the chart. Wong shook his head in disagreement.

When Lisa brought their food, Bullfrog rolled up the chart to get it out of the way. Bullfrog ignored Lisa while she set their food down. I could tell Lisa was relieved about that. Bullfrog seemed to be focusing on Wong now. They continued talking as they ate, Bullfrog getting more agitated by the minute. "I just let you use the plans, I didn't give them to you permanently…" said Bullfrog, his voice trailing off in a whisper.

Wong spoke quietly and kept shaking his head, disagreeing with Bullfrog. Bullfrog tried unsuccessfully to keep his voice low. I saw him lean over the table toward Wong and hiss, "They're mine Wong, mine!" He glanced around, noticing people looking at him. He ran his hand over his face, trying to regain control.

He continued talking to Wong, trying not to raise his voice…trying not to shout. Finally, he set his half empty water glass down on the table with a bang that sent melting ice cubes flying, "Give them back!"

The room went silent. All eyes were on Bullfrog. Wong sat back in his chair and smiled at Bullfrog. It was a weird smile; satisfaction, revenge, hate…all written on his face, in his eyes. I looked at Bullfrog. He was steaming. I hated Bullfrog too, but Wong scared me. That look in Wong's eyes…that evil look.

Lisa, not thinking ahead at all, picked just that moment to service her table. "Will there be anything else?" she asked politely.

Bullfrog and Wong continued staring at each other, Wong smiling, Bullfrog fuming. They ignored Lisa.

Lisa tried again. She was pretty dense. "Can I bring you anything else?"

Wong broke the silence. "You can bring Mr. Bullfrog the check," he said, then rose to his feet.

Bullfrog exploded, "You son-of-a-bitch!" Then, bellowing like an animal, he raked his left arm backhanded across the table, causing all the dishes, cups and glasses to go flying, clattering, spilling all over poor Lisa and the floor around her. Lisa screamed and started backing away. Bullfrog leaped to his feet, his chair flying backwards. He lunged forward, upsetting the table, toppling it on its side, depositing the teapot and what little was left on the table onto Wong's shoes.

Lisa backed up, still screaming, and stumbled on Todd Camper's table, losing her balance and sitting, unceremoniously, on Todd's bacon and eggs. Todd, smelling a story, grabbed his camera before Lisa knocked it to the floor.

I glanced quickly at the six snobby ladies and saw four of them frozen in mid-application, compacts lifted, lipstick tubes in hand, eyes wide, staring in disbelief at Bullfrog's outburst.

I looked back at Bullfrog as he stumbled forward over the fallen table reaching for Wong, shouting "Give them back! Give them back!" He was totally whacko! I think he wanted to kill Wong.

Todd's flash started going off. A scoop at last for the Comical Record.

Jim and Linus, our protectors, leaped into action. Linus knocked his chair backwards into one of the snobby ladies as he ran to break up the fight. Her lipstick tube, jarred when Linus' chair toppled into her shoulder painted a slash that looked like red Indian war paint across her cheek. The cops reached Bullfrog just as he put his fingers around Wong's neck, knocking Wong's wire-rimmed glasses across the room into a coffee cup on the snobby ladies' table, red lips on the rim, pouting their silent protest.

Jack and Pete came running out of the kitchen to see what was going on. Todd continued to (flash!) snap pictures to capture the action. The officers subdued Bullfrog, one on each arm, Bullfrog struggling and muttering something about wanting them back...whatever "they" were.

Wong brushed off his jacket, regained his composure, and reached for his glasses in the pouty cup. "I must go," he said simply, wiping his glasses with a handkerchief he pulled out of his breast pocket.

Jim Fletcher had other things in mind, like a trip to the police station, handcuffs on the assailant, that sort of thing. "But this guy. We've gotta arrest him. You'll have to press charges."

Wong held up his hand. "No. I don't want to press charges. It was an unfortunate misunderstanding." Then he looked into Bullfrog's eyes with that intense stare of his, "Wasn't it Mister Bullfrog?"

Bullfrog, still angry, stopped struggling. He looked at Wong, breathing hard.

Wong said, "I'm sure Mister Bullfrog will pay for the damages." He looked at Bullfrog again, then enunciated very clearly, "Won't you Mister Bullfrog?"

Bullfrog shrugged off the officers grip and smiled at Wong. He had that weird ability to change moods in an instant. "Of course I'll pay for the damages." He looked around, only then realizing that he had created quite a stir. "Oh my, yes. The damages. I'll certainly pay for the damages."

Wong nodded at Bullfrog and started to leave.

Bullfrog stopped him. "Wong!"

Wong turned.

Bullfrog continued. "This is not over Wong. I'll see you again."

"Yes, Bullfrog," admitted Wong. "I'm sure you will." He turned and quickly headed for the door followed closely by Todd Camper, chasing his story.

I watched Wong outside through the window, shaking his head at Todd's questions as he walked out of my view. He was probably walking back to Bullfrog's gallery to get his car. It looked as if Todd wouldn't get a story out of Wong.

Bullfrog took his wallet out of his breast pocket. He took two bills out and handed them to Jack. Two hundred dollars. "This should cover my check," he said. "But next time I come in, I shall expect a proper pot of tea." He left. I watched out the window. Todd ran up to Bullfrog as he got into his squashed car. He had a spiral notebook in his hands and I guess he was hoping to get a comment out of Bullfrog. He didn't. Bullfrog drove away.

I pedaled fast down Ferry Street, a winding road following the Kalamazoo River. I was heading for Oval Beach where I was gonna meet

Suzie and the other kids. It took an extra half hour to clean up after Bullfrog's fight, but I was finally out of there, finally in the sun.

I got to the Oval Beach Road and turned left. This road winds around through the forest and over the dunes separating Saugatuck from Lake Michigan. The pedaling was slower here, at least going up the dunes, but even the downhill parts were slower than you would think because the road turned so much.

The afternoon sun was coming through the thick forest canopy, decorating the road in irregular blobs of light and flashing sporadically in my eyes. It was my favorite road in Saugatuck, snaking through a dense forest growing out of the dunes.

I pedaled up the last dune and saw the lake glistening on the horizon, heard the sound of waves washing on the shore. A little hut was at the end of the road at the bottom of the hill. Cars have to stop at the hut and pay to park in the beach parking lot, but bikes get in free.

I raced past the hut, waving at Ed Stemple, a cute college sophomore who worked Oval Beach as a lifeguard during the summer. I couldn't wait to tell Suzie about Bullfrog. When I got to the snack bar, I parked my bike and scanned the beach, looking for Suzie. The best way to find Suzie was to look for a group of boys. She would probably be in the middle of it. Sure enough, a volleyball game was just breaking up and Jason was taking down his net. I saw Suzie flirting with all the guys who had played in the game, mostly guys from our school.

"Suzie!" I called.

Suzie looked up and saw me coming down the dune to the beach. "Hill! God, Hill, you missed the volleyball game."

I joined the group. French Fry Freddie bounced a volleyball off my head. "Yeah, Hill, you missed the game." Guys are so stupid.

"Suzie," I said. "You won't believe what happened at the Auction House."

Jason joined us. "We heard there was a big fight there this morning."

"Yeah," added Eric, a cute junior with his locker down the hall from me, "My brother told me a Chinese gang came into the Auction House and beat up that weird guy, Jeremiah Bullfrog."

"Were you there, Hill?" asked Bill Jergen, a guy from my English class.

"Yeah," I answered. I couldn't believe they heard about the fight already. It only happened a couple of hours ago.

"We heard all the furniture got wrecked and Bullfrog's in the hospital," added Suzie.

"Is Bullfrog dead?" asked Freddie, eyes wide with excitement.

"God! You guys! Who told you all that stuff?" Word really travels in a small town. I couldn't believe how the story got so exaggerated already. It was like Sandbar and the burglar.

I told everybody what really happened at the Auction House. Of course, they were all pretty disappointed. The story that had developed here on the beach through word-of-mouth was much more interesting than the story I had to tell. The guys wandered away, one by one.

"Come on, Suzie," I said. "Let's go for a walk." I wanted to tell Suzie a lot more about Bullfrog and the Chinese guy. We started walking north along the water toward the harbor entrance.

The north end of Oval Beach was mostly guys sitting in little groups, sunning themselves and taking an occasional dip in the Lake…mostly good-looking guys with good tans and skimpy bathing suits. Not many of them looked up as we passed. Suzie missed the attention. She was really getting to be guy-crazy, but this was the gay beach in Saugatuck. These guys were more interested in each other.

When we got to the end of the city beach, a guard stopped us. He was kind of an unofficial beach guard, a gay guy, stationed there to charge admission to the private property right next to Oval Beach. Guys who wanted more privacy could pay a few dollars and find it in the rolling dunes. He was really good looking, slim with blonde hair. He didn't notice when Suzie started flirting with him. "Hi!" she said, smiling broadly.

"Hi," he said. "I'm sorry, girls. This is a private beach. There's an admission charge to use this beach." He was very polite.

Suzie pouted, opening her eyes wide, flirting, "But we don't have three dollars. Can't we just walk on the beach?" She knew we could. Walking on the beach wasn't restricted, only spreading out a towel and sitting down.

"Well, yes," he answered patiently. "You can walk on the beach, no problem. You just can't stop."

"Oh thanks," gushed Suzie, batting her eyes, using all her charm.

"But I must warn you girls," he continued, not noticing Suzie's fluttering eye lashes. "This is a gay beach. Just stick to the shore, along the water. Don't go into the dunes."

"Oh, we won't," whined Suzie, still trying.

We continued on past the guard. "That guy was cute," said Suzie. "You think he liked me?"

"Yeah, right, Suzie," I teased. "He couldn't keep his eyes off you."

We giggled and continued walking down the beach, scanning the dunes, looking for some activity. The gay beach in Saugatuck was a scandal to some of the more conservative people in Saugatuck. Every once in a while someone wrote a letter to the editor of the Comical Record about seeing nude men, exposing themselves in the dunes. Usually these sightings were from boats off the shore, through binoculars. My Dad laughed when he read these letters. He said it probably took hours of scanning the dunes before these puritans could express their moral outrage.

I told Suzie about the chart and the argument. "I think they were arguing about speed tiles."

"Really?"

"Yeah, Bullfrog sounded desperate, like at Ursulla's that day."

"God!" she said. "I wonder why he wants them so much?"

"I have no idea."

"You think he's really as old as Ursulla?" asked Suzie.

"Dad says no. He says Bullfrog's younger than him."

"Why do you think Ursulla said that? You know, about being so old?"

"I don't know. Maybe she's confused. Maybe she's got Alzheimer's Disease or something."

We walked all the way to the pier head where the boats entered the Kalamazoo River. Suzie was kind of disappointed that we didn't see any nude men in the dunes, even though we kept looking as we walked. It was getting to be late afternoon now, and the sun was getting closer to Lake Michigan. We sat on the breakwater, watching the boats come in off the lake. I looked across the channel where Singapore once stood. I saw some activity way off in the distance. I stood up and squinted, trying to see what it was. "Look, Suzie, across the channel, up in the dunes."

Suzie jumped to her feet, hoping it was a naked man. "Where?"

"Over there, on the side of that hill," I said, pointing.

She looked. "It's a man, Hill. What's he doing?" He was pretty far away.

I watched the figure, the setting sun glinting off something shiny, reflections slicing across our eyes. Yes. It was a man. "I think he's digging, Suzie. I think he's got a shovel and he's digging in the sand."

We sat back down on the rocks and watched the boats, the water, the cawing seagulls. We watched the digging man. Gradually, I realized who it was. He was far away. I couldn't be sure, but I thought it was probably Dick Beaver digging in the sand again…searching for speed tiles in the ruins of Singapore.

Chapter 13

Slabs and Sirens

I stared at the picture on the front page of the Commercial Record, thinking, remembering. Hilllary had told me about the fight at the Auction House, about an Asian man named Wong...a common name. Could it be the same man I met in Helmut Schmidt's office in Chicago so many years ago? Could it be the same Wong Ted told me about who would be studying gravity anomalies on South Manitou Island? Why would a scientist be meeting with Bullfrog? Why would he be fighting with Bullfrog? Hilllary thought it had something to do with speed tiles.

I stared...trying to see inside the photo. Trying to see more.

I closed my eyes, thinking...seeing a drawing, a sketch of speed tiles, lined up in neat rows, my sketch...hearing the architect, Helmut Schmidt ranting about flowers, Kaminski, the developer, his "fuck the Earth"...echoing in my memory...looking up, seeing the dark eyes of Doctor Wong staring at my sketch, leaning forward, his forehead creased in thought...

I left that memory, stored it away. Eyes open, I focused on the photograph in the newspaper that Todd Camper took at the Auction House. Bullfrog, eyes wild, stringy hair flying behind him, leaping over a fallen table. Wong, stepping backwards, an instant of fear captured in his eyes. Was it him? (Dissolve) Back to the memory in the architect's office. The intense black eyes. (Closer) Was it him? Was it him?

"Dad!" shouted Hannah from far away.

I kept staring at the picture, trying to think…"Yeah?" I said absently.

"Dad, I'm going to ballet. Okay if I take the car?"

That face. Could it be?

"The car, Dad. Can I take the car?"

"Huh?" I dragged my eyes away from Wong and put the paper down on the counter. (Later) "Yeah, Hannah. The car. Yeah, fine. Take the car."

"Is that the guy Bullfrog tried to kill?" asked Hannah, grabbing up the paper.

"That's him, but I don't think Bullfrog tried to kill him, Hannah."

"Ha!" she shrieked. "Oh my God! Look at Bullfrog! He looks like a junk-yard dog!" Life was a joke for Hannah. Her laughter was infectious.

I looked again, laughing with her. "My God, I think you're right."

"He's almost foaming at the mouth!"

"Let's see." I grabbed the paper. It was a good action picture. Todd was really in the right place at the right time for this one.

"And look at that lady behind him. She's so annoyed." We both laughed again, studying the comical elements hidden in the picture.

Finally, it was time for Hannah to leave for her ballet class in Grand Rapids. "Gotta go now." Hannah gave me a quick kiss on the cheek, then she kneeled down on the floor to say good-by to our dog. "Oh Sandbar…Pupalupagus…" She gave Sandbar a long, lingering hug and a loud kiss on his jowls. "I'll be back later, Sandbar. Don't worry." I knew where I stood in Hannah's hierarchy.

She grabbed a doggy biscuit out of a box in the mud room and tossed it to Sandbar. Snap! Perfect catch. I was glad Hannah didn't throw one to me. "Bye, Dad."

I put the Commercial Record down and went out to the garage to work on some three dimensional pieces that would hang (literally) in Bullfrog's gallery. I was a little worried about Bullfrog's irrational behavior, but I had been focusing on this show, looking forward to it. I couldn't back out now. I had to get some reaction to my work, some feedback. Bullfrog's gallery would provide that.

I only had a few more days before it was time to bring everything over to the gallery. There was still a lot of work to do. Many pieces were partially finished and all the paintings needed framing. I went into the garage and maneuvered through a maze of aluminum bars, wooden pedestals, discarded constructions and empty paint cans. The place was a mess. It would be a long time before cars parked in this garage again.

In the center of the room was a massive Styrofoam block, two feet thick by three feet square. It was hanging by chains from eye bolts in the ceiling. I worked the surfaces of the block, shaving and sculpting the Styrofoam to resemble the slab that burst out of my attic. I painted my slab gray with latex paint, sealing the surfaces. I spray painted splotches of black, brown and white simulating burn marks and irregularities. As I worked I thought of the lightning flashes, the jagged hole in my roof, the impossible slab floating north. It had to be massive, my slab. It had to be intimidating, frightening. I worked and sculpted and painted for hours but I could barely approach the horror of the real thing.

"Hi, Dad!"

"Oh, Hi, Hill. Come look at my slab."

"Oh, wow, Dad. It's really looking great. It's so…so nasty!"

"Really? That's what I was trying to get…Yeah. Nasty."

We looked at the nasty slab together, walking around the hanging thing.

"Dad?"

"Yeah, Hill."

"Who's gonna buy this…this Slab?"

"Hmmm. I don't know, Hill. You don't think there's a market for slabs around here?" I joked.

"I like it!" she said

"Yeah, but would you hang it in your living room?"

"Definitely!"

"Well I hope there are a lot of art lovers like you coming to the show." I gave Hilllary a big hug. She was my biggest fan.

"Really, Dad. How much are you gonna sell this for?"

"I don't know, yet, Hill. Why? You want to buy it?"

"Sure! I'll buy it."

I paused, looking at the slab. "I guess I don't really expect to sell this. It's more to set the mood. It's what's called an installation piece. I'm hoping it will hang in the middle of a room and give viewers a sense of intimidation."

"Intimidation?"

"Yeah. I think of it as a kind of symbol…for runaway development. Unchecked technological advancement. I don't know…"

"Dad, you're weird."

"I'm also trying to simulate that slab I thought I saw outside the hole in our roof."

"Is that what it looked like?"

""A little. This one's not as scary."

"Dad?"

"Yeah, Hill."

"Did you really see a slab floating outside the hole that night?"

I looked at her innocent face, her inquiring eyes. I knew she was trying to come to terms with all the odd speed tile nonsense going on around here, trying to make some sense of it. I was too. "You know, Hill, I thought I did. But how could it really be. How can a thing like this float? It's impossible. It was probably my imagination. My mind was probably playing tricks on me."

She looked a little relieved.

I continued. "Whatever I saw that night, it gave me the idea for this…this beautiful slab."

"Beautiful?" she asked.

We laughed, trying to find beauty in the intimidating gray chunk hanging in front of us.

"You want to help me, Hill?"

"Yeah!" she said enthusiastically. "What can I do? I'd love to help!"

"You do?" Dad looked surprised. "You really want to help me?"

"Yeah, Dad, I really do."

"Wow, that's great! I can use all the help I can get right now."

"What can I do to help with your slab?"

"Well, now that it's painted, I have to put the wires in it."

"Wires?"

"Yeah. The slab I saw…or thought I saw…had dangling tendrils and wires kind of hanging off the bottom surface. That's the next step…the wires."

Hilllary helped me remove the slab from the chains. It was remarkably light in weight for its bulk. We turned it upside down and set it on the floor. I grabbed a big roll of heavy red wire I bought at Wilkins, the local hardware store in Saugatuck. I started cutting it into pieces about twelve inches long.

"You can help me cut this wire. Each piece also has to be stripped. I want the red plastic covering to be stripped off about an inch from the end of each piece. I'll show you how to do that."

I stripped the plastic off, then shoved the wire into the Styrofoam. It was easy to penetrate the Styrofoam surface and the wire stayed securely in the slab, sticking straight up. When I turned the slab over and hung it from the chains again, it would look like the wires were hanging off the bottom.

"That looks easy, Dad. I could do that."

Hilllary sat on the dusty, Styrofoam strewn floor and started cutting wires to length. I started stripping the plastic off the ends of the wires, then sticking them into the bottom, one by one.

I heard a car drive up outside the garage. Probably Hannah coming home from ballet. She came into the garage. "Hey! What's going on?" She stopped when she saw the slab on the floor. "God! What the heck is that?"

"That's the slab, Hannah," answered Hilllary, mischief in her eyes. She got very serious. "That's the slab that got out of our attic, Hannah. Dad got it back."

"Really?' asked Hannah, believing her completely, coming closer to the Styrofoam block.

I smiled, wondering how long the joke would last. It was easy to tease Hannah. She was very trusting.

"Yeah, now we're taking it apart to get the speed tile out," whispered Hilllary.

Hannah, eyes wide, came closer, carefully reached out to touch the slab.

"Don't touch it!" I yelled. I couldn't resist joining in the joke.

Hannah jumped back and looked at me, frightened. Hilllary started laughing and I joined in. Anger registered on Hannah's face as she realized she was being teased again.

"Hilllary! I'm gonna kill you." she said.

"You're such an easy target, Hannah." I said. "You're so much fun to tease." I pointed at the slab. "You could touch it. It's made out of Styrofoam."

"Is that what it looked like, Dad?" asked Hannah, "The one you saw that night?"

"Yep."

"What's Hilllary doing?"

"I'm helping Dad, Hannah. I'm helping him with his slab."

A look of dejection came on Hannah's face. She felt left out. "Can I help too?"

"That would be great, Hannah." I was beginning to worry about how much time it would take to cut all this wire and cover the whole surface with it. "We could really use your help."

Hilllary shot me a glance, jealous that she'd have to share me and my slab with her sister. Hannah noticed the glance. "Shut up, Hill. I want to help too!"

"I didn't say anything!"

Hannah sat down on the floor. She took over the job of cutting wire to length. Hilllary stripped the ends. I installed the wires in the Styrofoam. We worked that way until Marcia came home from work at Sally's Nook. She came into the garage. "God, what a mess. When are you gonna clean this place up?" She noticed Hannah and Hilllary on the floor, cutting and stripping. "Oh, jeez...look at you guys. You're all full of Styrofoam. What's going on here?" She noticed the slab. "Oh my God! What is that?" She pointed at the slab thing upside down on the floor.

"That's a slab, Mom," answered Hannah. "We're helping Dad with it."

"Yeah, Mom," added Hilllary. "You want to help too?"

Marcia frowned, looking at the mess. She was wearing a nice outfit. A kind of felt-like, ankle-length, purple dress. I tried to imagine her sitting on the garage floor in that outfit. She smiled, probably thinking the same thing.

"Come on, Mom, help us." pleaded Hannah. "We have to cover that whole slab with wires. It's gonna take forever."

Marcia looked at me and the girls. She frowned at the slab. "Okay! I'll just go in and change my clothes."

"Why do you have to change?" I joked.

Marcia changed her clothes and joined us in the garage. She took over the job of ramming the wire pieces into the slab. I went on to another piece, a grid structure I was making that looked kind of like the grid where I found the speed tile in the dunes so long ago.

We laughed and joked as we worked...a real bonding experience. Marcia said, "Isn't this cozy. The family that slabs together, stays together."

"Maybe we should bring a slab on the boat with us, Dad, when we go on our cruise," suggested Hannah.

"Yeah, we can work on it while we're sailing," added Hilllary.

"Oh yeah," said Marcia. "Lots of room for slabs on a boat."

I thought of our cruise...of South Manitou Island. I thought of the slab that was already there. My slab, with my speed tile locked within. Would I find it there? Would I find my lost speed tile?

The slab was covered with wires in no time. Each wire stuck out of the surface about six inches, each with a jagged copper tip emanating from a bright red plastic casing. We turned the slab over and hung it back up on the chains.

"Oh God," said Marcia. "Is that intimidating or what?"

"That's the idea," I said.

Hannah and Hilllary were brushing themselves off, stretching and getting the kinks out of their legs, stiff from sitting cross-legged on the floor all this time.

"You gonna make any more slabs, Dad?" asked Hannah.

"Yeah, Dad," added Hilllary. "We'll help you."

"Actually, I do have to build one more slab to hang over the Gaming Table," I said, looking at the hanging thing.

"Gaming Table?" asked Hannah.

"Yeah, didn't I tell you about the card game?"

"What card game?" asked Marcia, patiently.

"Digital Spoons," I said. "I'm also creating the cards on the computer...Digital Spoons Cards."

"Cards, huh?" said Marcia.

"Yep, cards." I confirmed.

"I'm kind of running out of time. Maybe you guys can help me with that slab, too? Actually, you better get used to it. When these slab things start selling, we're gonna have to set up an assembly line."

"Ha!" shrieked Hannah. "That's great! A slab assembly line."

They all left, laughing and joking, Hannah poking Hiller, Hiller punching Hannah, causing trouble, as usual, teasing each other, Marcia grabbing them, holding them apart, hugging them, loving them. They left me to go into the house, left me alone in the garage with my slab.

I turned to my grid. It was spray-painted gray using a latex texture paint which gave the wood structure a multi-colored softness, like mold, suggesting life, growth (or decay, neglect). I enhanced the visual depth of the square compartments with a quick spray of blue in the bottom of each cell. There were one hundred cells, each about three inches square, the structure ten cells high by ten cells wide.

I added speed tiles, starting from the center. I elevated Tiles in the middle four compartments (growing, birthing) almost to the top of the compartment sides, floating, suspended. The next twelve cells, emanating from the middle, held speed tiles not as fully developed, closer to the floor of the cells. The twenty cells surrounding those inner compartments contained speed tiles made of one-eighth-inch aluminum, half the thickness of a mature speed tile. In the next twenty-eight squares, only faint brass nubs were evident, four in each cell, pushing, sprouting, growing out of the bottom surface of the grid.

This was a speed tile Birthing Grid...a machine for manufacturing speed tiles. Was it like the one I saw in the dunes? The grid where I found my speed tile? I looked at it, studied it, thinking about how it might be activated, thinking about the power being focused in the center, emanating out. I looked across the room at the slab, hanging from the ceiling, at the red wires reaching down, the copper tips ready to send dashes of static, sparks of light, sending them down, down.

In a flash of insight, I grabbed the Birthing Grid and slid it under the slab, on the floor, precisely in the middle of the slab's influence. Yes, yes. Of course! The wires, the slab. Providing power, influence, encouragement...mothering the sprouting tiles, nurturing them, feeding them...making them grow, teaching them its terrible secrets.

I sat watching the slab, the grid. Of course, this was an interpretation, an imitation of the real thing. Nothing was growing here. It was my invention. (A memory) But it would hang in Bullfrog's gallery, just like this, suggesting power, mystery, horror. Perhaps a warning, a signal.

I left the slab and the grid, left them alone with each other to get acquainted. I decided to take a break and call Will Reed to ask him what he knew of the mysterious Dr. Wong, Bullfrog's visitor, Bullfrog's sparring partner.

I went in the house and dialed the phone. Marcia was in the kitchen making dinner. Hannah and Hilllary were in the back yard throwing a Frisbee, playing with Sandbar. "Hello, Will?"

"Yeah, this is Will Reed."

"Will, this is John Hunter."

"John! John, how are you? I haven't talked to you for a long time. How've you been? How's Saugatuck?"

"Great! Saugatuck's great, Will. How's the family?"

"Oh, they're fine, John.

Will had been working for many years on some kind of slippery molecule project at Argonne National Laboratories. He explained it to me very patiently one day over a bottle of beer as a kind of Teflon research. He said the more slippery you could make surfaces, the less friction there would be. He said his research had widespread applications in everything from motors and transportation systems to ice-skating rinks and cooking surfaces.

"Will, I've got a crazy question to ask," I said.

"Crazy question? What is it?"

"I wonder if you know a scientist, a physicist, I think, by the name of Wong? Doctor Jan Wong."

"Wong? Yeah, I know Wong. Gravity research. Yeah, I know him. Not very well, but I've talked to him a few times. He works in a research and development company in Chicago. Wong Laboratories. It's owned by his father, as I remember. It's a Chinese Company. Hong Kong. They have a contract with Argonne. Several, in fact. Why? How do you know Jan Wong?"

Bingo! It was the same guy I met in Chicago. Wong Laboratories. That was the name of the building Helmut designed. I had to find out everything Will knew about Wong. "I heard from a friend here in Saugatuck. He read about it in a Scientific American article on the Internet. He told me this Wong guy is coming to Michigan to investigate a gravitational anomaly on South Manitou Island."

"South Manitou? Yeah. Yeah. That's right. I remember. It was in the Argonne newsletter. As I remember, Argonne's paying for the expedition with a grant. In fact I think he's already left. He might even be up there by now."

"So, what do you know about Jan Wong?" I asked.

"Hmm. Not much. He's kind of an odd duck. Like I said, I don't know him very well. But he's got a reputation for being kind of offbeat. He's a recluse. Even in his own company, I heard he's kind of a loner."

"Is he a good scientist?"

"Good? Who knows. As I remember, he opened the Chicago office here when he first came. After all, it is his father's company. A big operation. Lots of money from Hong Kong. They even built a building in Chicago to house the offices and laboratories. Wong was in charge at first, but he's made some changes over the years. I can't remember the circumstances, but, I don't think he's in charge any more. Something happened. I can't remember what it was."

"Isn't gravity research kind of far out? Esoteric?

"Well, I guess it is. It's what you would classify as pure research. There really aren't any immediate applications for the results. But the company, the lab in Chicago, does some good work. They specialize in coming up with industrial applications for pure research. They've developed some good applications for my slippery molecule research in industry, among other things. I think the company is pretty profitable."

"So, why is Argonne interested in Wong's gravity research?"

"Incredible applications, that's why," replied Will. "Just think about how much easier it would be to build a bridge or a skyscraper if you could control the gravitational pull of the earth. The applications are endless." Will paused for a second. "What's this big interest in Wong anyway? Why are you so curious about him?"

"Well, a couple of things. That trip of his to South Manitou. I'm going there on my sailboat in a couple of weeks. He's probably gonna be up there when I get there."

"Yeah, I think he will. But you said a couple of things. What's the other thing?"

"This one's kind of strange, Will," I began. "I just read a local newspaper article that came out today about a fight that broke out between one of our gallery owners and a guy by the name of Doctor Wong. It happened last week. The editor of the newspaper just happened to be there and he took a picture while it was happening."

Will started laughing. "Wong got into a fight? That's kind of out of character for him. He's kind of quiet and reserved. What was it a barroom brawl, or what?"

"No, it was during the day at the Auction House. You remember that place. We had breakfast there last time you visited."

"Oh yeah. Nice place. Good breakfast."

"Yeah. Hillary works there now. Bussing tables. She was there when Wong had his fight. A lot of excitement for a small town like Saugatuck."

"You say there's a picture of him in the newspaper?"

"Yeah. You got a fax machine there? I can fax it to you."

"I'd love to see it. Wong's a pretty common name. Maybe it isn't Jan Wong. Why don't you fax it to me?"

I put Will on hold while I went into the study to fax the article.

I went back to the phone. "Will, you get it?"

"Just a second, It'll show up on my computer. Ahh. Here it is. Let me just open it up…There. It's kind of fuzzy, but…Well I'll be damned. That's him, all right. That's Wong. Ha! Wait 'til I tell the others at Argonne. We'll have to put this in the Argonne News."

"Tell you what. I'll mail this article to you. You'll have a better original to work with."

"Okay. But there's something I heard about Wong. I can't put my finger on it right now. Something about Wong Laboratories." Will paused, thinking. "I'll tell you what. I'll call you if I can remember what it was. I'll make a couple of phone calls and see what I can find out."

"Great! Bye, Will. And thanks." I hung up the phone.

My mind buzzing with thoughts of speed tiles and gravity research, I went into my studio to paint. All the paintings that would be in my show were about technology and its effects on people. The painting on my easel now was a large one, one of the largest that would be in the show. It was called The Siren of Progress.

I squeezed some paint onto my palette. I use acrylic paint and a heavy metal cooking pan for my palette. It gets heavier every time I use it, dried paint building up to an inch thick or more on the bottom.

The Siren is a woman in my painting. She is right in the center of the painting. She's very beautiful, with long blonde hair blowing wild in the wind. I dream as I paint. I imagine this woman, this siren. Her eyes are closed. She's very serene, unperturbed by the chaos around her. Her clothing. How strange it is. Her coat, oversized. A man's coat. A clown's coat. It's garish red and yellow checkered pattern in sharp contrast to her beautiful face, her flowing blonde hair, her mystical expression. She wears a red tie, like a man's tie. Is she mocking man?

Suspended over her head, a hat. A propeller hat. The propeller is turning. Is it a thought? A hat imagined? The hat is technology. As long as the propeller turns, everything is all right. Even though a city burns in the distance, the propeller turns. Progress is being made. Or, is it the illusion of progress that is being maintained?

She's sitting, legs crossed, hands folded calmly in her lap...sitting on a carpet. A magic carpet, floating in the air. Below the carpet, a meticulous arrangement of speed tiles, marching backwards in space toward the burning, smoldering city, a road, paved with speed tiles. A road leading to destruction, hopeless chaos, the speed tiles keeping the Siren suspended on her magic carpet.

Suiters stand on either side of the speed tile road. Red ties, gray overcoats. Bald. They are bald-headed suiters. They wear glasses. They are watching, waiting. They do nothing in these paintings, these suiters. They only watch. The suiter on the left watches the Siren, hands stuffed in the pockets of his overcoat. The suiter on the right has his head turned toward the burning city. I paint him. I imagine him. Wire-rimmed glasses. Asian eyes, bald, shaved head. A familiar face. A face from the Commercial Record. The suiter is Wong, watching the destruction behind him, calm, unmoved, emotionless.

Ring!…The phone, breaking my concentration. Ring!…

I dropped my brush into the coffee can filled with water and grab at the phone. "Hello?" I croak.

"John?"

"Yeah."

"John, you sound like I just woke you up."

"Oh, hi, Will. No. I wasn't sleeping. I was painting. I go into a daze sometimes. I'm awake."

"Yeah, well, I made a couple of calls to some of my colleagues at Argonne about Wong. You know that grant he was getting from Argonne? It was canceled. Withdrawn."

"Canceled? Why?"

"I don't know. It's kind of mysterious. It almost sounds as if Wong Laboratories might have turned it down, refused to accept it."

"Why would they do that, Will?"

"Hmmm. I don't really know. I just hear the rumors around here. But sometimes, if the research looks especially promising and potentially profitable, a company like Wong Labs might choose to keep it to themselves. Not share it with another lab. Maybe Wong is on to something."

"Yeah?"

"But here's the really puzzling thing. I called Frank Pluto, over at Argonne. He's managing a couple of grant contracts with Wong Labs. I asked him about Jan Wong. He told me Jan Wong doesn't even work there any more. Jan Wong has been kind of excommunicated from his family business. Apparently, the elder Wong, Jan's father, kicked him out.

Chapter 14

The Opening

The days leading up to Dad's opening were really busy. His art show was going up at The Ecclesiastical Absurdities Foundation, Bullfrog's gallery, and Dad was frantic. Mom and Hannah and me were all busy too, finishing up all the little details that nobody thought of until the last minute.

Dad got all his paintings hung. He talked Bullfrog into letting him put hooks in the ceiling to hang his slabs. He even sent Hannah and me to Oval Beach to get some sand. He put his birthing grid on the floor right under one of the hanging slabs we helped him build. Then he wanted to put sand around the grid to make it look like it was in the dunes. Bullfrog didn't like the sand idea, though.

"Now sand?" he asked Dad. "Sand? I just had this carpeting installed and you're putting sand on it."

"It's for the birthing grid," explained Dad.

"First you put holes in my ceiling, now you're filling my gallery with sand," moaned Bullfrog. Then he changed instantly, like he does, this time from angry to curious. "Birthing grid?"

"Yeah, Jeremiah. It's where speed tiles are born," Dad explained.

"Speed tiles born…" mumbled Bullfrog and walked away, deep in thought.

The grid looked great when Dad was finished. It was like the grid was half-buried, growing out of the sand. Bullfrog looked at it, stroking his beard, smiling, mumbling something to himself. I think he liked it too.

After most of the pictures were hung, Dad still had some left over. There wouldn't be room for all of them in the gallery. Dad knew the old Bat House had a big basement, so he asked Hannah and me to take the extra pieces down there for storage.

"God, Hill," said Hannah. "Why did Dad make so much stuff?"

"I don't know, but if it starts selling, he can always replace the ones he sells with these."

I went to the basement door and tried to open it. It was stuck.

"God, Hill! You're so helpless," said Hannah. She started pulling on the door, jiggling the knob, trying to get it open. Just then, Bullfrog came running in, eyes wide, angry.

I stepped backwards when I saw him, remembering how he acted at the Auction House. "What do you think you're doing?" he shouted, putting his back to the basement door and extending his hands, blocking us.

"We're just gonna put these extra things in the basement." said Hannah.

"B-B-Basement?" he blubbered. "You want to go in my basement?"

"Yeah. Just to store these things," said Hannah. "The door's stuck."

"Store things?" he said, eyes wide, eyebrows arched. He looked at us suspiciously. "You can't go in the basement. No, no, no, no. No!"

"Why not, we..."

"It's out of the question. The, ahhh...The ahhh...basement, ahh..." He sounded like he was gonna sneeze or something, but he was just trying to think of something to say. "The basement's full. It's completely full. With my personal effects. It's off limits. The door's locked. You can't go down there."

I looked at him guarding the door, eyes wide, arms outstretched, blocking it from us. It was typical Bullfrog behavior, he was overacting again. I looked at Hannah and saw her fighting back a smile. Bullfrog looked silly.

"You'll have to take them away," he said. "You can't keep them here."

Dad was getting used to Bullfrog's irrational behavior. He just shrugged and said, "Just put them back in the van. I can always bring them back here if we need 'em."

Dad built this big thing called the Digital Spoons Gaming Station that filled up a whole room in the gallery. It was awesome...by far, his biggest and weirdest piece. It took him months to build. He called it an installation. The silliest thing about it was that he built it just to stage this stupid card game called spoons...digital spoons, he called it. We were gonna play digital spoons at the opening.

In the middle of the room, Dad put a dorky square table with a red felt top. It had aluminum brackets and speed tiles, kinda like armor, protecting all the edges and corners. It was a low table and Dad had Mom make four pillows to sit around it. Dad picked out the fabric for them. It had big red and blue squares...like a checkerboard pattern.

He also made these crazy three-foot-high pie-shaped pillars to put at each corner of the table. The curves faced out and were painted with texture paint. The flat, inner surfaces had red felt, just like the table top...blood red. All the edges had armor and speed tiles, like the table. They looked like some mad scientist's electrode things, like Frankenstein or something. The four pillars were connected to each other with heavy chain. I don't know if Dad meant the chain to keep players in or to keep spectators out. All five of these pieces sat on a big round rug, also blood red.

Over the table, hanging from big, heavy chains, was a slab; sticky, pointy red wires, poked out of it, the ones we helped Dad cut in the garage. They looked like red worms, crawling out from inside the gross slab. Dad hung the slab low over the table. He wanted people who played digital spoons to feel intimidated, he said. It worked. You almost had to duck to sit at the table, otherwise the red wormy wire things might crawl in your hair...Yuck! It felt like this slab thing was looming over you, crushing you.

After Dad moved it in, he was kind of bummed. He worked hard on his gaming station but he didn't like the way it looked. "It needs something else," he said. "Something to set it off. The room's too plain. It's not threatening enough." Dad sent me to Wilkins Hardware to get a gallon of red paint and a roller…blood red paint.

Bullfrog hit the ceiling. "No! I just had these rooms painted!"

"Jeremiah," said my Dad. "I'll repaint them myself when the show's over, I promise." Dad pointed at the gaming station. "Look at it. Imagine that wall painted red."

Bullfrog thought about it, raised his eyebrows, eyes wide. "I'll hold you to that. You'll repaint it. I'll hold you to that after this show comes down." Bullfrog left the room, muttering to himself.

I helped Dad paint the wall red, but Dad was still disappointed. "It's not enough," he moaned, sitting on the floor across from the red wall. I sat in his lap, looking at the gaming station with him. "Something else," he said. "It needs something else, Hill."

"How 'bout if I paint one of my caterpillars on that wall…you know, like in my room," I suggested, smiling up at him. "A man-eating caterpillar with fangs."

Dad didn't answer. He just tickled me under my arms and hugged me. Then we sat there, resting for a while. "I got it!" said Dad. "It needs speed tiles on that wall. Big speed tiles."

Mom came into the room. "What's the matter?"

"That wall," said Dad, pointing. "It needs big speed tiles." Dad thought for a minute, looking at the wall. "But they're not speed tiles, are they? Speed tiles are small."

Mom looked at me. I looked at her. We both shrugged and Mom left the room.

"I know!" he continued. "We'll call them slab tiles." He looked at me with his eyes wide, excited. "They're like a cross between speed tiles and slabs, Hill. Slab tiles!"

I leaned back on his chest, not quite knowing what to say, but Dad was flying. He had a solution to his problem. The solution, apparently, was called slab tiles. He got up from the floor, dumping me off his lap. "Gotta go, Hill. Gotta go make some slab tiles. I don't have much time."

Dad rushed out the door of the gallery. "Where's he going, Hill?" asked Hannah.

"To make some slab tiles," I answered.

She looked at me suspiciously, thinking it was another trick.

"No, really, Hannah. He said he was gonna make some slab tiles."

Mom came in. "Doesn't he know that the show is opening tomorrow?"

I shrugged.

Dad apparently rushed to the lumber yard and bought a bunch of Styrofoam panels. Later he told me they were originally made for insulation, not slab tiles. When we got home that afternoon, Dad was busy in the garage. He was cutting the panels on his saw. Styrofoam was flying everywhere. I watched him for a while, cutting the panels into squares, but then Mom called me in for dinner. Dad didn't want to eat. "I don't have time to eat, Hill. Gotta make slab tiles."

When I came back later, he was hacking away at the edges like a mad man. Chunks of Styrofoam were everywhere. "They're too regular, Hill, too perfect." I went in to watch TV.

When I took Sandbar for a walk, Dad was slopping gray latex paint in big runny blobs all over his slab tiles. "This Styrofoam really sucks up the paint, Hill."

"Uh huh," I said.

Between TV programs I checked on him again. He had a big, long, round piece of wood and he was cutting it into little pieces on his saw. He had hundreds of 'em cut. Hundreds of little round pieces. Huh? I thought. "Dad, what the heck are you doing now?" He was totally out of his frickin' mind.

He showed me a piece he had finished. "Makin' these, Hill." It looked like the head of a bolt, like the brass bolts he put in the corners of his speed tiles, except it was way too big. It was a giant bolt head. "I rounded the edges using my belt sander," he said. "I need four of these for every slab tile."

God! How could he work so long? He was obsessed. "You sure you need these, Dad?"

"Positive!"

"I'm goin' to bed, Dad. You're makin' me tired. See you in the morning."

"Okay. Good night, Hill."

I started toward the door.

"Hill?"

I turned. "Yeah?"

"Thanks for all your help today. I really needed it." He smiled.

I laughed. "God! You sure did!" I waved and went back to the house.

The next morning when I got up, Dad was asleep on the couch. I went out to the garage, curious about what he had done. I couldn't believe he got so much done in one night. He had built a bunch of slab tiles, sixty-four in all. Each one was painted gray with black and brown splotches spray-painted on the surfaces. Each had four brass-colored bolt heads. One in each corner. They looked like over-sized speed tiles.

Later, when Dad woke up, I helped him take the slab tiles over to Bullfrog's gallery. "Now what?" moaned Bullfrog as we carried in the slab tiles.

"The Digital Spoons Gaming Station," said Dad, bleary-eyed. "I have to finish it."

"Finish it?" asked Bullfrog. "It is finished. It's done. You've painted my wall blood red. It's finished."

"These slab tiles, Jeremiah," said Dad. "I have to put these slab tiles on the red wall."

"Slab tiles?" he asked. "What the Dickens is a slab tile? Will you never finish?"

"Almost finished," said Dad wearily.

I followed him into the Gaming Station room carrying a stack of slab tiles.

Dad worked for the rest of the morning measuring and hanging slab tiles. He over-estimated how many he would need. He hung them in neat rows, eight tiles wide and seven tiles tall. They looked spooky. They made the room look like a metal chamber, blood red paint oozing out between the rows of slab tiles. It was scary.

Next, Dad hung his playing cards around the top of the other three walls, near the ceiling. Each playing card was framed in a cherry wood frame. They looked really cool. Dad made the cards on his computer and had them printed somewhere in Holland. He had 24 decks of cards printed, but he couldn't afford to have them cut to size and trimmed, so he did that himself with a knife and a pair of scissors. He trimmed nice rounded corners off of all the playing cards, one at a time. I watched him do some of them. It took him forever.

Besides the framed playing cards, he also made these six-sided Plexiglas cases. He stuck a deck of digital spoons cards, a digital spoon and three wooden spoons in each little case. He also put little latches and two padlocks on each case. He said he didn't want the cards to get out. What a freak!

"Dad?"

"Yeah?"

"Give me a clue. What's this all about? This gaming station, these spoons cards. What does it all mean?"

Dad laughed. He sat on the floor, looking at his wall, at the table and the corner wedges. He looked satisfied now, finally. "I don't know, Hill. It's really a big, elaborate joke. Another one of those things that just came to me. It's something to do with the speed tiles. Something to do with that time…that time long ago, when speed tiles were everywhere, used by everyone."

"Was there really a time like that, Dad?" I asked.

Dad shook his head, rubbed his temples with his hands. He looked at me. "I don't know, Hill. Probably not. I think I'm making all this up. But it all seems so real to me sometimes. Especially when I'm building it…when I'm making this stuff. I get lost in it."

"But we've played spoons before, Dad. It's a stupid game. It's fun, but it's really stupid."

"I know, Hill. That's what makes this gaming station so absurd, so overstated. Look at it. This is really an elaborate set-up, especially with the cards I made on the computer. It's like a stage set for a performance. And its all for the staging of this stupid game…Digital Spoons."

"Uh huh," I said, trying to understand.

Dad tried again. "You know how kids find it pretty easy to use computers? You know, they're not afraid to just click away, experiment, try things. But adults. The older they get, the more afraid they are to try, to experiment. They just don't have the energy or the curiosity. That's what this game's about, Hill. You'll see at the opening tonight, when you start playing."

"Who's gonna play?"

"You and Hannah and Suzie will be three of the players. And Mom, sometimes. You all know how to play Spoons. You're all aggressive, blood-thirsty players. The fourth player will be anyone else at the opening who wants to try it. If they win, they get a free playing card of their choice. But not many will win."

"Why not?

"Because you won't tell them the rules. Or, I should say, the lack of rules. They're gonna have to pick up the rules themselves, while they're playing."

"I still don't get it."

"It's like technology, Hill. New stuff, new programs, new gadgets come out all the time, but we don't know the rules. We don't know what they're for. We don't even know that we need them until we have them.

This is an allegorical game, Hill. You'll see. It'll be fun. Your job at the game will be to beat whoever sits down."

I looked at Dad, trying to understand, trying to figure out what "allegorical" meant. "Dad. I have no idea what you're talking about. You're such a dork!"

Bullfrog opened the gallery that night at 6:30. The opening party was scheduled to start at 7 o'clock. Mom was still rushing around hanging a tag next to each piece of artwork with the name and the price. Bullfrog was in the kitchen, icing the wine or something. I was at the Digital Spoons Gaming Station, under the slab, practicing the game with Suzie and Hannah.

Our first victim was Todd Camper from the Comical Record. He came in early to check out Dad's show and maybe write an article about it. "So, what's this about?" he said as he sat on the floor, looking around cautiously. "I feel a little…ahh…intimidated in here. Is this some kind of execution chamber, or what?" He looked up at the slab. "This thing with the wires…"

"The slab?" asked Hannah.

"Slab? Is that what it is? God! That looks heavy. Is it safe? Is it gonna fall on us? What's with these wires sticking out? It looks dangerous."

Todd sure asked a lot of questions. But I guess that's what a newspaper man is supposed to do.

"Don't worry. It won't fall…" said Hannah. "I hope."

Todd ducked his head, keeping clear of the wires. "So what's this game? How do you play?"

Hannah started dealing the cards. There were three wooden spoons in the middle of the table, all painted black. She dealt five cards to each player.

"Wait a second," complained Todd. "You gotta tell me how to play this game."

We all just smiled as Hannah started the game. "You'll just have to pick it up as we go," said Suzie.

"Yeah, Todd, that's the point," I said.

"That's the what?" asked Todd, visibly confused as cards were being picked up and discarded at a furious rate. He didn't know what to do. By now a couple other people had wandered into the room and were watching the game, smiling and trying to understand. Hannah was smiling too, enjoying the power of her knowledge.

Spoons is really a very stupid game. The dealer picks cards from the deck and discards unwanted cards to the left. Other players pick up discarded cards from the player on their right and keep the ones they want, also discarding to the left. The cards continue rotating around the table until one player collects four of a kind. That player then grabs one of the three spoons from the middle of the table. When that happens, all the other players dive for the leftover spoons. It can get pretty fierce, sometimes. The player left without a spoon is the loser.

Cards were flying around the table, Todd was sitting there, wondering what to do. "You need four of a kind," said Suzie, giving Todd a hint.

Hannah grabbed for a spoon. Suzie and I grabbed the remaining spoons. All activity in the game stopped and the room got quiet. All you could hear was Todd who continued looking through his cards, still trying to get four of a kind.

We looked at Todd and started laughing.

"What? I don't have four of a kind yet."

"The game's over, Todd. You lost."

"What do you mean, I lost? How do you win?"

"You win by having a spoon, Todd. You don't have a spoon."

More people came into the spoons room, attracted by the laughter and the activity. It was clear that this opening would not be a typical, refined cultural event in Saugatuck.

We gave Todd another chance, but Suzie drew four of a kind in no time and grabbed a spoon off the table. Hannah and I followed, leaving Todd spoonless again.

We gave Todd a third try and this time he almost got it. In fact, he drew four of a kind first and started reaching for a spoon. Of course, we were much too quick for him. All three of us saw him reaching and we dove for the spoons, snatching them right out of Todd's grasp. "Hey! That's not fair. I won. I got four of a kind."

"Yeah, but do you have a spoon?" asked Suzie.

Todd, laughing and a little embarrassed, got up from the floor, making room for another player. "I give up. You girls are too quick for me." He stayed to watch another player's humiliation. This was really getting to be fun.

Mom was helping with the spoons game by giving us a break every once in a while. She was an especially fierce player, using her nails as weapons, sometimes snatching spoons out of other players hands, even after they grabbed one first. She took over for me so I could get something to eat. I was also curious about how Dad was doing.

Hannah's shrieking laughter filled the other rooms of the gallery, making the event seem like a crazy party, not an art opening. But the mood in the rest of the gallery was completely different from the spoons room. People from town were milling around and drinking wine. Some seemed to enjoy Dad's art, mostly the younger ones. They laughed at Dad's crazy pictures and sculptures. Dad likes it when his work makes people laugh.

But a lot of town people, especially the old-timers, the people who have lived in Saugatuck forever, didn't seem to get the humor. That really surprised me. Some were really pretty upset by Dad's art. I listened to people talking as I wandered around the gallery looking for Dad.

"Oh, this poor artist," said one, smiling. "He is so sick."

"What a nightmare," said another.

One man, looking at Dad's painting of the suiters in a balloon said, "That's how I feel sometimes…at work."

Some people were actually pissed off about Dad's speed tiles. Like one group of men I passed. They were looking at a painting with speed tiles arranged under a floating slab. One of the men was George Steffans, the owner of a local marina. He also owned the Keewatin, a big three hundred-foot passenger ship built in the '30s. The Keewatin was a familiar site in Saugatuck, beached on the south shore of Lake Kalamazoo. It was now a kind of museum and tourist attraction. "He shouldn't have done this," said George, shaking his head. "He shouldn't have painted these pictures."

"How does he know about the speed tiles?" asked another man in the group.

I passed another couple, an older man and woman. They were looking at one of Dad's sculptures. It was called Captured Slab and it showed a small slab hanging from chains, suspended above an arrangement of speed tiles. It was all enclosed by an elaborate Plexiglas case. "Maybe it's about time. Maybe it's better to get it all out in the open," I heard her say.

I saw Bullfrog at the front door of the gallery talking to old Reverend Stillwell, the pastor of one of the local churches. The reverend looked agitated, upset. Bullfrog was beaming, loving all the attention his gallery was getting. I casually strolled closer to see what Stillwell was saying.

"You can't do this Bullfrog!" said Stillwell. "You must close this show down."

"Close it?" asked Bullfrog. "You must be insane."

"It will start up again. Don't you see? These paintings are the devil's work."

"Oh, come now, Reverend."

"Close it, Bullfrog. In the name of God, close this show before it's too late."

"I'm afraid it is too late, Reverend. Yes. Look around. Everyone knows now. It is too late."

Stillwell left in a huff. I wondered what he thought would start again. I remembered that Ursulla said something like that too. And "the devil's work,'" What did Stillwell mean by that? My Dad was kinda weird, but he was definitely not the devil. One thing I knew now for sure, from all the reactions, speed tiles were nothing new to a lot of the people around here. And speed tiles scared them.

I saw Todd Camper walking around, watching the reactions. He had his reporter's pad out, gathering comments from the crowd. His eyes were intense. He looked kind of excited. He smelled a story here, I could tell.

Bullfrog, a smug smile on his face, walked by me, greeting people, doing his gracious gallery owner act. He was trying to act charming with all the visitors. I watched him for a minute. I could tell he was only half charming. He would be, like, chatting with one person, but trying to eavesdrop on the people next to him. I guess he just wanted to hear what people were saying about Dad's work.

I stayed away from him and continued looking for Dad. I found him with Ted Clark. They were looking at the Hanging Slab and the Birthing Grid. Ted had a very serious look on his face. "That's where speed tiles grow?" he asked.

"That's right, Ted," laughed Dad.

But Ted wasn't laughing. "John, how did you come up with that? How did you know?"

"Know what? I made it up."

"No way, John. No way. I almost had a heart attack when I came in here and saw that."

"What do you mean?" asked Dad.

"Dad, remember?" I interrupted. "I told you Suzie said her Dad has a real speed tile."

"Shhh!" said Ted, looking around to see who might have heard her. "Not so loud."

I looked around too and noticed that Bullfrog overheard us. He turned away when he saw me looking at him. "Huh? Why?" I asked.

"I don't know," he answered, looking around. "It's just something we don't talk about around here, Hill." He looked at me, talking quietly. "Suzie told you I had a speed tile?"

"Yeah, why?" I asked.

"I didn't know she knew," answered Ted, gloomily. Ted turned to Dad, whispering, "The speed tiles. They're gonna cause quite a stir around here."

"Yeah?" said Dad, smiling. "Great...I think."

"Dad, he's right," I said. "Reverend Stillwell said your paintings are the devil's work."

"Devil's work?" laughed Dad. "That's great, Hill. The devil's work!"

"I think lots of people know about speed tiles around here, Dad."

Ted looked around, studying people's faces, a look of sad resignation on his face.

"What's the matter, Ted?" asked Dad, smiling and taking a sip of his wine.

Ted looked at Dad and shrugged. "I don't know. It's the surprise of it, I guess." He looked up, scanning the room, trying to gauge the crowd's reaction to Dad's work. A little old lady came up to Dad just then. I didn't know who she was, but she nodded at Ted. "Hello, Ted. How's Mabel? How's your, ahh...your mother?"

Ted nodded politely. "She's fine, Agnes. She's just fine. She'll probably be here later. Sally's bringing her."

Agnes turned to Dad. "So, you're the artist."

Dad smiled. "Well, I guess I am. How do you like my work?"

Agnes turned serious. "Your work?" She looked around the room, taking it all in. "I don't know, Mister Hunter." She shook her head, her expression turning sour. "I didn't expect this. No, not at all. I think this took all of us by surprise, Mister Hunter."

Dad's smile slowly faded as he listened to this lady's criticism.

"I don't think this town will appreciate this show, Mister Hunter. You shouldn't have done it. You shouldn't have brought back all these..." she gestured around the room, "...these bad memories." Agnes gave Dad a cold stare and walked away, shaking her head.

"Brrrr..." said Dad, shaking as if he had a chill. "What was that all about?"

"I think you've tapped into some pretty sensitive imagery, John," said Ted. "Whether you know it or not, speed tiles…real speed tiles, have a long and sorry history around here. Most people don't talk about it."

It was time for me to get back to the Gaming Station to give somebody else a break, but I was pretty curious about what Ted knew about speed tiles.

"Ted," said Dad, getting serious. "I just stumbled on this speed tile stuff, myself. What do you know about speed tiles. Like that Agnes lady. What's her problem?"

"Maybe we should have a long talk over a beer sometime soon," said Ted. "You could tell me a few things too." He looked at the grid. "Like this grid. I don't know how you came up with this grid."

"You like it?" asked Dad.

"Sure, I guess. But here's the mystery. I've got drawings of that grid, John."

"Drawings?"

"It's the same grid…exactly."

"I didn't make any drawings. I just made the grid."

"No, the drawings I've got are over a hundred years old. They're drawings of that grid. Engineering drawings. I found them in Mabel's attic. The same day I found the speed tile." Chapters or other Divisions

Chapter 15

The Grid

I had known ever since I found it ten years ago. I suppressed the knowledge but I knew there was something compelling, something bizarre, something alien about the speed tile, something that made me do things, think things. But Ted's revelation about the drawings gave me quite a jolt.

I had thought the grid came from my memory, my brief encounter with a decaying structure buried in the sand. I only saw a small section of the grid that day. I constructed the rest in my mind, filling in the pieces, completing the structure in my imagination...I had thought. But Ted's story about the drawings suggested another possibility. The speed tile was using me. I was merely its playback mechanism. It played back as a sculpture through me, while 100 years ago, it played back through another person as engineering drawings. What did it want, I wondered?

"Dad. Dad!"

"Huh?"

"Dad. I better get back to the Spoons game."

"Okay, Hill. See you later. And Hill?"

"Yeah?"

"Try not to hurt anybody, okay?"

"You should tell Hannah that, Dad. She's the maniac."

Hilllary went off to the Spoons game. I turned to Ted. "Speaking of maniacs, I've gotta see those drawings of yours, Ted. This is too weird."

Ted laughed. "You're telling me. Why don't you come over after the opening for a nightcap. I'll show them to you."

"You gotta date."

"In the mean time, put a red dot on that thing. I want to buy it."

"Hey, great! My first sale."

"I don't think so, I've seen Bullfrog putting dots on a few things."

I looked up at the door to the gallery and saw Sally come in. She was with Mabel and Ursulla. Sally came over to us to say hello while Mabel and Ursulla started looking at the paintings, one by one. I watched them as they shuffled from one painting to the next, pointing, frowning, shaking their heads, discussing each one. I was especially interested in Mabel's reactions. She was an artist, herself, and I respected her opinion.

"Congratulations, John," said Sally. "You did it." She gave me a hug and a kiss on the cheek.

"Thanks, Sally. I guess I did, didn't I?"

"Where's Marcia?"

"You could probably find her in the next room. She's playing cards."

"Cards?"

"Yeah, Digital Spoons. Go check it out. Let me know what you think."

"Digital Spoons?" she asked, laughing. "This I gotta see."

"I think I'll check out the Spoons game too," said, Ted. "I'll talk to you later."

Sally and Ted took off for the Gaming Station just as Todd Camper strolled over with his spiral notebook in hand. "This is quite a show, John," he said. "It's very impressive."

"Thank you Todd, I appreciate it."

"But there's something more than art going on here, isn't there?" he asked me, getting right to the point.

"What makes you say that?"

"Oh, I don't know," he said, scanning the room. "This work is very original, very amusing…to me. I really like it. It makes me laugh. But look around. There are a lot of people here who are not laughing."

"That's very perceptive of you, Todd."

"It's almost as if they're afraid of something."

"Afraid of what?" I asked.

"Afraid of those speed tiles you put in all your work," he said, looking me in the eye. "That's what."

We stared at each other for a few seconds. I was trying to think of what to say to him. "They're a symbol, Todd. For technology. They're like microchips. They do everything in this world I've created. They're in everything."

"Are they real, John?"

"Real?" I asked, feeling uncomfortable in Todd's gaze.

"Yeah, real. Why did you draw so many speed tiles in your work? Why did you make so many of them? You must have gotten the idea somewhere."

I sighed, wondering why I felt so secretive about speed tiles. Here they were, all over the walls. I hung them up all over the place. I stuck them on everything. Over the past year I regurgitated speed tiles. I spit them up. I shit speed tiles. I sweated speed tiles. They were coming out of my ears. What's the secret? "What's the secret?" I asked out loud.

"That's what I'd like to know," answered Todd.

"Okay, Todd. Maybe there is something going on around here with speed tiles. I think that a lot of these people didn't see their first speed tile when they walked in here tonight. But, I swear, I'm as surprised by some of these reactions as you are."

"Where did you see your first speed tile?" he asked.

"In the dunes. In the sand where Singapore used to be. Ten years ago, I found a speed tile in the sand. It was before we moved here. I put it in my pocket and took it home."

"Where in the dunes?"

"Just north of the harbor entrance."

"Okay…go on."

"Well, I guess my imagination just ran away with me since then. I've been imagining this bizarre history. And I've been playing these mind games with the powers that these things have."

"What kind of powers?"

"Ahhh…they make you want to have them," I started cautiously. "You ever read Tolkien? You know Golem, the creature with the ring? It's like that. You feel like they're precious or something…powerful."

"What else?" he asked, starting to look skeptical.

"Anti-gravity powers," I blurted. "They make things lighter. They can make a house float."

Todd stopped writing. He looked at me, shook his head. He snapped his book closed. "Yeah, right."

"I told you. Maybe it's just coming from my imagination."

"Uh huh." He looked around. "There must be some value to speed tiles, though. Something real." He looked at me again. "Something that's not a fairy tale." He started to walk away then paused. "Nice show, though. I like the work. I'll write a good review in the paper."

I smiled. Todd probably thought I was some kind of weirdo artist. Oh, well. I wandered around the room chatting with people I knew, enjoying the attention my work was getting, puzzled by the hostility it brought out in some people.

I watched Mabel and Ursulla for a little while. They were quite a pair. Ursulla was long and thin, her gray hair pulled back severely in a bun on top of her head. She wore black. A long black dress. She had a black lace shawl around her stooped shoulders. She wore no make-up. She looked rather stern.

Mabel was Ursulla's opposite. She was almost as tall as Ursulla, but heavier. She wore a bright flower print dress and had her short hair done in soft waves down to her neck. She colored her hair, a reddish tint, hiding the gray. She used rouge, brightening her cheeks, and lipstick. Her features were soft and kind. Her eyes sparkled. Although she walked with a cane, she didn't look as if she needed it. She was quite energetic and out-going. She was as old as Ursulla and you could tell she was once quite beautiful.

They were both visibly upset by the work. Bullfrog walked by them on some kind of urgent mission. He nodded politely at Ursulla. As he walked by, Ursulla pointed him out to Mabel and whispered something. They both frowned and shook their heads. I joined them.

"Hi, Ursulla, Mabel. Enjoying the show?"

"Well, hello, John," said Ursulla, looking up sharply.

"Yes, yes…" said Ursulla.

"Well…" said Mabel, looking around the room and smiling nervously.

"It's okay," I said. "You won't hurt my feelings. I know this stuff isn't for everyone."

"Well," said Mabel, trying again, "It's really quite well done, John. You're a talented artist. I can see that."

"Thank you Mabel. That's kind of you to say."

"But," she continued as she looked around the room. "The subject matter. I just don't know…"

"Yes, yes," interrupted Ursulla. "It's the subject matter, yes. I'm afraid of what this will do to us, John, yes, I'm afraid."

"You mean the speed tiles?" I asked.

"Yes, John," said Mabel, looking me in the eyes. "The speed tiles will make them mad again. They do that to men, you know."

"Mad?" I asked. "You mean angry?"

"I mean insane," said Mabel.

"Yes, yes…insane, John," added Ursulla. "They cause insanity, John. Yes, they do."

"Greed," continued Mabel, her eyes bright, her pupils darting back and forth between my two eyes, reading them, gauging my reactions. "Speed tiles are like a narcotic…like gold fever. They make men want more. We had hoped we were done with them. Done with the speed tiles."

"Yes, yes," repeated Ursulla. "Done with them for good."

"What do you mean, men?" I asked. "Do they only affect men that way?"

"Oh yes, yes," answered Ursulla. "They drive men mad. Yes, quite mad."

"Women are stronger than men," added Mabel. "In many ways, we're stronger than men."

I smiled to myself. "You mean they don't drive women mad?" I teased, smiling.

"Oh, you could laugh about it, John," said Mabel. "But you're playing with fire here." She got very serious and looked into my eyes again. "But I can see that you don't know. I can see it in your eyes." She became quite mysterious, studying my eyes. "Your fever is quite low. The yellow light is very dim. Yes. Quite dim."

"Yellow light?"

"Yes, yes," said Ursulla. "The yellow light. You've seen it, haven't you, John? You've seen it. Yes, yes, you have."

"We must go now," said Mabel abruptly. "We must prepare." She turned to me. "Your eyes, John. You don't know what you did here. With this show of yours. There's innocence in your eyes. It could be that you are a conduit, a messenger. I've seen it before." She thought for a few seconds, remembering. She looked back at me. "Yes, that's what it is. Be careful, John. Be strong." She looked around and saw Jeremiah across the room, beaming, waving his arms about, acting the gallery owner. "Be careful of Jeremiah Bullfrog, especially."

They left without saying another word.

George Steffans joined me in front of a large painting I had finished just before the show opened. It showed a man in a gray suit strapped to a chair. He was bald. The floor was covered in speed tiles. In back of him were four windows. Eight men, all bald, were looking in through the windows. They wore trench coats, ties. They were emotionless, waiting. There was a propeller hat sitting on the floor of the chamber in front of the seated man. A superimposed, misty, ghost-like image of the man was reaching for the hat. A memory? A thought?

"Is that you in that painting, Hunter?" asked George.

"Maybe it is, George," I said, reaching out to shake hands with him. "Thanks for coming." I had kept my sailboat, Dancer, in George's marina for many years before moving to the Saugatuck Yacht Club. He was a good businessman, but he had a reputation for being ruthless, stubborn. He was used to calling the shots, doing it his way.

"It's quite a shock, this show," he said. He looked back at the painting. "You can't decide, can you?"

"Decide? Decide what?"

He pointed at the hat in the painting. "Decide whether to pick up the hat." He pointed at the men in windows. "Who's that back there?"

"Oh, I don't know. Society, I guess. Bureaucrats. Faceless, emotionless bureaucrats. They want me to pick up the hat, I guess." I looked at George. "I guess I am trying to decide. What about you, George. Did you pick up the hat?" I joked. "What did you decide?"

"Ha! Are you kidding?" He laughed. A fake laugh. His face, strained. Suppressed fury in his eyes. He turned from the painting to face me. "I picked up the hat years ago. You bet I did." His fury beginning to surface. "How do you think I got the Keewatin down that river, Hunter? How do you think I got a 300-foot ship down a river with a depth of only 12 feet in some places? How do you think I did that?"

I stared at him. A little spittle was on the corners of his mouth. He was agitated. Why? Was he sorry, perhaps, that he "picked up the hat?" But it wasn't a hat that he picked up, I realized. It was speed tiles. My eyes widened as I pictured the Keewatin coming down the river, floating, suspended above the water, speed tiles making it possible.

George looked around the room. "You really stirred up the pot here, Hunter. You shouldn't have done it." He turned and stomped off toward the front door.

I heard the screech of Hannah's laughter coming from the Spoons room and the commotion of people scrambling to grab a spoon...a desperate scramble to avoid the shame, the humiliation of being alone, of being the spoonless one.

Bullfrog, eyes bright, big smile on his face, came rushing up to me. He pointed at George, leaving the gallery. "Unpleasant fellow, isn't he?"

"Yeah, well, that's George Steffans. What can you do?"

"He has speed tiles, I can tell," said Bullfrog, smiling.

I looked at him, wondering what he meant.

"Oh, yes. He has speed tiles. Real speed tiles," he repeated. Then he pointed at another man across the room standing in front of the Birthing Grid. The man was frowning, shaking his head. "So does he." He pointed at a man and woman standing in front of the Siren painting. "They have speed tiles too. Oh yes. I could tell. Yes, yes, yes."

Bullfrog was giddy with excitement. He pointed at another couple looking at a painting of a hanging slab. They were laughing, enjoying the painting, the humor of it. "They don't have speed tiles. No, they don't. They think it's a joke. Yes. Look at them laughing."

"Jeremiah," I said. "What? Are you taking a survey or something? What's the difference?"

He turned to me, changing instantly to a more serious look, a suspicious look. "Nothing. No difference. It doesn't make any difference at all. No. No difference."

Marcia came up to us. She was excited. "John, you're doing pretty well. Several pieces have sold already."

"Oh yes, of course," confirmed Bullfrog. "We have sold some pieces. Ted Clark bought the Birthing Grid piece."

"Yeah, I know, he told me he wanted it."

"He also bought the Siren, John," said Marcia. "The Siren of Progress. He said it looks just like Mabel...when she was a young lady, that is. He said the Siren looks just like a young Mabel."

I smiled, thinking of Mabel.

"And several smaller drawings have sold, and one of the sculptures," added Bullfrog.

"And three of the Plexiglas cases…the Spoons Games. They sold too," said Marcia, smiling broadly. "And a bunch of the little framed cards around the ceiling sold too."

"Well, I guess a glass of wine is in order, right, Jeremiah?" I said.

"Yes, well, I don't have that Gallo wine that you like so much," he joked, "but we'll see what we can do." Marcia and I followed him into the kitchen to toast the success of the exhibit.

Marcia and I stopped at Sally and Ted Clark's house after Bullfrog closed the gallery. Hannah and Hilllary went home. I was pretty excited about the success of the opening and I wasn't ready to call it a night yet.

Sally and Ted lived on the Kalamazoo River in a contemporary cedar house that Ted built mostly himself. He had converted a small cottage into a big, rambling, multi-level home with massive picture windows overlooking the river. You couldn't see any sign of the old cottage any more.

It was a comfortable place. It always had a disorganized look to it as if Sally and Ted were just moving in and trying to decide where to put stuff. Ted blamed Sally for the mess. Sally didn't disagree. They were sipping wine and laughing at the tree frogs when we arrived. There must have been twenty frogs, all stuck to the outside of the picture window, probably attracted by the light, or by the insects that the light attracted. Some were as big as my fist.

"So, let's see these drawings, Ted," I said as he handed me a glass of Merlot.

"Drawings?" Marcia asked. "What drawings?"

"Ted accused me of plagiarism at the opening," I joked. "He said another artist got the grid idea over a hundred years ago."

"Marcia, Ted's right," said Sally. "Wait 'til you see these drawings. It's quite a coincidence."

"I found them in Mabel's attic a long time ago," said Ted. "They just really intrigued me. I never really knew what they were for until I saw John's grid."

Ted unrolled the old drawings on his dining room table. They were yellow with age and the paper was dry and brittle, but they were drawn on heavy paper. They were still in pretty good shape. He pulled books off the bookshelf to use as weights for the corners. We approached the table to inspect the ancient drawings.

"They're like working drawings, engineering drawings," said Ted. He had reading glasses perched on his forehead. He gave his head a little jerk and the glasses dropped down on his nose. He bent over the top drawing. "They show how to make a grid just like yours."

The grid in the drawing had a hundred compartments, just like mine. I looked at the dimensions. Each compartment was three inches square, again just like my grid. I flipped to the next drawing for an elevation view. The depth indicated on the drawing matched my grid too. "This is spooky, Ted...very spooky."

"Here, look at this part." Ted flipped to the next drawing. It showed how each wall was to be engineered with tongue and groove joints with detailed instructions on the thickness of the walls and the depth of the grooves.

"It's like I used these plans to build my grid," I said to Ted.

"Not quite," said Ted. He looked up at me, gazing over the top of his glasses. "If you did, you left a few things out. Here, look at this."

Ted turned to the next drawing to show the floor of the grid in cross section. It showed what looked like electronic circuitry sandwiched in the middle of two layers in the floor. "This is one of the things that always puzzled me about these drawings," he said, leaning closer. "These look like microchips to me. There's one in each square."

I leaned closer. Sure enough, the circuitry drawn there was primitive by today's standards, but it looked like little microchips.

"I thought these drawings were a hundred years old," said Marcia. "How could the artist have drawn microchips? They weren't even invented yet."

"Bingo," said Ted.

"Bingo?" asked Sally, pouring herself another glass of wine.

"Yeah, bingo," repeated Ted. He reached up and propped his glasses on his forehead. "The person who made these drawings didn't know what these things were, either. He drew them because he had some kind of inspiration, like John. A vision. A premonition."

"But where did it come from?" asked Marcia. "The inspiration, I mean."

"I think it's obvious where it came from," said Ted. "From the speed tiles. The same place John's inspiration came from."

I flipped to the next drawing in the stack. It showed a bank of odd looking electric light bulbs sitting under the grid in an elevation. "What do you think this is?" I asked.

"I don't really know, but I think the engineer who drew this was trying to interpolate...trying to make sense of his inspiration. Those light bulbs look like the first ones Edison made. In 1880, Edison was a famous inventor. He was worshipped by engineers as a kind of god. Maybe he was imagining that Edison's strange and wonderful electric lights could somehow power this contraption."

"In my piece, the slab is powering it," I said.

"Yes," said Ted "And like the primitive microchips this engineer drew in his drawings, perhaps your slab is a primitive rendering of something that isn't in existence yet...something that hasn't been invented."

"Oh, it's in existence all right," I said.

"What do you mean?" asked Ted.

"The slab is a representation of something I saw, Ted. It grew out of my speed tile. The one I found in the dunes ten years ago. Remember that lightning strike on my roof?"

"Yeah, I remember."

"That night I saw this disgusting slab like thing floating in the sky, between lightning flashes, floating, heading north. It exploded out of my attic…"

"John!" said Marcia. "You don't know that for sure. You were pretty upset that night. Who knows what you saw?"

"You mean there is a slab?" asked Ted. "Like the one in your sculpture?"

"As far as I know, yes," I admitted. "There is a slab, Ted."

"Oh, brother," said Marcia. She turned to Sally. "Would you listen to these two crazies. Talking slabs, floating slabs. Come on, you guys, get real."

"These two have very active imaginations," said Sally. "Come here, Marcia, I want to show you that picture of Mabel. The one that looks just like John's Siren of Progress."

Marcia went with Sally. Ted was excited. "John, I can build this thing."

"What do you mean, Ted. I already built it."

"No, I mean a real one. Yours is like a mock-up, a model," continued Ted. "The drawings show how to make a real working grid."

"A working grid?"

"Yeah, a Birthing Grid that actually produces speed tiles."

"You gotta be kidding."

"Your version adds some insight into how to do it. Like the sand. I think the sand is an important element. And the power source…the slab hanging above it…"

"But Ted. Why would you want to build a real one?"

"To make speed tiles," he said matter-of-factly. He took off his glasses and used them to point at the drawings. "I think this guy just didn't have the technology to build it when he made these drawings a hundred years ago…a real working grid, I mean… Maybe now we do."

"But Ted, these drawings aren't that detailed. Like the wiring. What are all the microchips connected to?"

"I don't know yet, but I think I can build this thing. All I need is the slab to power it."

"You need the slab?"

"Yeah, the slab. Where did you say you saw it?"

"It was floating over the trees, in the storm. It was heading north, Ted."

"North?"

"Yeah, Ted," I confirmed. I looked at Ted, at the excitement in his eyes. He was chewing on one of the temples of his glasses. It scared me, the thought of him building a real Birthing Grid to manufacture speed tiles, but I told him anyway. "I think it was heading for South Manitou Island, Ted."

"Of course!" he said, getting even more excited. "South Manitou. The place with the gravity anomalies. There's something on that island that has something to do with this. There's gotta be."

"John!" called Marcia from the other room. "You gotta see this."

"What?" I asked.

"Mabel," answered Marcia. "Look at these pictures of Mabel. She was really beautiful in those days."

Ted and I joined Marcia and Sally in the living room. I sat next to Marcia, put my arm around her and gave her a hug and a kiss on the cheek. "Got room for one of us 'crazies' over here?"

"Sure, just behave yourself," she said. "Check out these old pictures."

I picked up the first picture on the stack. It was very old. It was framed in a cardboard mat with elaborate designs embossed around the edges. It looked like it was shot in a studio. Mabel was sitting in a chair, posing. She was strikingly beautiful, with blonde hair arranged meticulously in a bun on her head. But her face. It was, indeed, the face of the siren in my painting. My siren had long, flowing blonde hair cascading down and blowing in the wind. I felt sure that if Mabel had taken her hair down, it would have matched my Siren's hair. "My God, you're right. Mabel's my Siren."

I picked up another picture. There were a whole box of them on the table in front of the couch. Mabel was one of three women in this picture. They were all beautiful and elegant.

"That's Mabel's two sisters," said Sally. "It's really fun to look at these old pictures, isn't it? All these elegant clothes, this formal posing."

I looked at another and another, then it dawned on me. The age of these pictures. They were very, very old. I looked up to see Ted staring at me, waiting, his reading glasses perched on the tip of his nose, his eyes peering over them. "Ted, how old are these pictures?"

"Pretty old," he said.

I picked up another one and turned it over to look at the back. Photographers would often stamp their studio name and date on the back of prints in the early days of photography. I picked up another and another, looking for a date, a clue as to the age of the pictures. I found one with Mabel sitting in a horse carriage, the reins in her hands, in front of a wooden building. There was another woman sitting next to her. Lake Michigan was in the background. I turned it over. A date was stamped on the back. September, 1880. "Ted. This can't be Mabel. Here, look at the date on the back of this picture." I handed it to Ted.

He took it and smiled. "Oh, that's Mabel all right. And that's Ursulla sitting next to her."

I looked at Marcia. She looked at me, confused now. I remembered Hilllary's claim that Ursulla was over a hundred years old. "But, but..."

"John, Mabel's not my mother. She's my great grandmother. She's 137 years old. A year older than Ursulla."

Chapter 16

Ursulla

I practically had to drag Suzie up the stairs to Ursulla's bookstore. She didn't want to go with me. Dad sent me there to pick up some books he wanted to take on our cruise.

As we walked up the stairs, I heard a piano playing. It was a recording Ursulla liked, a spooky piece that I recognized, Claire de Lune by Debussy. I had the music for this piece and I wanted to learn how to play it on my piano. It was very quiet and dreamy and it made the trip up the stairs feel like we were climbing into another world.

"We oughta get Ursulla some Metallica," whispered Suzie.

"Beats chanting monks," I replied.

We reached the top of the stairs. "Ursulla!" I called softly. "Ursulla, are you here?"

We looked around the store but we couldn't find her.

"She must have flown away on her broomstick," whispered Suzie.

"Shh! She must be in her apartment." I had a sinking feeling as I opened the curtain and called to her again. All we heard was the haunting piano of Debussey. It reminded me of fog on a deserted Lake Michigan beach.

"Let's go in," I suggested.

"You sure, Hill?"

I nodded. We tip-toed quietly into her living area. I went first, passing through the small room with the table where I once found Ursulla's journal and her speed tiles. The journal was still sitting on the table under the Tiffany lamp but Ursulla's red purse was nowhere to be seen.

I went into the next room and gasped, holding back a scream. I pushed backwards into Suzie, stepping on her foot.

"Hill, what the heck."

Suzie recovered and looked over my shoulder, a soft squeak coming from her mouth as it dropped open.

The room was a shambles. Drapes were pulled off the walls, chairs overturned, drawers pulled out with their contents spilled carelessly on the floor. Ursulla's messy but cozy apartment had been turned into a stormy disaster. The dreamy music of Claire de Lune played beautifully, the notes flowing, rolling like fog over the chaos in front of us.

"Wrong music," whispered Suzie.

"Ursulla!" I called, frightened now.

The music ended but the arm on Ursulla's record player didn't shut off automatically. It stayed on the end of the record, scratching loud then soft, loud then soft, as if searching mindlessly for the next tune.

We stepped over the mess, into the room, looking for Ursulla, the old phonograph now playing the right music in its endless, scratching rhythm.

"Looks worse than your room, Hill," said Suzie.

"Ursulla! Are you here?" I called.

We went through the living room and into Ursulla's bedroom, the mess continuing in there. I heard a soft moan from the bed.

"There she is, Suz. Ursulla! Are you okay?" I said, knowing she wasn't.

My heart beating loudly in my ears, I sat on the edge of the bed and pulled the covers down off Ursulla's face. I jumped back, scared, almost falling off the bed, seeing her eyes wide, frightened, staring back at me. Her watery eyes were surrounded by the wrinkles and the sagging skin and the white matted hair of old age.

"Euughhh," said Suzie.

Ursulla was old, but she never looked this old.

"Suzie, call 911," I commanded.

"God, Hill, what happened to her?"

"Suzie! Shut up. Go call 911!"

"911?"

"The phone's in the living room, Suzie. Go call 911. Get an ambulance."

Suzie left the room and I heard her on the phone calling the emergency number, the scratch, scratch, scratch of the phonograph continuing a fitting tempo.

I didn't know what to do with Ursulla. She scared me. She looked so old and wrinkled. I was afraid to touch her, afraid that her old age would infect me. I sat helplessly on the bed next to her, staring into her wild, fearful eyes. I looked toward the living room, tears flowing from my eyes, sobbing softly, hoping the ambulance would not take long. I forced myself to look back at Ursulla, this time seeing something else in her eyes. Did she recognize me?

She reached out from under the covers with an aged and bony hand. It looked more like the claw of a bird than a hand. She gripped my wrist suddenly with more strength than she looked like she had. I moaned, afraid of the claw, not wanting it touching me, infecting me.

The claw pulled me closer. Ursulla tried to speak, her lips gray, her white, stringy hair framing her face, her eyes wide, knowing. "Hillary," she croaked.

"Ursulla. Suzie called an ambulance. They'll be here real soon."

Suzie came into the room. She stayed by the door, her eyes wide, frightened. She kept away from the bed, away from the old, wrinkled thing on the bed that was Ursulla.

"Bullfrog…" she whispered. "My speed tiles, yes, my children…"

"Bullfrog?" I asked.

"They're gone now. Yes, they're gone. Oh my. Oh my."

"What happened, Ursulla. What did he do?"

"It's over for me now, yes, yes. It's over."

"No it's not Ursulla. The ambulance will be here soon."

I heard the siren of the ambulance in the distance, coming closer, the scratching of the needle keeping its senseless tempo.

"But the madness. Yes, madness. Starting. Yes, yes."

I heard the ambulance stop at the street below, the siren trailing off to silence. I heard the door open and heavy footsteps running up the stairs. Suzie ran to meet them.

Ursulla suddenly gripped my arm tightly, hurting me, pulling me closer. "Hillary! The journal. The journal, Hillary."

Crying openly now, scared she would take me with her, I tied to pull away.

"The book! Take the book!"

Sobbing, pulling, fighting the death grip of Ursulla's claw, I cried out, "No! Ursulla, No!"

"Give the book to your father!"

The ambulance people burst into the room just as Ursulla released her grip with an eerie moan. I pulled away, sobbing, crying hysterically, running from the room. I had to get away from her, away from her suffocating grip of death.

I tripped on the cluttered floor and went sprawling into the living room. Suzie ran up to me, dropped down to the floor beside me and held me tightly. We both sat there, rocking softly to the tempo of the scratching phonograph, sobbing, sobbing.

We heard the purposeful sounds of the ambulance people working in Ursulla's room, working fruitlessly to keep death away. We heard more footsteps on the stairs, more people entered the room. We sat there, on the floor, in shock, rocking, crying, seeing our own future reflected in Ursulla.

The ambulance crew carried Ursulla's unmoving body out of the apartment and down the stairs. I knew they were too late. I knew she was dead. The police arrived, Jim Fletcher and Linus Beagle. They tried to hide it but even they looked frightened by the chaos and madness in

Ursulla's rooms. One of them took the arm of the phonograph off the record, stopping the constant scratching.

They didn't know what to do with two sobbing teenage girls. We told them what we had found between tears, leaving out Ursulla's mention of Bullfrog and the speed tiles. They called Suzie's house, then mine but Suzie's parents were at work and Dad was at the boat getting it ready for the cruise. We finally stopped crying and told them we would go to Sally's Nook to our mothers, who were both working there that day.

We got up off the floor and started for the stairs. In the hallway separating the apartment from the bookstore, I saw Ursulla's journal on the end table. I stopped and stared at it.

"Come on, Hill. Let's get out of here."

I remembered Ursulla telling me to give the journal to my Dad.

"Hill! Let's go!"

I looked back at Jim and Linus. They were busy looking around, probably destroying evidence. I picked up the journal and put it under my arm.

"Hill. What are you doing?" whispered Suzie.

"Shhh. Ursulla told me to take it."

"What?"

"Just before she died. She told me to give it to my Dad."

"God, Hill."

We walked quickly down the stairs and into the street. The sun was shining and tourists were everywhere, laughing, joking, strolling aimlessly, enjoying the summer sun and the quaint streets of Saugatuck. My knees felt weak and rubbery. I felt light-headed. Suzie was still crying soundlessly, tears rolling off her cheeks. We dodged the tourists on the way to Sally's Nook. I looked at their faces, the laughing, vacationing, ice-cream eating faces all around us. Why couldn't they see the misery I felt? How could they be so happy? How could they look so normal? How could they not feel the agony of Ursulla's death?

My Mom and Dad had to go to a stupid dinner party and Hannah was staying in Grand Rapids with one of her snooty, anorexic ballet friends. Mom didn't want me to be alone so Sally and Mom agreed to a sleep-over at Suzie's house that night. I didn't have a chance to give the journal to Dad, so I still had it when I went to Suzie's house.

"Wow, this is really old, Hill."

"I know, Suze. Be careful with it. I have to give it to my Dad."

"I'll be careful. We can at least look at it, can't we?"

We were lying on Suzie's bed, on our stomachs, the book in front of us. There was a lot of writing but it was impossible to read. It was written in another language. Suzie remembered that it was Dutch. Some of the pages had pictures that were hand drawn. Some pages had photographs pasted on them.

"God, Hill, look at this drawing. It looks like your Dad's grid sculpture."

"Yeah, it does. It looks like my Dad could have drawn it."

"My Dad's got big rolled up pictures of this grid thing too. He showed them to your Dad the other night."

"I wonder what it means?" I asked.

"It probably says so right here, if you could read Dutch."

We struggled with it for a while, but all we could figure out was that the grid was for manufacturing speed tiles, the same purpose my Dad's grid sculpture was supposed to be for.

We flipped some more pages and came to the picture of Bullfrog on the porch in front of a wooden house.

"I'll bet Bullfrog stole the speed tiles in that bag," said Suzie. "There's been all these weird burglaries around here lately too."

"You think Bullfrog has something to do with them?"

"Duh, Hill. Didn't Ursulla blame Bullfrog?"

"Yeah, but she was dying, Suze. Maybe she was, like, delirious or something."

"I think Bullfrog's been stealing speed tiles."

"Why? What's he gonna do with them?"

"Maybe he needs them to stay alive, Hill. Look what happened to Ursulla after her speed tiles were stolen."

"Yeah." I thought back to the afternoon, to Ursulla's wasted, wrinkled face. "Ursulla said she was the same age as Bullfrog, Suze. Maybe he needs them to stay young. Maybe that's why he's stealing them."

"I wish there was some way to find out."

"There is, Suzie. We could go to the Bat House and look around. I'll bet he keeps them in the basement."

"Hill, what are you suggesting?"

"Listen, Suzie, Hannah and me tried to go down in his basement to store some of my Dad's artwork. Bullfrog went nuts. He wouldn't let us down there. It looked like he was trying to hide something."

"His basement? God, Hill, that's spookier than Ursulla's bookstore."

"I know. It was spooky even when my Dad owned it."

Suzie stared at me, her eyes getting wider as she realized what I wanted to do. "Uh uh! No way, Hill. No way you're gonna talk me into this one."

"Pluck, pluck, pluck!" I teased, standing up on the bed, acting like a chicken.

"Hill! Shut up! I'm not going. No way!"

"Okay, Suzie. Then I guess I'll have to go myself. Can I borrow a flashlight?"

"Hill! No!"

"Suze, Yes!"

"No!"

"Yes! Suzie, I owe it to Ursulla. I have to find out if he stole her speed tiles."

Suzie looked at me, turning the adventure over in her mind. I could see she was weakening.

"How we gonna get in? What are ya gonna do, just knock on his door and ask to see his frickin' speed tiles?"

"I know a secret entrance to the basement. It's in back of the house. Bullfrog probably doesn't even know about it." I looked at Suzie expectantly.

"God, Hill! How do I let you talk me into these things."

We waited until after midnight. Suzie's parents were asleep in another part of the house. It would be easy for us to quietly tip-toe down the hall and go out through the garage. Suzie had done it dozens of times.

Giggling nervously, but trying to keep quiet, we took our flashlights and left the house. It was about a half mile walk to Bullfrog's gallery. Every time a car went by, we would duck behind a bush or something to stay out of sight. Suzie was really into this expedition by now. She looked like a commando, all dressed in black, sneaking around behind bushes.

"You oughta be a spy or something, Suzie. You're good at this."

"I know, Hill. Let's go."

She dashed across the street, diving dramatically behind another bush. I followed her.

"Suzie, aren't you over-doing it?" She ignored me.

"Follow me, Hill."

Crouching down low, she dashed from bush to bush, obviously enjoying the adventure. I followed her, giggling and enjoying it just as much.

"Get down, Hill!"

A car was coming. We hid between a stairway and a tree, keeping in the shadows while a car approached slowly down the street. It was a police car on patrol. I saw Linus Beagle in the passenger seat eating a donut.

"Shhh!" commanded Suzie.

We crouched low and followed the car with our eyes as it drove past.

Smiling, Suzie dashed to the next bush, then the next, staying out of sight as much as possible. We probably would not have attracted any attention at all if we simply walked out in the open to Bullfrog's gallery. Saugatuck was hardly a police state. But it was more fun to do it Suzie's way.

Finally we reached the house next door to Bullfrog's. The gallery was dark. It didn't look as if anyone was there.

"Okay, Hill. Where's the secret entrance?"

"It's in the back. Come on, I'll show you." I ran from behind the bush to the back of the house where the storm door entrance to the basement was. Suzie followed me.

I switched on my flashlight to find the door under all the bushes. "Here it is," I whispered.

"God, it's really hidden back here," replied Suzie quietly. "You think Bullfrog knows about it?"

"I don't know. We'll soon find out."

I reached down and found the handle to the door and pulled up on it. It was heavy and there were branches and roots and stuff grown around the edges. It wouldn't budge.

"Let's clear out some of these stupid weeds," suggested Suzie.

We dug around the outside edges of the door, brushing off dirt and branches and anything else that could be holding the door closed.

I gave it another tug. This time it gave a little. "Help me, Suzie. It's loose."

We both tugged at the door, lifting it and swinging it open. It gave off a loud squeaking sound and it fell open with a thump.

We stopped, afraid that we had made too much noise. We looked at each other, eyes wide, expectant, waiting, listening.

We didn't hear a sound so I shined my flashlight down into the black hole. Spider webs criss-crossed the opening and a puddle of water reflected the light from the bottom stair. A mouse, startled by my light, scurried into the darkness.

"Ughhh," said Suzie, wrinkling up her nose. "You want me to go down there?"

"Just a mouse, Suze. No big deal."

"What about the bats, Hill?"

I had forgotten about the bat. I prayed that we wouldn't run into any bats. "Bullfrog got rid of them, Suzie. There aren't any more bats."

I moved the beam of the light and saw the doorknob for the inner door. Dad never locked this door. I hoped Bullfrog didn't either.

"Let's go Suze." I started down the stairs but she grabbed my arm.

"No, Hill. The spider webs."

I grabbed a stick from the bushes outside and opened a path through the spider webs. "Happy now?"

My heart beating faster, I climbed down the stairs and reached for the knob. Crossing my fingers, I turned the knob and pushed. The door opened with a soft creak. I looked up at Suzie. Her eyes were wide with fright. My commando friend was chickening out.

"Come on, Suzie," I whispered.

"God, Hill. Why? Why do I let you talk me into these things?"

She followed me into the darkness of Bullfrog's basement.

It was dark in this room, a small, damp room off the main basement, but I could see a glow under the door ahead of me. It was yellow. Dirty yellow. The glow made me uneasy. It made me think of my Dad at the dining room table, hypnotized by his speed tile arrangement, the moonlight reflecting onto his face.

"Look, Hill. There's a light in the next room."

"Shhh. I know. I can see, can't I?"

We crept up to the door and listened. There was a soft hum coming from the next room, like a florescent light hum, but there didn't seem to be any movement. I reached for the door knob and turned it, pushing the door open slightly so I could see.

I peeked in and saw the edge of a low table or platform. I could only see a small part of it. A partition blocked my view. The glow seemed to be coming from the platform. To the left of the platform was a taller table with a big canvas bag on it, the same bag, I thought, that Bullfrog was holding in Ursulla's journal. There were also an assortment of small boxes and purses. I looked closer and saw Ursulla's purse, her red purse. The purse she kept her speed tiles in.

"There it is, Suzie. The purse."

"Let's see."

We traded places and Suzie looked through the crack.

"I don't see it," whispered Suzie.

"It's on that table, next to the canvas bag."

"Is that it? Are you sure?"

"I think that's it. Let's go get it."

"But that glow, Hill. What's that glow in there?"

"I don't know, Suzie. But I'm gonna find out."

I pushed the door open and, crouching low, I slid into the room slowly. I kept my back to the partition, trying to stay out of the light from the glow.

"Come on, Suzie," I whispered.

"Okay, okay."

I kept my eye on Ursulla's purse. As I came closer to the table I saw speed tiles haphazardly lying next to the boxes and bags that once contained them. I realized these were speed tiles Bullfrog had collected from his burglaries all over town. My heart beating wildly, I stood at the end of the partition, staring at the red purse. Wanting it. Needing it.

I was afraid of the yellow light but the purse hypnotized me. It called to me. I stepped into the light and approached the table slowly, seeing only the purse. I felt like I was moving in slow motion as I came closer and reached for Ursulla's speed tiles. I picked them up, surprised, again, by their light weight. I held up the purse and looked at it.

"Hill!" hissed Suzie, still behind the partition.

"Huh?" I looked back at Suzie with a jerk, then turned my head to the left, to the source of the dirty yellow light. I froze with terror. Suzie watched me as my eyes widened and my mouth formed a silent scream.

"What is it, Hill?"

There, over the platform, floated the still body of Jeremiah Bullfrog. He was face down, his head closest to me, his stringy hair flowing, dancing, bobbing slightly in the light. He was stark naked, his skin a dead, pale blue where the light wasn't reaching it, but a sick yellow on the bottom, flooded by light from the speed tiles meticulously arranged on the surface of the platform. His penis hung down loosely almost touching the speed tiles on the platform giving the impression that Bullfrog was balancing on the tip of his wiener. I was frozen in place. I couldn't move.

Suzie's curiosity won out over her fear. She stepped out from behind the partition and looked at Bullfrog's floating body. Her eyes went wide in disbelief. "Oh my God," she whispered. "Okay, I'm gonna leave now, " she said shakily and turned to leave.

"Wait, Suzie," I whispered.

"Why?" she asked.

"Wait, Suze, wait. I think he's in some kind of coma."

"He's naked, Hill."

"Duh, Suze."

"Ughhh, gross," she whispered.

We both stood there, hypnotized by this impossible sight.

"Is he dead, Hill?"

"I don't think so."

We crept closer, attracted by the glow. Bullfrog was kind of drifting above the tiles, his face turned away from us. It was as if a stream of air was keeping him suspended. His body flowed from one side of the table to the other, moving only slightly, undulating in the light. I looked down at the speed tiles. The golden nubs were alive, squirming. I remembered looking at them in Ursulla's purse. The light came from these wormy golden things. They were giving Bullfrog life, regenerating his ancient body.

We silently slid around the other side of the table. I had to see his face. I had to look into Bullfrog's face. He didn't seem to be breathing.

His eyes were closed and his face expressionless. Maybe he was dead, I thought.

We were hypnotized by Bullfrog's unearthly trick. I bent down to take a closer look. Suzie bent down too. We looked past the floating strands of his long, stringy hair. We glanced down his naked body, grossed out by his Oscar Mayer wiener. We peered into his dead, unmoving face and studied his yellowed features.

Then his eyes opened.

We both jumped back and screamed. His evil eyes stared accusingly at us, first swirling with confusion, then recognition; eyes smoldering with anger, dripping, oozing with a filthy yellow glow. Ancient eyes. Sick, diseased, furious eyes, raging with a hundred years of insanity.

We turned and ran, screaming, toward the door, but there, blocking our exit was a huge man, a monster, his shadow looming down on us. The beast came toward us, but we couldn't see his face. Trapped between Bullfrog and this new menace, we chose the new. Suzie to the left, me to the right, we stumbled around him, wailing, crying, scared out of our wits. The beast let us by.

We ran from Bullfrog's basement. We ran into the dark night, ran from the horror behind us. We didn't think. We didn't notice the stairs or the bushes or the street or the cars passing slowly. We ran; our town an indistinct blur around us, a smudge of dark but familiar shapes. We ran to the safety of Suzie's house, locking the door behind us. Locking out the naked evil that was Bullfrog.

Chapter 17

The Journal

I hated that damned phone, especially when it rang at night. That insistent, irritating, electronic bell…never good news at this hour.

"Hello?"

"John, this is Ted. I think you better get over here."

"Huh? Why? What's the matter?"

"It's the girls. They're hysterical."

"The girls? Somebody get hurt?"

"No, they're okay. They're just upset. They apparently had a very traumatic experience."

"What do you mean?"

"They went to Bullfrog's gallery tonight, John. They snuck in through the basement."

"Bullfrog's gallery?"

"They discovered some very disturbing things. You better get over here."

"I'll be right there."

I hung up the phone. Marcia rolled over, curious about the call.

"Ted Clark. Get this. The girls broke into Bullfrog's place tonight. Ted says they're hysterical."

"Good grief! Broke in? Why?"

"Ted wants me to come over. He says they're pretty upset."

"I better come with you."

At three a.m. after hearing Hilllary and Suzie's bizarre story, we called the police. Ted and I met them at Bullfrog's gallery. Hilllary and Suzie stayed with Marcia and Sally. The place was dark. Linus Beagle knocked on the front door, trying to wake Bullfrog. Jim Fletcher and I walked around to the back of the building. Bullfrog's car was gone. The basement door where Hilllary and Suzie broke in was closed.

We joined Ted and Linus at the front door. Linus turned the knob and found the door open so we went in. "What were they doing breaking into this house, anyway?" asked Linus.

"They think Bullfrog had something to do with Ursulla's death," I answered. "They were investigating. The crazy kids were investigating."

"Investigating?" asked Jim. "Investigating what?"

"Bullfrog," I answered. "They were investigating Bullfrog. Don't ask, Jim. You know how kids are."

"Speaking of Bullfrog," added Ted. "I wonder where he went at three in the morning."

"Yeah, Jim," I said. "Isn't it kind of suspicious that Bullfrog's not here?"

"No crime to be out at three a.m."

We went through the darkened gallery, past my slabs and speed tiles, followed by the unseeing eyes of my sirens and suiters. My paintings and sculptures, all silent and dark, imitating reality, pretending knowledge, mimicking wisdom. I had a premonition that this gallery would never be open again.

"Okay, we better get out of here," said Linus. "We don't have any right to be looking around here without a search warrant."

"We'll talk to Bullfrog when he gets back," said Jim. "I just hope he doesn't want to register a complaint about your kids breaking in here."

Bullfrog was definitely gone. There were signs of a hasty departure. Doors were left open, including the door leading down to the basement, the door Bullfrog was so careful to keep locked. "I'll check downstairs before we go," I offered.

Looking for the mysterious speed tile platform Hilllary described, I walked slowly down the stairs into the dark basement. I fumbled for the pull chain at the bottom of the stairs and heard a soft moan and shuffling sound. Frightened, I flailed around at the ceiling, beginning to panic, searching for the light, thinking of the monster beast Hilllary told us about.

I found the chain and pulled it, showering harsh light and deep shadows into the gloom. Looking at me, squinting at the glow, was the towering figure of Dick Beaver. He was getting up off the floor, rubbing his head, a trickle of blood running down his cheek. "Dick! What the…"

"That son-of-a-bitch stole my speed tiles!" he blurted.

"Bullfrog?" I asked.

"That bastard. That fucking bastard."

Ted came down the stairs with Linus and Jim close behind. "Dick. What are you doing here?"

"He must be the monster beast the kids described," I explained.

"Dick Beaver?" asked Linus stupidly.

"What?" asked Dick.

"Dick, what are you doing here?" asked Jim, repeating Ted's question.

"Came to get something that belongs to me," answered Dick, still rubbing his head. He dabbed at the blood on his cheek, looked at his hand then rubbed the blood on his jeans.

"Where's Bullfrog?" asked Linus.

"That son-of-a-bitch is gone!" answered Dick, shaking with rage.

"Gone?" asked Linus, a look of confusion on his face.

"What are you doing down here in the dark?" asked Jim, again.

"He took 'em all. I couldn't stop him," continued Dick, his anger mixing with helpless confusion, frustration.

"Took what?" asked Linus.

"Ahh, nothin'," answered Dick in disgust. Dick didn't have a lot of patience with our police department. "I'm goin' home."

Ted and I exchanged glances. Linus and Jim braced themselves.

"Now hold on there, Dick," said Linus. "We're gonna need a few answers here before you can go."

"You gonna stop me, Linus? I got nothin' to say to you. Bullfrog's gone. I done nothin' wrong. I'm leaving." Dick started for the stairs, his towering form dwarfing the two policemen.

Trying to head off a confrontation, Ted stepped between Dick and Linus. "You guys know where Dick lives. If Bullfrog wants to file a complaint or something, you know where to find him."

Linus and Jim looked at each other, considering this option. I think they were relieved to hear Ted's voice of sanity. "Well, maybe Ted's right," agreed Jim. "Okay, Dick. You can go. But we know where to find you."

"You sure do, Jim." answered Dick, climbing the stairs. "I'll look forward to seeing you again real soon, Jim! You too, Linus! Real soon." Dick didn't try to hide his disdain for the two.

I followed Dick up the stairs and out to his van, parked in the shadows across the street. "Dick, what happened tonight? Can you tell me?"

"I don't know what happened. He bopped me in the head. Knocked me out. But I know where he went. And I'm goin' after him. I'm gonna find that son-of-a-bitch. I'm gonna get my speed tiles back."

"Where, Dick? Where did Bullfrog go?"

"To the island. He went to South Manitou Island."

The next day I struggled with Ursulla's journal. I thumbed through the pages, looking at the pictures, frustrated by the foreign language I could not read. I decided to take it with me to Ursulla's wake. Maybe Mabel would be there. She was fluent in Dutch. Maybe she could help me.

"Hi, Dad."

"Oh, hi, Hill. How's my little burglar?" I gave Hilllary a big hug.

"Lookin' at Ursulla's journal?"

"Yep. Most of it doesn't make any sense."

"I know. Weird language."

"I'm gonna show it to Mabel. Maybe she can make some sense of it."

I looked at Hilllary. She looked tired, stressed out. "How you feeling, Hill? You had quite a night last night."

"I'm okay. Just tired. I can't stop thinking about Bullfrog floating over that platform."

"I still think you're fricking nuts, Hill," said Hannah, coming into the room. Hilllary had told Hannah the whole story when we got home early that morning.

"No, I'm not, Hannah! It's true! You should have seen it!"

"Yeah, right! I really wanna see Bullfrog naked."

"You better get dressed, Hill," I interrupted. "We have to leave for Ursulla's wake pretty soon. Mom's getting dressed now."

Hannah had to go to a ballet rehearsal, but Marcia and Hilllary came to the funeral home with me where Ursulla would be laid out.

There was quite a crowd when we arrived. Ursulla had a lot of friends in Saugatuck, including Mabel, who was sitting quietly in the front row, her cane in hand, dressed uncharacteristically in black. I sat next to her and noticed the leopard print scarf around her neck, her only extravagance on this sad day. I mumbled some senseless condolences. Mabel and Ursulla were close friends. I knew Mabel would miss her.

I looked up at the casket and realized with a shock that it was closed.

We sat quietly while several townspeople stopped by Mabel to pay their respects. Ursulla had never married, so she had no real family in Saugatuck, only friends like Mabel. "I warned her, you know," whispered Mabel.

I leaned over to hear her better. "Excuse me, Mabel?"

"I told her to hide them. To keep them from Bullfrog."

"You mean her speed tiles?" I asked.

"Yes. He came to my house too. The same night."

"Bullfrog?"

"Yes. He cleaned out the town. He sniffed them out somehow."

"Did he get your speed tiles, Mabel?"

"No, he didn't. The day after your opening, I put them in my safety deposit box. At the bank." She looked at me sympathetically. "He used you, John. You know that, don't you? He used your paintings of speed tiles to find out who had them."

"Why, Mabel? How did you know?"

"Bullfrog is an evil man, John. He always has been. The worst of them. His greed, his need. His overwhelming need."

"Ursulla said his name was Butler."

"Yes. He was with us in Singapore. A long time ago. In Singapore, before the sand."

I took out Ursulla's journal. "Mabel, Hilllary took this from Ursulla's apartment the day she died."

"The journal."

"Yes. Hilllary told me Ursulla wanted me to have it."

"Yes, she told me that too."

"But maybe you should have it. You see, it doesn't make much sense to me. It's written in Dutch."

Mabel sighed. She turned her head and looked at me. "Sense, John? No. It's never going to make any sense, no matter what the language. No. Never."

"What happened in Singapore, Mabel? What is all this about the sand?"

She looked into my eyes, thinking, deciding. I saw uncertainty in her eyes. Finally, she closed them and took a deep breath. "Not here, John. Come to my house tonight. Bring the journal. Bring Ted with you. I'm worried about Ted."

I picked up Ted at his house just before dark. There was fog rolling in off of Lake Michigan, billowing slowly up the river, brushing past Ted's house. The fog seemed to amplify the mournful wail of the fog horn. It blared in the distance where the Kalamazoo River emptied into Lake Michigan, moaning, crying at the grave of Singapore. Ted climbed into the car for the short drive to Mabel's house. "So, what do you think?" he asked.

"About what?"

"About Bullfrog and the speed tiles."

"I guess they're pretty important to him," I answered. I put the car in gear and backed out of Ted's driveway.

Ted took a speed tile out of his pocket. I glanced at it, the yellow nubs glowing softly. I felt a familiar longing mixed with revulsion. I wished it were mine, but I resented its power over me. "I can see why," said Ted. "They're beautiful."

The foghorn blared.

Surprised by his description, I looked at Ted's face. The faint glow was reflected in his eyes. He looked at it longingly. "Ted, back off. You're gonna get hooked on those things."

"Hooked?" He laughed then put it back in his pocket. "I don't think you've quite grasped the importance of these things. They're very powerful."

"Powerful? Yes. But also dangerous."

The deep bass foghorn sounded again.

"Agh!" he scoffed.

"Ted, you've seen what they do."

"John, they're like a gift. They're like a miracle…the promise of eternal life, John. Think of it."

"Yeah, and it scares the hell out of me."

The foghorn moaned.

I turned onto Holland Street on the way to Mabel's house. She lived up-river, closer to the insistent moan of the foghorn.

"You know," said Ted. "Bullfrog's going about it all wrong."

"What do you mean?"

"Hunting them down, prospecting for them, stealing them, hoarding them."

"I still don't get what you mean."

"The grid, John. Why collect a few here, a few there when we can simply manufacture them?"

"Ted, it's just a sculpture. A fiction. It's not real."

"But it is, John. It is real."

The foghorn wailed.

We pulled into Mabel's driveway and stopped. I put the gearshift in park and looked at Ted. "Ted, what the hell are you talking about?"

"I built one, John. A speed tile birthing grid. It's in my workshop at home. A real one."

"Ted, how..."

"I used the plans from Mabel's attic. I used Pentium processors, a hundred of them. One in each compartment."

The foghorn moaned.

I couldn't believe my ears. He actually thought he built one. A working grid. His eyes were wide, ecstatic. He was bursting with excitement. "Ted, you gotta be kidding."

"All I need is the slab to power it. All I need is the slab from your attic."

"But it's gone, Ted. The slab's gone."

"But I'm gonna find it. I'm gonna install my grid on Whalesback and take it to South Manitou Island. I'm gonna harness it and manufacture speed tiles...mold them out of the singing sands of South Manitou Island."

The foghorn groaned.

I looked at him, afraid. I thought of his forty-foot houseboat, Whalesback. I remembered the big open living area below. With a shock of unexpected clarity, I imagined the grid sitting on the floor in a pile of sand...(A premonition?) I pictured the slab, the awful slab, straining at the steel beams of the ceiling, the dripping, slimy tendrils hanging down, tickling, teasing, brushing the empty compartments of the grid, oozing unnatural life into the sand below. I saw Ted's face, kneeling on the floor, watching, waiting. I saw madness in his eyes. "Ted, no..."

"John, yes."

The foghorn bellowed.

Mabel had changed out of her black outfit into a cheerful, brightly colored, flower print dress. She was brewing a pot of tea when we went into her house.

"How are you holding up Mabel?" I asked.

"Oh, I'm okay, I guess. I'm going to miss Ursulla, though. We go back a long way you know."

"All the way back to Singapore?" I asked.

"Yes, Singapore. A long time ago." She looked past me, seeing the past, remembering.

Ted went up to Mabel and gave her a gentle hug. "Hang in there, Mom."

Mabel looked up at me. "You know, I'm not really Ted's mother."

"I know."

"His mother died the day he was born."

"You raised me like a mother," said Ted. He looked at me. "I only learned the real truth a couple of years ago, when I found that speed tile in Mabel's attic."

"Oh, speed tiles, speed tiles…" moaned Mabel. "I'm so tired of hearing about speed tiles." Mabel leaned shakily on the back of a chair.

Ted put his arms around her shoulders. "Why don't we sit down?" The teapot started whistling. "I'll get the tea, Mom. Sit down. It's been a long day."

Ted helped Mabel to a seat, then went into the kitchen to get the tea. Mabel looked up at me. "I'm afraid Ted is much too interested in speed tiles for his own good. I'm worried about him."

I was worried about him too. "What are speed tiles, Mabel? Do you know? Do you know where they came from?"

Ted came into the room with the tea. "Does that journal of Ursulla's provide any hints?"

"Maybe. It's just kind of hard to decipher." I looked at Mabel. "I was hoping Mabel could help translate it."

"I'm afraid the journal doesn't tell you where they came from," said Mabel. "But it does tell what they did to Singapore."

I handed Mabel the journal. She opened it and flipped through a few pages. "I've studied this journal before. Ursulla and I have read every page. It was written by Ursulla's father. He was a banker and business-man in Singapore before the sand."

"What's all this about the sand?" I asked.

"The sand is what destroyed Singapore. Buried it."

"The dunes are moving all the time," I explained. "They're constantly shifting. But it took years, decades, for the sand to cover Singapore."

"Years?" said Mabel. "No. Singapore was covered in less than a week. Buried. It was horrible."

"A week?"

"Let me start at the beginning," said Mabel, thoughtfully. "As you probably know from Kit Lane's books, Singapore was a lumber town. Quite successful for a time. Ships would sail out of Singapore loaded with lumber from the sawmills, especially after the dry summer of 1871. That was the year Chicago burned, and Holland, and Manistee. Manistee burned the same day as Chicago. Did you know that?"

"So all these towns needed lumber to rebuild," said Ted.

"That's right. And the forests around here were thick with trees. We thought they would never run out."

"But they did, didn't they?" I added.

"Yes, they did, and Singapore fell into hard times." Mabel got very serious. She frowned. "And then, the speed tiles were found."

"In the dunes?" I asked.

"Yes. A few at first, here and there. Men found them very helpful. They seemed to make things weigh less. They made men feel powerful, inde-structible. Men traded them and kept them locked up, either at home or at Ursulla's father's bank, the Singapore Bank. They were considered very valuable. But they did bad things to people, too. They made men drunk with greed." Mabel shook her head and frowned, remembering.

"But not women?" I asked.

"No, not women. You see, women liked them too, but for different reasons. Women liked them for their beauty, not for their power…for the companionship they provided, for the stories they would tell."

"Stories?" I asked.

"Each speed tile has its own secrets, its own personality."

"Do your speed tiles tell stories?" I asked.

"Oh yes," Mabel smiled, a sad smile. "They are very interesting. But most of all, women liked them because they make us feel younger and more beautiful. Look at me. I'm 137 years old. My speed tiles have kept me young." She looked up at me proudly.

"Bullfrog too," I added.

"Yes. Bullfrog too," she frowned again. 'But he hasn't aged at all since Singapore." Her brow wrinkled in thought. 'That's very peculiar."

"So, what happened in Singapore?" asked Ted.

"Many speed tiles were discovered around the dunes of Singapore. They were most often found with Indian artifacts, shards of pottery, arrow heads, primitive tools used by the Ottawa and Potowotomie Indian tribes that lived in this region for centuries. Some think speed tiles are magic charms made by the Indians. But I don't think so. I think they were left here for some other purpose. Left here even before the Indians.

"Men found them in the dunes. They treasured them. They traded them and used them in their work. They used them as you would currency. They bought and sold things with them. And they even gambled with them. Speed tiles became a symbol of power and wealth."

Mabel opened the journal to the picture of Bullfrog holding the canvas bag. "This picture was taken after a desperate night of gambling at the boarding house that you can see in the background of this picture. Bullfrog's bag is full of speed tiles. He won them in a card game. Many people resented Bullfrog and suspected that he used marked cards in the game, cheating them out of their precious speed tiles." She shook her head sadly, then brushed her hand absently over the old picture of Bullfrog.

"But people just went looking for more speed tiles. As the sands shifted, new pockets of speed tiles would be uncovered. But fewer and fewer speed tiles were found in the dunes as time went on, so, eventually, people stopped looking. Of course Bullfrog's speed tiles became even more valuable.

"But Bullfrog couldn't get enough of them. He was more greedy than most." Mabel seemed to direct this last comment at Ted. "He needed them like most of us need food."

I glanced up at Ted but he didn't seem to relate Mabel's description of Bullfrog's need with himself. I looked back at Mabel.

"He bought an old schooner, the F. B. Stockbridge. He bought it from the Stockbridge family before Francis Stockbridge went off to Washington. He was a U.S. senator, you know."

I thought of the Sea Captain painting, of Captain Jeremiah Butler and his sandwich board resume. The Stockbridge. That was one of the ships on his resume.

"He used it for hauling freight from port to port around Lake Michigan, mostly lumber, but he kept searching for signs of speed tiles at other locations. He looked mostly on the eastern shores of Lake Michigan, in the towering dunes that line this coastline. Finally, he found them. First in Leland where he discovered people trading speed tiles and using them in their work. Much like we did in Singapore.

"People were naturally secretive about where they got their speed tiles." Mabel leaned forward and whispered: "They have that effect on people you know." She leaned back again. "But Bullfrog was persistent. He finally discovered that the speed tiles came from South Manitou Island, from an area of drifting sand and abundant forests, an area much like Singapore.

"Bullfrog's boat, as well as most of the ships on Lake Michigan, used the natural harbor of South Manitou Island as a resting point, a place of shelter from storms at sea. They would also carry wood from the sawmills on South Manitou Island. In those days, there was quite a thriving community on the island. Hundreds of people. Farmers, lumber men, and a life-saving station run by the government.

"Bullfrog spent a summer on South Manitou, prospecting for speed tiles. Oh, his ship did continue the business of shipping lumber from the island. He hired a captain and crew to work the ship." Mabel shook her head and looked up at Ted again. "But Bullfrog was obsessed with speed tiles. He had to have them." She turned to me. "And finally, he found them.

"It was on the far western tip of the island, an unpopulated area in the dunes. As you know, the sand hills are very high on that island. Hundreds of feet high. The highest dunes in the State of Michigan except for the Sleeping Bear dunes on the mainland. The dunes separated a vast forest of cedar trees from Lake Michigan...a virgin forest of monumental trees that is there, even today.

"He found it in a dune leading down to the forest. The shifting sands must have uncovered it. Among Indian artifacts and primitive tools was a large cache of speed tiles. They may have been stored there centuries ago, held in reserve...maybe hidden for some purpose we will never know. From what Ursulla's father wrote, they were stacked loosely in grid-like structures like the one you built, John. The structures were old and decayed, but the speed tiles were in very good condition, silvery with golden nubs, shiny and seductive."

I saw Ted's eyes brighten at the mention of grid-like structures.

"Bullfrog secretly mined the trove of speed tiles. He packed them tightly in stout wooden boxes built from the cedar trees on the island and he waited for his ship to make port. It was the autumn of 1889. Bullfrog loaded his speed tiles onto his boat and set sail for Chicago, his wealth and his power safely below.

"But he never got to Chicago. The weather forced him into Singapore. It was early winter and the snow and ice kept the Stockbridge sealed into the harbor, the speed tiles packed away in the hold of his ship. When it became apparent that he would not sail, he dismissed his crew, but Bullfrog stayed on in Singapore to be close to his ship, close to his speed tiles.

"But speed tiles don't take well to tight packages. They have to breath and be free."

"Yes, I know," I said, remembering my speed tile. "The speed tile I found in the dunes burst out of my briefcase, and through my roof."

Mabel continued. "Speed tiles are very powerful. You could imagine the repressed power of several thousand speed tiles, kept captive in boxes in the hold of a ship…"

Mabel paused to take a sip of her tea, thinking, remembering. She looked sad.

"By 1889 Singapore was falling into ruin and losing its population to nearby Saugatuck. My father and Ursulla's father were already making plans to move to Saugatuck, but they wanted to take their buildings with them. The use of speed tiles to move buildings was not uncommon and the few speed tiles Bullfrog could not horde, the ones left behind in Singapore in the possession of families like mine and Ursulla's, were going to be put to use to move us to Saugatuck.

"Bullfrog stayed at one of the boarding houses near the deserted sawmill. I remember him being very nasty and irritable. He wanted to get to Chicago, but the weather wouldn't let him. All winter he fumed and sulked, every day, going to his ship to check on his precious cargo. He drank heavily, and gambled and bragged about his wealth and his power. My father would occasionally play cards with him. So would Ursulla's father. But they didn't trust him. Not many did trust him.

"The weather was especially harsh that winter. The snow blew in drifts making the dunes look like massive mounds of ice. The wind blew constantly, in icy blasts off the lake. The ice formed for as far as the eye could see, a barren landscape of white over Lake Michigan.

"But for reasons we could not understand, the ice did not form around the Stockbridge. There were three other ships in the harbor and they were solidly locked in, frozen in place by the ice. The Stockbridge floated free at her dock, a pool of water six or eight feet around her. But that wasn't all."

Mabel's eyes opened wide with wonder. "The Stockbridge scared us. It rocked and it pitched, it pulled at its moorings. At first we thought it was the wind, the waves, but the boat seemed to be alive, restless. Bullfrog's swaggering manner, his bragging ways, soon gave us hints to the mysterious cargo on the Stockbridge, but Bullfrog hoarded his secret along with his speed tiles.

"Finally, one stormy night, the Stockbridge pitched and rolled more than usual in the icy wind. She strained at the lines that held her. She actually lifted clear out of the water and slammed down hard on her hull, again and again. Bullfrog was in a panic. He didn't know what to do to contain his unruly ship.

"The speed tiles encased in their cedar cases could be contained no longer. Finally, they exploded. Speed tiles burst out of the hold of the Stockbridge, instantly sinking her at her mooring. Then the storm worsened. It was as if the speed tiles, angry at the greed of men, brought that awful, blinding white blizzard." A tear came to her eye and she absently dabbed it with her handkerchief. She whispered angrily. "The speed tiles brought devastation to Singapore. Bullfrog's greed buried us."

She looked up, her memories stoking her emotions. "Swirling tornadoes of snow and sand and ice beat mercilessly on our doors, pelting our windows, ripping off our shingles. For five days, snow and sand piled high on our homes, massive dunes moving relentlessly like living creatures, encompassing us, burying us. Desperate men shoveled night and day, hoping to keep the sand at bay.

"In a panic, seeing the doom that was enveloping Singapore, my father used his speed tiles to lift our house in the howling wind, lift it out of the suffocating sand, onto the ice of the river, away from the wind and the dunes. He moved us upstream, helped by friends and neighbors, to the relative safety of Saugatuck, to where we sit right now. Ursulla's family did the same."

Mabel's emotional telling of the demise of Singapore was hard on her. She closed her eyes, remembering, resting. She looked tired and drained, but Ted and I were mesmerized by her story.

"That sounds horrible, Mabel," I said. "You must have been terrified."

She shook her head and looked up at us. "Terror? Oh yes. Terror. It was frightening. I thought the sand would kill us. I still remember the wailing and the screams as we left for Saugatuck in the blinding snow, the stinging sand on our faces. Families desperate to save their homes shoveled and dug until they were exhausted. Some were lost, falling exhausted into their houses, trying to escape from the mountain of sand moving over them." Mabel sobbed quietly, then continued. "Some families were never seen again, buried alive in the silent tombs of their homes."

"What happened to Bullfrog?" asked Ted.

Mabel sighed. She looked up at Ted. "Bullfrog? I don't know. I thought he was lost too, until I saw him here, in Saugatuck. I thought the sand buried him and his destructive greed for good."

"What about the speed tiles?" asked Ted.

She shook her head, impatient now. "Yes. The speed tiles. Always the speed tiles." She sighed and opened the journal to a new page. "It's right here. The speed tiles. Ursulla's father saw it. I didn't. He wrote it down here. But I don't know if its true. I don't see how it could be. You see, Ursulla's father saw it through the blinding snow, as he readied his building for the trip up the river. He saw swirling tornadoes of sand and water and ice rising up out of the sunken Stockbridge. He said he saw speed tiles in the maelstrom, speed tiles rising with the wind, twisting and turning and flying around and around, a dull yellow glow coming from the eye of the storm."

"So they must be there," said Ted. "They must be under water, in the river."

"No, Ted, they're not there. Months later, men from Singapore, the survivors; they dragged the river bottom looking for Bullfrog's unruly cargo. Oh, they found a few speed tiles, here and there, in the sunken wreckage of Bullfrog's ship, but not the shipload they expected.

"Ursulla's father wrote that on the night the Stockbridge sank, he saw these speed tile tornadoes, these unnatural whirlpools, rise up out of the water and move slowly north and west, out over Lake Michigan. He wrote that these tornadoes somehow moved against the weather. They moved impossibly north."

Chapter 18

The Voyage

Vacation time…finally. Mom and Dad spent that whole morning loading stuff onto Dancer. Hannah and me were still packing, trying to limit our clothes to one small duffel bag each. There's not much room on a 30-foot sailboat. The space is smaller than my bedroom at home and four of us would be sharing it for three weeks. Dad says it promotes togetherness.

"All you need is a swim suit and a couple of T-shirts," said Dad.

Dad was already wearing his sailing uniform: a pair of red shorts and a gray t-shirt, the same outfit he would be wearing for the next three weeks.

"Dad, I hope you brought more than one gray t-shirt," I teased, holding my nose.

"Why? It's summer. Who needs clothes?"

Mom rolled her eyes and shook her head.

We dropped Mom and Dad off at the boat. They wanted to spend the morning putting stuff away and getting the boat ready for our voyage. Hannah and I drove back home to finish packing and to pick up the morning mail.

"Hill, let's sneak Spinnaker onto the boat."

"No, Hannah. Dad'll kill us. He doesn't want any animals this trip."

"Yes he does. He just won't admit it."

"He'll make us come all the way back here when he finds out."

"He won't find out, Hill. At least not until we're out in the lake. Then it'll be too late. He won't turn back just to take the cat home."

Hannah packed some kitty litter and a few cans of cat food in the bottom of a boat bag. She called Steve and Mary, our neighbors, to tell them that there would be one less animal for them to feed while we were gone. Then she got a pillow case to hide Spinnaker in.

We finished packing our clothes and threw them in the back of the car. I went out to the road to get the mail. The weekly issue of the Comical Record was supposed to come out that morning and Dad wanted to see what Todd Camper wrote about his show at Bullfrog's gallery. Of course, a lot had happened since Todd wrote the story. The gallery wasn't even open now that Bullfrog skipped town.

"Come on, Hill. It's getting late. I want to go sailing."

"Shut up, Hannah. Dad told me to bring the mail."

Hannah threw the duffels into the back of the car and went inside to say good-by to Sandbar.

"I wish we could bring Sandbar too," she said as she hugged him.

"Yeah, right."

I thought about the last time we brought Sandbar on the boat. Every time we tacked, the boat would heel over in the other direction and Sandbar would slide across the floor of the cabin to the other side looking confused and sad with his ears down and his tail between his legs. Sandbar hated sailing.

I went into my room to see if I had forgotten anything. I stood at the doorway and looked around. I walked over to my dresser and kneeled down. I opened the bottom drawer where I kept stuff I never wear any more and reached way back into the far corner and pulled out Ursulla's purse. The speed tiles. I should bring the speed tiles. They had just begun talking to me, giving me hints of their different personalities. I was starting to understand why Ursulla called them her "children." I opened the purse and saw the golden yellow glow of the nubs softly pulsing. Maybe I could learn more about them on the cruise. I stuffed the purse in my pocket and ran out to the car.

Hannah handed me Spinnaker.

"How are we gonna get this cat past Dad?"

"Leave it to me, Hill."

We drove to the Saugatuck Yacht Club and parked the car under a tree. It would sit there for the next three weeks until we got home. Hannah tried to stuff Spinnaker into the pillow case, but he was all legs and claws, hissing and yowling. He didn't want to go in the pillow case.

"Hannah, don't hurt him."

"I'm not hurting him. He's just being a jerk. Spinnaker, calm down. We gotta hide you from Dad."

Hannah finally got the cat in the sack, then she twisted the top and put a twist-tie around it so Spinnaker couldn't get out. Spinnaker yowled. We looked at each other and started laughing.

"It's okay, Spinnaker," I said, trying to soothe the savage beast.

"Spinnaker, shhh," said Hannah.

Spinnaker hissed.

"Now let's stuff him in the boat bag," said Hannah. If he cries, we'll just make lots of noise while we get on the boat."

I looked out at Dancer at the dock. Dad was waving to us. "Come on girls, time to shove off," he yelled.

Dad had the diesel engine on, so maybe he wouldn't hear Spinnaker. We locked the car and started toward Dancer. Hannah carried the boat bag with our cat in it. Spinnaker howled. We looked at each other and started giggling uncontrollably.

"It'll never work, Hannah."

"Yes it will. Come on."

We walked down the dock. I was following Hannah and I saw the boat bag bulging and moving. How would we ever get away with this?

Spinnaker moaned.

"Start singing, Hill. Real loud."

"Singing what? What should I sing?"

She looked at a row boat tied to the dock and started singing, "row, row, row your boat, gently down the stream…"

"Come on, Hill. Sing loud."

Spinnaker joined in, howling in protest.

"Merrily, merrily, merrily, merrily, life is but a dream…" we sang, giggling and laughing down the dock, the bag squirming and bulging.

Dad was on the bow ready to cast off the lines. Mom was at the wheel ready to back out. Dad looked at us as if we were insane, but he didn't seem to notice the bag, alive with a yowling, wriggling cat. We sang louder but the cat meowed louder too.

"Let's go sailing," yelled Dad over the sound of our song and the diesel.

We got on the boat and went immediately below, laughing and trying to muffle the sound of our cat. Just as we got Spinnaker to the V-berth, he burst out of the bag, arched his back and hissed loudly.

"Shhhh," said Hannah to the cat.

"I think we made it," I said.

I heard Dad moving around the boat, coiling lines and getting the sails ready to raise. When he finished, I saw him heading for the companionway to come below.

"Quick, Hannah. Here he comes!"

Hannah pushed the hissing cat behind the bulkhead, out of Dad's sight. Dad came down the stairs into the cabin.

"So, girls, did you forget anything?"

"No. We got everything," I said looking nervously into the corner.

"Yeah, everything," said Hannah while with one hand she tried to keep Spinnaker in the corner.

"How about Spinnaker?" asked Dad. "You didn't forget to bring Spinnaker, did you?"

Hannah and I looked at each other in surprise. He knew all along. Spinnaker hissed and jumped out from behind the bulkhead.

"Dad! " said Hannah. "How did you know?"

"You guys do this every year. You always sneak an animal on board. I'm just glad it's not Sandbar this time."

"I couldn't fit him in the boat bag," said Hannah.

"Hill, did you get the Commercial Record?"

"Yeah, it's right here." I fished the mail out of the boat bag and handed it to Dad. "How are people gonna see your show if Bullfrog's gallery is closed?"

"You know, Hill, now that I'm on the boat, I don't even care. I'll worry about it when we get back."

We went up to the cockpit and Dad sat next to Mom at the wheel. We were just passing the Coral Gables on our way out to Lake Michigan. Dad thumbed through the paper and found the article Todd wrote about the show. I watched him as he read it.

"Ha!" he said. "Todd liked the show. He says it was 'a thoughtful and mysterious body of work.'"

He read some more, smiling.

"He says something about my 'fertile imagination,' and how 'incredible it is that all of Hunter's work was sparked by a little metal artifact he found in the dunes.'"

Dad kept reading, then his smile faded.

"Oh oh. He tells about the dunes and describes where I found the speed tile. He writes about the powers that I imagine the speed tile to have."

"So?" asked Mom.

"He kind of pokes fun at me."

"Well, it is a pretty outrageous story."

"Yeah. I guess."

Dad kept reading, more serious now.

"He writes about the grid I built and how I found the speed tile in a similar grid in the dunes. He says the speed tile is supposed to have far-reaching powers that defy gravity and that speed tiles contain the secret of eternal life."

"Whoa, heavy stuff," said Mom.

"He kind of writes it tongue in cheek. There's a picture of the grid with the slab hanging over it." Dad held up the paper to show Mom.

"Good picture," said Mom.

"Let's see," said Hannah.

Dad handed Hannah the paper, a look of concern on his face. "People around here either know about speed tiles or they don't. The article's harmless for the people who don't know, but for those who do know…"

"What do you mean?" asked Mom.

"It's like gold fever, Marsh. People might read between the lines and think there's more speed tiles out there."

We rounded the bend in the river and started down the channel that cut through Singapore. Dad raised the mainsail and looked out over the lake. There was a 15 knot breeze blowing from the west. It was a perfect wind for sailing north.

As we came to the dunes where Singapore once stood, I noticed a lot of people and activity. At first I thought it was a picnic or a beach party.

"Dad, look."

Dad went below for the binoculars and scanned the dunes.

"Unbelievable."

"What is it?" asked Mom.

"They're digging."

"Digging?"

Dad shook his head and handed me the binoculars. I focused on a man digging frantically. I think it was George Steffans, the man who owned the Keewatin. Behind him I saw a Jeep drive up with two men in it and shovels sticking out of the back. I didn't recognize them. I panned to the left and saw a family digging in the sand, searching. It looked like Courtney from my class with her brother and her father. I panned some more and saw Linus Beagle. He didn't have his police uniform on, but he did have a shovel. He was digging next to an old house foundation sticking out of the sand. I panned back to the right and saw two men arguing. They both had shovels. They both wanted to dig in the same place. One of them was Jack Lancaster, my boss from the Auction House Restaurant.

"Dad, what's going on?"

Dad looked kind of sad as Mom steered the boat out of the channel and turned north. The wind filled the mainsail and Mom shut off the engine. Hannah pulled on the jib sheet, unfurling the big head sail. It opened with a whoosh and the boat accelerated, heeling to the right, leaning toward Singapore.

We watched silently as our friends and neighbors dug in the sand, their voices muted but urgent. Their shouts sounded frantic, desperate. I put my hand in my pocket and felt Ursulla's purse, safe, secure.

"What are they looking for?" asked Hannah.

Dad turned to her. "Eternal life, Hannah. They're looking for eternal life."

We sailed north, away from the madness in Singapore. The sun was out and the wind continued to blow from the west. It was a perfect day for sailing. Dancer soon put Dad in a better mood.

"Do you believe this day?" said Dad. "We haven't touched a sail since we came out of the harbor. This is great." He was sitting in his favorite position, at the wheel with his back to the Lifesling and his feet stretched out across the aft cockpit seat. From there, he could scan the horizon every once in a while to see if we were gonna hit any other boats. But the lake was pretty empty. We passed another boat once in a while, but most of the boats were near harbors. "This sailing stuff is hard work, huh Hill?" Dad yawned.

"Tito's doing all the work," I said, pointing to the auto pilot.

Dad looked up at the sky. "Yeah, but we'll pay for this. Lake Michigan is never this perfect. It'll get us back."

"Enjoy it while you can," said Mom, who was lying on the port cockpit cushion, sunning herself.

We passed Holland harbor first with the "Big Red" lighthouse to starboard. Next came Port Sheldon, only about five miles further.

Another ten miles and Grand Haven's lighthouse went by on the right. Slowly, the naked image of Bullfrog floating over his speed tiles faded to the back of my mind as the sun traced an arc across the sky.

Six hours into the sail we passed Muskegon, about thirty miles from home. It was getting late now. We sailed for two more hours, then Dad took over from Tito and pulled into White Lake. We had logged about 38 miles on our first day of sailing. Not very far for a car, but it seemed like a thousand miles on Dancer.

As the sun set into Lake Michigan, Dad dropped the anchor in a protected cove in White Lake. The wind had died to a whisper and Dancer rocked us gently to sleep.

The next morning Hannah and I slept late but we heard Dad pulling up the anchor at dawn.

"What's the hurry Dad?" asked Hannah, sleepily.

"Gotta take advantage of this great wind," answered Dad.

We slept for another two hours but Dad dragged us out of bed as Pentwater went by. Eating a breakfast bagel, we watched the endless Michigan dunes roll by along the shoreline. We passed Ludington and waved at the huge 500-foot car ferry just coming into the harbor from Manitowoc, Wisconsin. Dad produced a documentary about the Ludington carferry service once. It still played for the passengers every day during its crossings.

The wind was still blowing steadily from the west pushing the trauma of Ursulla's death further from my mind. We passed Manistee with the sun directly overhead, our skin turning brown. Spinnaker eased into the routine of boat life, napping under the dodger covering the companionway. Hannah napped too. Mom read a book. Dad fussed and fiddled around with things on the boat, fixing things and organizing the stuff in the boat's lockers. I worked on my journal, writing about the voyage and drawing pictures like in a comic book. I thought of Ursulla's journal and wondered if someone would be reading mine 100 years from now. I kept my speed tiles hidden in a locker under my bunk.

Tito steered us north, past Portage Lake, then Arcadia. The harbors on the Michigan shore are pretty close together, so pleasure boats like ours are no more than 15 or 20 miles from a safe harbor if the weather turns bad. In a power boat, 15 miles can take a half hour or less, but in a sailboat, 15 miles takes two and a half or three hours, depending on the wind. Dad says sailboats have a limit to how fast they can go because of the shape of the hull. Even under diesel power, Dancer can only go about six knots, or seven miles per hour. "It's the voyage, not the destination," said Dad.

The sun was setting. We had been sailing since just after 6 a.m. that morning…15 hours. We were all exhausted from being outside in the sun all day, even though we didn't really do anything but lay around. We had already covered about 80 miles that day.

"Let's pull into Frankfort," said Dad. "It's too late to sail for the island."

As Dad took over steering from Tito, we could barely see South Manitou Island on the horizon, about 20 miles away, straight north.

Dad turned into the Frankfort harbor channel and turned on the engine while Hannah and I took down the main and furled the jib. Mom called the harbor master at the Frankfort Municipal Marina on the radio and asked if they had a slip for the night. They directed us to a vacant space and Dad eased the boat slowly into the slip.

It was always exciting going into a new harbor. It felt like we had sailed across an ocean to an exotic new port even though we were only about 120 miles north of where we lived. It was only three hours by car, but it took us two days to get here by boat.

A man from the slip next to us helped us dock. "Where you from?" he asked.

"Saugatuck," answered Dad. "Sailed here from White Lake today."

"Long ways in a sailboat. Where you headed?"

"South Manitou. We're gonna sail there tomorrow."

"Don't think so. Wind's supposed to shift, come out of the east tomorrow."

"Is that right?"

"Yep."

There are no marinas on South Manitou Island, but there is a big crescent-shaped bay for anchoring that offers protection from all directions except the east. Dad says it's dangerous to anchor there with an east wind. The waves get really big and without protection, Dancer could wind up on the beach.

"Well, we'll just have to see how it looks in the morning," said Dad.

Mom had started marinating some chicken strips in teriyaki and honey earlier in the day. Dad started the grill that hung on the stern rail and Mom opened a box of Uncle Ben's wild rice. We had dinner while the sun sizzled into Lake Michigan.

Mom looked at Dad and sipped a little wine. "Exactly why are we going to South Manitou?" asked Mom. "Is it about speed tiles or slabs or what?"

Surprised by the question, Dad looked up from his plate. "Slabs?"

"Yes. Are we chasing your slab or are we on vacation?"

"Why do you ask that? We always go to South Manitou. We're on vacation."

"We never covered 80 miles in one day on vacation. That was a long sail today. It's like you're in a hurry."

Dad looked thoughtful, then he smiled and blushed. "I don't know. I guess I'm still curious…deep down I'm still curious. But another part of me just wants to let it go. Sometimes I wish I had never seen a speed tile."

"Are you gonna keep making speed tiles, Dad?" asked Hannah.

"I seriously doubt it, Hannah. I think I got speed tiles out of my system now."

I looked up at him, thinking of Ursulla's speed tiles, her purse. Now they were my speed tiles.

"You got speed tiles out of your system, Huh?" said Mom. "So, what are we gonna do when we get to the island? Look for speed tiles? Search for your long lost slab?"

Dad laughed. "No, we're not gonna search for speed tiles. I've had enough speed tiles for a lifetime. I told you, we're gonna just hang out on the beach, drink beer and hike the island. We're gonna vacation...we're gonna relax."

"And lie in the sun and get a great tan," said Hannah.

"What about Wong?" asked Mom. "You gonna look for Wong?"

Dad looked up, blushed again. "Wong?" He shook his head, looked up at the ceiling, looked down at his wine glass. He looked like he was trying to avoid the question.

"Yeah, Wong. Are you gonna look for him on the island?"

"Wong, Wong, Wong!" he said. "Okay. Yes! I am gonna look for Wong. I told you. I'm still curious about all this. Aren't you?"

Mom set her wine glass down. "Curious? No. I'm not curious. I'm just scared. I'm afraid of all this speed tile stuff. It's so...unnatural." Mom leaned over the table closer to Dad. "John, let's skip South Manitou Island this year. Let's sail to Beaver Island."

Dad's head snapped up at Mom's suggestion. "Skip South Manitou? No way, Marsh."

"Why not? If not Beaver, then we could sail into Grand Traverse Bay. We can go to Northport."

"I don't want to skip South Manitou." Dad looked at Hannah and me. "You guys don't want to skip the island do you?"

"I don't care," said Hannah. "I just wanna get some sun."

"I like South Manitou," I said. "I'd rather not skip it."

"See, Marsh," said Dad. He reached over and held Mom's hand. "Okay. I'll admit it. I didn't really even think about it until you brought it up. I'm curious about this Wong guy. And Ted. He said he was gonna come to the island too, with Whalesback. And Dick Beaver said he was coming here to look for Bullfrog...,"

"Oh great!" said Mom, pulling her hand away. "We can have a big reunion." She poured another glass of wine.

"It'll be more like a rematch if Bullfrog and Wong get together," I said.

"Whatever," said Dad. "It should be interesting, whatever happens. I'd like to see what Wong's after." He looked at Mom again. "Probably nothing will happen. Wong's probably not even here. Will said his grant was canceled. We'll just stay for a couple days, then we'll go to Northport. Okay?"

"Okay!" said Mom, getting up from the table. "You're the captain. Aye, aye, sir. May I be excused, sir? I'd like to go to bed now."

Mom was pissed. She went into the V-berth to get ready for bed.

Dad sighed and looked at Hannah and me. "I'm really beat. I'm going to bed, too. Don't forget to do the dishes before you go to bed."

"Aye, aye, sir," said Hannah.

Dad gave her a dirty look.

As the sky darkened, Hannah and I did the dishes and cleaned up the galley area. One thing about living on a small boat is that it doesn't take much to clean it.

I got the cave that night. That's the berth that's tucked in right under the port cockpit seat. It didn't have much head room, but it had a thick, soft cushion; and my speed tiles were hidden under it. When everyone else fell asleep, I would take them out and play with them, hold them in my hands, feel them, one at a time. Maybe I would learn some of their secrets.

Hannah put the table away. It swung up on hinges and attached to the main bulkhead. With the table up she was able to pull the port quarter berth out and extend it into a double bed. It was the biggest bed on the boat but it took up most of the room in the main cabin.

We went to bed, stretching out head to head. Spinnaker circled the foot of Hannah's bed and finally settled down, purring loudly. I heard heavy breathing from the V-berth too. Mom and Dad were asleep.

"Hannah," I whispered.

"What do you want, dork?"

"Did you ever see a speed tile?"

"Dad made lots of them. Sure, I've seen 'em."

"No, I mean a real speed tile. Did you ever see one?"

"No, I never did. Why?"

"You want to see one?"

"What? You got one?"

"Shhh! You'll wake Mom and Dad. Yeah, I've got more than one. But it's a secret. You can't tell."

Hannah sat up and looked at me in the dim light. "Are you kidding, Hill? You really have speed tiles? Where'd you get 'em?"

"Shhh! From Bullfrog's basement. The night Suzie and I went there. They're really Ursulla's speed tiles. Bullfrog must have stole 'em."

"Let's see. I want to see one."

I pulled Ursulla's purse out from under my bunk. A dim yellow light escaped as I opened the purse. I shook one of the speed tiles out.

"Wow!" said Hannah. "Let's see."

Hannah reached for the speed tile. The yellow nubs brightened as Hannah took it in her hand. "It's so light, Hill"

"I know."

She looked closely at the speed tile. I could see the yellow light reflected in her eyes. "Ughhh," she said and dropped the speed tile on her pillow. "It moved."

"The nubs look like they move, but I don't think they really do."

"They look like worms, Hill, squirming little yellow worms…Which one plays Frank Sinatra?"

We giggled, remembering Dick Beaver's joke, trying not to be loud enough to wake Mom and Dad.

"I think its just something inside that makes 'em look like they're moving."

"Maybe we should take one apart, Hill."

"No, Hannah, I don't think so."

"How many do you have, Hill?"

"I don't know. A whole purse full."

"Can I have one?"

"No, Hannah, they're mine."

"You've got a whole purse full, Hill. Let me have just one. Please."

"No. Hannah, I can't. I need them. Each one's different."

"What? Need them? Need them for what?"

"I don't know. I just know that I need them. Ursulla wanted me to have them."

"Right. How would you know that? There's no way you could know that."

"I just know it. Now give it back, Hannah."

"Wait, let me look at it some more." Hannah stared at the speed tile. She kept squinting her eyes. "It's, like, blurry or something."

"I know. It's hard to keep it in focus."

"It feels…like, ahh, sad or something."

"I know, but some of them feel more happy."

"They do?" asked Hannah, looking at the speed tile again.

Dad yawned real loud and we heard him getting out of the V-berth.

"Quick, Hannah. Give it back."

"No, Hill. I want to keep it."

"Give it back!"

"Give what back?" asked Dad sleepily.

Hannah looked up at him. "Nothing, Dad."

I grabbed the speed tile off of her pillow and dropped it back in Ursulla's purse. I didn't think Dad could see it in the darkness of the cabin. Hannah looked back at me sharply. She really wanted it.

Dad went into the head. After he relieved himself, we heard him blow his nose. Dad sounds like a bellowing moose when he blows his nose and it always makes Hannah and me laugh.

"What are you guys laughing about?" he asked when he came out of the head.

"Your nose, Dad," said Hannah. "You probably woke up the whole marina."

Just then, a light went on in the boat in the next slip. Hannah and I went into hysterics when we saw the man who helped us dock stick his head up out of his hatch. We knew he was looking for the moose.

Chapter 19

Storm at Sea

I looked out over Lake Michigan…a gray summer morning. Low clouds and an offshore breeze confirmed our dock neighbor's forecast: east wind. Marcia and the girls were still sleeping. I woke up early so I took a walk to the Frankfort beach to look at the sea conditions first hand.

I sat on the sand and looked out over the gentle water. In Michigan, an east wind meant wave-free sailing. The biggest waves came from northerly winds which can build angry, rolling waves as high as ten to twelve feet over the two hundred mile length of Lake Michigan.

I couldn't see South Manitou Island from here. There was a big dune jutting out into the lake protecting the harbor entrance from northerly winds and blocking my view of the island. I thought of South Manitou and realized that Marcia was right. I wanted to go there so bad I could taste it. I fooled myself into thinking it was a vacation I was after on the mysterious island. As usual, Marcia cut through the crap and found the truth. I was looking for my slab…my lost speed tile.

But it was just curiosity that drove me, wasn't it? I wasn't addicted like Dick Beaver or Jeremiah Bullfrog. Or was I fooling myself about that too? I thought about Ted Clark. I wondered if he was bringing his grid. I looked out over the calm waters and realized that this would be a perfect day for Whalesback on Lake Michigan. The water was flat, and Ted's flat-bottomed River Queen houseboat liked flat water the best.

Ted could cruise at twelve knots in these seas, twice the speed as Dancer. He could get here in a day.

I hiked to the grocery store and filled up a cart with food. Sausage and eggs and cold cuts for sandwiches and more bagels and cream cheese and a big steak to cook on the grill, some big baking potatoes and some more wine and beer. I got two more blocks of ice for the cooler and a bag of cubes. I loaded all the groceries into one of the courtesy carts the store provides for visiting boaters and went back to the boat.

Marcia was relaxing in the cockpit with a cup of coffee when I got back. The girls were still sleeping. Our dock neighbor was standing next to our boat holding a cup of coffee and chatting with Marcia.

"East wind," he said, looking up at the sky.

"Yep," I said.

He took a sip of his coffee and scratched his head. He looked thoughtful. "You ever hear of moose up here in these parts."

"Moose?" I said.

"Moose?" repeated Mom.

"Didn't you hear it last night? The moose call?"

"Moose call? No. I slept like a baby."

Marcia and I gave each other a questioning look.

"Where you been?" Marcia asked me.

"Went to the beach. Then I went to the grocery store."

"Great! I'm hungry. What did you get?"

"Sausage, eggs, bagels."

I excused myself and started cooking breakfast, clattering pots and pans loudly to wake up my lazy daughters. Hannah covered her head with a pillow.

I turned on the VHF radio to get a weather forecast. I tuned in to a NOAA station to hear the monotone droning of the announcer delivering his no-frills forecast.

"Dad! Turn it off. I'm sleeping!" moaned Hannah, her head right below the radio.

"Shhh. I'm listening to the weather."

"Dad," said Hilllary sleepily. "We going to the island today?"

"I'll tell you in a minute, Hill. Let me listen."

As I cooked the sausages, the announcer cycled through his ten-minute forecast, recorded earlier that morning, and started repeating it again.

"You can shut it off now, Hannah."

East wind, ten to fifteen knots, clocking around to the south later in the day. Cloudy with a 50% chance of thunderstorms...typical summer forecast. There was almost always a chance of thunderstorms in the summer.

I put the sausages on a paper towel to drain some of the fat and scrambled up a bunch of eggs.

"Get up, Hannah. We need the table."

"Dad! I'm sleeping."

"Not any more you're not."

I cut the bagels in half and put them under the broiler to toast.

"Hurry up, Hannah. Breakfast is almost ready."

"God!"

Hannah finally got up and folded her big double bed back into the bulkhead, stuffing her bedding into the locker behind the cushions. She folded down the table, which occupied the same space that her bed was just in. Mom came down from the cockpit.

"We sailing today, Dad?" asked Hilllary, crawling out of the cave.

"I think so."

"We could stay here today," suggested Mom. "Frankfort's a fun town."

"No Indians to entertain us," I joked. The last time we were in Frankfort, the entire park in front of the marina was filled with Indians and frontiersmen. They were here for a weekend celebration and a re-enactment of a historic battle from the French and Indian War. We stayed for the whole weekend, setting sail only after the last teepee came down.

"Let's not stay," said Hill. "Let's go to the island."

"East wind," said Mom. "We can't anchor there in an east wind."

"It's supposed to shift to the south," I said.

"You believe that guy on the radio?" asked Marcia. "When was the last time NOAA got it right?"

Forecasting the weather on Lake Michigan was more chance than science. The best forecast came out of what you could see for yourself.

I dished out the scrambled eggs and sausage and put the bagels on a plate on the table. We all sat down to eat breakfast.

"Smells great, Dad," said Hannah.

"We could sail toward the island and if the wind doesn't switch, we could go to Leland," I suggested. "The east wind will make for some easy sailing today. No waves."

"Yeah, Mom," said Hilllary. "Let's not stay here. Let's go."

"What about the thunderstorms?" she asked. Mom was the cautious one in our family.

"There's always a chance of thunderstorms," I said, looking out the companionway at the gray sky. "I already restocked the ice and got some wine and beer. Let's go sailing."

The water was flat as we came out of the Frankfort channel. The east wind pushed us effortlessly northwest, around the big dune blocking our view of South Manitou. We rounded the dune and turned north, the island now in view. The sky was gray. It looked like rain.

Tito steered directly for South Manitou and Dancer glided quietly through the water at about five knots on a starboard tack. A light drizzle started and we put on our yellow foul weather gear: bib pants with suspenders, rubber boots and raincoats. Sailing in the rain was annoying but comfortable if we could stay dry.

As we sailed north, the wind didn't clock to the south as predicted, but cheated more to the northeast putting us on a beat into the wind instead of the more comfortable beam reach we had been on for the last two days. Dancer picked up speed and heeled at a dramatic 30 degree angle, slicing through the flat waters as the wind increased.

The drizzle turned to a more steady downpour and we heard the ominous sound of thunder in the distance.

Marcia looked at me. "Uh oh."

"What happened to the south wind NOAA promised us?" I asked.

"Dad!" said Hannah, excited by the possibility of a storm at sea. "Are we gonna have a storm?"

"Could be, Hannah."

I looked at the darkening sky. It looked like some weather was approaching from the west; a low pressure system rolling in to meet the high pressure we'd been enjoying these last few days, thunderstorm conditions for sure.

The wind continued to increase, heeling the boat more dramatically. I partially furled the jib and reefed the main to reduce sail and bring the boat more upright. The wind continued to increase, kicking up short, angry little waves.

"Dad," said Hilllary. "I'm scared."

"Nothing to be scared about," I said more confidently than I felt. "It's just a storm. No big deal."

"Yeah, Hill," said Hannah, the adventurer. "No big deal. This'll be fun."

"Should we turn back?" asked Marcia.

"Too late, Marsh. I wouldn't want to be in the channel with hard stuff all around us in this kind of weather. We're safer out here."

Spinnaker came to the companionway, looked at the pouring rain and meowed. He retreated back into the dry cabin. A gust of wind hit us and we heeled over even more.

"Whoa," I said. "You girls go below until this passes. And pass up my harness."

"I want to stay up here, Dad," said Hannah. "I can help."

"Okay. I could probably use some help. Marsh, pass up two harnesses."

Hilllary and Marcia went below. I relieved Tito at the wheel and turned more west to ease the pressure on the sails. Marcia passed up two harnesses. Hannah put hers on first, a snug nylon affair that fit over the shoulders and around the chest. It ended in two sturdy D-rings. Hannah clipped a six-foot tether onto the D-rings. She connected the other end to the toe rail. I did the same. If we were swept overboard, we would stay attached to the boat.

"Hannah, take over the wheel. I'm gonna reef again. Keep it at about 330 degrees, a little left of north."

Hannah steered while I went to work. I let the jib sheet loose and the sail flapped noisily in the wind. The boat snapped upright. I pulled on the furling line, rolling up the jib completely. I tightened up the mainsheet so the boom didn't have far to travel.

"Turn into the wind a little, Hannah," I yelled over the noise of the wind.

The mainsail flapped in the wind and the boom whipped back and forth over our heads. Without the pressure of the wind in the sail, it was easy to reef the main down to the second reef point.

"Okay, Hannah, turn right now."

We now had very little sail up, but the wind was howling at over 30 knots. If it got any worse, we could turn downwind and put the wind behind us. I thought about our location and was relieved to know that we had plenty of sea room if we turned downwind.

The thunder boomed and rain pelted our faces as we sailed into the storm. Lightning lit up the dark sky in the distance, coming closer. The storm was approaching.

I looked at Hannah. She was smiling, excited. Her eyes dancing, alive. "Dad, this is so cool."

"Yeah, right, Hannah."

She trusted me completely. She knew Dancer and she was confident that we could handle anything Lake Michigan could throw at us. I wasn't so sure. We were in the Manitou passage, a narrow, dangerous stretch of water littered with two hundred years of sunken ships once sailed by over-confident captains.

With a bang, the boom crashed over to the right. Dancer was knocked over on her starboard beam, throwing us off balance and onto the lifelines. I looked down to see water pouring into the cockpit over the gunwale. It was a sudden wind shift bringing a cold north wind. The storm had arrived. Lightning lit the sky as Dancer struggled back upright, a foot of water at our feet thankfully draining out the cockpit scuppers.

The knock-down sent books and dishes and everything loose flying down below. The companionway hatch opened and Marcia's frightened face appeared.

"Are we sinking?"

Hannah laughed nervously. I tried to appear confident, in control.

"Everything's okay. Just a wind shift."

I turned south, going back the way we came. The wind was now coming from the northwest and the seas were building fast. I decided to put the wind behind us on a broad reach, the most stable angle in these conditions. The wind was gusting at forty knots or more. I hoped the storm would pass quickly.

Hilllary joined Mom at the hatch. "You okay Dad?"

"Fine, Hill. Just a little wet."

Then I heard the loudest sound I've ever heard. It penetrated my body, filled my mind, made my hair stand on end. A lightning bolt. I ducked my head. So did Hannah. Afterwards, Marcia and Hilllary said it hit the water about twenty feet behind the boat. They said it was huge, wider than the boat. A big, bright, jagged column of white.

I looked at Hannah. She was pale, her smile gone, fear in her eyes. Marcia and Hilllary stared out at us in shock.

"We're okay, Hannah. It's just lightning." I tried to reassure her with a weak smile. "I'm gonna buy a lottery ticket as soon as I get to land!" I shouted to Marcia and Hilllary.

We sailed southeast through the driving rain and over the building waves. It wasn't the direction I wanted to go, but the boat was stable now and we could change directions when the storm passed. I couldn't believe this was the same lake we started sailing on that morning. The waves were six feet high now and still building. Thunder rumbled and crashed, lightning revealing the gray, churning landscape in brief, irregular flashes.

Off the port beam I noticed a shape, the dim profile of a boat struggling into the wind, a companion in the storm. A power boat. As we sailed in the opposite direction, surfing down the waves I watched as the shadow boat rode up the crests and pounded down into the troughs. A flat hull. Not a good boat to be on in these conditions. A boat like Ted Clark's Whalesback.

As the shadow passed, lightning lit the sky and I realized with a start that it was Whalesback. It was Ted Clark.

"Marcia!" I called.

Marcia came to the hatch.

"Look," I pointed. "It's Ted's boat. Call him on the radio."

I couldn't believe Ted would be out in Lake Michigan in a houseboat in those conditions. Sailboats are much better suited for nasty weather than powerboats. Flat-bottomed houseboats were made for flat water.

Hannah took over at the wheel while I went to the open hatch to talk to Ted.

"Whalesback, Whalesback. Come in Whalesback," called Marcia into the microphone. Then she identified us and announced our ship's radio license number, proper protocol, even in this weather. "This is Dancer, WSA 4885. Come in Whalesback."

No answer.

"Try again, Marsh. He's probably a little busy right now."

She tried again and still got no answer from Ted. Marcia handed me the microphone. I called one more time, then gave up. Ted was either hurt and couldn't get to the radio or he was busy surviving the storm. In the dim light I saw a wave hit Whalesback on the side. Ted's boat leaned over precariously.

I handed Marcia the microphone. "I hope he's all right. Maybe we should come about and follow him."

She signed off. I went back to the wheel, the rain coming down harder now, the waves getting bigger.

We were surfing down waves that looked to be seven or eight feet high, the miniature mainsail, straining, driving us forward in the gale. I decided not to come about and follow Ted. We could find him after the storm passed.

Hannah screamed in delight as the knot meter hit ten knots at the bottom of one huge broiling, churning wave. Apparently my thrill-seeker daughter had recovered from the fright of that lightning strike.

I looked over the stern rail and watched the dinghy we were towing dangerously surfing down the waves after us. The dinghy would build up more speed than Dancer, catching up to the bigger boat and sometimes slamming into her hull at the bottom of the waves. As Dancer climbed the next wave, the Dinghy would trail behind until the line attaching her to the bigger boat snapped taut and yanked her violently to follow. To make matters worse, the downpour was quickly filling the dinghy with water, making her heavier, putting more strain on the painter and its attachment points.

Like an obedient dog, the dinghy tried to keep up, tried to follow Dancer's insistent lead. But like an impatient master, Dancer kept yanking her chain, punishing her, insulting her, insisting that she follow, that she keep up.

Finally, our dinghy tired of Dancer's stern admonishments to follow. With a loud bang, the painter snapped.

"What's that?" shouted Hannah in alarm.

The hatch slid open. Marcia poked her head out, fear in her eyes. "What happened?"

The explosion sounded as if we hit something. I read their minds. They thought we were holed, that we would now be sinking.

"It's okay. We're safe. It's the dinghy. The line snapped."

Hannah and I looked back. Free at last, the dinghy drifted away hiding in the troughs, getting smaller with each passing wave, finally disappearing in the distance.

Without the dinghy trailing behind and acting as a brake, we were now going too fast. The wheel was useless as the waves took control of the boat. I worried about Dancer broaching, digging bow first into a wave and flipping head over heels upside down.

"We have to slow down," I shouted. "We're out of control."

I also thought about land. In the direction and speed we were sailing we would soon run out of water. I could see the massive hulk of Sleeping Bear Dunes ahead off the port beam, getting bigger, looming over us in the gray light. We had to come about soon.

I turned the engine on and tightened up the mainsheet. Between waves, I turned Dancer into the wind, heeling at first, then letting the sail luff noisily. We slowed to a crawl immediately, pounding into the waves at a 45 degree angle under diesel power. We could only go about two knots into the wind. Dancer rose high on the crests and crashed dramatically into the troughs, the hull shuddering in protest. We finally found the right angle into the waves and gained better control of the boat. We were moving slowly, but we were safe and stable.

The storm continued for another two hours. Instead of sailing north for the island, the wind was pushing us further and further east. I still worried about running out of water. Sleeping Bear Dunes continued to loom menacingly on our right. The seas were too high and the wind too strong to go directly north, into the wind. Finally we rounded Sleeping Bear Point and I was relieved to have more sea room to the east. Dancer sailed more upright and rode the waves more easily when I steered more to the right. I decided to give in to the weather, turn east and head for Leland. We couldn't go to the island without a dinghy anyway. I thought Ted would probably do the same thing with Whalesback.

Slowly the wind and seas moderated and the downpour changed to a drizzle. As the sky brightened I saw South Manitou Island off our stern. The island would have to wait another day for our arrival.

We limped into Leland harbor, exhausted and humbled again by Lake Michigan. Leland is a small harbor, but a harbor of refuge in the dangerous waters of Manitou passage. No matter how crowded Leland got, they continued to accept boats, stacking them up and rafting them off of each other.

We gratefully accepted the help of the dock boys, skillfully maneuvering us into place next to another sailboat. We were six boats deep off the end of a finger pier but thankful to be safe and secure.

Leland, especially at times like this, is like a floating community. Fellow boaters help each other, intermingle, socialize, share horror stories and brag about their travails at sea. When asked about the storm I joked that we just came into Leland because we ran out of ice.

I saw Whalesback docked nearby, only the third boat out from the dock. Ted wasn't anywhere to be seen. He must have been sleeping. Ted probably had arrived a couple of hours earlier. I was happy to see Whalesback was safe.

"How about a beer?" asked Marcia.

"Absolutely!" I replied.

The rain stopped so we sat in the cockpit, winding down, sipping our beer. Hilllary sat next to me, snuggling close, needing the security of my touch. I put my arm around her and hugged her.

"That was scary, Dad."

"It was, but Dancer kept us safe."

"It was exciting!" bubbled Hannah.

"It was also expensive," said Marcia. "We lost our dinghy."

"Maybe we could find it," I said. "It probably washed up on the beach around Sleeping Bear Point."

Marcia made a tuna fish salad and heated up a couple cans of clam chowder. We ate quietly as the sun honored us with a spectacular sunset through the breaking clouds. We didn't see Ted until the next morning.

"I heard your call on the radio, but I couldn't leave the wheel," explained Ted. "It was all I could do to keep Whalesback from flipping."

"I saw you in the rain," I said. "I was glad to be on Dancer and not Whalesback."

"Yeah. The storm caught me by surprise. I was so anxious to get to the island."

"I know. Me too. Are you going today?"

"As soon as I can get free." We were standing on the dock. Ted looked out at Whalesback and silently counted boats rafted off of her. "There are four more boats that have to leave before I can get out. How about you?"

I looked up at the sky. The sun was out and the wind was blowing out of the northwest. "Conditions look good for anchoring off the island. I'd like to leave today, but we lost our dinghy in the storm."

"Really? Where?"

"Just off Sleeping Bear Point. I was hoping to talk you into helping me find it."

Ted looked torn. I knew he was anxious to get going. "You think you can find it?"

"There's a good chance. It's probably on the beach somewhere. We can get pretty close on Whalesback."

He looked out at South Manitou Island, only fourteen miles away, gleaming in the morning sun, a jewel on the horizon. "Sure. It's worth a try. We can leave as soon as these other boats get out of the way."

An hour later, Ted and I motored out of the harbor, hugging the shore. Marcia and the girls stayed on Dancer. I brought my binoculars to scan the beach. Whalesback bullied her way through the three-foot waves, groaning and slamming off of every peak. The motion of the boat was jerky and uncomfortable. I couldn't imagine being on Whalesback in that storm.

We rode in the cabin, the steering station being enclosed and out of the weather. A canvas tarp covered Ted's invention, sitting on the floor of the cabin, lines tying it securely to eye bolts sticking out of the floor.

"How's the grid?" I asked. "Come through the storm okay?"

"It's fine. You want to see it?"

"Yeah."

"Here, take the wheel. I'll undo the tarp."

Ted untied all the lines and whipped the tarp off with a flourish. He was obviously proud of his contraption. "Voila!"

I turned and looked down at Ted's grid. It was similar to mine in proportion, but Ted's grid was built out of aluminum and buffed to a gleaming shine. It was thicker than mine in the floor to accommodate the Pentium processors. I looked more closely and saw that the floor of the grid must have been glass or Plexiglas; some kind of transparent material. In each of the grid's compartments, I could see a microchip, one hundred of them, securely encased behind the transparent floor of the grid.

"All those processors must have cost a fortune, Ted."

"It wasn't cheap."

"What about the sand? I thought you needed sand?"

"I'm gonna use South Manitou sand."

"What about the slab? What are you gonna use to power it?"

"The slab…yes. I don't know what to do if I can't find the slab. I'm just playing it by ear. I'll go to the island and see what happens. Maybe you can help me find it."

"If it's there," I said, shaking my head. I didn't have much hope of finding the slab. In a way, I hoped I wouldn't find it. And even if we did find it, how would we harness it? How would we get it onto Ted's boat? I thought Ted's trip to South Manitou was a desperate move, a shot in the dark, but I couldn't bring myself to tell him that.

"How's this thing work, Ted?"

"I haven't the slightest idea. I just built it. I just followed the directions in the drawings."

"You're kidding."

"No. I think the grid will take over. I think that the speed tile inside the slab has somehow been pre-programmed to complete the process. It's gonna be interesting to watch."

"Aren't you afraid it'll blow up or something?"

"It might. Who knows. I'm not gonna know what happens 'til I try."

"You're nuts, Ted."

"Maybe."

I looked out over the lake as we pounded over the waves. "Here, Ted. Why don't you drive. I'll go out on deck and see if I can spot the dinghy."

For the next two hours, Ted motored along the shore while I scanned the beach with the binoculars. Finally, I spotted it, well past Sleeping Bear Point. It was turned over and covered with sand, wedged between a log and a rock about ten feet from the water's edge. A big wave must have thrown it up there during the storm.

Ted stayed on Whalesback while I rowed to shore in his inflatable dinghy. It took me a little effort to unwedge my little boat and drag it to the water's edge. I was glad to see that the dinghy appeared to be structurally undamaged. The frayed painter and a few gashes in the fiberglass bottom seemed to be the only evidence of the dinghy's adventure in the storm. Boston Whaler made a sturdy boat, my dinghy being their smallest model at seven feet.

I replaced the painter and towed the dinghy back to Ted's boat. I felt pretty good about the recovery.

An hour later we were back in Leland. Marcia and the girls cheered when they saw us motor in towing our errant dinghy. Ted dropped me off at Dancer and went right back out into Lake Michigan. He was anxious to get to the island. Filled with trepidation, I watched him motor out into the lake. I thought Ted was messing with something that was beyond his comprehension, beyond his control. But I knew I would follow him the next day.

Chapter 20

South Manitou Island

"No, Hannah. They're mine."

"Come on, Hill. You've got lots of 'em. Let me have just one."

"I need 'em."

"For what, you dork? What do you need 'em for?"

"I don't know yet. I just know that I need 'em all."

"God, Hill. You're such a selfish bitch."

"Shut up, Hannah."

"I'm just gonna take 'em all then."

"No you won't. You don't know where they are."

I had my speed tiles hidden under my bunk in the cave. There was a hatch toward the back that Hannah didn't even know about. I put the purse under an electric drill Dad had stored there a year ago.

"I'm gonna tell Dad you have 'em."

"No Hannah. Don't."

"I'm gonna."

"Yeah? You'll never get one then, will you?"

She looked at me. She was pissed. Then she finally gave up and went on deck, throwing one last insult at me.

"You whore."

I laid on my back in the cave, feeling the speed tiles under me. I was confused. Why didn't I just give her one? I felt guilty about not sharing, but I couldn't face the thought of giving one up. I was just getting to know them now. And I really enjoyed their company.

I guess I felt a little guilty about keeping the speed tiles secret from Mom and Dad too. I remembered the lightning that put a hole in our roof earlier in the summer. I wondered if yesterday's lightning was aimed at the speed tiles I was hiding. Maybe these speed tiles were dangerous. Maybe they could get us all killed.

But they were so beautiful. And…I don't know…fun to be with, to listen to, to feel in my fingers. I had to have them. I had to have them all.

"Hey Hill," yelled Dad from the dock. "Come to the grocery store with me. I need your help."

I crawled out of the cave and went on deck. The dock was crowded with tourists and boaters. In Leland, the docks were kind of like the zoo. Tourists could stroll down the docks with their ice cream cones and their fudge and stare at the exotic wildlife. That would be us, the boats and the crews. The biggest boats got the most attention.

"Where we going, Dad?"

"I want to stock up on food. I want to be able to stay on the island for a few days. There are no stores on the island you know. Grab the boat bags."

I took the two big canvas boat bags out of a locker and joined Dad on the dock. Hannah was sitting on the deck, still sulking.

"What about Hannah," I asked.

"She's gonna wash the boat…aren't you Hannah?"

"Dad!" moaned Hannah.

"Do it now, before we get back with the groceries."

Mom was already in town doing some shopping…clothes shopping. There were a lot of cool shops in Leland. She went into town before Hannah and I even woke up.

We walked down the busy dock dodging the gawking tourists. There were less boats in the harbor since the storm the day before but it was still a busy place. Dad paused to watch a big powerboat pull in to the gas dock. It was driven by a black man. The boat was kind of nasty. It was more like a work boat than a pleasure boat. It had a big flat deck cluttered with lots of lines and tools and chains and stuff. Dad stared at the boat like a tourist.

"Dad, come on."

"Wait, Hill."

The man was talking to the boss of the harbor, the harbor master, pointing at the boat, then pointing out into the lake. It looked like he wanted to dock the boat there. The harbor master nodded, then called a couple of those cute dock boys.

"Dad!"

"What, Hill?"

"Come on."

Dad shrugged and we continued down the dock on our way to the grocery store. "That guy looked familiar, Hill. That black guy on the work boat. You ever see him before?"

"Nope." Dad was seeing ghosts everywhere these days. Ever since he recognized Bullfrog from that bridge in Chicago.

We loaded up our cart with food at the grocery store. Ground beef, bratwurst, eggs, pancake mix, cereal. I was starting to worry about how we would carry all this stuff back.

"How 'bout corned beef hash, Hill?"

"Ughhh. You mean dog food?"

"Hill…corned beef hash is a delicacy."

"You mean a smellicacy," I said, holding my nose. Dad and Hannah liked corned beef hash. Puke. Mom and I hated it.

"Speaking of dog food, Hill, you better grab a few cans of cat food for Spinnaker."

I grabbed six cans and dumped them in the cart.

We rounded the corner at the end of the aisle and Dad almost bumped into another cart coming the other way. It was the black guy from the work boat.

"Oh, excuse me," said Dad.

"Pardon me," said the guy.

But then the man did a double take. He looked at Dad, surprise in his eyes. Dad looked at him too. It only took a second. The man quickly backed up his cart and went around us. Dad's eyes followed him, suspiciously, as he passed.

"I swear I know that guy from somewhere, Hill."

"He looked like he recognized you, too, Dad."

We paid for the groceries and tried to stuff them into the canvas bags. No way. We bought too much. We had to cram the overflow into two of the store's flimsy paper bags. I looked around for a courtesy cart like they have in Frankfort, but no luck. They didn't have any. We left the store overloaded, struggling, shuffling down the street with our provisions. "Maybe we should have made two trips," I suggested to Dad. His arms were stretching noticeably longer from the heavy shopping bags.

"It's all that cat food," moaned Dad. "You had to bring that cat..."

"What about that smelly corned beef hash," I said, "I won't even mention all that wine you bought."

"You just did," said Dad as he put his bags down on a park bench, rubbing his shoulders.

I gave Dad a dirty look and put my bags down next to his.

Just then an old rusty van screeched to a halt in front of us, rattling and belching gray smoke. "Want a lift?"

I looked up. Through the smelly cloud I saw Dick Beaver sitting behind the wheel smiling.

"Dick!" said Dad. "I thought I might see you up here."

"You planning to feed an army?" he asked, looking at our bags. He got out of the van and opened the back door.

I looked around inside the van for some place to put the groceries. It was crammed full of old dirty gears, dusty machines, and greasy tools. It looked like a bomb had exploded in there. "You want me to put actual food in that mess?" I asked.

"Looks like your room, Hill," joked Dad.

"Plenty 'a space," said Dick as he threw an old belt sander toward the front of the van. He pulled a broken ceramic lamp out of the back with an ugly purple shade. He must have found it on the road somewhere. He held it up and looked at it, then walked over to a nearby trash can and pitched it in. "Didn't need that," he mused. After a couple of minutes he had created an open space big enough for our bags.

"You can always come back for the lamp," said Dad.

"Nahhh."

We loaded our bags and I opened the passenger door to get in. In the passenger seat sat a wheelbarrow and a collection of shovels and picks. There was no room to sit.

"You'll have to walk, Hill. Where do you want your groceries?"

"Why don't you drive down to the dock," said Dad. "We'll meet you there."

Dick drove off and we walked down the hill to meet him. "Do you believe his van?" I asked.

"Yeah, Dick's quite a collector, isn't he?"

Dick helped us carry the groceries to the boat. Hannah was still hosing it down.

"I need a shower," yelled Dick. "Can you hose me down, Hannah?"

I saw Hannah smile. It looked like she was gonna take him up on his request.

"No Hannah," said Dad, seeing that look in her eyes. "We've got all these groceries."

Mom came up on deck. "Dick. How you doing? John said we might see you up here."

"Yep."

"Going to the island?" asked Mom.

"Yep." He looked over toward the ferry dock.

"Ferry's gone for the day, Dick," said Mom. "Next run'll be tomorrow morning."

"Oh," said Dick, handing Marcia a bag.

"Why don't you come with us?" asked Dad. "We're sailing there tomorrow morning."

"Yeah, Dick," joked Hannah. "You can ride in the dinghy."

Dick looked down on our little Boston Whaler dinghy. "Think I could fit?"

"Not if you bring your wheelbarrow," I said.

"I need my wheelbarrow," said Dick, reaching over and tousling my hair. "Maybe you can tow me in the wheelbarrow."

"Why don't you bring your stuff on the boat now," said Mom, "while your van's right here."

"Sounds like a plan."

Dad and Dick went back down the dock to get Dick's stuff. They came back wheeling his wheelbarrow filled with digging tools, a tent, sleeping bag, and an old khaki duffel with some extra clothes.

"Gonna do some prospecting?" asked Hannah.

"Yep."

Dad lashed the wheelbarrow to the deck and stuffed Dick's other stuff in one of the cockpit lockers. "You can sleep out here on the deck tonight, Dick…unless it rains."

"Hope it does rain," said Dick, smiling. He looked up at my sister with the hose. "I need a shower…right Hannah?"

Hannah gave him a quick squirt, hitting Dad with some of the spray, too.

"Hannah!" yelled Dad.

"More, Hannah, more," taunted Dick, laughing.

Dick did take a real shower at the marina the next morning. We all did. There were no bathrooms on South Manitou. Not real ones, anyway, just the smelly hole-in-the-ground ones. Dad said we would be on our own when we got there. That's one of the things he liked about going there. We would have to be self-sufficient.

We left around ten in the morning. I glanced at the fuel dock as we motored out and noticed the old work boat was gone. It was a sunny day and the wind was blowing, but Dad said it was coming out of the west, right where we wanted to go. Dad didn't even try to set the sails. We motored into the small, one foot waves, the island a small bump in the distance.

Two hours into the trip, the wind shifted to the southwest and we raised the sails. Dad said the two hours of motoring topped off our batteries. With the sails sheeted in tightly, Dad shut off the engine. We sailed silently toward South Manitou Island, watching it grow slowly larger on the horizon.

Hannah and I sat on the forward deck in the sun leaning against Dick's wheelbarrow. There were puffy white clouds hanging over the island. It was a beautiful day.

"Maybe we'll find some speed tiles on the island," said Hannah.

"That's what Dick's lookin' for," I said.

"And Bullfrog. Dick really wants to get his hands on Bullfrog."

"What do you think he's gonna do to Bullfrog if he finds him?"

"Kill him."

"Hannah!"

"Really! Dick's really pissed at him."

"Hannah, he just wants his speed tiles back."

"That too, Hill…Hey! Why don't you give him some of yours."

"Shut up, Hannah."

"Shut up, Hannah," she mocked. "You know, if I find any speed tiles, I'm not gonna give you any."

"I wouldn't want any of your stupid speed tiles, bitch."

Spinnaker came on deck and sat in Hannah's lap, soaking up the warmth of the sun. We watched North Manitou Island pass on our right, an island even more primitive than South Manitou.

It only took us about three hours to cover the fourteen miles from Leland to South Manitou. The southwest wind was blowing steadily. It was a perfect day to sail.

Dad said he wanted to scout the island, so, just for fun, Dad decided to sail around it instead of going directly into the harbor. The island is about five miles long and four miles wide. Dad figured it would take us four or five hours to go all the way around.

We could see a couple dozen boats anchored off the beach as we came closer, but Dad steered past the anchorage. The boats at anchor slowly slid behind the dunes at Gull Point as we sailed north and west. Thousands of seagulls cawed sadly at us as we sailed silently past. Gull Point is a protected rookery; a nesting area for seagulls.

Dick joined us on the forward deck. He sat on his upside down wheelbarrow listening to the wistful sound of the gulls.

"You know the legend don't you?" he asked.

"What legend?" asked Hannah.

"The Chippewa Indian legend about how these islands came to be here."

"Something about Frank Sinatra?" asked Hannah suspiciously.

"No, no, no…Perry Como," he joked. "It's about Perry Como."

"Who the heck is Perry Como?" she asked.

"No, just kidding, Hannah. Just kidding. But there really is an Indian legend. It seems that a mother bear and her two cubs jumped into Lake Michigan to get away from a big forest fire in Wisconsin. They swam all night across the lake. The mother made it across and that's her over there."

Dick pointed to the mainland, to a huge mountain of sand gleaming white in the mid-afternoon sun, the biggest dune in Michigan.

"That's Sleeping Bear Dune. She's still waiting there, waiting for her two cubs. It's a national park now. So are these Islands."

"What happened to the cubs?" asked Hannah.

"That's them. The islands. North and South Manitou. They didn't quite make it across. The islands mark where the cubs died trying to reach their mother. The islands were created by the great Indian spirit, Manitou, to mark their graves."

The gulls cried for the drowned cubs as Dad turned Dancer west, on our way around the island. We sailed past white sand beaches, rolling sand hills and waving dune grass. This part of the island was completely deserted. We didn't see a soul…just gulls…cawing, screeching, crying gulls. It was kind of spooky, but beautiful.

Dancer followed the shore until the sails started luffing. Dancer was facing southwest, right into the wind. Dad didn't want to turn on the engine so he turned right a little and sailed straight west, out into the lake for a few miles before coming about and tacking back for the island. That's how sailboats sail into the wind, by zig-zagging, keeping the wind to either side of the sails instead of directly ahead.

Dancer headed back to the island sailing south and a little east. We sailed right next to Perched Dunes, massive 500 foot high sand hills on the west side of the island. I felt small next to all that sand, a mountain of sand hiding the mysterious interior of the island from my eyes.

Mom took the wheel and Dad joined us on the deck. "I think that's where Bullfrog found all those speed tiles over a hundred years ago," he said, pointing to the dunes. "Actually, it was on the other side of the dunes, toward the cedar forest."

"That scum…" muttered Dick, looking out at the dunes, blinding white now, from the sun's reflection.

We rounded the southwestern tip of the island and sailed past the Valley of the Giants, just visible over the dunes. "Those trees are over 500 years old," said Dad. "Probably the only virgin cedar forest left in the United States. Some of those trees are fifteen feet around and eighty feet high. We'll have to hike there tomorrow."

The trees swayed majestically in the wind, the leaves rustling quietly. The island looked content, happy. It didn't need us. It didn't need people to give it purpose. It didn't want people. Dad said men raped this island in the 1800s, stripped its forests and left it nearly naked and bare. Now it was wilderness again. And it was content.

I looked over the bow of the boat and saw that we were coming up on some kind of crazy building sticking up out of the water near the shore. It was all funny angles and rusted metal. "There's the Morazon," said Dad. "It's a sunken ship. It ran aground here in a November snowstorm. In 1960."

The sea was slowly finishing off the Morazon, constantly washing over her rusting steel decks, pushing her deeper into the sand, pulling her apart piece by piece. "She'll be completely gone in another ten years," said Dad.

The gulls called her home now. As we got closer I could see hundreds of birds circling, cawing.

"It looks like the Morazon was just painted," said Hannah.

She was right. The exposed decks were blinding white in the sun. I shielded my eyes from the glare.

"That's bird shit," said Dick. "Guano, to put it more delicately. The gulls are constantly painting and repainting her decks."

On the other side of the Morazon I saw another boat, a power boat, anchored close to the aging wreck. As we sailed past, I realized it was the work boat Dad stared at in Leland. The same man was on her deck. The man we ran into at the grocery store. He waved. We waved back. Dad locked eyes with the man as we passed.

I noticed an inflatable marker near the power boat. "What's that, Dad?"

"That's a dive marker. Somebody's diving on that wreck. Scuba."

The sun was getting lower in the sky as we reached the south tip of the crescent that defined the harbor. We had come all the way around the island. There was an old, deserted lighthouse on this point. It gleamed white in the sun, bone white, like the bleached bones of a skeleton in the sand…like the deck of the Morazon. As we came closer I could see that the lighthouse was kind of wrecked. The cupola on top of the tower was gone. The stucco walls were crumbling and the paint was chipped and stained. I could tell this was once a pretty cool building but now it was abandoned. Dad said it was no longer useful for navigation so the Coast Guard was letting the sea reclaim it, little by little. A newer light, an automatic one, was out in the lake, marking the passage for ships. Dad said most lighthouses don't need to me manned any more.

We sailed past the falling down lighthouse, into the quiet harbor. The water was calm here, almost flat. It was a big anchorage. The beach curved around in a graceful curve, like a crescent, a big beach. Dad said it was over two miles from the lighthouse on the southern tip to gull Point to the north.

"Okay girls," said Dad. Time to arm yourselves."

We looked at him, confused. "Huh?"

"Water balloons, duh! We're gonna attack Whalesback."

"Yes!" shouted Hannah. She jumped up, heading for the galley.

Dad scanned the harbor with his binoculars and spotted Whalesback anchored near shore. "There he is. Prepare to attack."

Mom turned on the diesel engine and steered as Dad dropped the sails. Dick sat on his wheelbarrow with a big smile on his face.

"Dad! Dick! Help me!" said Hannah. She had a bucket full of water balloons in one hand and a big rubber sling shot in the other.

I followed Hannah up on deck, laughing, with a big bowl full of more water balloons.

Dad held one end of the sling shot and Dick held the other. Hannah put a balloon in the rubber basket and pulled it back, getting ready to launch it into the sky. I looked out at Whalesback and saw Ted climbing out of his dinghy. He hadn't seen us yet. Hannah screamed, "Fire one!" and let it go.

The balloon flew, carving an arc through the air and landing with a wet splat on the deck of Whalesback. Ted looked up in surprise.

Hannah let another one go just as Ted reached the deck, hitting the side of the cabin and spraying Ted with water.

"Hey!" shouted Ted. "What did I do?"

Marcia steered the boat closer and Hannah and I pelted Ted with water balloons, drenching him, giggling and shrieking in delight. Ted caught a couple of the balloons on the fly and tried to fight back. He hit Hannah on the shoulder with one of them, but he was severely outnumbered and underarmed. He should have known better than to come to South Manitou Island without balloons.

"Okay girls," shouted Dad. "Hold your fire."

"But he didn't surrender yet," said Hannah. She looked over at Ted. "Do you surrender?" she shouted.

"I surrender! I surrender!" called Ted, holding his hands over his head. His shirt and shorts were dripping wet from the attack.

"Hey, Ted!" shouted Dad. "Look who we found in Leland." He pointed at Dick.

Mom turned the boat around and found a nice place to drop the hook close to Whalesback. She put the diesel into reverse to stop Dancer as Dad dropped the anchor. Dad let out a bunch of line as the boat drifted slowly backwards. He gave the line a tug to set the flukes of the anchor into the sand. Mom gave the diesel one last goose going backwards to set the anchor even more. Hannah and me immediately dove into the crystal clear water. We had arrived.

Ted came over to Dancer for dinner. Dad started the gas grill on the stern of the boat and cooked up some bratwurst. Mom heated up a couple cans of baked beans in the galley. Ted brought a big bottle of red wine over from Whalesback and a couple of unbroken water balloons from the attack. "Maybe I shouldn't be surrendering my meager supply of ammunition," he joked as he handed me the balloons.

"We'll save these for tomorrow's battle," I said, giving him an evil stare.

Ted laughed and turned to Dad. "Yeah, Wong's here. He's staying in one of the Forest Ranger's buildings. He's got a helper. A big black guy."

Dad looked up. "Does he have a boat?"

"Yeah. A power boat. A flat deck work boat."

"Okay. We saw Wong's boat and that same guy in Leland. He must have gone in to get some supplies yesterday."

"That's right. He just came back this morning. I don't know where he went today though. Haven't seen him."

"We saw him," said Mom. "He's over at the wreck of the Morazon. He was anchored over there. There's somebody diving on the Morazon too. Maybe its Wong." Mom looked around at the three men. "Why don't you guys just leave him alone. Let this whole thing be. Let's just relax and have a nice vacation."

Ted looked away. He didn't even seem to hear her. "One of the rangers told me Wong's here doing his scientific study."

"The gravity study?" asked Dad. "He must be doing it freelance. He had a grant from Argonne, but it was canceled."

"He must be," replied Ted.

"Have you seen Bullfrog?" asked Dick. "Is Bullfrog here?"

"God!" interrupted Mom. "Let it be, Dick. Let him have your stupid speed tiles. Get on with your life."

Ted smirked and ignored her again. "Haven't seen Bullfrog. I don't know if he's here."

We heard a power boat in the distance. Dad grabbed his binoculars and looked south as a boat rounded the point on the way to the ranger dock.

"It's Wong," said Dad.

He watched as Wong and his assistant docked the boat and unloaded a bunch of stuff onto the dock. Dad handed Ted the binoculars.

"We'll have to go meet this Doctor Wong tomorrow morning."

"Good idea, Ted. We'll just go knock on his door."

"Why not?"

"You guys," said Mom. "Why don't you leave him alone."

"Just curious, Marsh," said Dad. "It won't hurt to just meet him, see what he's up to. After all, we're old friends. I met him in Chicago over ten years ago."

"Maybe we should attack him with water balloons," blurted Hannah.

Everybody laughed at the thought of the distinguished scientist, Dr. Wong, getting pelted with water balloons.

"I'm going to shore," announced Mom. "I can't take all this intrigue. Come on girls. Let's get a fire going on the beach."

"Yes!" yelled Hannah.

"Smoorz!" I said. Do we have marshmallows? How 'bout Hershey bars?"

"Got 'em," confirmed Mom.

"Graham crackers?" asked Hannah.

"Of course."

"Okay, let's go."

Mom and Hannah and I loaded up the dinghy with stuff for the beach. A blanket, some sweat shirts and two flash lights...and all the ingredients for the smoorz we planned to cook. The men stayed on Dancer, drinking wine and talking speed tiles. We rowed to shore in the failing light, visions of melting chocolate and toasted marshmallows dancing in our heads.

Chapter 21

Doctor Wong

Marcia and the girls stayed on the boat, soaking up the morning sun. Ted, Dick and I hiked to Wong's borrowed house the morning after we arrived on the island. The house was one of about a dozen houses the U.S. Park Service had restored from the old island settlement. We didn't know what to expect from the mysterious Dr. Wong. Would he send us away, jealously guarding his gravity research, or would he welcome us, anxious to learn of our experiences with speed tiles?

Wong answered the door. I recognized him immediately from our brief meeting over ten years ago.

"How do you do, Doctor Wong. I'm John Hunter, these are my friends..."

"I know who you are, Mr. Hunter," interrupted Wong, impatiently. "I was afraid you would be coming here."

Wong stared at me intently, ignoring Ted and Dick. I remembered his intense dark eyes, a stare from ten years past that bore a hole in my drawing and penetrated my mind. He looked at me, suspicious, searching for clues, reading me, his spectacles flashing reflections of light from the morning sun.

"You were expecting me?"

"Yes. What do you want with me? I'm very busy."

Ted interrupted. "Doctor Wong, I'm Ted Clark. We think we know why you're here. We think we may have some things in common."

"Things in common?" he asked imperiously. "I doubt it, Mr. Clark. Whatever can we have in common?"

"Bullfrog," said Dick. "Jeremiah Bullfrog."

Wong looked up abruptly at the mention of Bullfrog. "And who are you, ah, Mister…"

"Beaver. Dick Beaver. I'm here looking for Bullfrog."

"I know nothing of Jeremiah Bullfrog. Now, if you'll excuse me."

Wong started to close the door but Ted took a speed tile out of his pocket and tossed it up in the air like a coin. "Heads or tails, Doctor Wong?"

The tile twirled around in the air, flipping end over end, landing on the ground at our feet.

He stopped closing the door and stared down at the speed tile. It landed face up, the yellow nubs sparkling in the sunlight.

Wong looked up at Ted, studying his eyes, then back at the speed tile.

"They always land face up. It's always heads. Did you know that, Doctor Wong?"

"Where did you get that?"

"You do know what that is, don't you, Doctor Wong?"

Wong looked back at the speed tile. "Of course I do. It's a speed tile. Now, where did you get it?"

"From my mother's attic, Doctor Wong. In a house that once stood in the town of Singapore."

"Hmm," mused Wong. "Singapore."

"Doctor Wong, we really are sorry to disturb you," I said, trying to be diplomatic, "but we think your research here is centered around speed tiles. We were hoping you might be able to help us answer some questions."

Wong tore his gaze away from Ted's speed tile. "Questions?"

"Yes," answered Ted. "And maybe some of our experiences with speed tiles can help in your research."

Ted picked up the speed tile off the ground and put it back into his pocket.

Wong sighed heavily. "Questions," he said under his breath. He looked up at Ted. "With speed tiles, I'm afraid that's all there is, Mister Clark. There are very few answers."

"Can we come in, Doctor Wong?" I asked.

He frowned, considering my suggestion. He reluctantly agreed.

"Yes. You may come in."

He turned to go back into the house. We followed him into the small living room. I heard hurried footsteps on a stairway. It must have been a basement stairway because we were in a single story house. The black man, Wong's helper, burst through a door, his eyes wide with panic. He must have heard our footsteps when we entered the house. He slammed the basement door and looked at us suspiciously.

"No need for alarm, Alex," said Wong. "They are all speed tile veterans, so to speak."

Wong turned to Dick and Ted. "Aren't you...Mister Beaver? Mister Clark?"

Alex eyed us distrustfully. "Yeah...that's what worries me, Doc," he drawled in a deep baritone.

His voice sparked a deeply buried memory. Where had I heard that voice before? The three of us stared at Wong and Alex, not knowing what to expect next.

"Well, gentlemen," said Wong. "I must admit, I have been keeping track of certain activities that have taken place around Saugatuck. I know a little bit about Singapore."

He turned to me. "And your artwork, Mister Hunter. Bullfrog shared some of your artwork with me. Very perceptive. Very insightful. I've learned a lot from your work. You've come a long way since we first met in Chicago." I was surprised to hear him refer to our brief meeting so long ago.

He turned to Dick. "Your house-moving exploits, Mister Beaver. I've heard about them, too. Very clever."

Then he turned to Ted. "And your mother, Mister Clark. That must be Mabel Clark. Yes. She's a very strong woman…most impressive. Your Mister Jeremiah Bullfrog…" Wong spit the name out like poison. "He's been keeping me well informed."

"Where is he?" asked Dick. "Is he here?"

"No, Mister Beaver. Bullfrog's not here. I haven't seen him. I hope I never see him again."

I was watching Alex, Wong's helper, trying again to remember how I knew him. He was a big man, as big as Dick. Broad chest, strong-looking. He had thinning hair, graying on the sides, a thick mustache also sprinkled with gray. He was silent, serious, suspicious. He was watching me, too.

"So," began Ted. "Gravity research is just a cover story then?"

"Not really, Mister Clark. My specialty is gravity, as you know, and speed tiles have very strange anti-gravity properties." He turned to Dick. "That's what makes them so useful in moving houses, Mister Beaver."

"They have a lot of other strange properties too," I said.

"Yes, they do. But my gravity measurement techniques have allowed me to identify this place as a likely source of speed tiles. Did you know that we weigh ten percent less on this island than we do on the mainland?"

"I've been trying to lose a little weight," joked Dick.

"I'm here to find those speed tiles," said Wong. "And to study their unique properties and capabilities."

"They're dangerous, Wong. I know that," I warned. "And they're addictive."

"Nonsense."

"Have you found any?" asked Dick.

"Some. But not nearly enough."

"Enough for what?" I asked.

Wong looked up at me, suspiciously. I saw him exchange a quick glance with Alex. They didn't trust us with their secrets.

"That's none of your concern, Mister Hunter."

"You said my work was insightful, Doctor Wong. Maybe my insight can help. Maybe we can help each other?"

"And this cozy place you have here, Doctor Wong," added Ted. "I wonder if the park service would still be willing to let you use it if they knew you weren't connected with Argonne any more."

Wong shot Ted a blistering glance. Then he looked at Alex and back at Ted again.

"We know you don't work for Wong Labs, anymore Doctor," added Ted. "This looks more like a personal project of yours than any kind of sanctioned research."

Wong looked at Ted angrily, then back at me, thinking, measuring. He shrugged. "Somehow you've been able to tap into the secrets of the speed tile instinctively, naively touching on many of its powers and capabilities. That's been helpful to me. It's as if your mind…your artist's mind, is a kind of receptor."

"Doctor Wong," said Ted. "John's work has been an inspiration to me too."

"I'm sure it has," replied Wong, off-handedly, still angry at Ted's veiled threats.

"How many more speed tiles do you need," continued Ted, "for your, ah, research?"

"Thousands, Mister Clark. We need thousands more."

"I might be able to help," said Ted.

Doctor Wong was skeptical. "I doubt it, Mister Clark. No one has access to that many speed tiles…"

"Except Bullfrog," interrupted Dick.

"Bullfrog's a fool," said Wong impatiently.

"I didn't say I have that many speed tiles, Doctor Wong, but I may have a means of manufacturing them," continued Ted.

Wong looked up suddenly. "What? Why, that's impossible."

"Maybe not. Like I said before, John's work is an inspiration to me. He created a sculpture. He called it Speed Tile Birthing Grid."

"Yes, a sculpture," said Wong, wearily. "Mister Hunter's work is interesting, but it couldn't work. At best, it could only be a mock-up, a facade…"

"I built one," interrupted Ted. "I'm an engineer, Doctor Wong. I built a real one."

"You built a birthing grid? That's absurd. How? How could you? Where is it?"

"Not so fast, Doctor Wong. How about a little give and take here?"

Wong exchanged glances with Alex again. He sat down, deep in thought. Finally, the thought of an unlimited supply of speed tiles weakened his resolve and tempered his arrogance. He looked up at Ted. "What do you want from me?"

"Some answers," I said. "Maybe if we pooled our experiences we might be able to explain a few things."

"And I'd like to get my speed tiles back," said Dick.

"I can't help you there, Mister Beaver. My guess is that Bullfrog took your speed tiles. He's a ruthless man. I haven't seen him since our, ahem, delightful lunch in Saugatuck several weeks ago."

"What is your connection to Bullfrog?" asked Ted.

"I bought some drawings from him many years ago in Chicago." Wong looked at me. "It was about the same time I first met you, Mister Hunter. I met him outside of a train station. The fool was looking for a job. He was desperate for money. He had some old drawings, brittle with age. They were engineering drawings."

"Sounds familiar," said Ted.

"What do you mean?"

"I have old, brittle engineering drawings that I found in Mabel's attic. They're the drawings I used to build the birthing grid."

"I see." Wong's eyes opened wide. He was slowly gaining more respect for us.

"What do Bullfrog's drawings illustrate?" asked Ted.

Wong looked at Ted, then at Alex. He rose from his seat and said, "I might as well show you."

Alex stiffened. "I don't think that's a good idea, Doctor."

"Alex, it's all right. Show the gentlemen into the basement. They may be right. We may be able to learn from each other."

Alex frowned. It didn't look as if he wanted us here at all. He certainly didn't want to share the secrets of his basement with us.

"Open the door, Alex."

Alex finally relented and led us slowly down the stairs into the dark basement. He pulled a chain at the bottom of the stairs and a bare light bulb illuminated the space. On the dirt floor was a large platform made of wood. It looked like the platform in Bullfrog's basement. But it wasn't the platform that got our attention.

"Holy shit," said Dick under his breath.

There must have been a hundred of them, all lined up in neat rows. A hundred speed tiles, shining, glowing, the yellow nubs gently pulsating, squirming like little worms in their unnatural metallic homes. I gasped, remembering my own speed tiles…my home-made speed tiles…remembering my obsessive need to get them lined up just right on my dining room table, the yellow moonlight pouring in through the skylights reflecting that sick yellow light off the nubs.

I thought of Hilllary's description of Bullfrog's basement, his speed tile platform, his naked body suspended, floating above the neat rows of tiles. I looked down on Wong's platform and realized he was right. He didn't have enough speed tiles. He needed more to cover the platform. He needed a lot more.

Ted was drawn to the old engineering drawings that sat on the platform apart from the speed tiles. The drawings looked like the same vintage as Ted's grid plans. "These look as if they could have been drawn by the same hand as my drawings, Doctor Wong."

Next to the old drawings was a sketch made with a ball point pen on a piece of lined note paper. It looked familiar to me. It was wrinkled and had been folded several times. Now it was lying open on the platform. My heart beating, I went closer to the drawing, bent down and took a closer look. With a start I realized what it was. I looked up quickly at Alex. He was watching me intently. Now I knew where I had seen him before.

The drawing was mine. I made it over ten years before, during my meeting with the architect, the day of my swan dive into the Chicago River. I looked at the speed tiles on the platform, then back at the drawing. The tiles were lined up in rows just like my drawing. I looked up at Alex again. "You're the guard. The guard from the building. I remember now. You took my drawing. You folded it up and put it in your pocket."

My head was swimming. The memory of that day flooded my mind…memories of my own madness, my fear and my paranoia. I sat shakily on the edge of the platform. Alex continued to stare at me, silent, suspicious.

Wong saw that I noticed the drawing. "Alex brought that drawing to me. I asked him to take it from you after our meeting in the architect's office."

I looked up at him, confused.

"I had been researching speed tiles for several years," confessed Wong. "I had been collecting them from small archeological digs all over the world. Your speed tile drawing was quite a shock to me."

Wong continued. "You can see the correlation between your drawing and these plans. I'm not sure how you knew. The alignment of the tiles is uncannily accurate. It's very much like the plans I got from Bullfrog."

Wong joined Ted, who was studying the ancient plans. "Your plans, Mister Clark. I must see them. You say they show how to manufacture speed tiles?"

"Well, not exactly. They show how to build a device. I think the device is supposed to generate speed tiles somehow."

"What does it look like?"

"A grid containing 100 compartments. It's here, on my boat in the harbor."

"It's here? Does it work? And why did you bring it here?"

"Like I told you, John built a grid, but he also created a sculpture of a boxy slab-like thing hanging over the grid. I think this slab, somehow, powers the grid. You see, there are speed tiles growing in the grid compartments. Not real speed tiles, John's interpretation of speed tiles. He made them out of aluminum and brass."

Wong turned to me. "And this slab you created. Does it have a basis in fact?"

Wong's question snapped me out of my reverie. "The slab? Yes. The slab." I got up off the platform and exchanged glances with Alex. "As a matter of fact, the speed tile I found in the dunes grew into a slab…a very real slab…over a period of ten years. It happened in my attic. But it escaped in a lightning storm. It burst through the roof and floated away. I think it came here, to the island."

"Slabs, of course," whispered Wong, thinking to himself. He looked up. "Stone tablets in Mexico, hieroglyphics in Egypt, even some of the ancient cave paintings in France…In many of the places we recovered speed tiles, we found evidence of these slabs. I didn't know what they represented."

"I want to place my grid under the slab," said Ted. "If I can find it. If John's artwork is an indication, it should begin the process of generating speed tiles."

Wong was looking at us in amazement. "I had no idea. The power of these things. The implications." He turned to Ted. "I must see your grid."

I looked at Dick. He appeared hypnotized. He was staring intently at the speed tiles on the platform. I saw him slowly bend down and reach for the tiles lined up there. He wanted them badly. I could see that he had to have them.

Just as Dick's hand neared the speed tiles, Alex grabbed Dick's wrist, snapping him out of his trance. Surprised, Dick looked up at Alex. Their eyes locked. They remained that way for several seconds, Dick's hand extended, his fingers reaching. Alex holding Dick's wrist. Alex was very protective of these speed tiles.

"So, you wanna go steady?" asked Dick, finally standing up.

"In your dreams, Beaver," mumbled Alex.

Alex let go of Dick's wrist, frowning and watching Dick intently.

Dick turned to Wong. "So, what's this thing for anyway? What does it do?"

"I don't know, Mister Beaver. I'm following the plans. I'm building it, hoping that it's purpose will reveal itself."

"That's how I built the grid," confessed Ted. "I'm guessing about the purpose. I'm hoping the speed tiles take over."

"Doctor Wong," I said. "This structure you've built here. This peculiar arrangement of tiles. I've seen it in my mind. That's why I made the sketch you have. But I've also arranged tiles like this…my own tiles, not real ones."

"And the platform," added Ted. "It looks like Bullfrog's platform, from his basement in the gallery."

"Bullfrog had the plans. He could have built a platform like this," admitted Wong.

"He did more than that, Doctor Wong," I said. "He got the whole thing to work."

"Nonsense, Mister Hunter. Bullfrog's a brainless idiot. He couldn't have."

"I think you may have underestimated our friend Jeremiah Bullfrog, Doctor," said Ted.

"Bullfrog's a fool," insisted Wong.

"He may be a fool, Doctor Wong, but a very crafty one," I said. "Did Bullfrog sell you the plans?"

"Yes."

"He sold them to you because he was finished with them," I said. "He didn't need them any more."

"Did he tell you about Singapore, Doctor Wong?" asked Ted.

"What does Bullfrog know of Singapore?" asked Wong.

Ted and I exchanged glances. "He doesn't know," whispered Ted to me.

"Know?" asked Wong. "Know what? What don't I know?"

"You don't know, Doctor Wong, that Bullfrog already has thousands of speed tiles," said Ted.

"Enough speed tiles to cover a platform like this," I added.

"And he uses the platform," continued Ted.

"He uses it to stay alive," I said.

"Bullfrog has been collecting speed tiles for over a hundred years," said Ted.

"He's been stealing them for a hundred years," corrected Dick.

Wong looked like he was watching a tennis match. His glance bounced from one to the other of us, trying to take in these revelations. Trying to understand.

"Our daughters found Bullfrog suspended above one of these platforms in Saugatuck," I said. "He was floating over it, face down, naked. Apparently, Bullfrog needs his unholy bed to sustain himself, to stay alive."

"Bullfrog is over 130 years old, Doctor Wong," said Ted. "He should have been dead years ago."

Wong sat down unsteadily on the edge of his platform. "This is impossible, absurd," he said, looking up at Ted. "How could you know that? How could he be so old?"

"Mabel," Ted answered. "She's not really my mother, Doctor. She's my great grandmother. Speed tiles have, somehow, kept her alive for all these years, too. She's 137 years old. She knew Bullfrog in Singapore before it was destroyed."

Ted took a step toward the platform and Doctor Wong. "What you're building here, Doctor Wong, is a machine that can sustain life."

I stepped up next to Ted. "Eternal life, Doctor Wong."

It took some explaining, but we told Wong about Singapore and the journal and Mabel's extended life. We told him about Bullfrog's short stay in Saugatuck and his larcenous ways. We described Bullfrog's gallery and how he used my show to ferret out the local speed tile users…about his burglaries and the ugly death of Ursulla.

We were sitting in Wong's living room now, away from the partially constructed speed tile bed.

"So, Bullfrog's been deceiving me," said Wong.

"He's a desperate man," said Ted. "My guess is that speed tiles somehow expend themselves. They don't last forever. Whatever energy they use for sustaining Bullfrog's life gets used up. He needs more and more speed tiles to keep going."

"That's why he went to Saugatuck, then," said Wong.

"To find more speed tiles," I said. "And my guess is that he'll be back here, where he found his original stash."

"I can't wait to get my hands on him," said Dick. "I'll be waiting for him."

"So, where are you finding your speed tiles, Doctor Wong?" asked Ted.

Wong looked at Alex, wondering if he should reveal another one of their secrets. I saw Alex shake his head no.

Wong shrugged. "From a sunken ship, Mister Clark. The Morazon."

Alex sighed heavily.

"We saw you diving on the wreck yesterday," I said.

"I thought the Morazon was carrying a cargo of plastic shampoo bottles," said Ted. "At least that's what the history books say."

"Shampoo bottles, yes," replied Wong. "It was carrying shampoo bottles. But it was also carrying a cargo of speed tiles, thousands of them. I suspect that was one of the reasons the Morazon sunk."

"So, you got those speed tiles in your basement from the Morazon?" asked Dick.

"Some of them," answered Wong. "They were buried deep in the sand under the wreck. But we also found some in the dunes…maybe in the same place where Bullfrog found his speed tiles a hundred years ago."

I looked at Dick. I knew where he would be going with his shovels and his wheelbarrow.

"You mentioned a cargo of speed tiles," said Ted.

"Yes. The ship's manifest. I found the original manifest of the Morazon in the library in Traverse City, in the nautical archives stored in the basement. The manifest lists plastic bottles, shampoo bottles, but it also lists a container of native Indian artifacts. I think they were listed as artifacts so as not to attract undue attention. Or maybe they just didn't know what else to call them. I think the artifacts are really speed tiles."

"You say you found speed tiles around the wreck?" asked Ted.

"Yes. there were a few scattered around…maybe twenty-five or thirty of them. They were buried deep in the sand near a metal cargo container I found under the wreck when I was diving yesterday. I suspect that container is filled with speed tiles."

"Can you get into the container?" asked Ted.

"I have a barge and a crane on the way here. Alex arranged for a salvage crew to arrive with it sometime tomorrow. By tomorrow evening we should have the whole cargo of speed tiles recovered."

"Then what?" I asked.

"Then I can finish the platform. I can begin my research. I can study these odd devices and learn about their powers."

"Then you can live forever, right Wong?" asked Dick, sarcastically.

"Oh no, Mister Beaver. Eternal life is not my motivation. Science is what drives me."

"Right..." said Dick, skeptical, as usual. He turned to Wong's helper. "And what about you, Alex. Do you want to live forever?"

Alex continued to frown and stare at Dick. He remained silent.

"These things have a way of taking over, Wong," I said. "Surely you know that by now."

"Yes. They have addictive properties. But I'm sure this addiction can be controlled."

"Sure, all it takes is practice," said Ted. "Look at Bullfrog. He's had over a hundred years to practice control."

Chapter 22

Ursulla's Purse

Mom and Dad left Hannah and me on Dancer alone. They went hiking to the cedar forest on the west end of the island. After spending yesterday with Wong, Dad decided he better spend this day with Mom. Dick went there, too, with his wheelbarrow. He was gonna prospect for speed tiles in the dunes.

Ted was with Wong on Whalesback. They motored out to the Morazon in the morning to meet the salvage barge Wong had hired. Also, Ted was showing Wong the crazy grid thing he had installed on Whalesback. Wong's sidekick, Alex, stayed at their cabin with their speed tiles.

I was kind of daydreaming on the forward deck of Dancer, playing with my speed tiles, arranging them this way and that, lining them up in rows, picking them up one by one, rubbing my fingers over the golden nubs, dreaming, thinking...

This one is nice...friendly. Waves of laughter bubbling out from inside of it sometimes...just a feeling. It's my favorite one. It seems kind of girlie, somehow. I don't know why...kind of feminine. Kind of like a girl...a young girl. A happy girl. Something sad, though. In the background...something sad, tragic...

This one seems old, wise. Hmm…female too? Maybe. Lots of feelings in this one…can't tell. Confusing, deep feelings, really complex. It kind of gives me a headache. I can't understand it…

Oh, this one. It's kind of different from the others, somehow. I'm not crazy about this one. It's feels more male than female. Kind of naughty…a touch of evil, waves of jealousy, envy…I don't know…

I was starting to see why Ursulla called them her children. Each one was different. Each one felt like it had a lot to share, a lot to tell…But how? Why?

"What are you doing Hill?" asked Hannah. I didn't notice her come up behind me.

I frowned at Hannah as she approached. "None of your business, Hannah."

"Oh, playing with your precious speed tiles, huh, Bitch?"

"Shut up Hannah." I had all the tiles out of Ursulla's purse now. There were twenty-five of them. I had them lined up in neat rows, five high and five wide. They were beautiful, glistening in the sun.

"God, Hill, look at all the speed tiles you have! I didn't know you had that many. You're such a selfish bitch, Hilllary. Why can't you give me just one?"

"'Cause I need them all. Can't you see that?"

"See what?"

"This pattern. It's symmetrical."

"So what, dork. What's the difference? Just give me one."

"I need them, Hannah!"

"God damn it, Hilllary! You better give me one or else I'll take them all!"

My heart beating faster, I looked up at my big sister, coming closer. I put my hands protectively over my speed tiles. "Find your own, you whore."

She grabbed me by my arm and dragged me away from the neat rows of shiny speed tiles. She pulled me over the hand rail and into the cockpit, bouncing my head on a winch. "Ouch!"

"Okay, then I'll take them all."

She turned and started back to the deck but I grabbed her by the ankle and tripped her. "No Hannah! They're mine!"

She was stronger than me. She pushed me away and started back on deck. "Not any more, you dork."

Furious, I jumped on her back. I had to protect my speed tiles. I couldn't let her touch them.

The boat swayed and tilted, throwing Hannah off balance with me on her back. She fell against the lifelines, turning so that I hung out over the water. She tried to regain her balance, but it was no use, I was too heavy and I wouldn't let go. We both toppled over the lifelines into the crystal clear waters of South Manitou harbor.

"You jerk. Now look what you've done," spluttered Hannah as she came up for air.

I pushed her head under water again and started swimming toward the ladder on the stern of the boat. Hannah grabbed me by the leg and pulled me back. I grabbed her and we struggled in the water, each of us trying to get to the ladder first.

Finally, the silliness of our struggle hit us both at the same time and we started giggling uncontrollably. I couldn't stop laughing. We stopped struggling and started hugging each other, instead.

My back was to the boat and we were floating and treading water, about fifteen feet off the port side. "Hilllary, You idiot. I'm gonna…"

I watched Hannah's face change from a smile to horror as she looked over my shoulder at the bow of the boat. I turned quickly to see what she was looking at.

"Spinnaker! No!" she shouted just as our cat sprang from a crouching position on the deck to the lifelines, trapping an unsuspecting sparrow in his lethal claws.

"Oh my God, Hilllary. He caught a bird."

Hannah started swimming toward the swim ladder, hoping she wasn't too late. Hannah was a real animal lover. She hated to see any animal get hurt. I watched as she scampered up the swim ladder and dash forward to the scene of the attack.

Spinnaker saw her coming and grabbed the bird in his mouth and dodged Hannah on the starboard side, taking the wounded bird below into the cabin. It was Spinnaker's prize. He had caught the bird fair and square and he meant to keep it.

I climbed up the swim ladder just as Hannah dashed below after Spinnaker and his catch. Hannah was crying now, angry and frustrated by the injustice of it all. She wanted to save the bird.

I heard a commotion below as I stepped on deck; then I saw Spinnaker, ears back and tail puffed up, dash back up out of the cabin, bird in mouth, Hannah close behind. There were feathers everywhere.

Spinnaker ran forward where I had arranged my speed tiles. He dropped the bird on top of them, looked up at Hannah and hissed. I came forward to join them.

"Spinnaker, you murderer!" wailed Hannah as she kneeled down next to the dead bird. Spinnaker hissed again, then went below, finally giving up his prey.

I kneeled down next to Hannah. The bird was all limp and ruffled. Little streams of blood dripped over its feathers and onto the speed tiles. It's neck was kind of loose and hanging at a funny angle. It didn't move. Hannah sobbed.

"God, Hannah, it's only a bird."

"Shut up Hilllary. That fricking cat killed it. I hate that cat!"

"That's what cats do, Hannah. They hunt."

"I don't care, Hiller. I hate that cat."

I knew she didn't. I knew she would eventually forgive Spinnaker. Hannah likes animals better than people and sometimes she gets sappy and overly emotional...like now.

Spinnaker came back up on deck and sat on top of the dodger, looking down on us, his ears back, still angry about losing his prize.

Slowly, Hannah stopped sobbing and we sat quietly, looking down at the dead bird, listening to the wind in the shrouds and the waves quietly lapping at the hull of the boat.

Then it moved.

"Did you see that?" I asked.

"What?"

"The bird, Hannah. It moved."

"It's dead, Hill."

It kind of spazzed again, its neck popping back to where it should have been. Hannah jumped back, "What the…"

I watched as the golden nubs on the speed tiles below squirmed under the bird, glowing, pulsing, casting a dull yellow glow on the feathers of the sparrow.

"God, Hill, what's going on?"

"I don't know, Hannah."

The bird convulsed again, sending feathers flying in the breeze. Spinnaker arched his back and hissed.

"I guess it wasn't dead after all, Hill."

The bird struggled to its feet, shaking its wings free.

"Oh, it was definitely dead, Hannah."

"Well, it's not any more, Hill," said Hannah, smiling.

The bird spread its wings and took off.

"It's the speed tiles, Hannah. They brought the bird back to life."

"Oh my God…" said Hannah as she backed away from the tiles on the deck. "This is too weird. It can't be."

I jumped up from the deck and ran to the cockpit. "I'm gonna try something."

I scooped up the carcasses of six or seven dead flies off the floor and went back on deck. I sprinkled the dead bugs on top of the speed tiles and waited.

Hannah came closer, mesmerized by the pulsating speed tiles, activated again by the tiny carcasses. We both watched as the flies came alive one by one and flew away.

"No way," said Hannah.

"Way!" said a voice from the cockpit.

We both jumped at the unexpected visitor and looked up to see Jeremiah Bullfrog, dripping wet, standing next to the steering wheel. We were so hypnotized by the flies that we hadn't noticed him climb on board. Spinnaker welcomed him with another hiss.

"Why must you torture me with that infernal cat?" asked Bullfrog.

Hannah got up and grabbed Spinnaker protectively. "He's not an infernal cat..." said Hannah, "whatever that means."

"What are you doing here, Bullfrog?" I asked, afraid of what the answer might be. He looked older, somehow. Maybe it was because this was the first time I had seen him without a coat and tie. He was shirtless, with bare feet, but wearing long pants, kind of tattered and dirty. I looked at him more closely and, with a shock, noticed that his skin had a grid-like pattern etched into it, like a total body tattoo...speed tile burns I realized, from his unholy bed.

"I might ask you the same question, young lady," he answered. "But if you must know, I've come for the purse you stole from me." His eyes turned to slits and he growled, "I want it back. Now."

"That was Ursulla's purse," I protested. "You stole it from her."

"Get off our boat, Bullfrog," warned Hannah.

Bullfrog smiled and started toward us. "You're not making me feel very welcome, but very well. I'll leave. Just give me the purse."

"Don't give it to him, Hill," said Hannah.

"It's mine now," I said, scooping up the speed tiles from the deck and dumping them in Ursulla's red velvet purse. "Ursulla wanted me to have them."

"You don't know what to do with them, you little idiot. And Ursulla was a doddering old fool."

"Shut up, Bullfrog," I said angrily. "She died because of you. You killed her."

Hannah and I both backed away, moving toward the bow of the boat. Spinnaker hissed again at the approaching Bullfrog.

He had us trapped. I thought about jumping in the water to try to escape but I was afraid Bullfrog would jump in after us and drown us. I held the speed tiles close to my chest, my heart beating wildly. I couldn't give him my speed tiles. They were mine now. They were my friends. I needed them.

"Hill, you better give him the fricking speed tiles," said Hannah shakily.

"No Hannah! They're mine."

"You should listen to your older sister, you little wench," said Bullfrog, coming closer.

"Hill…I think he means it."

"They're mine!" I shouted defiantly, tears of frustration pooling in my eyes. I couldn't give them up. I loved them. I needed them.

We looked into Bullfrog's dark, hate-filled eyes, his mouth twisted into a growl, his teeth clenched. We backed into the bow pulpit, side by side. No where to go. Trapped. He reached for the purse. "Give me the purse!"

"Fuck you!" shouted Hannah and threw Spinnaker at Bullfrog's face. Mrowww! Hisss! The angry cat exploded into a fit of flailing claws and biting teeth. It only lasted a second before Bullfrog, wailing in agony, pealed the furry monster off his face and threw him to the deck, but the damage was done. The cat left behind long jagged welts…angry open scratches down Bullfrog's cheeks and neck.

I ran past Bullfrog and dove over the lifelines into the water with Ursulla's purse in my hand. Now I could get away. Now I could keep my speed tiles. In a panic, I stuffed the purse into my pocket and swam for shore. My speed tiles. Safe. I could keep them. I had to keep them.

"Hilllary…Help!"

Hannah's voice. Didn't she follow me into the water? I stopped swimming and turned to see Bullfrog holding Hannah on the bow of the boat. Bullfrog had one of the mooring lines wrapped around Hannah's throat.

"I want those speed tiles," said Bullfrog calmly. Hannah squirmed in Bullfrog's arms. He tightened the rope and I heard Hannah gag.

"I can't!" I hollered. "I need them!"

Hannah gagged again.

"But I need them," I sobbed. "Hannah…I need them."

I stayed there threading water, watching Bullfrog…watching Hannah. He was strangling her. He was killing her. He was killing my sister. But the speed tiles. I had to have them. I couldn't give them up. I needed them. I watched as Bullfrog tightened the rope. Hannah finally stopped struggling and kind of went limp in Bullfrog's arms.

"No!" I wailed. "Stop!"

Bullfrog loosened the rope and I started swimming back to the boat. I was confused. I felt my stomach churn. I felt ill at the thought of giving up my precious speed tiles. But my sister…

I climbed the ladder and pulled Ursulla's purse out of my pocket. I dropped it on the deck and stood there shaking with rage and confusion. I looked at Bullfrog and Hannah. He let her drop, unconscious, to the deck and came toward me to claim his prize. I watched him as he picked up Ursulla's purse. He opened it and looked inside, his eyes bright, dancing with madness. The welts on his face were bleeding now. Spinnaker's wounds were ugly and deep. I watched in horror as he dripped blood on the deck of Dancer…yellow blood. Sick, dirty yellow, pussey blood. Alien blood. The blood of a man who I knew was already dead. I realized then that Bullfrog needed the speed tiles more than I did. And I hated him.

He pushed past me for the stern ladder. In disgust, I spit on him as he passed. He turned his dark, angry eyes on me and slapped me with the back of his hand, sending me sprawling into the cockpit. I lay there sobbing as he dove into the water and swam for shore.

Rubbing the red bruise on my face and still crying, I ran forward to where Hannah was lying. She was out cold, with red marks around her neck where Bullfrog was choking her with the rope. She was breathing unevenly. Still alive. Oh God, she was still alive. Bullfrog didn't kill my sister.

"Hannah. Hannah, wake up!"

I started patting her cheeks like they do in the movies with unconscious people. She wouldn't wake up, so I dropped a bucket with a line attached to the handle into the water and pulled it up. This always works in the movies. I threw the full bucket on her face.

It worked. Spluttering and coughing, she came to. "What the…" she said, confused and dazed.

I dropped to my knees and crying in relief I hugged her. I hugged my sister, sobbing and laughing at the same time. She was all right.

"God, Hilllary," she said after a few minutes. "You whore. You almost got me killed."

"I know, Hannah. I'm sorry."

"I thought he killed me. I thought I was dead meat. Why didn't you just give him the fricking speed tiles, you bitch?"

"I don't know. I couldn't."

"You couldn't? Are those stupid speed tiles more important than me?"

"Shut up Hannah. I gave him the speed tiles, didn't I?"

"God, Hill…It took you long enough." She looked around the deck. "Where's Spinnaker?"

"He ran below after Bullfrog peeled him off of his face."

We looked at each other and smiled, remembering Spinnaker's explosion on Bullfrog's face. Then we started laughing…a little too loud. The laugh turned to a nervous titter. Then silence. We heard thunder in the distance. Dark clouds were rolling in from the west. We sat there hugging each other for a long time after that, deep in thought, looking out over the darkening beach in South Manitou harbor. I missed my friends. I missed my speed tiles.

Chapter 23

The Slab

"John…get a clue," pleaded Marcia. "Look what he's done already. He almost killed one of your daughters."

Hannah and Hilllary sat together below, looking sad and petulant, watching their parents argue. A stubborn drizzle of rain added an urgent patter to the roof of the sailboat's cabin. "What is it that you want me to do, Marsh? Kill him? Kill Bullfrog? Believe me, I'd like to do that right now."

"No, I don't want you to kill him. You reported him to the Rangers. Let them and the Coast Guard take care of Bullfrog. I want you to leave all this behind. I want you to forget about speed tiles. Let that son-of-a-bitch have the damned things."

I sat down next to Hannah to take another look at the rope burns on her neck. I glanced at Hilllary and caressed her cheek lightly where Bullfrog had slapped her. "You guys feeling better?"

"We're fine now, Dad," said Hannah. Then with fire in her eyes: "But I think you should kill that son-of-a-bitch."

"Hannah!" scolded Marcia. I wasn't sure whether Marcia objected to Hannah's foul language or her homicidal instincts.

"He's evil, Mom!" said Hannah.

"Anyway, you can't kill him," said Hilllary, matter-of-factly. "He's already dead."

I looked at Hilllary with a questioning look in my eyes.

"He bleeds yellow blood, Dad. I saw it."

"She's right, Dad," confirmed Hannah. "He's like the walking dead."

Marcia looked at them with surprise, then at me with anger. "Look what you've got them thinking."

"No, really, Mom," continued Hilllary. "Before Bullfrog came, Spinnaker killed a bird but the speed tiles brought it back to life…Ursulla's speed tiles."

"And a bunch of bugs too," added Hannah. "We put some dead bugs on the tiles and they came alive."

"I've heard just about enough of this supernatural bullshit," said Marcia.

"It's not bullshit!" said Hannah, pushing her luck with her potty mouth.

"It's true, Mom," said Hilllary.

"So Bullfrog's speed tile bed actually brings him back to life every night," I mused, getting up off the settee and looking out one of the ports.

The rain was coming down harder now and the wind was tossing Dancer back and forth on her anchor. It was still daylight but the dark rain clouds gave the landscape a gray cast. I saw Whalesback crashing over the waves in the distance coming around the lighthouse on the way back to the anchorage, scattered flashes of lightning showing her the way. "Here comes Ted."

"Let's get out of here, John," pleaded Marcia. "This place scares me."

"This storm scares me too, Marsh," I said. "We can't leave in this weather." We were safely anchored in the crescent-shaped harbor protecting us from the heavy weather blowing fiercely from the west. From the looks of it, there would be eight to ten-foot waves and gale force winds in the open waters of the lake. No sailor in his right mind would purposely venture out into Lake Michigan in this weather.

I went to the VHF radio to hail Ted. "Come in, Whalesback. This is Dancer, WSA-4885, come in, Whalesback."

Ted answered right away. "Hello Dancer, this is Whalesback. Switch and answer on six-eight."

I switched off of channel sixteen, the hailing and emergency channel and went to sixty-eight. "Dancer on six-eight."

"Hi, John. Lovely weather we're having, isn't it? Over."

"Yeah, great. How's the salvage operation? You get the cargo container?"

"Yeah, we got it all right. They had to dig down about fifteen feet into the sand to find it. But the container was empty. The speed tiles must have blown a hole in the bottom of the container. Wong's pretty disappointed."

"You want some more good news?"

"Oh oh. What is it?"

"Bullfrog. He's on the island. He was on my boat before I got back. Bullied my kids. Tried to strangle Hannah. Over."

"Why did he do that?"

"For speed tiles. Hilllary had a purse full of them. She got them from Ursulla. I didn't even know she had them. Over."

"Why does everybody keep those things a secret?"

"You tell me, Ted. You kept yours a secret."

"Yeah, well…"

"Anyway, Ted, I reported him to the Rangers. When the weather clears, a Coast Guard boat is gonna come to the island to look for him. Over."

"Unless we can find him first," said a different voice. It was Wong.

Marcia looked up at me. Our eyes met. I went back to the radio. "What do you mean, Doctor Wong?"

"His speed tiles, Mr. Hunter. If we can find him first we can get his speed tiles."

Marcia rolled her eyes, than shook her head.

"Yeah, well…ahh…"

"John? You there?" It was Ted again.

"Yeah, Ted. I'm not sure I want to deal with Bullfrog. He just tried to kill one of my daughters. Tell Wong. He's dangerous. He's desperate."

Ted and Wong were silent for a few seconds thinking about what I just said. I knew speed tiles had a way of pushing your priorities around. To Ted and Wong, speed tiles were now at the top of their list.

"Okay, John," said Ted. "We'll talk about it later. Gotta go now and get this tub anchored."

"Dancer, WSA 4885, back to sixteen. Out."

The girls sulked as I watched out the port at the growing storm. I was watching for Dick. We had left him on the trail earlier that day when he took the right fork on the way to the dunes and we took the left fork to the cedar forest. He was rolling his wheelbarrow filled with shovels and picks and buckets. He also had his tent and his sleeping bag so I wasn't sure if he meant to come back to the boats or not. In this storm he might want to sleep on one of the boats rather than inside his flimsy tent.

Marcia's comments made me uncertain about my motivations. Why was I here on this island with a murderous maniac on the loose? What was I trying to prove? Why was I putting my family in danger?

I knew speed tiles still had a hold on me. I told myself it was just curiosity, but I still longed for my speed tile, my slab. But I was sure I could do without it. I didn't need it any more. Or did I?

Finally, I saw Dick's lumbering figure on the beach, waving to get our attention. It was still raining, so I put on my rain gear.

"I'm going to the beach to pick up Dick. I'll probably bring him to Whalesback. Ted's got more room for him than we do."

I jumped in the dinghy and headed for the beach. Dick was dripping wet. He looked agitated, excited.

"You OK, Dick?"

"Fine, John,…can't say the same for Alex."

"Alex?"

"Yeah, just stopped at Wong's cabin. Door was open. Alex is dead. Blood all over. Looks like there was a struggle. Someone bashed his head in."

"Bullfrog," I said.

"Bullfrog? Is he here?"

"He attacked my kids while we were gone. He's here all right."

We dinghied out to Whalesback in the rain. Dick repeated his bad news for Ted and Wong.

"And the speed tiles?" asked Wong.

"Gone."

I looked at Wong wondering whether the grief-stricken look on his face was for the loss of his friend or his speed tiles.

"But I think I know where he took 'em," continued Dick.

"Where?" asked Ted and Wong in unison.

"Lighthouse. Deserted building. Perfect place for Bullfrog to hide and set up his crazy bed. Nobody goes there. All boarded up."

"Lets go," said Ted as he pulled on his raincoat.

"Go?" I asked. "Go where?"

"To the lighthouse. To find Bullfrog."

"Ted. He's dangerous. He just killed a man."

"He's also got the speed tiles," said Wong. "My speed tiles."

"I'm ready," said Dick. "I hate that son-of-a-bitch."

I looked at their faces. It was the speed tiles. They needed the speed tiles. So did I.

"Dancer, this is Whalesback. Come in Dancer."

"This is Dancer. What's up John?"

"Hi, Marsh. We think we know where Bullfrog is…at the lighthouse."

"Good. Let the Coast Guard take care of him."

"We're going there now, Marsh. We're gonna go find him."

"John. No you're not. You come back to the boat."

"I'll be right back Marsh. There are four of us. We can handle him."

I purposely kept the news of Alex's death from her. I didn't want to worry her more than she already was.

"John, no!"

I looked at the microphone, torn between returning to my family and finding Bullfrog's speed tiles. "This is Whalesback, signing off. See you later, Marsh."

"John…" I clicked off the radio.

"Let's go."

We took both dinghies to the beach in the rain, pouring down harder now. Even in this protected cove, the seas were getting violent. Lightning flashed in the darkening sky, illuminating whitecaps crashing over our gunwales.

We secured the dinghies and started down the beach toward the lighthouse. The light was no longer in service, replaced by the Coast Guard with automated lights out in the Manitou passage. It was a deserted building now, at least before Bullfrog took up residence. The round tower rose dramatically into the night sky, painted stark white against the black clouds. There was no sign of Bullfrog. Maybe he went somewhere else.

We forced open the doors and went inside, flashes of lightning showing the way. The entryway was strewn with broken plaster, chipped paint and splintered wood. The structure showed years of abuse by vandals.

A rusted spiral staircase wound around the crumbling walls to a hole in the ceiling about twenty feet above us. Water from the driving rainstorm streamed down the discolored walls to muddy puddles at our feet. We went up the stairs, single file, looking for Bullfrog. Looking for speed tiles.

We found them on the second level: speed tiles, not Bullfrog. There was his wooden platform, right in the middle of the round room, speed tiles arranged meticulously over its surface. The tower rose another hundred feet above us, the staircase spiraling dizzily around the inner walls to the chamber above that once held the beacon and the French-made Fresnel lens. But what brought us here wasn't the architecture.

"Speed tiles," mumbled Wong.

"Look how many there are," whispered Ted.

We stood staring at Bullfrog's bed, mesmerized by the precious artifacts. Lightning continued outside, flashing unholy shadows through the spindly stairs and onto the walls of the room. Rain leaked down, leaving a glistening greenish slime on the walls and floor.

Then, a blinding white light. A deafening explosion.

The building shook. Bricks, mortar, metal fragments from the cupola above came raining down on our heads and on Bullfrog's bed.

We dove under the stairway to avoid being crushed by the falling debris. Lightning must have hit the tower.

I looked out from under the stairs to see rain pouring down through a new opening slashed by the lightning strike. As lightning flashed I saw a jagged, gaping hole with the spiral staircase hanging precariously off the walls at an impossible angle, mocking its previous purpose.

Then I saw something else. I gasped in horror as a dark shape hovered over the hole blocking the dim light from the sky. More lightning…a rectangular shape descending slowly down toward us. The slab. My slab. Long, slimy tendrils, hanging off of it, dancing in the rain, flailing around, dripping death, destruction. Ominous, sick, disgusting.

I looked at the horror in the eyes of my companions. Dick turned to me. "That belong to you?"

It was my slab. The same slab I saw bursting out of my attic in Saugatuck, floating in the storm, heading north.

"Oh my God," said Ted, his eyes wide with horror.

"What's keeping it in the air like that?" wondered Wong, his scientific mind trying to make sense of the slimy, mutated thing in front of him.

We watched, frozen in fear as the thing descended the tower, stopping about three feet above Bullfrog's bed. The speed tiles below it started pulsating, the yellow nubs absorbing power from the slab. The tendrils lashed back and forth, flailing in wind gusts funneling down the tower from above, brushing over the tiles causing sparks and miniature lightning flashes. The smell of ozone, like an electrical fire, permeated the air.

"Fascinating," whispered Wong.

"Disgusting," said Dick.

"Now's our chance," said Ted.

I looked at Ted, his face smeared with muddy plaster dust and drips of rain. I looked into his eyes, bright with wonder, intense with purpose. "Our chance for what, Ted?"

"To try the grid. I've gotta get it over here. I've gotta put it under the slab. Your sculpture, John! Just like your sculpture."

"Ted. You're nuts! You don't want to go near that thing."

"But look at the power it's generating. We gotta do it now. Who knows how long it'll stay."

"He's right," confirmed Wong, desperate for speed tiles. "I think the electricity generated by the storm is somehow powering it. We have to try it now before the storm subsides."

Dick agreed, discouraged by his fruitless day of prospecting. "Let's do it. Let's make some speed tiles."

"You and Dick stay here," ordered Ted. "Wong and I will go get the grid."

"Right," said Dick. "We'll make sure it doesn't try to get away."

I looked at Dick in amazement. How in the world did he think we would stop it if it tried to get away. These people were crazy. Ted and Wong hurried down the stairs and out into the storm. Dick and I crouched in the shadows under the spiral stairs, watching the repulsive thing doing its devil's dance on Bullfrog's bed. The storm raged on. We waited.

SLAM! The door below us crashed open. A shuffling noise below. It was too soon for Ted and Wong to be back with the grid. The stairs. Someone dragging something up the stairs. I looked at Dick. His eyes turned cold.

"Bullfrog," he whispered.

We stayed in the shadows, hiding, waiting.

A shadowy figure crawled up out of the hole in the floor dragging something. A sack. He entered the room and let out a muffled scream. We could see him recoil in terror at the sight of the thing before him. We could hear him sobbing in anguish.

A flash of lightning. Bullfrog, kneeling on the floor, whimpering before his unholy alter, his mutated god, shuffling backwards on his knees, backing away from the horror of it.

"Welcome to the party, Bullfrog," said Dick, coming out of the shadows and approaching the pitiful figure.

Surprised, Bullfrog fell backwards onto his sack. He looked back at his bed, at the slab. "My bed. What have you done?"

In his confusion, Bullfrog somehow thought we had caused this to happen, spoiled his nap time. I looked closer at Bullfrog and realized he was badly hurt, probably from his fight with Alex. His leg was twisted at an impossible angle, broken. He must have crawled here over the sand, dragging his broken body over the rocks and the dunes. The gashes in his face from Spinnaker's attack were oozing yellow puss. He looked older and worn. He needed a strong dose of speed tiles to regenerate his aging and broken body.

More thunder. More lightning. The storm continued, sending streams of rain down the open gash in the tower. The flashing lightning continued its unearthly light show, sporadically illuminating the horror in the circular chamber we were in.

"You don't look so good, Bullfrog," said Dick, shouting to make himself heard over the rain and the thunder.

"You must help me," begged Bullfrog. "I must get to my bed."

"Right. You want me to help you," said Dick sarcastically.

"I'm dying. Can't you see that. I'll give you anything. Anything! Please help me."

"Looks like you'll have to share your bed tonight, Bullfrog," said Dick, looking at the slab, whipping its tendrils back and forth in the wind. "Speed tiles make strange bedfellows."

"Make it go away!" cried Bullfrog.

Crash!

Another lightning strike sent more bricks and mortar cascading down the chamber. I watched Dick dive for shelter under the stairs and

Bullfrog shy away, covering his head with his hands. Big chunks of the wall fell on top of the slab, exploding into dust on impact, sending a white dusty mist through the soggy air.

Bang! The downstairs door again. Ted and Wong, back with the grid. I heard them struggling up the stairs with it.

"Honey, we're home," sang Ted nervously as he appeared through the hole. Wong followed carrying the other end of the heavy grid Ted had built. It was wrapped in a canvas tarp. "Had a hell of a time getting this thing on the dinghy," said Ted. Then he noticed Bullfrog cowering on the ground against the wall.

"Well, look who's here," said Ted.

Wong turned and saw him. "Bullfrog! You murdering animal."

"I didn't mean to kill Alex," he stammered. "He attacked me. I was defending myself."

"Helping yourself to my speed tiles as well, weren't you?"

"I was going to give them back to you, Wong. I was."

"You disgusting creature."

"My bed," sputtered Bullfrog. "You must help me with my bed. I'm dying."

"You don't deserve to live," said Wong with a sneer, then he turned to Ted and the grid.

"Hurry," said Ted. "We need sand from the beach. Just like John's sculpture at the gallery. We need to put the grid on a bed of sand."

Dick kept an eye on Bullfrog while Wong grabbed Bullfrog's sack. It was filled with Wong's speed tiles. The ones Bullfrog murdered Alex for. He dumped them on the ground next to Bullfrog. Wong and I worked together filling the sack with sand and building a mountain in the circular chamber, well away from the sparking, smoldering slab, still dancing eerily over Bullfrog's bed.

"I'm hoping the slab will be attracted by the grid once we get it set up," said Ted.

Ted fiddled with the microprocessors and activated the batteries under the grid, readying them for their upcoming marriage to the floating slab. Bullfrog lay whimpering in a heap at Dick's feet, muttering to himself, pleading with Dick to help him.

"That should be enough sand," said Ted. "Let's give it a try."

Ted and Wong carefully placed the grid, now humming with its activated microchips, on top of the hill of sand.

Then we waited to see what would happen.

Chapter 24

Mom

God, was Mom pissed.

"That son-of-a-bitch hung up on me!" she said as she slammed the VHF microphone down.

She didn't want Dad running around the island looking for Bullfrog. She was afraid for him. She wanted him here with us. Safe. She wanted him here, protecting us.

"I'm gonna kill him!"

She paced up and down the tiny cabin, frustrated, steaming with anger.

"I'm gonna get a divorce. I can't compete with those damned speed tiles."

"Mom, calm down," said Hannah. "Look, you're fogging up the windows."

"What does he think he's doing?" she fumed. "Who does he think he is, some kind of movie hero…some kind of John Wayne?"

"Who's John Wayne?" I asked.

"If he comes back here alive, I'm gonna kill him."

Hannah and I looked out the window at the driving rain, waiting. We could just see the top of the lighthouse over a dune on the beach. Then we saw it. A sudden bolt of lightning, almost as wide as the tower itself, came straight down out of the sky and with a deafening crack, shattered the top of the cupola. We recoiled in horror. "Dad! No!" I cried.

Mom ran to the window. "What happened?"

"A fricking huge lightning strike, Mom," said Hannah.

Sobbing, afraid for my father's life, I blubbered, "The lighthouse. It just got hit by lightning. Dad…that's where he went…"

Mom held us both and we stared out the port at the smoldering tower. The waves tossed us back and forth, Dancer groaned in the wind and jerked at her anchor in protest.

There was nothing we could do but wait out the storm…wait for Dad to return, hoping that the lightning didn't get him.

"What is it about those things?" asked Mom to no one in particular. "Why do seemingly intelligent people do such crazy things for those idiotic little metal things."

"They're habit-forming, Mom," I answered. "Like cigarettes."

"Ha!" she responded. "You can't even smoke, 'em. What's the thrill?"

"The ones I had…Ursulla's speed tiles…were each a little different. When I held them, one at a time, they made me feel things…like they were connected to…ahh…"

"Connected to what?" she snapped. "The moon? Mars? What are you talking about, Hill?"

"…to people. One was like a little girl. That was my favorite one. It's hard to explain. I really miss them." I started to cry, thinking about the pleasure and companionship Ursulla's speed tiles gave me, and also thinking of my Dad, trapped in the tower.

Mom sighed and sat down next to me, hugging me, trying to comfort me. "Hill. I don't think they were good for you, no matter how much pleasure they gave you."

"Yeah, Hill," added Hannah. "You almost got me killed because of those things."

Hannah was looking out the porthole at the lighthouse when she saw two men climbing into Ted's dinghy on the beach. The rain was still coming down in buckets. "There's somebody on the beach!"

Mom and I jumped up to look out the port. We watched nervously as Ted and Wong motored over to Whalesback.

"Maybe I can find out what's going on," said Mom as she rushed to the VHF radio.

"Whalesback! Whalesback! This is Dancer. Come in Whalesback."

Silence.

"Whalesback! Come in!" yelled Mom into the microphone. "Come on…answer the call…"

"Dancer, this is Whalesback," answered Ted.

"Ted, what's happening? Is anyone hurt? We saw the lightning!" Mom's face was contorted into a worried frown.

"Nobody's hurt, Marcia. Everything's fine."

"Everything's fine?" asked Mom, looking out the port at the continuing storm.

"Yeah, fine. We just came back for the grid."

"The grid?" Mom couldn't believe her ears.

"Yeah, Marcia. We have to put it under the slab."

"The slab?" Her voice hitting a higher octave with each response.

"The slab is in the lighthouse, Marcia," said Ted patiently. "It's hovering over Bullfrog's bed"

"Bullfrog's bed?" She looked at the microphone like it was a piece of Sandbar's excrement.

"Yeah, look, I gotta go now. I'll explain later…"

"Ted!"

"Whalesback, out."

"Damn it! What's going on?" Mom slammed the microphone down on the navigation table. Hannah and I jumped.

"At least we know Dad's all right," said Hannah, taking up her position at the port, looking out at the lighthouse.

Then boom! Another impossibly loud thunder clap. Hannah lurched back from the porthole, with fear in her eyes. "God!"

"What happened now?" cried Mom, jumping up to see for herself.

"The tower got hit again. I can't believe it."

We looked out the porthole at the crumbling lighthouse. "What a nightmare," whispered Mom.

Chapter 25

The Lighthouse

Ted's grid sat humming quietly on the pile of sand. The slab continued its unearthly dance over the speed tiles on Bullfrog's bed, making them glow and squirm in the dim light. Thunder and lightning flashed sporadically. Rain streamed down the open gash in the tower, hitting the slab and instantly vaporizing into a gray mist. The inside of the tower was like the devil's steam bath with hissing steam and snapping tendrils. Incongruously, I thought of Helmut Schmidt's skyscraper design from long ago in Chicago and realized the flailing tendrils were the slab's version of his pistil and stamen towers…a mutation of power and communication lines…angry, malevolent, looking for purpose, searching for a place to take root.

Slowly at first, one tendril, than a second, snapping and popping, searching and feeling…moved toward the grid, exploring. Then movement. The massive slab, steam rising off its surface from the vaporized rain, floating, bobbing in the night, coming toward us, leaving the comfort of Bullfrog's bed.

"Oh oh!" said Dick.

"It's working," whispered Ted.

Wong and Dick scrambled around the circular wall of the tower to get away from the snapping tendrils, the monster slab. Ted sat mesmerized, watching his invention mate with the thing.

"Ted, you better get out of its way," I said, grabbing his arm.

"Wait…"

"Ted, come on…"

It was like Ted was hypnotized. He stood up to get a better view of the inside chambers of his grid, actually leaning closer, closer to the zapping, hissing nightmare.

Too close. With a bright flash, one of the tendrils lashed across Ted's chest and sent him flying backwards into the rubble of the falling walls. He actually glowed briefly when he got hit. I ran to him.

"Ted, Ted! Are you all right?"

He was still conscious, but a dark, jagged burn across the front of his shirt marked where the tendril hit him. His shirt was smoldering. I grabbed him under his arms and dragged him to safety, out of the slab's reach.

"Ted!"

"Yeah…I'm all right."

I unbuttoned the front of his tattered shirt to see a mean red welt slashing diagonally across his chest. I expected worse. "Ted. You lit up like a Christmas tree when that thing hit you."

"It talked to me."

"Ted. Just relax. We gotta get you out of here."

"No, John, really! It talked to me."

"Yeah, yeah…"

The slab was now hovering over Ted's grid and it seemed to calm down a bit. The tendrils seemed to have more purpose as they danced and popped over the grid chambers. Something was happening. We watched in wonder as a yellow mist rose silently out of the sand around the grid. The mist organized itself into small amorphous cube-like clouds, one over each grid square, one hundred of them. Then they began to glow from within.

The zapping tendrils changed their ways. Softly, almost tenderly, they probed and shaped and massaged the tiny clouds, each cloud raining tiny sparks down into the grid chamber below it.

"It's making speed tiles, John. Look at it."

"I know, Ted…I know."

Distracted by the wonders of Ted's speed tile womb, we didn't notice Bullfrog's activities on the other side of the room. He had, somehow, dragged himself up to his bed. When I finally noticed him he was lying on his side on the platform, his broken, misshapen leg hanging uselessly off the side. He was desperately rearranging the speed tiles and cleaning off the broken plaster and bricks. His face was wrinkled and worn…the face of a seventy-year-old man. He was grunting and whining, working furiously to arrange the life-giving speed tiles just so.

Finally, he rolled his decimated body onto the speed tiles, his skin hissing with the contact. He laid there face down for a few seconds, then slowly rose, floating, six-inches above the surface, his scarred and battered face turned toward us. His eyes were closed. He looked peaceful there, even with the hissing, sputtering slab doing its birthing thing only a few feet away.

I grabbed Ted's arm and motioned toward Bullfrog. We watched in amazement as his misshapen leg popped back into place, the wrinkles and welts in his face, becoming smooth, soft.

"Oh, no, you don't!" shouted Dick.

He noticed Bullfrog's miraculous recuperation too. He got up from his hiding place under the stairs and went toward Bullfrog to ruin his nap. But he didn't get far.

The slab turned suddenly, its deadly tentacles flying. The maternal attitude of the slab changed abruptly as it moved in jerks and starts back toward the speed tile bed. Dick dove back for cover, barely avoiding the whips of the flailing tendrils. But Bullfrog wasn't so lucky.

The slab descended on him, trapping him suspended between speed tiles and tendrils, sparking, flailing angrily, oozing yellow puss. Bullfrog awoke and turned to see the deadly tentacles envelop him. They twisted around his arms and legs, wound around his neck, burning his skin, setting his clothing smoldering and smoking. His eyes wide with horror, his mouth twisted in a grimace of pain, he wailed a prolonged cry of terror as the slab, with its new prize, started rising unevenly back up toward the gash in the tower.

We watched it rise jerkily, bouncing off the curved walls, sending new chunks of plaster and bricks down on us and on Bullfrog's bed. I didn't think he would need that bed any more.

The slab reached the opening above with Bullfrog's body firmly woven into it's intricate grip. It continued to rise with the storm lighting the way. We ran to the center of the room and looked up to see Bullfrog's writhing body in the slab's embrace. A pitiful "help me..." was the last we heard of Bullfrog as the slab disappeared from view.

"That son-of-a-bitch," mumbled Dick.

Chapter 26

Hilllary

Sailing home has been great. Dad's in no hurry. We've just been harbor-hopping from port to port, heading south, covering the 120 miles of shoreline 20 or 30 miles at a crack, hanging out for a day or two in some of the more interesting ports. Sailing, soaking up the summer sun, relaxing…and trying to forget the horrors we experienced on South Manitou Island.

Hannah met a boy in Pentwater. We were there for two days. He was on another sailboat heading north. He's a real jerk…a perfect match for Hannah. They promised to write to each other. Right. The jerk will have to learn how first.

Dad's been hugging me a lot. Hugging Mom and Hannah too. Mom's still pissed at him…a little.

Dad finally stopped screaming at night. His arm's getting better now too. He scraped all the skin off his forearm leaping out of the V-berth in the middle of the night. Scared the crap out of us. Slab dreams, he said. Nightmares, I guess. I've been dreaming too. But good dreams, about that little girl I met in the speed tile. I really liked her. I miss her.

We left Ted and Dick and Wong back on the island. We left them with the speed tiles and Ted's crazy grid thing. We left them to deal with the police and the sheriff and the Coast Guard and the rangers. I don't know how they're gonna explain the slab. Of course it's gone now.

Hiding, I guess. Bullfrog's gone too. Good riddance to him. Him and the slab deserve each other. The last we saw of Dick, he was heading back to the dunes to prospect for speed tiles again. I hope he finds what he's looking for. But I hope he comes back to Saugatuck. I like Dick. He's funny. I'll bet his family misses him.

Ted's grid really did make speed tiles, a hundred of them, but they're not the same. They're light-weight like the others, and they're pretty, and the little nubs squirm and glow when you hold them, but they're empty. They're blank. Nothing like Ursulla's speed tiles.

Dad says he's kinda got it figured out. He says speed tiles are like data storage things…like computer floppy disks or CD-ROMs or something. He says they're also like batteries. Ted's speed tiles, the ones the slab made with his grid, don't have any data on them yet. Dad says they probably never will, unless Dr. Wong learns how to record stuff on them himself.

He thinks the one he found so long ago in the dunes was programmed for manufacturing. When the slab lashed Ted in the lighthouse, it told Ted that. Okay Ted, if you say so…

Anyway, Dad's speed tile manufactured that ugly slab using the plans in the briefcase. Whoa…what kind of sicko architect would draw plans for that? Dad said Helmut was a pretty weird guy, but it's my guess that he wasn't drawing a building to be built by a speed tile.

Dick's speed tiles were for heavy construction. Dad's guessing about that too.

Ursulla's speed tiles? He didn't know what Ursulla's speed tiles were programmed for. He couldn't guess. But I could. I knew what they were for. They told me when I held them.

They were for holding a life…for storing the history of a person, a real person. Each one like a journal, or a diary, but much more too. It's like the mind of a person, all the memories and feelings, all the emotions and ambitions, all the happenings of that person's life…recorded on this little thing. I don't know how they did it…or who did it. I don't know why.

But they did it at the moment of death. A memorial maybe, like a tombstone? Just a record like a birth certificate? Or is it some way of sustaining life? Some way of making that person live forever…like an old Fred Astaire movie keeping alive the memory of an old time movie star. Creepy, huh?

How do I know? I just do. From holding them. Its like they're playing back in my mind. Like a VCR. I wish I could hold one again. I wish I could go to that place inside the speed tile. It's really different from here, from this world. I wish I could be with the people in there…

But Mom won't let me near speed tiles again.

When we left, Wong and Ted were talking about building some kind of playback machine for speed tiles, like a VCR or a CD-ROM drive. That would be cool, I guess, but I don't know…how do you play back a life? What kind of picture would he get out of all those jumbled emotions and experiences and feelings…all that stuff that's mixed up inside one of those things.

Wong says he wants to unlock their mysteries. He wants Dad and me to help him. He says we're like human playback machines. With practice, he thinks we could learn to read what's on them.

Mom says no. She says they're too dangerous.

I guess they are…dangerous, I mean. But I can't seem to get that little girl off my mind. The little girl in that speed tile…

About the Author

John Leben was born on October 17, 1945 in Chicago. He has been married since 1971 and has two grown daughters. John Leben is an active writer and artist, but he is also the owner and president of Leben Productions, Inc., a media production company. He has a BFA in Painting from the University of Illinois in Champaign (1968), an MFA in Painting from the School of the Art Institute of Chicago (1971) and a 25 ton Captain's License from the United States Coast Guard.

As an artist, John's passion has always encompassed a wide variety of media. He learned the ancient arts of fresco and glass mosaic in the woods of Northern Maine as the University of Illinois' Raymond Fellowship student at the Skowhegan School of Painting and Sculpture (1968). At the School of the Art Institute of Chicago, he built robots, experimented with Xerox technology in paintings, and inched closer to electronic media, in both his imagery and his tools. He graduated with honors in 1971 winning the Kuniyoshi Traveling Fellowship which paid for a 6-week tour of Europe.

John's growing interest in the technology of media led him to the video industry in 1973 when he worked commercially as an art director. He formed Leben Design in 1978 to build models, design studio sets and produce animation sequences for Chicago-area producers. He formed Leben Productions in 1980 to write and produce video programming for corporations and public television.

In 1988 he moved to Saugatuck, Michigan splitting his time between video and fine art. He honed his writing skills on numerous documentary projects which were embraced nationally by Public Television and the History Channel. A successful Public TV series followed as well as a special showing at the Urban Institute of Contemporary Art in Grand Rapids. His fine art was exhibited at the Grand Rapids Art Museum, Midland Center for the Arts, The Kalamazoo Institute for the Arts, Paint Creek Center for the Arts, and the Muskegon Art Museum.

His love/hate relationship with technology and his growing interest in literary media combined as he began incorporating the use of narrative elements in his fine art work. The storylines for his visual work blossomed into a novel called SPEED TILE which took his imagery a step further into the realm of fiction. Started as a serialized story on Leben's website, it blossomed into a full blown novel dealing with the themes of technological stress and dependence.

John's varied career combining fine arts and high tech media production gives him a unique perspective on using all media for artistic expression. He often credits his fine arts background for teaching him the techniques he uses in all his artistic endeavors. He approaches writing and filmmaking in much the same way he attacks a painting, building images and impressions layer by layer, words, sounds, time and imagery his paintbrushes. His many years of working in high tech media have given him an appreciation of the devastating effects technology can have on the human condition and has provided him with the raw material for his artistic explorations of technology in both print and fine arts media.